THE IMPOSSIBLE GIRL

THE IMPOSSIBLE GIRL

LYDIA KANG

LAKE UNION
PUBLISHING

Published by Lake Union Publishing, Seattle

www.apub.com

Amazon, the Amazon logo, and Lake Union Publishing are trademarks of Amazon.com, Inc., or its affiliates.

ISBN-13: 9781503903388
ISBN-10: 1503903389

Cover design by PEPE *nymi*

Printed in the United States of America

For Richard

The widest land
Doom takes to part us, leaves thy heart in mine
With pulses that beat double.

—"Sonnet VI," 1850, Elizabeth Barrett Browning

PROLOGUE

January 12, 1830
Long Island, New York

The baby was small. Not so small as to concern Charlotte, but small enough to announce itself as precious.

"Aye, she's a wee thing!" Leah said, swaddling the infant in a thin blanket. The maid had said the obvious, as usual, but Charlotte didn't mind. She liked to be reminded that the details of the world were real, and warm, and worth speaking of. Her cousin, Elizabeth—the baby's mother—had never been petite herself, but babies had a way of disregarding what was expected of them.

The stub of cut-and-tied umbilical cord was beginning to shrivel, but it was still pink—a sight that shocked Charlotte. She'd given birth once, but the babe had been cold and gray. Stillborn. Alexander had wept at the birth, then never spoke of the child again. The dead child had done nothing to convince Charlotte to marry him. He was still an artist and still unworthy—and nothing to redeem her status in her family. At the first sign of her swelling waist, the Cutters had sent her away from their mansion on Chambers Street to this cottage on the edge of Gowanus Bay, in Brooklyn. The wealthy might arrive in carriages to the pastoral loveliness of nearby hills and valleys on weekends, but none visited Charlotte or Leah, who'd followed her mistress from marble halls to these dirt floors.

This was the life destined for Cousin Elizabeth too—if she survived the birth. Elizabeth lay on the bed, the pool of bloody birth water staining the sheets between her knees. Her chalky visage reminded Charlotte of a ghost she'd dreamt of once.

"She's not well. Three weeks too early! And now the afterbirth won't budge, and the blood is still comin'," Leah said nervously. They'd been given explicit orders by the Cutter family not to call upon a midwife or apothecary. And since the family held the purse strings, Charlotte and Leah did as they were told.

Charlotte stared at the widening pool on the sheets. There wasn't enough money for a doctor plus food that week.

She threw a dirty sheet over Elizabeth's legs to cover her decently. "Leah, go find Dr. Grier. He might be at home."

"But, Miss Charlotte, they said not to—"

"Just go. I'll find the money somehow, and we won't tell the family. I have an amethyst parure I've been keeping by; I'll sell the set if I must. Call for him."

Leah pushed greasy tendrils from her temples and handed the babe over. On went a gray shawl, and she was out of the cottage and into the bitter, uncaring January night. For a second, the brisk wind coming through the valley blew the door open and held it. Moonlight streamed from behind the clouds before winking out again.

Charlotte wiped the tenacious, waxy white stuff from the infant's body and swaddled her inexpertly. It wasn't just the baby's small size that was unusual. She was odd looking. Hair like burnt molasses, eyelashes the same color surrounding eyes shaped more like a baby rabbit's. The father was one of several handsome men Elizabeth had met in the oyster saloons near the east docks, the absolutely worst place a lady of consequence could find herself. It was a miracle she had not been attacked.

She'd escaped her elder chaperone on four occasions. A mere one of those occasions, however, was enough to ruin her.

By the time her family refused to allow her attendance at any evening parties or theater events, Elizabeth was already with child. The moment her dresses had to be let out to fit her expanding waist, she was banished to Charlotte's care.

The baby cried again, and Charlotte jiggled her in her arms. She dipped a rag in the new milk they'd bought that morning and offered a corner to the infant. Suckling half air, half milk, the babe soon tired and burped before slumbering. Charlotte placed her awkwardly in a box upon the floor. Elizabeth was sleeping soundly, her blonde hair ropy and sweaty against the pillow. Charlotte draped another blanket across her legs. At least the blood had stopped seeping through the bedding.

An hour passed before the doctor thrust open the door. The odor of stale beer entered before him. So, he'd not been at home; he'd been at the tavern, and seemed none too pleased to have left it on a cold winter's night. Leah shuffled in behind, red faced and puffing.

Charlotte wrung her hands. "She's sleeping, but the afterbirth—it hasn't come, Doctor. We've done the best we can. Leah has delivered a half-dozen babies in her time, and surely—"

"Be silent," he snapped.

The doctor was old—older than he'd seemed when she last saw him in town—but his gray eyes were sharp, though reddened from drink. An extra odor of musty hay and burnt tobacco trailed in his wake, mixing with the metallic tang of blood in the room. After removing his cloak, he bent over Elizabeth's sleeping face to touch her cheek, then her neck, with the back of his fingers. He held one wrist in his hand, then the other.

"Her afterbirth—" Charlotte began, but the doctor straightened.

"No need. She's dead as can be, probably before your servant even fetched me. Mercy, can you not tell the living from the dead? What a waste of my drink and dinner. And I had me a decent pork joint, at that."

Charlotte cried out. She went to Elizabeth's side. Surely she was sleeping; surely the doctor was wrong. She lifted her cousin's chilled hand to her cheek and found it was stiffening ever so slightly in the cold room. Elizabeth's eyes were open to tiny slits, but they stared without purpose. Charlotte dropped the hand, aghast at the truth. Elizabeth—curious, bright Elizabeth—wasn't here anymore.

"Well, I might as well take a look at the child, since I've come all this way," the doctor said. "Bring the child to me."

Leah jumped to attention. Later, Charlotte knew, she'd cry over Elizabeth's death while scrubbing out pots behind the cottage. Elizabeth had been clever and merry, even in her confinement, and Leah had adored her for it.

Leah bent to lift the sleeping child and handed the bundle gingerly to the doctor. He set the child down on the rough-hewn table by the window, with that fickle moonlight and a pale-yellow glow from the oil lamp nearby. As soon as he unwrapped the swaddling, the baby erupted in a shrill cry, and the doctor nodded in approval. Ignoring the black, muddy stool already staining the fabric, he lifted the child, flipping her over.

"There is a large birthmark here on the buttocks. Very odd," he murmured. He flipped the baby sideways, examining the umbilical cord stump tied firmly with a cotton cord. His large hand covered the tiny rib cage, smaller than a year-old roasting hen's. Suddenly, his breath caught. "Ah. But what's this? Extraordinary!" The baby wriggled and bleated her discomfort from hunger, or the loss of her warm swaddling, or both.

"What do you mean?" Charlotte stepped near the light of the oil lamp. The oil was cheap, and she had to wave away the smoke so as not to cough.

"A pulse." He lifted the baby and put her chest to his ear. "Right here. Just beneath the rib cage, on the right side." He laid the child down again and pointed with a broad fingertip.

There, just between the tiny ridges of the infant's rib cage, Charlotte saw a rhythmic rise and fall, as if a bird were hidden under her skin, attempting flight. She touched the warm, silky skin. Beneath her fingertip was a beat, beat, beating. It was a familiar cadence.

"I don't understand," Charlotte said.

"One can feel her pulsations where her heart is, but there is an identical one here. On the right." When Charlotte shook her head, not understanding, he added, "Why, the child has two hearts. It's plain as day."

"Impossible," Charlotte said.

"What? Did she steal it from her mam?" Leah suggested, glancing at the corpse. She was superstitious and too imaginative.

"Stop it, Leah," Charlotte said, her tone harsh. She turned to Dr. Grier. "Two hearts? Impossible," she repeated.

"Many things are possible. The human body's mysteries are finite but not yet solved. Your feminine mind couldn't possibly understand." Here, Charlotte bit her tongue hard. These were the swallowed exclamations that had gotten her into trouble with her family in the first place. Dr. Grier continued. "But I must know—who was her father? Was he ill in any way?" The liquor seemed to have left him completely; he was sober as sharpened iron, and his eyes sparkled as they hadn't before. In the lamplight, his expression was grotesque.

"I . . . I don't know," Charlotte said, shrinking at his words. "We think he might have been a dock loafer. Or a sailor."

"A Chinese tar! Why, that would explain it. The child looks almost as if she'd been delivered from Canton itself. Every day, the ports bring tea ships from China and all manner of oddities. I have heard of such things. Fascinating!"

Charlotte's skin prickled with alarm. She quickly swaddled the little girl, who had stopped crying, and held her tight. "Oddities? She's just a child! What things, exactly?"

"Think of those connected twins, Chang and Eng! Marvelous!"

"But they are from Siam, not China," Charlotte said. "And I don't believe they had mixed parentage . . ."

"If the child lives," he said, ignoring her comment, "she might be barren, for one. But the child shall die, most likely. And then we will know what the nature of her malady is. Internal examination will bring the answer."

"Internal," Charlotte murmured. She had the desperate thought of taking the baby and running as fast as possible away from this man. He threw on his cloak, not noticing her reticence.

"Some good can come of an unwanted, bastard child. When the child dies, give the body to me, as it will be of no use to you. It might fetch as high as fifty dollars."

"For what?" Charlotte asked, her nose curling in disgust.

"For dissection, of course. She's an anatomic jewel. She'll be useful to study. In New York, she'd fill an amphitheater of students and learned men. Imagine, five hundred seeking to learn her secrets, with tickets at fifty cents each. It would be a wondrous gift to medicine."

Leah covered her mouth with a handkerchief and shook her head.

"No," Charlotte replied coldly. "Never."

"If you don't give her to me, another will take her. Word will get out about the girl with two hearts. They'll snatch her straight from the grave, and you'll get nothing. Not a cent." He glanced about the dilapidated cottage. "And you need more than nothing, I've good enough eyes to see that."

"Leah. Fetch the crock," Charlotte ordered. Leah did so, scurrying to the open hearth and returning with the tiny white porcelain bowl that had been sitting on the mantel. Charlotte freed a hand from under the baby and scooped out the scant few half dimes, the one quarter, and scattered copper pennies—all they had to pay for their bread and such for the next week. "Take this. For your fee. We owe you nothing. And don't return. This child is not for sale, alive or dead."

The doctor scowled but tipped his hat, leaving behind his yeasty odor of liquor. The door banged shut behind him, and the lamp flickered. He was gone, but the women's alarm would not dissipate.

"What if he returns?" Leah asked, wringing her hands.

"We'll move. Out of Brooklyn, and back to Manhattan, though the rent will be dear."

"But your family—they'll only give us brass if we stay away from the island!"

Charlotte looked over at Elizabeth, whose slit eyes still stared at nothing. The emptiness that her cousin's passing had left behind made her heart ache. All that bright laughter, gone. Then she looked at the child, so strange, so beautiful. The little girl bleated yet another cry and cracked open her eyes. Unfocused, they were beautiful, shining like wet stones. Charlotte's lone heart thumped in response.

"We'll lie. We'll tell everyone it's a boy, healthy as can be. We'll treat the child like a boy. Dr. Grier loves his drink more than air itself. Everyone knows it. No one will believe his story upon seeing a robust boy, when he claims he attended a sick baby girl. We shall say he was a fool of a drunk throughout the evening. The rumor will disappear. When we can save enough money, we'll move away. Back to the city, perhaps, or south somewhere. We'll raise her as a proper lady then."

"What shall we name her? The wee thing," Leah said. She was tickling the baby's toes.

"We need a boy's name. Henry? Samuel?"

"I like Jacob," Leah offered. Charlotte's chin trembled; it was the name she would have given her stillborn son. Leah had so looked forward to caring for a little boy.

"Jacob." Charlotte let the name sit with her and found that it pained her not; it nestled about her heart just so. "Very well. Jacob.

We'll give her a different family name. Lee, I believe, is what Elizabeth called the baby's father. If she belonged to the Cutters, she'd be named Allene, in keeping with family tradition, but she's ours, not theirs. For her real name—Cora."

"Cora?" Leah asked, uncertain.

"Yes. *Cor* is Latin for *heart*. I recall that, at least, from my lessons. That shall be her true name. But we won't speak of it until Dr. Grier is dead and gone, or we've left this terrible cottage behind us. And for that, we'll need to earn some money, and soon." There would be work, and there would be heartache ahead. Nothing new to Charlotte, but Cora had no such history to toughen her. Not yet.

"Cora," the maid cooed, ignoring her mistress's frown. "The impossible girl with two hearts."

TWENTY YEARS
LATER

CHAPTER 1

There were days when Cora Lee loathed her job, but this was not one of them.

It was cold and rainy, too cold for the middle of September. Cora stepped onto the green lawn of Marble Cemetery near First Avenue. Tuckahoe marble obelisks and stones, newly popular with those who could afford to buy their plots in advance, dotted the green.

A proper lady like Cora ought to be on Broadway, bedecked in finery beneath a silk umbrella, promenading before the so-called Marble Palace that housed Stewart's Department Store. But instead, she was here, at the place where God welcomed the young and the old, equally dead as they were. It was a neighborhood of the deceased, with no fewer than eight cemeteries within a four-street radius. But most were no longer accepting burials. Graves were being disinterred and moved to rural cemeteries, as the island was becoming simply too full of the living. Out to Randall's and Ward's Islands they went, and to Green-Wood on Long Island, and to the second Trinity Cemetery at the north end of the city. New York accepted the hungry, poor souls from any ship, but when they died, they didn't stay. Only the wealthy did—like lucky Mr. Hitchcock here.

Or unlucky, perhaps.

Cora bowed her head, face covered under a veil as she joined the mourners already gathered about the coffin freshly polished with beeswax. She was a shadow amongst the mourners—an appropriate shadow, in case anyone looked closely: medium height, with a sturdy build and a narrow waist confined beneath a whalebone basque, and a face that was decidedly not Irish but otherwise difficult to place. Her eyes were dark; the braided knot of hair at her crown was the color of tea that had been steeped too long—though in truth, her real hair was shorn short beneath a rather expensive, matching colored wig. There was no chapel on the cemetery grounds in which to conduct the service, so instead, a thin priest, looking like he'd not yet recovered from the recent cholera epidemic, cleared his throat and began. The ground had yet to be turned, for the Hitchcock family owned a below-ground crypt, hidden beneath a few feet of soil and a heavy marble slab that covered the entrance.

"We leave to rest our very amiable Randolph Hitchcock the third."

Not very amiable, Cora thought. His two grown children appeared more bored than upset at their patriarch's passing.

"A man of God—"

Who died bedding his favorite prostitute at Madame Emeraude's abode on Elm Street.

"And a devoted servant to his family, Randolph Hitchcock left us too soon. He will be remembered for his generosity."

Generosity, or did he mean greed? At least the priest was correct about one thing: Randolph Hitchcock III had indeed died before his time. Cora hadn't known when he would die, but she'd known it would be soon. The doctor treating him had told her so, for the price of a quarter eagle. Hitchcock had been ripening an aneurysm within his vast abdomen, his aorta stretched out to the size of a large apple, at the ready for a catastrophic rupture. The doctor could feel it pulsating under his fingertips, enlarging as the months went by.

According to his favorite girl at Madame Emeraude's (also paid in coins), Hitchcock had laughed off the doctor's warning to quiet his life. Stop drinking, stop his daily trips down to Wall Street, and forgo visits to Madame Emeraude's. And for goodness' sake, stop gobbling down those enormous plates of roasted oysters at the saloons. But it was at Madame Emeraude's where he'd collapsed, insensate—on the upper floor, atop Belle. Apparently, Belle had screamed and thrashed for ten minutes before someone freed her from under his three hundred pounds. Belle always yelled when she was with clients—it was hard to tell when there was a valid crisis.

Hitchcock might not have been a prize when alive. But he certainly was a prize dead. A ruptured aneurysm within a corpulent body would fetch a pretty penny for dissection. Bodies like Hitchcock's were Cora's specialty—a corpse containing a curiosity. The anatomy professors and anatomical museums were willing to pay for the extraordinary. The more that could be learned of the body's errant ways, the better for society. And the more it lined Cora's pockets.

She eyed the burial site. Most resurrectionists did not have the patience to deal with rifle-wielding guards at the private cemeteries, or the marble vaults, or the rare iron mortsafes. Potter's Field was easier to scavenge, but its contents were also rather boring. Consumption. Stillbirth. Apoplexy. Scarlet fever. The poor died in such dreadfully ordinary ways. But even those bodies fetched five or eight dollars apiece, the same sum earned by a week's work of unloading steam boilers at the docks.

Marble Cemetery was unlike a normal cemetery—no headstones, and only a few obelisks and carved marble plaques on the wall indicating the locations of the family crypts. The marble slab on the Hitchcock crypt was a deterrent for unprepared, inexperienced body snatchers. The cemetery's fence was pointed and painful to scale, more so with a three-hundred-pound body. Not that it mattered. Cora had paid a goodly amount last year for a key to the gate's lock.

Cemeteries were where Cora did her best work. She knew them as she knew her own reflection—the ways in, the rotations and vices of the guards, the layouts of the crypts and vaults. She knew which coffins featured an iron knob at the end where the head would be, which suggested the corpse wore a neck ring to prevent it from being pulled out. She noted whether bodies were being kept in a mort house instead of interred, so that they might rot well before they ever went beneath the ground. Cora detested mort houses—they ruined fresh bodies and ruined her profits.

The priest had finished speaking, and a prayer had begun. Cora bowed her head, and the rain lessened, no longer pattering her ruffled umbrella. The mourners began to disperse, and she focused on one of the sons. Warren, the younger son, was the only mourner with reddened eyes. (Although, she noted, even his eyes were not quite sad enough to shed tears.) He was speaking with the priest, and the spaces between him and his family began to widen. Excellent.

As he turned to follow the mourners, Cora collapsed her umbrella and hurried forward. Just as she strode past him, she pretended to trip, and let out a gasp.

"Oh. Oh dear," she said, fumbling as if she'd twisted an ankle on the grass.

The younger Hitchcock reached for her elbow. "Are you quite all right?"

"Ah, no. Not so well." She leaned on his arm and looked to him, lashes sparkling with tears. He was brown haired, mustachioed, and smelled of expensive cigars. His eyes went to hers, then to her bosom above the black lace trim of her bodice.

When his eyes rose again, his breath caught. This was how men often reacted to her. Unable to stop staring at their first meeting. Wondering how her beauty could be labeled and organized within their minds. Was she foreign born? Was she Spanish? How did such a woman, with such eyes and hair, come to be? But this was where she lived, on the edges that defied classification.

"Thank you," Cora said. "I need only a moment."

"Of course." He hesitated. "Do I know you? Did you know Father?"

"Yes. I believe we met last year at the Schermerhorns' December ball." They hadn't, but he'd be too polite to admit he didn't remember her. "Mother would have come herself, but she was ill."

"Of course," he said again.

She let him put his hand on her waist to steady her, and they stepped toward the gate. "Mother wished to know—she's so very worried—if you were planning to make sure your father would rest safe here. Because of . . . Oh, I hate to say it!" Cora put her handkerchief to her nose.

"What? Do you mean grave robbers? Oh yes. We have a guard arriving before sundown, for the next two weeks. Father shall be in a marble vault, in any case."

"That is a relief. I'm so very grateful for your assistance." Cora stepped away from him. "I'm quite well now. And there is my hack, and I must be going. My condolences, sir," she said primly, before walking away.

"Of course, Miss . . . Miss . . ."

But Cora was already gone. The driver took her gloved hand as she stepped into the two-wheeled cab. "Back to Irving Place," she ordered. At the crack of the reins, the horse started, and the hack jiggled its way back up Second Avenue, passing block after block of marble and ubiquitous brown sandstone homes.

Cora sighed with satisfaction. With her perfectly beribboned clothes worthy of the finest ladies in town, she knew how to slide into the finest establishments, stealing a quick word with her favorite high-society physicians, or observing the crowd for signs of strange ailments. And then, she could slip away before anyone asked if she truly belonged.

No small feat, considering she'd lived the first fourteen years of her life disguised as a boy.

She closed her eyes as they wound through the wet streets, loud with newsies on the corners hawking their stories and the clocking of hooves on cobblestones. The smell of fresh rain made everything feel new, though it didn't fool Cora. This evening, she'd be surrounded by the freshly dug, ancient soil of the island, and old Mr. Hitchcock would be her prize.

Her fingers went to her right rib cage. There was nothing, really, to touch, but she knew what lurked beneath the layers of fabric and whalebone. A slight thrilling beneath her fingertips. A pulse, where one ought not to be.

Of course, none of the doctors she paid off, or the doctors she sold the bodies to, knew the truth—that Cora herself was a prize so precious, she'd become legend. The girl with two hearts, too impossible to have truly been born.

<hr/>

The clock on the mantel chimed. Five o'clock. Time to make money. Finally, after a dry spell of weeks without any work.

Knuckles rapped lightly on her chamber door, and Leah entered. Smaller than Cora but with thick and sturdy shoulders and hips, she carried an armful of clean linens. Her yellow hair was in a tight twist on the top of her head, and her apron was crisp and clean. Cora smiled fondly. Leah had been in Cora's life since time out of mind, and in the three years since Aunt Charlotte had died, she'd become as good as a mother.

"Well, Miss Cora. And will you be goin' out tonight, or will Jacob? No sitting about on your arse anymore, eh?" Leah asked. This was a compliment; Leah disliked people who were idle, but the lack of work was not Cora's fault. She was no reaper herself, after all.

"Jacob need not make his appearance until later. My brother can rest for now," Cora said. "And anyway, this job needs a delicate hand."

"That you have. Two, I might add." Leah's pale-blue eyes crinkled. "Did you fill your belly good and full?" Her accent had grown fainter over the years, but her brashness had bloomed.

"Yes, Leah." Leah was always looking to keep her appetite well appeased.

"Be careful, lass. There's only one of you, and your auntie would come back from the grave and give me a lashing if anything happened. If I'd bollocks, she'd chop 'em off."

"Don't be so crude, Leah. Anyway, Alexander would be happy to lecture me in her stead, I'm sure."

"Oh, Alexander." Leah waved her hand. "Of course. We'll wait for a Sunday lecture, won't we?" Leah was actually fond of Charlotte's previous on-and-off lover. A sculptor by trade, he paid his bills by creating anatomic wax figures for the museums downtown and was in high demand. He'd brought a basket of pastries every Sunday since Cora was an infant. Leah liked Alexander best on Sundays, as she had a sweet tooth.

"Please call for a cab, Leah. I'll be down in a moment."

Leah left the room, and Cora sat at her vanity, adding only a hint of rouge to her cheeks. When she stood, her hand went to her right rib cage. It was a bad habit of hers.

Never let anyone know. Ever. This secret will steal you out of your grave someday. And it will take you to your grave, if the wrong person knows.

Her aunt had said these words, time and time again. Even on her deathbed, yellow from the infection, she still rasped these final words of caution. What frightened Charlotte, more than the thought of oblivion, was that someone might find out that Cora was worth more dead than alive.

Cora descended the stairs, hearing the family on the other side of the wall arguing over the price of flour. Cora wasn't wealthy enough to own or rent an entire building, but she wasn't poor enough to crowd into a place with two or three or twenty others. Like the soap boilers and shoemakers whose businesses thrived so they might become the shopkeeping aristocracy, she, too, lived in that twilight in which many of the working class found themselves. Too rich to reside in the Five Points; too poor to be accepted in the best boxes at the Park Theater. But she had Leah, and she had her secrets. That was good enough.

Leah held the door for her, while the hackney cab waited outside. "Be careful, lass. You've been goin' out as Cora too often. It's only been two years since Dr. Grier died, and only three since Charlotte left us."

"I know. I'll be careful." She grinned. "Just a regular night's work. That's all."

Leah kissed her cheek, and the scent of newly baked bread embraced her until she climbed into the cab. Hopefully Leah wouldn't get drunk again. She'd had a habit lately of disappearing and reappearing with an empty bottle of spirits, snoring on the bed.

Cora had already sent word to her boys to meet at the cemetery later tonight. Before then, she had work to do. Often, she wasn't needed at this point on a job—Jacob could handle it. But sometimes, a woman's touch was best. She ordered the cab to drive past Stuyvesant Square and its grand twin fountains, past Saint Mark's Church and down Second Avenue. Above the gate of Marble Cemetery, the sun was bobbing low, its gold beams filtering through the tree boughs that sheltered the iron fencing.

Cora stepped down from the cab. She ignored the driver's remark about her odd choice of drop-off point and reminded him to wait for fifteen minutes. She stood before the gate. It was closed but still unlocked. Through it she spied a large, brutish gent, a Bowery b'hoy—a species of single men well known for their riotous behavior and tendency to dress in too-bright clothing. This specimen sported a yellow plaid vest over his broad chest, an ill-trimmed mustache, and hair slicked behind his ears with soap. (Cora loathed soap-locked hair; it made her think of insects caught in dirty sap. Jacob wore his hair plainly.) The b'hoy leaned against the stone wall beneath an oak tree, ten feet from the newly turned soil above the Hitchcocks' crypt. He held a rifle. Physically, a bullet would only wound one of her gang before they overwhelmed him, but one shot would attract unwanted attention.

She sidestepped away from the gate for a moment, gently squeezed the purse of money hidden in a pocket of her dress skirt, pinched her cheeks, and took a breath. She was ready.

Without looking, she pivoted toward the gate and slammed face-first into a wall.

Or what she thought was a wall. It was a man. Her nose smarting from the blow, she drew her hands to her face from the pain. Though startled, she didn't cry out. She'd learned ages ago to muffle her surprise at anything—it attracted too much attention.

The gentleman shot out an arm to steady her. "Oh! I'm so sorry! My apologies—I didn't see you there at all."

Cora gathered herself. Her eyes cast downward, she saw a good set of leather shoes, gray wool trousers that were worn but clean, and clean hands. Young hands that had yet to meet any labor. She peeked up over the hand still covering her nose.

He was quite tall, with a slightly ginger tint to hair that had both chestnut and brass highlights, and hazel eyes, the kind that were neither bright green nor brown, but a muddy, middling color. His mouth was straight with concern, but his eyes seemed to be laughing at her.

That was how she would always remember Theodore, looking back on this first meeting—how he seemed never to be one thing, at any one time. But her first thought was, My, he's handsome. The second was, He needs to go away. Immediately.

She removed her hand, saw that there was no blood, and nodded. "I'm quite all right." She sounded congested. "Thank you. Good day." She began to walk past him and into the cemetery, but he followed.

"I can't leave until I'm sure you're well." His voice was mellow, almost teasing. She began to think that perhaps she actually disliked this man.

"I'm very well, as you can see. Good day to you."

"It must be a good day, as you've said it twice. And here I've smashed your pretty face by accident. At least let me apologize formally."

"It's not necessary." He was still so close to her. Close enough to touch her waist. This might take some more direct words. "I'm quite all right. Goodbye, sir."

"Or rather, hello. I'm where I need to be, so I'm going nowhere for the moment." He spread out a hand to display the cemetery grounds, empty except for the paid guard, who was watching them suspiciously.

"I see." But Cora didn't see. She decided to ignore him, but every step she took, he seemed to match. Maybe he was a member of the Hitchcock family. It was the only explanation, the way he followed her like a shadow. She would just ignore him. Surely he would leave soon.

"Say, don't we know each other? You look awfully familiar." He smiled again, and she had the strong urge to run. Cora threaded through all classes of society—with the dockworkers at the oyster saloons as Jacob, and at the ticketed grand openings at the museums as Cora. It was quite possible he'd seen her before, but her work demanded that she maintain her anonymity. Only a few doctors in town knew of what she did; if the uppertens knew, she wouldn't possess the stealth to search out new medical anomalies.

The Bowery b'hoy in the plaid vest seemed rather entertained by their exchange. Which was doubly irritating, because Cora liked to be professional, coolly in control of negotiations even before negotiations began.

Irritated, Cora turned to the stranger. "Leave me be, or I'll call for help."

"I seriously doubt you mean that. No copper stars or watchmen walking around here. Maybe you're the one who should leave."

She stared him straight in the eye. He held her gaze but then quickly looked over to the guard.

Oh.

He wasn't trying to flirt, and he wasn't there to mourn. He was competition.

How odd. She knew most of the resurrectionists in town. This one was an unknown, and rather too well dressed for the position. (Cora's dress, of course, was terrible for digging, but she wasn't here for the labor.) Besides, new burials below Eighty-Sixth Street were exceedingly rare, so most resurrectionists went north for bodies.

Cora didn't grace his words with a reply. Business was business. It was time to ignore this upstart. She approached the guard directly.

"Cora Lee, at your service. I—"

"Never mind her. I've ten dollars here if you'll look away for one hour tonight."

The guard stared at him. Cora stared at him. The price was ridiculously high. An interesting body might fetch twenty dollars; giving away half to the guard didn't make any sense. He was being paid by the family to watch the grave anyway. The guard seemed suspicious, and rightly so. It sounded like a trap. Clearly this boy didn't know a thing about Cora's line of work, nor did he know the language.

The guard shifted his rifle to the other hand so he could point rudely in his face. "Who's this jack dandy?"

Cora waved her hand, as if to shoo away a fly. "Aye, he's an archduke and needs to dry up." She stepped in front of her competition, who suddenly seemed confused. "Listen. I've a dawb and a good bean for that quaroon. Got a school comin' at midnight to get under this earth bath. We'll be right shady."

The guard nodded, thinking, but he was taken aback at hearing flash spoken by a lady. It wasn't an everyday occurrence, if at all, especially north of Canal Street.

"What did you say?" the young man asked. "I already offered ten dollars!"

Cora tipped her head toward her companion, whose confidence had melted away. "He's a napper! You'll get your two dews in the reign of Queen Dick." At this, the guard laughed out loud, and Cora smirked. "I've got half in my moll-sack, and you'll get the second half after."

"What did you call me?"

But the young man was so distanced from the conversation, neither heard his complaint. The guard shook hands with Cora, who gave him a handful of coins out of her reticule. He tipped his hat.

Cora smiled. "Look for Jacob, my brother. He'll bring the rest."

"Jacob Lee?" the b'hoy asked. Cora nodded. "Ah. I've heard of you two." He seemed impressed, and relieved. The Lees had a reputation for discretion and fair pay.

Cora turned on her heel and walked back to the gate. Twilight had darkened the whole cemetery. One by one, the gaslights on the street were being lit, sputtering and hissing their welcome to the evening. Behind her, the guard spoke some rude words to her competition, who then trotted to catch up to Cora like a whipped dog.

She smiled and got into her waiting cab. Before the horse could walk off, the young man grabbed the reins. The driver yelled in protest, and Cora peeked her head out the side.

"What is it?"

"What did you say back there?"

"If you don't know, you'd better get out of the business."

"Tell me."

"Only if you let go of these reins."

"All right."

Cora sighed. "I said you were a liar and a fool, and he's getting five dollars to look away. My men will be back later, so don't you dare come back. My brother will be with them, and he's not nearly as civilized as I am. You had best stay out of our way."

"Theodore."

"Excuse me?"

"My name is Theodore Flint. But you can call me Theo. In case you need to insult me again."

He let go of the reins, and the horse jumped to a start. Cora sank into the velvet cushions, glad to be away from the stranger. Just as she turned the corner, she heard a yell and a laugh.

"Cora Lee! I think I'm in love with you!"

Looking back, she saw Theodore Flint, halfway down the street, bow grandly. Cora had a feeling that staying out of her way was the last thing on his mind.

CHAPTER 2

Leah was asleep in the next room when Cora woke just before midnight. Leah's snores were so sonorous that Cora felt the reverberations in her pillow. On a night like tonight, Cora slept in parcels of three or four hours—tiring but normal.

She lit an oil lamp, its yellow glow warming the corners of the room. After washing her face in the basin, she stared into the looking glass on the wall. She touched the short hair on her head, smoothing it at the nape of her neck. No need for a trim; it was short enough, and messy enough too. Off came her nightgown, the cool air of the bedroom alighting on her bare skin and making her shiver. Leah had laid out Jacob's clothes on a chair in the corner. On went some loose drawers that covered her from knees to waist. Cora then wound a long, wide strip of gauze around her breasts until her feminine bust flattened into oblivion under four tidy layers. She wound one end over her left shoulder, then tucked in the ends so tight they would not budge, no matter how much she moved, heaved, and lifted.

She paused, her hand on her right ribs where that mysterious other center of herself throbbed to the same pulse as in her wrist. All these years, her other heart had sat within her, innocent. Once, only once, had it made her ill. For the briefness of an afternoon, Cora had listed to the side, drool dripping from her mouth as she slurred her dismay. Charlotte had been beside herself, and Alexander, who was over for dinner that day, attempted to bolt for the door and call for a doctor. He was reminded that never, ever, could Cora be seen by a doctor again.

So, thirteen-year-old Cora had shivered and cried, wondering if her numbed left arm and leg would work again, or her garbled speech would right itself. And they did—only a few hours later. It never happened again, but the incident reminded Cora that her body held dark sway over her existence.

She lifted her hand and reached for a slim-fitting shirt whose length stopped at her elbows, laced in the front so it was tight as a wet kid glove. Leah had constructed it of double-layered sailcloth, sewn with leather padding over the deltoid and latissimus muscles, to give her a more masculine, triangle-shaped torso. A hand clapped upon her clothed shoulder would feel a solid, sturdy, wiry frame.

On went a pair of trousers, a brown shirt closed high to the neck, and buttoned-on galluses. She slipped on an old silk vest, and pulled on sturdy boots constructed with an extra-thick layer of leather sewn in the outsoles. An inch and a half of dense felt sewn on the inner sole, sitting above the heel with a deep instep, gave her nearly two inches of added height. Under her long hemmed trousers, no one would know. Finally, on went a long coat with tails and plenty of pockets.

Cora went to her vanity and searched out a glass jar. She dipped her fingers in a gray mixture of charcoal and lard, and smeared a fine film over her cheeks, chin, and upper lip. Her eyebrows were darkened and mussed. More was rubbed into her knuckles and fingertips and beneath her nails, to disguise her lady's hands. Another swipe went under her eyes—Jacob didn't sleep as well as Cora. She dipped a boar-bristled brush into another jar, this one containing ink with the texture of tar. She stippled it lightly over her upper lip, chin, and near her cheekbones. In the dark of night or under the few gaslights around, it would look like she needed a good shave. One sticky black piece of sealing wax conformed to her right canine. She grimaced in the looking glass. Her smile was not welcoming.

A short knife was strapped to her right calf, and another hidden within her vest. The money for the guard and her boys was secured in her coat pocket, with more for some gambling after the job, if she felt the urge. Finally, on went a soot-colored stovepipe hat.

Jacob Lee was ready to work.

Leah continued to snore in the next room. She would not awaken; real or no, Jacob gave far less to worry about than Cora, clever as she was. Jacob knew exactly what kind of trouble would kill him, and it was the kind he could see from a mile away. Cora looked out for the kind of trouble that would kill her in a more insidious fashion, through the gossip of anatomists and doctors on the island.

She thumped down the stairs and out the front door. A few curtains draped shut when she glanced up. The neighbors didn't like Cora's brother much; he tended to grunt and looked too rough for that part of town, but as long as Cora's gentle smile shone during the daylight and her purse kept the rent paid, the landlord didn't complain.

The street was quiet, but for the lamp on the corner that hissed. A covered wagon sat just outside of the front door. Only two of Cora's boys—Friar Tom and Otto the Cat—were sitting in the seat. Just before abandoning him for California, Friar Tom's wife had poured a pot of boiling soup on his head, scorching his hair so that all that was left was a fringe orbiting his skull. Otto was leaner than a broom handle and wore a dead cat's tail tied to the back of his pants, for reasons unknown. He made a killing in the dog fights at Kit Burn's Rat Pit every weekend; grave robbing was his "regular" job.

Cora spat on the ground and pulled her voice low. "Where are the others?"

"They're already waiting at the cemetery," Tom said. He yawned and pulled out a meat pie from his pocket, not offering to share. Breakfast time.

"Where's the dimber-mort? Miss Lee coming tonight?" Otto said. He exchanged a lascivious glance with Tom. Cora was all too used to hearing how beautiful she was.

"No," Cora answered. She pulled out the knife from her vest and used it to pick her teeth. "She's family, boys. You keep your eyes to yourself, or I'll pluck them out and have 'em boiled in my morning tea."

Tom and Otto quieted. They were smart enough not to be impertinent, for fear of Jacob's wrath. A salacious comment about Cora had earned one of their prior colleagues a scar that went from forehead to cheek. His eye whitened with blindness after the infection settled. Last they heard, he'd left on a ship to work on the Erie Canal with "more civilized folk."

Cora sheathed her knife and jumped into the back of the wagon. She peeked at the pile under a coarse cloth. There were wooden spades (quieter than iron), an ax, several folded cloths, iron rods for breaking chains, and a good saw. A small lamp, lit low, swung merrily from a hook at the wagon's corner.

Tom jerked the reins, and they were off. As the horse's hooves clomped down First Avenue, they chatted about the dog fights happening this weekend, which pugilist was going to lose to the great Irish brute who'd been winning nonstop for the last month, and whose oyster saloon they'd visit after the job was finished. When the wagon slowed by the cemetery gate, Cora hopped out.

Three other men stood smoking and waiting. Cora recognized two of them. One was Puck, a large card player with enormous ears—he'd been a pugilist when he was younger, and his ears expanded with every fight until they looked like chunks of rotted cheese. He could barely hear out of those ears now.

The Duke had come too. No one knew what the black gent's real name was, but the Duke was a man of his word and held himself like royalty, so no one asked. There were rumors that he'd fled from a slave owner in Georgia somewhere. He was a good man and earned his coin.

Behind the Duke, a third man was squashing his spent cigar underfoot. Cora could already tell his clothes were too fine to belong to one of the regular boys, but Puck had a habit of bringing an extra friend desperate to earn a few coins. She'd tell him that needed to stop. After the hint of competition earlier that evening, she wanted to keep her team tight.

The stranger lifted his chin and nodded hello, eyeing Jacob with a grin.

It was Theodore Flint.

The Duke started, "Jacob Lee, this is—"

"What is he doing here?" Cora yelled, which was unlike her. And it was hard to yell and keep the register of her voice low, like a man's.

"He's new, but he's willing to work tonight, no pay. Just to get some experience, maybe help out later for another job."

"No. This isn't a damned school." She peered at Flint, who wisely stayed silent. "Cora said nothing about a new man. But she did mention a Sam trying to steal the job." Flint raised his eyebrows, unaware Jacob had just called him a stupid fellow.

Cora had to make sure Flint didn't recognize her. She needed Jacob as much as ever—for the income, and to protect those two hearts of hers. Although Dr. Grier had died, his insistence on the existence of a two-hearted girl with a Chinese father ensured that the gossip was still out there. And so, careful she must continue to be.

Cora cleared her throat and gave Jacob's voice steel. "My sister told me his name was Flint."

"Aye, one and the same," the Duke said, before whistling. "Never mind, then. Be off, you. Or we'll scragg ya." He made a hanging motion, conjuring an image of the executed in the Tombs.

Flint raised his hands. "Wait a moment. Now, that was a mistake. My mistake. I didn't know your sister worked a good gang here, or this one in particular. I told your man here if I could come, I'd have a buyer tonight. For forty dollars."

"Forty?" Cora leaned back on her heels. With these boots, she could almost look Theodore Flint in the eye. Cora could have him on the ground, a knife at his throat, in less than two seconds. Now that she was a man, society said she could hold his gaze all she wanted.

"I've a particular buyer in mind," Flint said, standing up straighter, as if trying on a new suit of confidence.

"Who?"

"Someone who will only buy if I'm there to help sell."

Cora crossed her arms. "I know every buyer in town, and they've all sold to me or my sister."

"Not this one. He's new. And he's willing to pay more than the others for particularly unique specimens. Look, I'm not the police. I'm just trying to learn, I promise."

Tom, Otto, and the Duke waited for their captain to speak. Puck was lazily picking a scab on his neck. A small gesture, but one that meant he wasn't vested in the job. Cora took note. She thought for a moment about Flint, and this body. She could still take the body and sell it to Dr. Phillips, or Jenkins uptown, if Flint's buyer didn't materialize. They'd been giving nearly thirty dollars lately for an excellent specimen. But still. Forty dollars.

"What's your cut?"

"Like I said, just the pleasure of coming along with you fine folk."

At this, the boys all laughed roughly, and Puck clapped Flint on the back so hard, he actually took a few steps forward to regain his balance.

"Come now, Jacob. A dollar's a dollar, and forty of them sound mighty good tonight. Better than our usual sum, eh?" the Duke said. His dark, intelligent eyes spoke to Cora, saying something different. Let's meet his contact, and then we'll never need Flint again. Cora nodded subtly.

"And I'll cut his ears off if he's a diver," added Puck. "Been too long since I sliced off a pair." Puck had a strange thing about collecting ears, since his were mangled. Every second or third job, he sliced one off the body and pocketed the pieces of cartilage. There was a rumor that he and Gallus Meg were lovers. The very Gallus Meg who bit men's ears off in fights and preserved them in a jar on the bar of her saloon. Cora never bothered to ask whether this was true, because she didn't really want to know the answer.

"All right," Cora said. "We're watching you, you hear? And it's getting late. We need to work. Otto, you keep a keen eye on our friend here."

Cora picked up the small lamp from the wagon's corner and went to the gate, using her key to unlock it. They pushed the gate aside (no creaking; the boys had already oiled the hinges). In the deep gloom along the far stone wall, the plaid-covered guard was slumbering against a tree trunk. Her boys carried their tools without so much as a clank and laid them quietly on the grass. Cora had taught them well.

She walked silently up to the guard, whose hat was pulled low on his forehead, and gently nudged his foot.

"Hello," she said. "We're here for our parcel."

"Don't mind me," the guard murmured. "I'm busy watching this trunker, remember?" And with that, the guard tipped over, pulled his hat off, and started snoring like a very large baby.

Several feet away, beneath the darkened patch of grassless ground, lay Randolph Hitchcock, ready to be used for something more than selling at the Stock Exchange and eating a half gallon of oysters at the best saloons. Cora felt a strange longing to speak to him, perhaps brought on by the slight flutter of her second heart. I'm just like you, or I may be someday, she thought.

"Let's get to work, boys," Cora said.

RANDOLPH HITCHCOCK III

There are two things I regret.

It's always too late when one thinks of these things, but I have never been one to plan ahead. My dear Emma keeps all the details of our lives tidy and in place. And now I've left her behind, with a shadow of scandal—I ought to have died in her arms, but alas, I was with another.

I should have told Emma that I loved her. I did love her, but I am not a man of great outward affections. I am a man of appetites, and those have consumed me utterly, it seems. For it wasn't the great mass of blood thumping in my belly that brought about my end, as my physician had cautioned me. No, a bitterness still lies upon my tongue, cold as it is now. A bitterness I ought to have noted in the pudding brought to me hours before my death.

It matters not. I was speeding toward this destination, no matter how I found myself here, and thus my second regret is my thoughtless misplacement of time. One always thinks one has forever, and that tomorrow will come to wipe away yesterday's misfortunes and mistakes so one can start anew. But tomorrow will come no longer. Not for this Hitchcock.

Instead, these men come for me. And one a woman, by God! She wears a man's clothing, but nothing is hidden to me now.

Well. Have at me, you hungry savages! This body does me no good anymore.

But then the woman touches my shoulder—a fleeting tenderness. She isn't indifferent to my death.

There is a door they cannot see, waiting behind them. I shall go to it now. Whether it leads up or down, I don't know. I do know there is no choice in the matter. My deeds on this plane are done.

Oh, my dear Emma.

'Tis far too late, but I am sorry.

CHAPTER 3

Cora stooped down and pointed. "This is where the entrance shaft is. Should be one or two feet down." She picked up a wooden shovel and tossed it hard to Theodore Flint, who caught it awkwardly. "Your education starts now. Dig."

Puck, Otto the Cat, the Duke, and Friar Tom smiled at one another. They watched Flint dig, quietly egging him on when he flung dirt too far.

"Now, be neat about it, boy. Messy makes more work for you later," the Duke chided. Otto played with his dead cat tail, swinging it temptingly near Flint's head. And Puck sidled next to Cora.

"I want more coin," he whispered. "You pay the others better."

"You're new," Cora growled.

"Not anymore."

Once more, she cursed the day the Duke had brought Puck on— one of the few times they'd disagreed—and she cursed herself for not turning him away sooner. She didn't trust him. And now, he'd learned all their tricks. As high-class resurrectionists, they'd had little competition. A disgruntled Puck might try to change that.

"I'll think on it," Cora said at last. Then she listened to Tom having a long, drawn-out discussion (with no one) over why blueberries were far more delicious than blackberries. Tom was always looking to keep his belly round, to match the curve of his bald pate.

After one and a half feet of excavated soil, Flint was sweating and out of breath, when his wooden shovel clinked faintly against something hard. The other boys got down on their knees and scooped away the last of the soil, exposing a two-by-two-foot marble capstone.

"Here it is. Door to the dead," Cora announced. The marble was ghostly white in the darkness despite the thin whisking of dirt on top. Everyone except Flint stooped to ease their fingertips beneath the edge of the marble. Only rich families had underground vaults. This one was shared between two families—one shaft, two vaults. Entering it would take some muscle.

Cora looked up at Flint. "What, you waiting for someone to serve you a squall now?"

"A what?" Flint asked.

"A drink. Liquor. Suet. Swig," Otto said helpfully. "He means, put your back into it, already!"

"Very well." Flint wiped the sweat from his brow and bent down next to Cora. Cora confessed to herself that she liked Flint better now that that smile was off his face and a good sweat had soaked his neat hair into points and curls. Also, he wasn't complaining about the labor.

"On my count. On. Duo. Tray!" Cora whispered.

They all pulled, jugulars bulging at the effort. The marble capstone weighed almost three hundred pounds, but Cora could lift her portion equally. The heavy work, night after night, had made her arms and thighs taut and strong.

After a small amount of grunting, they were able to transfer the capstone onto the lawn. Cora wiped her hand on her trousers and peered into the dark shaft. Several feet below were two dusty doors opposite each other. Cora lowered herself into the shaft with one swift movement, landing on hard dirt.

"Lamp," she ordered.

Otto used the tip of his tail to polish a milky spot on the glass, then handed her the lamp. Cora adjusted the wick. These doors didn't have locks, like some of the others she'd encountered. She opened the north door with a creak and held her lamp aloft.

The vault was small, just eight feet wide, with a curved ceiling. The packed-dirt floor was perhaps ten feet below turf level. The vault smelled damp, like good soil, not like rot. Several shelves of slate jutted from the walls, holding the crumbled remains of previous Hitchcocks. One large body lay conspicuously near the door on a low shelf. Randolph Hitchcock, wrapped demurely in cloth. The coffin had only been a temporary home for him at the funeral.

"Flint. Otto. Get down here," Cora ordered. "Bring the rope."

Flint lowered himself into the shaft, followed by Otto, holding a coil of narrow rope. Cora began unwrapping the shroud.

"Get his shoes and stockings off, Flint."

"Why?"

"No one ever needed a nice pair of shoes to be ottomised by a professor. His clothes are in the way. If you want to keep them, take them off with care. If not, use a knife."

Under the light shroud, the body wore a nice evening outfit, complete with silk embroidery at the collar and cuffs.

Otto pointed to Flint. "You heard Jacob. Get the shoes and socks off. And if they're my size, they're mine. If they're not, I keep the rags."

By rocking the body left, then right, Cora was able to get the rope beneath Hitchcock's torso and under his armpits. His limbs were stiff already, making the job more difficult. She finished tying the knot as Flint and Otto pulled off the last of the clothing. Hitchcock's body seemed bloated, but not from death. From too much drink and too many rich victuals. Wealth, it seemed, was not always a boon to life.

Cora handed the rope's end to the boys above, who prepared to pull. But Flint had paused, staring at the naked body with a nauseated expression.

"No one has time for your tender feelings," Cora said briskly. "Haven't you seen a dead body before?"

"I have. I've just never stolen one."

Flint continued to stare at the body God had given Hitchcock. No more silk or linen garments here to mask or impress anybody, or to stave off the rot that would eventually eat him into dust. The eyes were opened to slits, darkly staring into oblivion.

"Aw, it's his first time. Have a care, Jacob Lee," said Otto, clapping Flint hard on his back.

Cora stepped next to Flint, who was blinking quickly. "I'll tell you what I was told the first time I did this five years past. This chum is dead, and can't hear or feel a thing. He's as sad as floating wood in water. If you're going to cry, go to church and pray for the living. The dead don't need your tears."

Flint's eyes flicked up to meet hers. They were red, but he wasn't crying or sad. In fact, he seemed angry. The hazel had become an inscrutable color, almost the color of his namesake stone.

"Just tell me what to do next." His voice was cold and dry, and for a moment Cora had the distinct feeling that Theodore Flint wasn't exactly who she thought he was, or the individual she had met earlier. She'd expected him to snap, not to display this shred of resiliency.

"Grab his right shoulder. I've got his left. Otto, get his ankles," Cora ordered.

Flint did so without complaint or a wince. As the men above tugged on the rope, they shuffled the heavy body together into the narrow entrance shaft. As Cora pushed and heaved, Hitchcock's face drew closer to her. His jaw sagged a touch, and the tip of his tongue bulged slightly against his teeth. Even in the dim light of the lamp swinging from Puck's hand, she could see that his tongue was a vibrant shade of green.

How extraordinary. Why on earth would it be such a color? But she had little time to think about it, as she was soon heaving the rest of Hitchcock's slack weight upward. Tom and Puck tugged the naked corpse into the night air and onto an outspread cloth, rolled it up like a cigar, and carried it to the wagon. The others replaced the heavy fieldstone cap on the shaft and shoveled dirt back into the hole.

Cora dug into her coat pocket, pulled out a few dollars' worth of coins, and went to the guard, who was awake and sitting up.

"You've earned a peck and booze for tonight." She handed over the money, and the guard replaced his hat, touching it.

"Be off, now. I never heard nor seen you."

All six of them loaded into the wagon. There were no congratulations. Revelries would be succinctly articulated with a few belches later after some whiskey or a visit to one of the beer gardens. Cora turned to Flint, who was still steely faced.

"Well, Flint? Who's to buy our prize?"

"Drive north on Broadway," Flint said. The Cat shook the reins, and the horse began to clip-clop toward First Avenue. The gaslights had been extinguished, and only a dim sliver of moon lit the way. Bill stickers, with their paste-filled buckets, were at work along the street, gluing on fresh advertisements wherever there was flat space to be had. "Night scavengers" passed by, the unluckily employed men who carried the contents of public privies toward the river.

"I didn't ask for directions. I want a name. What's his affiliation?" Cora asked. "Physicians and Surgeons? University of the City of New York? The Grand Anatomical Museum?"

"The university," Flint responded. That was all.

Cora thought of the various physicians she'd sold to recently. Their class sizes were surging lately. Drs. Mott and Van Buren had both bought unusual specimens from her in the last month, but she also knew that their students smuggled in corpses dug up from Potter's Field. Her contacts told her that they were not bringing in the volume they'd like, but the question why this Flint boy needed to step into her corner of the game was unanswered.

Ten minutes later, the wagon pulled up in front of the Stuyvesant Institute, the current and temporary home of the University of the City of New York's medical school, across from Bond Street. The granite building was designed to impress, with four imposing Corinthian columns in the front. Iron gates blocked a side alley.

Flint stepped down from the wagon and wordlessly produced a key. He ushered the wagon to the back of the grand building. A stale odor emanated from piles of rotted garbage that a cook had thrown out. But it was nothing compared to some of the alleys farther downtown in the Five Points, where clogged sewers prevented even the rain from washing away the refuse. Cora looked left and right. There was no one waiting for them.

"And who's the buyer?" she demanded.

Flint smiled, the first time since she'd wiped the smug look off his face at the cemetery gate. "It's me."

Cora narrowed her eyes. "You."

"Yes. I'm a medical student, but I've been tasked with finding the most unique bodies on the island for the right price. Several of the anatomy professors are counting on me."

They *should* have been counting on her.

"Why not say so in the first place?"

"I have my reasons," he said stubbornly.

"Then why dig with us? To steal our methods?"

"Never mind that. We've got a body to stash upstairs. And I've got the money for it."

Cora crossed her arms and frowned. She glanced up at Otto and Tom, who were both scowling. The Duke and Puck were murmuring to each other. None of them enjoyed being lied to.

Cora lifted her chin. "Let's see, then."

Flint pulled out a handful of coins—gold five-dollar half eagles, quarter eagles, and more. He handed it all over to Cora, who counted.

Forty dollars, just like he said. Cora slipped the coins into her vest pocket. Half would go to her men; the other half she kept.

"Are we good?" Flint asked.

"Aye, that we are." She turned toward the wagon, noting that Flint had lifted a foot to follow her. She planted her right leg, pivoted her hip, and punched Flint square on the left cheek. The force of the blow rang up Cora's arm to her elbow, but she had momentum and preparation on her side. Flint, on the other hand, had walked into the punch.

He staggered back, eyes squeezed shut, arms reaching for purchase as he lost his balance. She took one clean leap upward and kicked him in the chest, and Flint landed on his back with a grunt. Gravel scattered around him.

The other lads jumped off the wagon and stood behind Cora.

"What was that for?" Tom asked.

"Yes, what was that for?" echoed Flint, gasping as he rubbed his jaw and moving it to make sure it still worked.

"We have rules. If you were the buyer, you should have said so. Come on, lads, let's give him what he's bought."

With that, they dumped Hitchcock's naked body nearly on top of Flint, who scrambled away from the pasty corpse.

"I guess that'll teach him. We'll not work with him again, eh?" Puck said, clapping Cora hard on the shoulder once they were in the back of the wagon.

"No, we won't," Cora said smoothly, though she couldn't shake the feeling that she would see him again, whether she liked it or not.

CHAPTER 4

It was past nine o'clock in the morning when Leah awoke her. Cora turned over and grunted, her dreams fleeing her groggy mind, save one detail.

A green tongue.

She shivered and pried open one lazy eye. Leah, scrubbed to shiny cleanliness with her apple cheeks aglow, maid's cap on her crown, was carrying a basket of wood. She swept out the ashes in the fireplace and placed more wood on the dying embers.

"I'm still sleeping," Cora said with an added groan. If she groaned enough, sometimes Leah would make coddled eggs.

"If you were sleeping, you wouldn't be speaking."

"True."

"Never mind that. The currant buns are already getting cold."

No mercy, this one. "But, Leah."

"Never mind you." Leah bent to pick up the dirty clothes near the bed, and her eyebrows rose half an inch. "Why are your knuckles bruised? Ah, have you been fightin' again? Cora Lee, your aunt and mother in heaven would cry!"

Cora shook out her right hand. Her knuckles were sore, and a purpling mess spread across them.

"It's fine. Get some liniment and I'll heal nicely."

"One of these days you'll get a bruise on your eye, and how will that look on a lady?"

"Wonderful! Then I'll have to be Jacob for weeks. How fierce I'll look!"

"Let 'em come here, and I'll blast them with my wind. That porter didn't sit right in my stomach last night." She waved a hand near her rump.

Cora laughed, and jumped out of bed to ready herself. Before long, she was downstairs in a day dress of pink-and-green lawn, corset on neatly, bustle accentuating her tiny waist just so, her favorite wig firmly on. The tendrils drooped over her forehead and temples, covering the edges of the wig beautifully. Even though it was only Leah and Alexander, she was careful to be Cora completely. Never halfway with her two lives.

She entered the dining room, where breakfast was laid out. And there were coddled eggs! Leah was a dear. And there was Alexander too. He didn't acknowledge her when she entered, his eyes fixed, through his reading glasses, on the latest issue of *Courier and Enquirer*. When she was little, she'd receive an embrace and perhaps a sweet kiss. Now, he was stiff and formal. She missed the old Alexander.

He was tall, handsome though nearing forty, and already with half a head of silver hair. He'd not yet attained the middling corpulence of others his age, instead cutting a trim figure like the dandies walking about Broadway at night. Unlike those rogues, he chose the sober dress of one who saw beauty beyond pearls and silk. What Cora loved the most about him—if she were rudely objectifying—were his hands. Alexander had sculptor's hands—long, tapered fingers that were strong and delicate at the same time.

"And how is the wax-sculpting business these days, Alexander?" Cora asked lightly, pouring him a cup of tea, then one for herself and for Leah.

"It is eminently meltable, malleable, and occasionally brittle." Alexander took off his spectacles. "And you're bruised. My goodness, Cora. What would Charlotte say?"

Cora put a currant bun on her plate, then sipped her tea. Whenever her behavior didn't please Leah or Alexander, it always came back to her aunt. Would Charlotte be displeased? Would Charlotte approve? Cora hoped that in heaven, her mother and aunt weren't gossiping over her choices. Even if her choices had been born of their decisions. Charlotte was the one who originally found a meaningful salary from watching over cemeteries, scouting out the newest burials for the resurrectionists in town. She had used her uppertens upbringing as an asset—in the cemeteries of the rich, no one doubted she belonged among the mourners. Charlotte made sure the rich were pillaged the same as any other soul.

"I believe," Cora said slowly, "that Charlotte would be proud of me."

"I doubt that," Alexander said coolly, folding his paper.

"You're wrong."

Leah walked in, brushed her hands on her apron, and sat down opposite Cora. "Don't be speaking to your uncle like that, Miss Cora. Manners."

Manners. Cora dug up corpses and punched men and bound her breasts into oblivion, yet Leah could make her bite her tongue with one word: *manners*. Alexander wasn't really her uncle, but he was as good as. He was there when Cora fell from a tree and broke her wrist. When she had the measles and almost died, he'd fetched the medicines and nearly knocked down the druggist's door at midnight. She might almost have seemed a substitute for the baby he and Charlotte had lost, but anyone could see that the heartbreak of it had never left them. While she was growing up, they'd acted more like siblings than lovers.

An artist by trade, Alexander had found work as a wax sculptor for the medical schools that wished to have various anatomical features recreated for study. Thanks to his prowess, the carotid bifurcation and complexities of a hand's tendons became as detailed in wax as in the real thing. Cora knew he'd rather make his living as a sculptor of marble and clay, but wax paid the bills. He'd once likened it to a poet paying his rent by publishing penny papers and weeklies.

And his work was in demand. The anatomist at the College of Physicians and Surgeons loved him, and every anatomy museum that cropped up begged for his work: reconstructions of hearts and lungs, open torsos that showed the inner truths of spines and spleens and aortas. *Under the skin, we are all the same,* Alexander would say. *The field is level for everyone. This is what Charlotte tried to do, keep the field level, even after death.*

"Cora," Alexander said firmly.

"Yes." She lifted her eyes and smiled. "I'm sorry, what?"

"Your aunt. You forget yourself. This position was not intended as something to do all your days. I make better money now. I could provide you and Leah income enough. You could stop, you know."

Cora bit her lip. Leah said nothing, only nibbling the currants out of her bun.

"I cannot," Cora said. "I don't wish to be dependent on you, Alexander. I thank you, but what if you were to marry? Or grow sick? No. I must do this."

"It's dangerous work. Someday, you may be found out. If a salary is that important," he added, "you could find other work."

"How?" Cora challenged. "Sewing collars, or embroidering, or tassel making, destroying my eyesight for fourteen hours a day and bringing in fifty cents a week? Being a maid and not making enough to support Leah? Working in Madame Emeraude's every evening after the theaters close?"

Alexander looked up at the ceiling. "I see your point."

"I don't have a family name to lean on. I can't marry well. The Cutter family thinks I'm dead. They stopped supporting Charlotte when she moved to the city, and they won't start again if I suddenly tell them I'm alive." And dying a slow death in a salon somewhere uptown was not her idea of living. Charlotte always said that the women of the Cutter family—and Cora was one, even if not in name—were never good at staying put within their limited sphere of gilt-molded ceilings and Grecian facades. Cora's maternal grandmother had married a rich Cutter heir and wrote sentimental novels. Her great-grandmother had abandoned a husband to become a ballet dancer. The Cutter women always got into trouble. Why go back to such a life, only to disappoint?

"I speak for Charlotte too," Alexander said, reaching out to take her hand. "I know you don't enjoy the work."

"You're wrong." Cora shied away from the warmth of his grasp. Though she called him her uncle, Alexander was still an unattached gentleman. She didn't think of him in such terms, but the rest of the world might. "I do not dislike it. It's a service to mankind. I'm helping someone who will learn from what I've provided. Fewer will suffer the affliction, with time and understanding."

"And what of Jacob?" Leah ventured to ask. She had stopped picking at her crumbs, an ominous sign.

"What about Jacob?"

"Are you ready to leave him behind? Maybe you should consider that you might want a family someday," Alexander added.

"Absolutely not. I need Jacob." What Cora didn't say was that though Jacob and Cora might never live in the same room at the same time, they couldn't seem to exist without the other. She'd spent so many formative years as Jacob. It was only when she turned fourteen, her feminine body arriving with quiet inevitability, that Charlotte had moved them to the island of Manhattan. It had been time to school Cora in how to be a lady. She'd loathed leaving Jacob behind—it was like trying to convince herself she no longer needed her leg or her arm. And so, her first act as a resurrectionist had been to exhume her former self, in the form of a twin brother. She touched the bruises on her knuckles. They were his. Hers. Theirs.

Leah and Alexander were still watching her. She smiled brightly and said, "Jacob has brought us more income than I could alone. He's the only reason we can afford to live here on Irving Place. It's that simple. So, no, I'm not saying goodbye to Jacob. And I need the safety he affords me." Here, Cora placed a hand over her second heart.

"Surely no one knows," Leah said. "After all this time." She scratched her nose—a nervous tic.

Alexander grunted. "If only that were true. Dr. Grier kept talking about Cora, until the day he died. The two-hearted girl with Chinese heritage."

"You see?" Cora said to Leah.

Leah cursed under her breath, and Alexander gave her a severe look that made her get up and leave the room.

"So," Cora said. "The new Grand Anatomical Museum. I've been there twice and have not yet met the curator."

"I don't like where this is going," Alexander said, returning to his paper.

"And I need to meet him."

"I see."

"And you have. You've had commissions."

"Cora, I'd rather take a manure bath than let you meet him. Frederick Duncan treats women worse than his dogs, and those he's subjected to vivisections. He's awful."

I'd rather meet him than see Flint again, Cora thought. Anyone but Flint. She flexed her bruised fist behind her back.

"Oh, Alexander. But many of the exhibits and lectures at his museum are educational, are they not? If they wish to compete with the other anatomical museums, they'll need material. I'll be discreet. I always have, and it's worked. They're open this afternoon. Be my escort?"

Leah walked back in, clearly having overheard everything. "You'll need supplies. A blade. At least two, I'd say, from the rumors flying about. I've heard that Duncan's a right scoundrel."

In one smooth motion, Cora stood. Her gown was frilled and laced about the hem, tucked beneath the waist, the bodice sleek and tight. Her corset fit perfectly, bosom peeping from beneath the gauzy triangle draped over her shoulders. "I'm sure Duncan will think I'm well supplied as is, but very well, Leah."

At Leah's wide eyes and Alexander's frown, Cora stifled a laugh, then went skipping upstairs to add some stone-sharpened accoutrements to her toilette. A day without seeing Theodore Flint would be good, and a day's work to keep her business going? Even better.

<hr />

Cora and Alexander took an omnibus the twenty or so streets downtown from Union Square. The four-horse-drawn vehicle was crammed with people, the side garishly painted with its name, "The Thomas Jefferson." They paid their fare to the driver, who yelled at everyone at once, "Get on, yeh hoody-doody! Hop the twig, make room!"—omnibus drivers were the angriest men on the entire island—and then they squeezed onto red velvet seats in the back. The cushions were well past luxuriousness, stained and crushed from the thousands of previous passengers.

"One day, they'll make a train that's up on legs, like a bridge across the whole island," Alexander noted. "I heard some men speaking of it. An elevated train. Or even one that goes underground."

"What an absurd notion," Cora said, wedged between Alexander and a plump lady. Cora perked up as soon as the horse-drawn vehicle stopped at the corner of Anthony and Broadway.

Alexander placed Cora's hand over his arm as they walked down the street, staying far from the piles of horse manure on either side. The cacophony of the omnibus drivers, the hundreds of hooves on the circular cobblestones, and the iron-clad wagon wheels was almost soothing. This was the heartbeat of the city, the common music that assailed any newcomer stepping off a steam boiler in port.

Alexander stared blankly ahead as they walked. He rarely smiled since Charlotte died. Cora suspected at times that his affection toward her—holding her arm, asking about her health—was only a duty he was paying to Charlotte. But Cora was grateful, nevertheless. She never stopped longing for the playful uncle she once knew, the one who built sundials out of paper for her, and made puppets out of ink drawn on his fingertips to keep her laughing endlessly on cold winter days.

To the right, New York Hospital's grounds were contained by a delicate wrought-iron gate. To her left was the beautiful Broadway Theatre, a flag waving merrily atop. And there on the next street stood the Grand Anatomical Museum, between a milliner's and a chemist's shop. Signs were propped outside, and a forlorn-looking boy wearing a sandwich sign advertising today's exhibits walked up and down the sidewalk. A line of men and women waited to gain entrance.

Cora read the boy's sign.

The Origin and Progress of HUMAN LIFE
Malformations AND Monstrosities
Intellectual and MORAL Curiosities!
Our Deity at Work!
Admission Price ONLY 20¢

"Twenty cents only?" Cora wondered fleetingly, Would I be worth so little? But she forced the idea away. As usual, she blurred her thoughts over words like *monstrosity* and *malformation*, as if they had nothing to do with her. "I suppose they're trying to steal Barnum's customers. He's charging twenty-five," Cora noted.

"Barnum has more to offer. Bearded ladies, and enormously rotund babies, and Faber's mechanical talking machine . . . It's quite the competition."

Down the street, just past City Hall, Cora could see Barnum's American Museum—gaudy flags of all nations flying from its rooftop; oval paintings of bizarre animals posted between the rows of windows. General Tom Thumb—a dwarf just over two feet high—had his tiny carriage and tiny horses on display outside the entrance.

Cora reached for coins in her reticule, but Alexander stayed her gloved hand.

"No need. I've my studio here now."

Cora stared at him. "You do? I thought your studio was over on Henry Street." It had been over a year since she'd visited him there.

"I only use that one for my marble and clay work, or the pieces I send to Philadelphia." Alexander smiled sadly. "Though that work is slow going. These days, the rich want oil paintings, not sculpture. And Duncan has been purchasing much of my wax work, so he demanded I move my work and living situation here so he can dictate his tastes more precisely. I hate to admit it, but he'll likely work with you too. He's always looking for new special exhibitions."

"And I am always looking for a new buyer."

She stopped abruptly, not wanting to mention Theodore Flint's name. His behavior last night proved he was there to steal her entire business, not just become a buyer. Yet she oddly felt shy about mentioning him to Alexander.

"Are you all right, my dear?" Alexander asked, touching the hand that lay on his forearm.

"Quite. I don't enjoy a long queue. Let's go in."

Alexander murmured to the man selling tickets, who recognized him and tipped his hat. Inside, two long galleries extended far back into the building. Signs read, "The Human System" and "Health and Disease." A staircase led to more displays of the animal world—birds and beasts, taxidermied, painted, and preserved. Stuffed porcupines and disembodied bear paws sat next to shark jaws and endless bottles of wrinkled rodents. Two-headed snakes coiled in jars, gaping askew in the only way they could.

"This way," Alexander said, leading her toward the back of one of the galleries.

"Are we going to your studio?" she asked.

"No, I'm looking for . . . Ah, here he is."

In the distance, they could see a gentleman—well dressed, in a silk embroidered coat and narrow-striped pants with golden buttons sewn up both sides. He wore a beautiful black top hat and carried a gold-topped cane. A lavish, heavy fob sparkled from his waistcoat. He was of average height, average build, with manicured sideburns. His age was hard to determine—as if he had the feminine habit of bathing his face in goat's milk every night. Older eyes in a young face, which was somewhat disturbing.

Still, this was the gentleman on whose account Leah thought she needed two knives to protect herself? What an idea. Jacob could smash his face in the mud in less than ten seconds.

But between Cora and the curator was an impediment. Two physicians, Drs. Tilton and Goossens, were in the midst of a heated discussion with a rather short woman, dressed neck to floor in sooty, smothering black wool, dark hair swept to the sides so that it covered her ears. The doctors caught Cora's eye, looking almost desperate for her to interrupt. Both physicians had helped her find unusual bodies to sell to the College of Physicians and Surgeons.

She whispered to Alexander, and he let go of her arm. The woman in the black dress stepped away from the physicians just as Cora arrived.

"Good day to you both," the lady said in a decidedly British accent.

Turning, the woman glanced at Cora. Her dark eyes sparkled, as if she'd formed an opinion of Cora in that single glance. For good or bad, it was hard to tell. But oddly, her left eye didn't move. It was glass.

"And who are you?" the lady asked.

How rude not to wait to be introduced! Cora was dumbstruck, and Dr. Tilton intervened to hurry the woman on her way.

"Very well, good to meet you again, Miss Blackwell."

"*Dr.* Blackwell," she corrected him.

"Yes, yes. Very well. It was good to make your acquaintance."

"Indeed. I shall look into the Tompkins Square Dispensary and see if they have work for me there." With a swirl of skirts, she left the room.

"The beautiful Miss Lee!" Dr. Tilton said, clearly happier to see her than Dr. Blackwell had been. He bowed and kissed Cora's hand. "And how are you?"

"Well, and looking for more work," Cora said, smiling fondly. The doctors both puffed out their chests, like mallard drakes. "My goodness, Dr. Tilton. Did I hear that lady correctly—she is a doctor?"

"Sadly, yes."

"Well, that is extraordinary. Is it true?"

"Apparently. She has just gotten her degree from Geneva Medical College. I can't imagine why the school would admit a woman. She now seeks a position in New York. Extraordinary."

Considering the look of disgust on Tilton's face, he didn't mean *extraordinary* in any positive sense whatsoever.

"And how are your patients?" Cora asked. In her mind, she ticked off the names of the patients she followed with both doctors—she kept a list in a ledger hidden in her room. No one saw it, save herself and Leah.

"No news," Dr. Tilton said, but Dr. Goossens raised his eyebrows.

"Here's a to-do, Miss Lee. Do you remember Miss Ruby Benningfield?"

"Ah yes, the lady with the tail."

It was true. She had been born with a tail, nearly four inches long—hairless and furless, boneless and soft as the skin between thumb and forefinger. Only her parents and Dr. Tilton knew of it. Her parents feared surgery at such a young age, but the lady was looking to have it removed before she entered society in earnest at the age of seventeen. Still, Cora did not think she would see her end up in a cemetery any-time soon—Ruby was too healthy, apart from the tail. Only a random act of bad luck would kill her early.

"How is she?" Cora asked.

"She's gone."

Cora inhaled in surprise. "Excuse me? What do you mean, *gone*?"

"She had gone to Stewart's to buy some silks, and as she left, she just vanished. Her companion said they were steps away from entering their carriage, and suddenly she wasn't there."

"How strange. Are the police involved?"

"They are. But you know those copper stars. They hardly know where to start. Her family fears that she is dead." Dr. Goossens paused and thought for a moment. "In the meantime, I have an update on one of our curiosities. The older lady with a beautiful mass in her neck?"

"Ah. Ida Difford," Cora said. The poor lady had been coughing up hair, of all things. Trichoptysis. Dr. Goossens had noted that he could feel teeth growing there. Cora had heard of such cases. Tumors with hair and teeth, eroding into the lungs.

"The patient's tumor is growing. We'll have to try to remove it soon."

"Thank you. Let me know if there is more news."

"My pleasure, Miss Lee," Dr. Goossens said.

Dr. Tilton bowed. "The education of our young doctors ought not to be such a behind-the-scenes affair, but so it must be. Medical students are best kept to studying their books and cadavers rather than spending time digging them up. It's not a gentleman's business to raise the dead."

It was Cora's, of course. And speaking of business . . .

She looked past the two doctors to see the curator walking away in the company of a gentleman. She motioned to Alexander, who extricated himself from a group of visitors discussing a wax figure of a foot he'd sculpted.

After polite goodbyes to the two doctors, they walked quickly to the corner of the gallery, where several wax models of abdominal organs were on display, blooming with shining brown livers and magenta spleens. Just as they reached the curator, the man he was speaking with turned to leave. Cora's heart thumped hard and seemed to skid to a halt.

It was Theodore Flint.

CHAPTER 5

"What are you doing here?" Flint asked Cora, eyeing Alexander the way one might regard moldy bread. Behind him, Duncan had turned toward the door, but a couple had stopped him in greeting. The lady's great bosom nearly overflowed her lace bodice, and Duncan fixed on it while he spoke.

"You're very rude," Cora said. "Excuse me." She kept Alexander's arm under hers and attempted to push past Flint. He hooked her other arm, and now they were an uncomfortable, awkward chain of three, straining under the tension of decorum to split in opposite directions.

"Aren't you going to introduce me?" Flint asked.

Alexander was enough of a gentleman not to raise his voice, but he took a step closer and put his extra two inches of height to good use. He stared down at Flint. "Release her immediately," he said, dropping the pitch of his voice. Cora smiled. Alexander was so even tempered, but when his voice went to these purring registers, he sounded absolutely lethal.

"Well! Are we having a row? And over a pretty girl?" Duncan had stepped away from the couple and sidled up to the commotion. He waved his gilt-topped cane toward Flint. "Alexander! Do you know this scamp?"

"I do not," he murmured.

"She does," Flint said, nodding to Cora.

She flushed, so much that perspiration prickled under the edges of her wig. This was not how she'd hoped to meet the curator. Usually, she had their attention, their full attention. And while they gazed at her, trying to attribute her odd beauty to a family of consequence, wondering perhaps if she might end up underneath them in bed, their questions swirled. But then Cora would turn the compass needle of the conversation toward a different desire—a body for dissection or display, a special one that only she and her men could procure. Absolute and confidential discretion. Excellent references, if need be. A fair price.

Cora felt her moment of advantage quickly ebbing away under Flint's bright grin. Alexander broke the silence.

"Mr. Duncan, this is my niece, Cora Lee."

"It is a good day when a beautiful lady has on her arm a relative, and not a husband." Duncan smiled—a slow smile that stretched into a full-fledged arc of ivory teeth. It was such an enormous grin, Cora wondered if he could swallow a rabbit whole. He reached out, and Cora withdrew both her arms from the men beside her. Duncan took her gloved hand. But instead of kissing the glove, his lips found the wedge of skin on her bent wrist. The kiss left a moist mark, and Cora wished she had some Fowler's arsenic solution to wash it off. "I am Frederick Duncan, the curator of this fine institution."

"It is a pleasure to finally meet you. I've sought an introduction for some time," Cora said.

"Have you! Am I so lucky? Well, you must come back and enjoy one of our exhibitions. I would be delighted to give you a personal tour."

Cora tried not to pout. She was no stranger to museums of this sort, or what she'd already provided for most of them. After a public dissection, specimens were often placed in alcohol-filled jars for display. The curved spine and webbed hands she'd found were at the

American Museum. But P. T. Barnum preferred living examples. He'd been wooing the conjoined twins of Siam, Chang and Eng, to become an exhibit, like his 576-pound lady, leopard-skin-clad wrestlers, and spinning "Shaking Quakers." Cora would make better money with an anatomic museum like Duncan's. And real anatomists would work on the specimens, enlightening the world with the discoveries instead of some of the quack showmen at the smaller museums who only gawked at findings.

"Mr. Duncan, I—"

"And how do you know Mr. Flint?" he asked. "Not a beau, I hope?"

"Not at all, but please allow me to—"

"Excellent, excellent. Flint, next time we do business, you must include introductions to your beautiful acquaintances in the bargain!" An assistant had rushed through a side door and now spoke directly into Duncan's ear. "I'm afraid I must be off. It was very good to meet the very beautiful Cora May." His eyes skimmed her from her hat to her hem, then back up, pausing at her bodice. Why was he staring at her rib cage in that way? He blinked, then waved at Alexander. "I must speak to you about your shipment of wax, as well, Alexander. It's scandalously overpriced. We should not order from them again. Follow me. We'll discuss it on the way."

Alexander gave Cora a helpless look, before following the curator and his assistant out the door. She was left alone with, of all people, Flint.

And she was furious. She'd barely been able to introduce herself. Duncan didn't even know who she was, what she did—he had even gotten her name wrong.

"Cora May?" Theodore chuckled. "Is that what he called you?"

"Oh, cheese it!" she hissed, irritated.

"Such language, Miss May!"

"Stop calling me that!"

Cheeks scarlet, Cora forced herself to keep her voice low and lady-like. She certainly couldn't yell and holler like she wished. She wasn't Jacob right now. "Let me be clear, Mr. Flint. The back alleyway of the University of the City of New York could have been graced with two corpses last night if my brother had so wished it." She flicked her finger hard against the bruise on his jaw. "You're lucky this is all you've purchased after your lies."

His impertinent face sobered. "I'm not fond of anyone laying death threats before me. I do apologize. But what, in God's name, have I done wrong today except tease you about Duncan's own mistake?"

She pointedly refused to answer, asking instead, "What are you doing here?"

"What am I doing here? Of all people, you should know why I'm here."

"I know why you shouldn't be here. My uncle works here. And the curator will only work with me, once I'm through discussing the terms with him."

"Once he actually knows your proper name, Miss May."

"*Stop it!*"

"You've missed your window of opportunity. I've already set the terms. Four bodies, each with a unique anatomic finding, dissected down to their most illuminating revelations. Half-paid in advance, I might add."

Cora actually lost her ability to speak for several seconds. "You . . . are a *thief*! This is my job!"

"You don't dissect. I can do it all, and ask the most preeminent anatomists to work with me. I can procure the bodies as well as your men can, I'm sure. And a portion of the ticket sales to the dissection event will end up in my pocket, not in your lace mitts."

Cora cooled her temper. Flint was no expert resurrectionist. He was nothing but an opportunity for her to pick, just one she hadn't encountered before. She simply had to figure out how to turn him back into a buyer, not competition. What have I got, she wondered, that he wants?

The answer was at the ready. Cora smiled slowly, and took Flint's arm in hers, leading the way into the next salon. She walked briskly, so that he could perceive the pull of his arm against hers. A small party was having a gay discussion over the bright-blue butterflies in the corner, pierced with pins in a display that made them look as if they were sprouting out of an artificial bouquet of roses. A blonde woman in the middle of the group stared briefly at Cora before turning back to the display.

"Tell me, Mr. Flint," Cora said. "Where do you plan on procuring these four unique specimens?"

"Oh, in time, they'll come."

"So, you don't even have your marks. You're waiting for fate to drop them into your lap."

"That's not what I said," he replied, irritated. Cora tugged his arm again, and this time they swung into a room containing insects from Madagascar—terrible creatures, big and black, the size of an adult human hand, the occupants of nightmares.

"What if I told you that I already had my bead on seven—seven anatomic curiosities—whose doctors have promised to inform me about their imminent demise so I can snatch them from the grave before anyone else does?"

Theodore stopped walking. Cora rested her arm on his and smiled.

"Seven. Seven! What kind?" He was slightly out of breath. Cora wasn't. Jacob kept her as fit as a fighting dog.

"My secret, not yours. Where will you find four more on this island? I have established contacts and a history of good, fair work. You do not. You'll need me."

Every last scrap of smirk and confidence had left Flint's face. Cora was right—he'd made deals without having anything to sell, really—just promises constructed of smoke and shadows.

"I'll think about your offer." He let go of her arm and shuffled one step away. "Maybe I could speak to Jacob about it."

Cora's face reddened. "You may speak to me. I handle the business, and Jacob does the labor. He hasn't the mind for it."

"I'd rather discuss it with Jacob. I suspect your brother is far more intelligent than you give him credit for."

Cora's eyebrows twitched upward. She'd crafted Jacob to be crude, simpleminded, direct, and not terribly complicated. Nevertheless, she was somewhat pleased that Flint regarded Jacob with more appreciation than most of his class who met him.

They walked into the next salon, followed by the party who'd been examining the butterflies. This room was full of anatomical wax displays. Oohs and aahs erupted, and many of the ladies covered their faces in astonishment. Only the blonde woman didn't seem fazed by the large glass enclosure containing a female wax model whose abdomen had been flayed open, and intestines pushed aside to show liver, spleen, and uterus. The figure's eyes were half-closed, pink lips parted to show white teeth and a dab of tongue. Alexander must have painted her to look as if her lips were wet; her inner organs also glistened with a shining coat of paint. The blonde wasn't looking at the anatomic display, though; instead, she'd fixed her eyes on Cora, as if she knew her.

"Is she a friend?" Flint asked, noticing the two eyeing each other.

"Not at all. Do you know her?"

"No, but I recognize the gent with her. Daniel Schermerhorn. Rich fellow. Their fortune is in shipping, I believe."

Everyone knew the Schermerhorns, so this was not fresh information. "You're changing the subject," Cora said.

"Aye, and I'll change it again. Do you know what I did this morning?"

Cora didn't particularly feel like guessing.

"Well. I dissected that fellow we procured last night, before my fellow classmates, in our largest operating theater. My first lead dissection, and as a medical student. It was fascinating."

Fascinating. In what way? Had they found other signs of vascular anomalies, beyond the aneurysmal swelling, ones that tempted her two hearts to flutter with fear and fascination? As Jacob, she often attended public dissections in the upper, cheaper seats. The truth was, she didn't truly enjoy these spectacles—though Jacob pretended to—but she learned from them. So very much. The human body was a revelation in every sinew, every branching artery and nerve plexus. The betterment of humankind through understanding was worth the cause. And maybe one day, they'd discover how to cure an anomaly like hers.

"Fascinating," Cora found herself repeating. She thought of Hitchcock's emerald tongue but said nothing.

"Absolutely. What did you say that he died from? An aortic aneurysm?"

"Yes."

"Well, you were wrong. It wasn't his cause of death."

This time, she couldn't mask her surprise. How could that be? Dr. Flannigan had been absolutely sure the aneurysm was nearly ready to burst. A mere extra serving of cake could be enough internal pressure to pop the thing, he'd said. True, not all of the people she procured died directly from the cause she sold them for, but most did.

Flint's slight grin had all but vanished. "Oh, it was there, the aneurysm, and it was on the verge of bursting. But it was intact. Entirely intact. Full of clot, but it hadn't budged or caused any trouble. Something else killed him."

"An apoplectic attack?" Cora suggested.

"No. The brain tissue was normal."

"A cardiac anomaly?"

"No."

"Dropsy?"

Flint's face brightened and relaxed. The language seemed to comfort him. "My, you're full of horrible ends, aren't you? No. None of the above. He was a puzzle to all. His tongue was a poisonous green color, though."

Cora's bottom lip dropped open. He'd noticed too. What did it mean?

"I should hope that someday, we doctors will have better tricks to evaluate the causes of death. Chemical tests, or some such magic. You know, I wish Jacob had been there to see. He'd have an idea."

"Women are allowed in such theaters too," she said, before realizing it sounded like she yearned for an invitation.

Theodore paused. "You're jealous, aren't you?"

She said nothing, her mind whizzing with other thoughts. What on earth had killed Hitchcock, if not that terrible aneurysm? What could that green tongue possibly mean? Could he have been poisoned? She'd never heard of a green poison before. It couldn't be. But what also surprised her was an unexpected sensation of grief. It came like a winter wind in September. She didn't know Hitchcock, not really. But the thought that someone might have hurt him, on purpose, tilted her world.

"Cora."

She spun around: Alexander was there, but the curator was nowhere to be seen. "It's time we were off," he said. He glanced at Flint, sizing him up as he might a large gutter rat.

Flint seemed to wither under the intelligent, hooded eyes of her uncle.

"Miss Lee," he said, bowing, before releasing her arm and leaving.

Wordlessly, Alexander took her arm. "I'm sorry to say that Frederick Duncan has left for an appointment down near the Bowling Green. I apologize for not giving you the meeting you'd hoped for."

"It's all right." They walked toward the grand staircase in the front of the building. More patrons entered the museum, clutching tickets and printed guides, and closing parasols. "You provided an introduction, and that is all I need. I'll try to meet him again soon to discuss terms before that Flint—"

"You know that ridiculous man?" Alexander interrupted.

Cora nodded. "He's another resurrectionist. He and I . . . and Jacob . . . had a bit of a misunderstanding last night."

"I see."

Once outside, Alexander stopped her. "Cora. Be careful. Flint seems like a fool, but the curator is a different beast altogether. He's a rampant adulterer. If he doesn't get what he wants, he'll take it anyway."

"I can handle myself, and him, Alexander. Both of them. You ought to know that."

Alexander didn't smile but nodded all the same. As they paused in the sunlight, the blonde woman and her party passed them. Once again, the woman gazed a little too long at Cora—at her pink-and-green lawn dress, at her dust-smudged hem, at her neatly trimmed faille bonnet. Had they met in one of the salons near Union Square last week? Cora never paid attention to the ladies, who had no business in her business. She put it out of her mind.

All the way home, she stared out the window of the omnibus, but she hardly noticed the scenery. She thought instead of Ruby with the tail. Where had she gotten to? Perhaps she'd simply disappeared temporarily with a young gentleman. It had been known to happen—it had happened to both her mother and her aunt, and they'd suffered the consequences of losing everything. Perhaps it would be in Cora's blood, too, to run away from everything settled in her life, and into the warm arms of someone wholly wrong for her. Against her wishes, Theodore Flint's grinning face flashed in her mind's eye. No. He wouldn't be her savior, nor her undoing.

There were other things to worry about. Hitchcock's manner of death and that emerald dye in his mouth remained an unwhispered secret that unsettled her. First Hitchcock, and now Ruby. The deaths and bodily disappearances of those on her watch list were never meant to surprise her. Her hands shook slightly—with fear or horror or sadness, she wasn't sure.

She did not like this at all. She found herself murmuring imperceptibly as the omnibus rattled homeward.

"Where are you, Ruby?" she whispered.

RUBY BENNINGFIELD

I don't know where Mama is.

In times like this, she would say, *Keep yourself neat, Ruby. Be sure your bustle is in place. Always sit to the side. We'll fix your ailment soon enough.* She calls it my fairy tail, though in truth it disgusts her like nothing else. Father never speaks of it.

I don't know where I am, and I find that it's a very strange feeling, to be lost like this. I am not hungry, I am not cold, I am not wanting of anything that used to push and pull me. The temptation of a delicious new novel, or ten yards of good voile for a summer dress do nothing to make my heart flutter.

My heart.

My heart.

It doesn't flutter at all now, does it?

One moment, I was exiting Stewart's Marble Palace, my maid's arms full of dry goods, and then I tripped and someone had their arm around me, and I turned to see if Mama had noticed, and then I was in an alley, and it was as if a ribbon were being tied too tight around my throat from behind. I felt it with my fingertips, though I could not loosen it. It was a ribbon that took my breath away.

In anguish, Mama and Papa search for me. And they are not the only ones. That girl who used to watch me from afar—the one with hair the color of burnt chestnuts—she still follows me. She still searches for me. I cannot see her—not exactly. But I am not afraid of her anymore. In fact, I feel certain that she should be afraid, though I know not why.

Oh, I believe I must go.

I don't know what for; I only know just now—I must go.

CHAPTER 6

Supper was a quiet affair, but Leah thrummed with anger. She hacked the small pork roast on the cutting board, then thumped the boiled potatoes, and snatched a flour biscuit and slapped the butter on.

Cora sighed. "Very well, Leah, out with it."

"You ought to find a husband and stop this business. Have a family. Be a proper lady."

"You are my family, Leah." Cora leaned over to embrace her, but she shrugged away. Cora was used to it—Leah preferred a dirty joke and a pint of cheap beer to morsels of tenderness. "Anyway, who would marry me?"

"Many good men. You'd never need to speak of that Chinese father of yours. You blend in well enough."

Well enough. It was only a hairbreadth away from *not well enough.*

"I'm not ashamed of who I am, Leah. It's everyone else that has trouble with it."

"I was talking about money!" Leah said, a little too quickly. She hated to discuss Cora's birth history—it brought back nothing but grief for her; for Cora's side, it elicited curiosity. Charlotte and Leah had been her mothers. She knew she missed Elizabeth far less than Leah did. And

Cora wondered about her father. Where was he? If he knew she existed, would he miss her?

"Very well. Well, right now we need the money from my work."

Leah sighed. It was true. The rent was expensive: three hundred dollars a year. Being able to live and walk amongst the "bon ton" meant needing a steady supply of bodies, and things had been slow. Health was terribly inconvenient for Cora, but she would not do anything to hasten death. It was one of her rules.

She went to bed and dreamt that the blonde woman met both her and Jacob, side by side in the way that dreams make the impossible true. The woman stared at one and then the other and said, calmly, and with a righteous firmness to her vowels:

"I know who you are. And you are a thief, Cora Lee."

In the background, Hitchcock laughed. He was fully dressed, with naught but a single red line staining his waistcoat from neck to pelvis.

"She doesn't even know what she stole." He laughed, green staining his teeth. He waved a fork that held a piece of cheese of all things; flies buzzed in a halo around his head.

Somehow, Jacob and Cora couldn't move from their spot of judgment. And yet, in the dream they knew—the woman wasn't talking about grave robbery, but something else entirely.

⸻⬥⸻

Leah was usually rather grumpy in the mornings, but the next morning she was smiling. Cora discovered the reason for her mood on the salon table.

Two bouquets of flowers, each with a card.

A note from Frederick Duncan accompanied a beautiful cluster of vivid yellow hothouse roses.

I shall be pleased if you would meet me for tea on Saturday at Sherman's, on Bleecker Street. Three o'clock.

Cora smiled. Good Alexander! He must have spoken to Duncan again and urged the meeting. Flint would not be very happy about this prospect.

She looked at the second bunch of flowers. These were small blue flags, and not from the hothouse. They grew where the wilderness was still lush—past the spoiled-milk stink of the swill dairies on Sixteenth Street. The hastily scribbled note said only, *Regards, Theodore Flint.*

Nearby was a separate note creased and sealed. She flipped it over. It was addressed to Jacob Lee.

> *Jacob,*
> *I apologize for not being more forthright—I blame my own senses for being muddled after a slight row with your sister. I should like to make it up to you, and discuss some more jobs in the future, as I have procured a good hand-shake with Frederick Duncan at the Grand Anatomical Museum. You must know him, I'm sure, though your sister only just met him.*

Cora seethed. Why would Flint assume Jacob knew the curator before she did? Had she not told him that she was the manager of the entire operation? It wasn't the first time she'd been informed, directly or indirectly, that her womb consumed far too much energy to allow for mental acuity. She bit her lip and read on.

> *I think you'd be interested in meeting some of my chums and attending one of our lectures. There is a splendid dissection this afternoon, with a curious abnormality present. Three o'clock, at the Stuyvesant Institute. Come meet me, and we'll have supper after.*
> *Yours, Theodore Flint*

It was cordial, and friendly, and a certifiable olive branch. All Cora got was flowers, but Jacob had an invite to friends and a lecture. He would answer and say yes, of course. How odd that Cora should be jealous of herself, but she was.

She gathered up the blooms from Duncan and Flint, and went into the kitchen, where Leah was scrubbing the morning dishes.

"That Duncan is an alley cat, but who's this Flint fellow—eh! Where are you going with those flowers?" she asked.

Cora opened the window and tossed them out, where they'd wilt under a wave of dirty dishwater.

Leah raised her eyebrows. "Well, I shan't be gettin' you flowers for your birthday."

In the early afternoon, Cora readied herself as Jacob. She thumped downstairs and bolted a meal of bread and cheese. She noticed that Leah had retrieved a single bloom from the two bunches she'd thrown out. It sat drinking in water from a brown glass emptied of liniment.

"Getting a little sentimental, are we?" Cora said.

"I like blue flags," Leah said defensively. "Hiram gave me flags once." Hiram was the grocer who gave Leah an especially good price on flour. Cora found out two years ago that Leah spent an extra hour there every few days when pretending to run errands, making god-awful cat noises in the back bedroom with Hiram. Leah caught Cora staring at her. "So, tell me about this Flint. Is he a good working man?"

"It's for the job, Leah. Nothing more. No more talk of this marriage business."

"If we don't bring in more money, perhaps we could ask—"

"No. We'll ask no one," Cora snapped.

Cora had never borrowed money, not once. She was too proud to write or call upon the Cutter family. Not that it mattered—when

Charlotte had moved too close to the Cutters on the island of Manhattan, the family had cut off all funds. But it was a necessary separation: the time had come to raise Cora as a girl, and there'd be no good explanation for her sudden appearance in their household and Jacob's disappearance. As a result, Cora had never felt much connection to the Cutters, and since Charlotte's death, she felt even less.

Alexander made a good income as a wax sculptor, but she would never ask him for money. He lived very simply, joining them for Sunday breakfast or on quiet evenings for a game of faro or reading after supper. Cora had discovered his secret vice almost by accident. On evenings when Jacob planned to frequent the oyster saloons and gamble, Alexander would press her for her whereabouts. Suspecting that he was spying on her for her safety, she'd searched for him amid the crowds. But she never saw him.

"Oh, Cora," Leah had said. "He doesn't want to be seen by his niece gambling and visiting the bawdy houses. He's a man, and he must have his enjoyments like any other man. It's been a long while since he's had a woman to warm his bed."

Oh. Well. After that, she told him where she would be, even days in advance.

Leah had long since left the kitchen. Cora finished her meal. She squinted into the overcast afternoon and frowned at the light streaming inside. Like an opossum, Jacob was a less savory breed that preferred the cover of night. Today, Cora would keep her hat on for as long as possible.

Eschewing the crowded omnibuses that lumbered behind their tired horses, Cora preferred to walk the length of Broadway below Union Square and its lovely oval green. Past the post office and the bustle of Astor Place, she arrived eventually at the Stuyvesant Institute.

No one asked why she was here. One of the enjoyments of being male was freedom of movement: Jacob could go where Cora couldn't, and only the cleanliness and class of Jacob's clothing might stop her.

Today she'd worn a slightly nicer vest of sober black satin, and her newest trousers. She was passable as a poor student, at least.

Luckily, the interior wasn't brightly lit, and it appeared as if the whole abode was in slight disarray—two workers were carrying worktables out through the front door.

"Jacob Lee!"

Cora turned and saw Flint descending the stairs in the small atrium. Two other students were behind him. She nodded briefly, relieved that the dim light obscured her face.

"What's this?" Cora asked, gesturing to the ebb of furniture out the door. One worker, carrying an entire articulated skeleton, gasped when the skull fell off and bounced down the exterior steps.

"Ah. We're moving. The medical school has a brand-new establishment on Fourteenth Street, near Third Avenue. Have you seen it? It has an excellent surgical theater. This one was far too small, and the viewing is poor. But it's what we have. Come! I'll show you. No tickets needed. I've already signed you in as a visiting student."

Visiting student. Cora liked the sound of that.

She accompanied Flint back up the stairs, and his two friends followed like shadows.

"Are your friends missing their tongues, or are they just brought up poorly?" she asked.

"Oh. My apologies." Flint stopped halfway up the stairs. "This is Robert Cane, and this is Howard Franklin. They've already been rounding at Bellevue, but they are down here for the lecture today. Should be an excellent one. We just got it in last night."

Both men snickered at the sight of Cora. "What's this rat doing here, Flint?" Robert said. He had yellow hair and a striped shirt, and he reminded Cora of a straw-tick mattress stuffed to the brim with hay. Howard had a snub nose that dominated his face.

Cora snarled. "You tell Strawtick and Snout to stubble their red flags unless they have something useful to say."

"You're here on Flint's invitation, not ours," Snout said. "We'll say what we like."

"You see this?" She pointed to the bruise on Flint's jaw. It was still purple and slightly swollen. "That's my work. You gents want one to match?"

They went quiet.

"Better. Let's see this mort. It had better be worth me losing my precious sleep."

"It will be," Flint said. He thoughtfully rubbed the bruise on his face and stepped up his pace to the top of the stairs. Soon, they rounded a corridor to a small surgical theater originally created as a two-tiered chamber for meetings. Students had already filled most of the seats, and Cora was relieved that their seats were at the very top, in the poorest lighting.

In the center of the small chamber, a long table held a very obvious corpse covered in a white cloth stained with yellow and pale brown. Feminine feet peeped out from beneath. Cora narrowed her eyes. The feet were well kept, with smooth skin and toenails used to regular baths and good shoes. They were the feet of a rich woman.

A wizened professor garbed in white, his mostly bald head festooned with white hair, entered along with a nervous-looking assistant who rolled in a tray of surgical instruments. All the doors were shut, and a hush fell on the room. A few windows provided the only illumination. Flint leaned in close.

"That's Professor Granville Sharp Pattison. Trained in Glasgow, and he's been at the university a good few years now. Famous."

Cora said nothing but leaned forward to listen as the professor began speaking in a gruff monotone.

"Gentlemen. I welcome you to one of the last dissections of this quarter, before we move into the new building uptown. We have a classic case for you, an unusual case, and we shall begin with the gross findings. This young lady came to us after having suffered for some time with a malady that we do not often see, as it is hidden from society at all costs."

Cora's spine stiffened. Why hadn't it occurred to her before? Her thoughts now went immediately to Ruby: Had the missing girl turned up dead? With a grand sweep, the professor snatched away the shroud.

A young woman lay bare on the stained wooden table, her hair cascading over the edge in ropy brown locks. She might have been pretty, but her face was darkened by a good deal of bruising—as if she'd died facedown and the blood had drained to her face in rigor mortis. Without turning her over, Cora wouldn't know if she had a tail.

"Do you see the abnormality, gentlemen? It's right there. Keen eyes should see it in a moment."

There was a long silence before he pointed at a tiny dot on the deceased woman's rib cage.

"Plain as can be. She has a third nipple."

There were a few murmurs of interest and some pointing. A few put on their glasses to see the speck of darkness, no larger than a fly.

"Is that all?" Cora said, shoulders falling.

Flint looked crestfallen at Jacob's disappointment. "Were you expecting something else?"

She went silent. Flint didn't need to know that one of her specialty bodies was decidedly lost.

The professor gave a sharp look up at the highest seats, and the entire lecture room hushed. The dissection ended up being a rather ordinary one. Despite her dainty feet, the woman wasn't one of the uppertens. She had fallen down drunk a day ago, and landed face-first in a puddle behind a loud and boisterous beer garden in the Tenth Ward.

Cora's mind wandered as the woman's torso was opened, rib bones sawed away to expose her heart and lungs. The stench wasn't nearly as bad as it could have been. She had not been dead long.

"Does this not interest you?" Flint asked. "A great specimen."

Cora only yawned.

"Ah, he's not bored. He has no idea what he's seeing, that's what," Strawtick said.

"Boredom ain't stupidity," Cora said, the hair rising on her neck.

"Isn't it, now? Tell me," Snout whispered. "What is he pointing out? The name of that vein right there?"

"I don't have to tell you anything," Cora said.

Snout snickered. "Because he doesn't know!"

"Do you have something to share, Mr. Cane? Mr. Franklin?"

"No sir. Just letting our guest here know that he needs to pay better attention to your fine lecture, Professor."

"Indeed. Well, if you can't pay attention, then you ought to leave, Mr. . . . ?"

"Lee," Cora said. Her face flushed from forty faces all turning simultaneously to stare at her. The makeup on her face felt smothering.

"And can you tell me, Mr. Lee, why the azygous vein here is missing the corresponding artery next to the inferior vena cava?"

"The answer is obvious, ain't it?" Cora said.

"He doesn't know, sir," Snout said. "He's not a student, just a visitor."

"And all visitors should pay attention," the professor boomed.

"Never mind," Flint whispered, turning his shoulder away from the onlookers. "We can leave. It's all right if you—"

Cora stood up. "The azygous vein does not have a corresponding artery. *Professor.*"

Snout and Strawtick shrank in their chairs.

The professor cleared his throat. "Go on."

"The name is Greek for *unpaired.* It's the only vein that's got no matching artery in the body."

"And where does it join the vena cava?" the professor asked. All forty pairs of eyes were still on Cora.

"That's a trick. It depends. Sometimes it empties into the right ventricle. This lady is ordinary as bread. Ends right in the superior vena cava, below the right innominate. You can see it, plain as day."

The professor smiled. "Excellent. Well, perhaps you should join our incoming class, Mr. Lee."

"No, thanks. Save the schooling for these kinchin who need it."

Cora sat down, and Snout and Strawtick stayed blessedly quiet for the rest of the lecture. After about two more hours, they rose to leave for the afternoon. Cora didn't mind when Flint's friends quickly egressed the tiny theater and didn't wait for them.

"You know your anatomy well," Flint said.

"Aye. And I don't need you to teach me. So that was a waste of a good three hours. Why did you bring me here?"

"I thought you'd enjoy it. For education. I didn't realize you'd already learned this."

Cora sped past Flint and trotted down the stairs, clamping her hat back on her head. The sun was low in the sky, casting long shadows in the entranceway. "I've been going to anatomic lectures for longer than you."

"Apparently. Why didn't you tell me?"

She shoved the door open into the late-afternoon light and nearly let it close on her pursuer. "Why should I?"

"Excellent point. And one we can ignore while we have a plate of oysters." Flint grabbed her elbow just before she was completely out of reach. "Come. I owe you a dinner for such an abominably boring time."

Cora paused, a pinch of her sleeve fabric caught in Flint's outstretched hand. "Why don't you go eat with your oafs?"

Flint let go and scratched his neck. A sign of discomfort. Bodies often revealed more than words did. Flint was hiding something.

"They're all right. I suppose they are oafs, as you say, but they're not friends. I don't really have friends."

Cora thought, I don't have friends either.

"Truth is, they don't have to do much to be here. They'll get a position as long as they do the minimum schoolwork. Their families are paying their tuition, and they have connections. They won't be working the dispensaries with the worst of the worst. I'm paying my own way. Which is why I've got the night work, you see."

It was explained rather simply, but she could see that there was something else. Flint was running. Running from what—a poor childhood, obscurity? Who knew. But she saw a similarity between being a Lee and being Flint. For the first time, she felt sorry for him.

"Anyway, I like it," he said. "Anatomy is the equalizer, isn't it? Shows we're all just clay and water, in the end, no matter if you're highborn or not. I like that."

"I'd rather be alive, though."

Flint grinned at this, and Cora couldn't help but grin too.

"Very well," she said. "Two plates of oysters, not one, and I choose my libation. On your bill. You tell me what my sister's babbling about with you having some deal with that curator over at the Grand Anatomical Museum, or we never speak again—and if I see you in my graveyards, I'll add another bruise to that very fine one on your face."

Flint nodded and smiled wide, like a child who'd just gotten his first peppermint candy.

CHAPTER 7

They walked down Broadway as the sun set behind the buildings in the west. It was a changeful hour, and not only due to the light. The dandies—sons of the wealthy, fancifully dressed—sought out supper and more entertainment. The ladies who had spent the afternoon promenading up and down Broadway to the millineries, silk shops, and glove shops were now crammed into omnibuses or their own private carriages, transported back uptown to dining rooms bedecked with Italian marble and crystal goblets.

In their place came the Bowery b'hoys and g'hirls in their gaudy and colorful threaded clothing, the painted faces of the evening ladies, and the eating house owners enticing patrons into their dark recesses.

"Roast goose shillin', roast beef shillin', clam soup sixpence, extra bread and butter three and sixpence, mutton and taters shillin'. Walk in, sir, walk in! Have a seat!"

As the darkness descended, Broadway became a bright, jeweled marvel, from the colored lanterns hanging on the edges of the carriages, to the gaslights flickering to life. They passed Lafayette Hall and the Chinese Building with its long-ponytailed workers, who noticed Cora's dark eyes and wondered why she seemed so vaguely familiar. Perhaps they knew her father, or grandfather, or aunt. Her ancestors, though unknown, were stitched into her very being. Cora reached to pull her hat lower on her forehead but couldn't help stealing a furtive glance their way. One young man caught her eye—and she saw the tiniest widening of his mouth—a miniature sunrise of a smile. She passed him by, but she would hold that flickering warmth within her for a long time.

Finally, Cora located one of her favorite oyster saloons, Bardy's, and paused.

"Here?" Flint asked. He actually looked a bit taken aback. Likely he frequented the nicer eating houses.

"Here."

She led Flint down the stairs to the cellar, where the saloon was already crammed full of patrons. In the corner, they found two empty spots at a table. Two men stood behind a bar, shucking as quickly as they could, piling oyster shells onto a growing barrel next to them. When it was full, they would roll it into the back and dump it right into the alleyway at the rear of the saloon.

A sign above the bar listed the menu: Oysters, oysters, and oysters. Raw, fried, baked, stewed. Oyster pie, oysters stuffed in fowl, duck in oyster sauce. Hunks of bread were served on platters to soak up the drippings, and fine Croton water was being poured almost as much as malt liquor, bad brandy, and the German lager brewed near the shipyards.

A black fellow wearing a thick apron sidled up to their table. "Jacob Lee! Been a good week since you've come to my saloon."

"I've been busy, Bardy." Cora shook hands with the owner. "Two plates of roast oysters, bread and butter, and one of your best butter cakes."

"Hob or nob?" he inquired.

"Two brandies," Cora said. "The good stuff, not your sixpence bathwater."

The owner turned and hollered the order, and soon plates with crusted loaves of bread, two generous lumps of butter, and drinks were on the table along with the steaming golden oysters.

They didn't talk for a while. Cora was too hungry. The bread and cheese from lunch seemed days ago. She shoveled in the oysters and washed them down with water until she burped luxuriously, and put her elbows up on the table with dual thumps. Flint had eaten half as much and was still chewing while watching with a wary eye the men at the next table, who were rowdily discussing a game of ten pins.

"Okay. I've eaten. What do you have to tell me?" Cora said.

Flint put his elbows on the table, too, tenting his fingers. Good God, Cora hated when men did that. It was so supercilious, it made her want to knock their teeth out and sell them each for a half penny. For a moment, Flint squinted at her, as if he saw something amiss. But then he fished an errant piece of oyster shell from the tip of his tongue, and the moment passed.

"As Miss Lee told you, I've made a deal with the curator of the Grand Anatomical Museum. Duncan has a large collection of natural curiosities—animals and insects and such—but wants to supplement them with more displays on human anatomy. He has a wax sculptor—"

"That would be my uncle," Cora interrupted.

"Oh! I believe I met him, then! Well, he's making some fine pieces, but Duncan says it can't all be wax. He wants preserved human specimens. Barnum's is making too much money, and they're only just down the road. Duncan needs more bodies to compete."

"I already know this," Cora said, picking flecks of pepper out of her teeth with a fingernail, careful not to dislodge the black wax over her canine.

"Ah. Well, what's more—the medical school will soon be at the new location. It'll be quite grand. Seating for six hundred students, with three lecture rooms and two museums. One is slated for specimens only. And they want me to help fill it." He paused to catch his breath, and Cora took a long drink of Croton water to soothe the swimming feeling she had from drinking the brandy. "If you'll help me with these jobs, I'll split my profits with you."

"Split the profits, eh? Why bother? I'll have Cora sell the corpses directly to the curator and Professor Pattison, who knows us already."

"He knows you? But at the dissection today—"

"You think a dapper professor of the University of the City of New York would acknowledge a resurrectionist under the roof of his establishment? Of course he knows me. He knows Cora too. She shared a glass of the finest raspberry cordial with him only a week ago." Which was true.

Flint looked flummoxed. "Well then, why did he ask you the anatomy questions?"

"Because he knew I knew the answer. He likes to show the other students that they aren't nigh as high and mighty as they think they are. I've gone to those lectures of his, as well as those at the College of Physicians and Surgeons, and the ones at the Anatomical Museum. I can outanswer you in any anatomy question, Flint, and then some." Her entire first year of work had been spent memorizing anatomy books. Quain and Sharpey's, Cruveilhier's, and Harrison's were her favorites.

"Then you know what killed Hitchcock, without having been at the dissection? Because I'm sure you weren't."

This time, Cora paused.

"Ah. I see you don't know, or that quick tongue of yours would have whipped me already. Well, I'll tell you what. If you split the next six resurrections with me for both the medical school museum and the curator's collection, then I'll tell you what happened to him. It's quite scandalous, actually." Watching the emotions flit across her face, he added, "Or do you need to speak to your sister about this first?"

"She's my sister, but no woman tells me what to do," Cora said sourly. Half the profits? That was a lot of money. She didn't want to split more than was necessary; the goal was to buy time to stifle Flint's competition, so that eventually all the profits went back to her. "Three resurrections," she said. "Take it or leave it. Then you can be on your way, and we'll be on ours."

"Very well. I'll drink to that." Flint waved the saloon owner over to refill their tumblers with more brandy. They both drew deeply of the amber liquid, and Cora enjoyed the sweet burn of it as it went down her throat. "But here's something I won't drink to. The bastard that killed Hitchcock."

Cora coughed and sputtered, nearly tipping over her brandy. "What? Killed Hitchcock?"

"Quiet now, hush!" Flint hissed. "After the dissection, I went to ask Dr. Pattison why the green tongue, and what was the cause of death. He wouldn't say in class."

"The aneurysm hadn't burst, as you'd said?" Cora asked.

"No. Even though it was the size of a small melon. It was that green color. It was on his tongue, and trailed all the way down his esophagus and stained his stomach. But his stomach was empty. Some cathartic perhaps—he must have vomited before he died, and emptied his bowels out too."

"What are you saying?" Cora said, not understanding. The green color was something she'd never seen in a dissection, not ever.

"I mean . . . I think he was poisoned."

"You really do? With what, exactly?"

"I don't know. We'll never know. I've never heard of green poison. Have you?"

Cora shook her head. "What about the mab he was with? At Madame Emeraude's?"

"Mab? What?"

Of course Flint wouldn't know. She had forgotten, for a moment, that his world was so very different from hers. Hitchcock's doctor had said nothing of vomiting. Just him falling down dead on Belle, while having his way with her. Part of the story was missing.

"Well, that makes for two strange things to happen to my people," Cora murmured.

"People?" Flint asked, and drained his tumbler. His eyes were glassy and his face pink.

"The ones that Cora watches."

"You said two. Was there another? Who?"

Cora hesitated. Was it worth telling him about Ruby's disappearance? The brandy had made Flint's hazel eyes less intense, but more genuine. Urgency and concern tinged his voice. This seemed more like the real Flint.

Cora finished her brandy and with a small burp, decided yes, it was worth telling him.

"There's a girl I know, lives well enough, but she has a vestigial tail."

"Tail! By Jove—"

The saloon owner seemed to think he was being summoned, and poured yet another six-penny tumbler full of brandy for them both. He paused at the table. "Go join the hockeys upstairs. Hop the twig."

"Let's go. There's a groggery up there where we can drink," Cora said to the befuddled Flint, tossing back her drink. "He wants this table, and we're not eating anymore."

They paid for their food and followed a few other men up a narrow, creaking set of stairs to a drinking saloon. Large-bosomed Lacey Stanton, "the Widow," stood behind the bar, and there were several tables of men playing euchre, brag, whist, and faro. Tobacco was offered around, and pipes filled the ceiling with a haze of smoke. Tonight, Lacey was delivering trays of whiskey punch to her patrons. Most of the men paid a weekly subscription to enjoy the Widow's upstairs, but Jacob didn't come regularly enough.

"Just tonight, thank you," Cora said, pushing ten cents toward the Widow. Flint did the same.

The Widow leaned over, showing her bulging wares above the lace of her neckline. "And will this young one be wanting some time with me in the back room, perhaps?"

Cora laughed. The Widow already knew Jacob wasn't interested in other *amenities*—after several refusals from Jacob, she'd simply assumed buggery was more his flavor, and never asked again.

"No, thank you," Flint said hurriedly.

The Widow leaned toward another more interested customer, and Cora and Flint went back to talking in the corner.

"A girl with a tail? That's a fine speshumen!" Flint said, a little too loudly. He was slurring now. "Where did you find her? Is she ill? Does she have other ailments?"

"None that I know of. I didn't think that she would fall ill—there's nothing else the matter with her. But she's gone missing," Cora admitted.

"You have dirt on your face," Flint said, and sloppily attempted to wipe Cora's face. But she was a touch more sober and easily dodged his hand. She waved his attention away.

"Do you know anything of her? Heard if she's been ottomised—" At Flint's blank look, she clarified, "I mean, dissected?"

"No, but she'd be a prize piece to have."

"Will you tell me if she has been?"

"I will." Flint looked into his tumbler. "Empty. You need to catch up. Because I have something else to tell you. 'Bout the curator. 'Bout a girl he's watching."

Cora put her cup down. "What girl?"

"Drink first. Tell later," Flint said, waving over the Widow for another round. "S'not a good thing, being drunk alone."

Cora dutifully downed another cupful, and when she wasn't seemingly drunk enough, Flint urged one more. Cora wasn't happy about her swimming head—she worried that she'd break character. But she didn't mind being drunk if it meant Flint was. Flint was so much simpler this way. She liked the absence of his bravado and posing and one-upmanship. He seemed lonely. He seemed afraid Jacob would leave.

By the end of that third punch, Cora was decidedly inebriated and laughed heartily at Flint's description of Professor Pattison carrying around his dueling pistols everywhere, including to the bathhouse and to bed, so fiery was he and ready for words with anyone. The idea of holsters built into his undergarments had them both undone. It was only after catching their breath that Cora vaguely remembered that she was supposed to ask something of Flint.

"Ffflint," Cora slurred. "Theodore. Teddy, my oaf. What was the curator looking for? What woman did you say?"

"A figment," Jacob said, licking drops of whiskey out of his mostly emptied glass. "A fairy tale. A tale!"

Cora scrunched her eyes together. "A tail? I already told you about the tail lady!"

"Tale! Fairy tale! It's complete rubbish, but he said he heard from an old doctor in Brooklyn—Brooklyn!—about a woman with the most p-priceless find." Cora had to wipe his spittle from her face, but it only made Flint laugh harder.

"What? What is it?"

"Not possible." Flint waved his glass and dropped it onto the carpeted floor. "Not possible."

"What's not possible? Tell me, you sot."

"He said . . . He said . . . that there was a girl in town with two hearts. They say she may have Chinese lineage. Can you believe it?"

Flint guffawed, then promptly vomited his dinner of oysters onto the floor, not even realizing his companion had abruptly stopped laughing.

CHAPTER 8

The next hour was a blur. Cora was so drunk that she could barely walk. She and Flint clung to each other's shoulders as they staggered out into the September night and up Broadway.

The gaslights hissed merrily, but in Cora's eyes, they were an evil illuminating her guise. She was conscious of Flint's hand on her shoulder and the padding just beneath her jacket. Could he sense, even in his inebriation, that it was fake muscle? At supper, had he been staring too closely at the false stippling of whiskers? If anything comforted Cora, it was that Flint kept calling her Jacob even as he slurred his words.

"Jacob Lee, you are a terrible person to let me drink so much of that punch."

"Jacob Lee, why is your sister so mean to me?"

"Jacob Lee, I believe I am going to regurgitate again. Right here, in front of this very fine Olympic Theatre."

Which he did.

Finally, they reached Flint's boardinghouse, several doors down from the Stuyvesant Institute. Cora had to snatch the keys from his fumbling hands to enter the front door. A nightcapped woman cracked open a door within and tsked her disapproval.

"Theodore Flint, you need a visit from the Temperance Society!"

"I need a visit from my mattress," he responded with as much dignity as possible. Which was not much, given he had a glob of vomit on his chin.

"Sorry, ma'am. Just dropping him home, and I'll be off." Cora was fairly impressed with how sober she could sound and act even though her head was swimming.

"Quickly then, and don't wake up the other boarders," she snapped.

Cora nearly dragged Flint up the stairs because he'd pause after two and start snoring. On the first landing, she slapped him.

"Ow! Why did you hit me?"

"Which one is yours? Which room?" Cora hissed.

"Top floor, number eleven."

Cora slapped him again.

"Aaaaah. Why'd you hit me again?"

"For living on the top floor, you sot."

They stumbled up two more flights. Room eleven was tiny, not larger than fifteen feet square. A thin mattress, neatly made with sheets and an old brown blanket, was squared into the corner. An oil lamp perched beside a stack of medical textbooks—outdated and very worn—atop a wood desk. A sheet was draped across the corner, behind which a few shirts and trousers sat inside a nearly empty trunk, so well used that half the rivets around the brass bands were missing.

One could learn a lot from a person's room. And at a glance, Cora knew that Flint studied hard, and had very little money and no family. There were no piles of letters to and from loved ones, no painted miniatures or pictures propped anywhere. But the room was impeccably clean, and what little he had was ordered to painful squareness.

Theodore Flint was lonely. The walls spoke about nights alone, and hours spent by the window looking out on Broadway and not participating. Wanting, but unable. Cora recognized the language of isolation in her own room at home. She saw it in the looking glass as well. Cora needed only to glance at herself to feel as if she didn't belong in any world she set foot in. At least Theo didn't have to hide, but poverty and friendlessness struck their own kind of blow. She wanted to laugh— a competition between who was lonelier was a terrible competition, indeed.

Flint released a loud burp, scented with the sour tang of stomach acid.

"Ugh, Flint. No one deserves to smell the insides of your belly. You owe me for this."

He was barely hanging on to her shoulder. Cora staggered over to the thin bed and considered throwing him down, but decided on gentleness. The result, however, was that after she lowered him onto the mattress, her arm was trapped beneath him.

Exhausted, and still foggy from drink, Cora sprawled half on, half off the lumpy mattress (which was shockingly comfortable), and closed her eyes against the clean cotton sheets. She would rest, just for a minute, then wrestle Flint off her arm and go home. Before that, though, she grabbed the edge of the sheet and gently wiped Flint's face and mouth clean.

She was so very tired. She'd rest only a bit.

Just one minute.

⟞⟝

Cora awoke to the sound of a door slamming somewhere at a distance. Which confused her—Leah was not the slamming-doors type, even when upset.

She stirred, and realized her head was pounding with pain at her temples, and something heavy was lying across her chest. Opening her eyes, she regarded a water-stained ceiling with peeling plaster.

Wait.

Where was she? She inhaled, and smelled something earthy, something that reminded her of work late at night, when she was Jacob—the smell of men whose sweat had dried in yesterday's clothes.

That was when Theodore Flint snored in her ear.

She froze, terrified.

She was Jacob. Not Cora. And she was still lying on Flint's bed. The dusky morning cast a buttery light into the far corners of the boarding-house room. Holding her breath and trying not to panic, Cora lifted her head and saw that one of her legs hung off the side of the cot, the other one nestled next to Flint's prone and sleeping body. Flint's arm was draped across her chest.

Not just across her chest—worse. Flint's arm was lying on Cora's sternum, and his hand had slipped under the edge of her jacket and was flat against her ribs, exactly over her second heart.

Cora's second heart.

The very heart that Flint had spoken of only hours ago in the Widow's upstairs saloon. After he had told Jacob that Hitchcock was likely poisoned, not dead of natural causes, and they had shaken hands over a deal that meant many more days ahead in each other's company, looking for odd specimens, like girls with two hearts.

Oh God.

How could she have been so thoughtless and careless?

Cora rubbed her eyes and face, dismayed to see that her makeup came off on her hand as a gray smudge. She had to leave, and quickly. Taking a slow breath, she carefully levered herself off the edge of the cot. As she did so, Flint's hand dragged across her left bosom, bound tightly beneath layers of linen. But even Cora was aware that there was a slight swell there that couldn't be hidden when touched.

She froze again, and her feminine senses seemed to take over, registering that she had never been this close to a man, nor had a man's hand ever touched these illicit places. She'd gone dancing in the past, yes, but then she'd been touched only on her shoulder, or waist.

When she couldn't bear it any longer, Cora carefully shoved Flint's arm off her body and stood. His sleeping eyes whizzed under satiny closed eyelids, and his hair was mussed in a fetching mess across his forehead.

Stop staring. Stop it.

Cora looked about quickly for her reticule, then remembered she was Jacob and didn't carry a purse. She headed for the door.

"Cora," Flint wheezed, his eyes still shut.

She whirled around and gaped at Flint, then exhaled slowly once she realized he was still quite unconscious. So, Theodore dreamt of Cora! It was both disturbing and pleasurable, and she had no idea what to do except leave.

Forty-seven Irving Place was quiet on the outside, its simple red brick and its white window awnings neat and respectable. But even from the outside, she could detect Leah's faint squeals and exclamations from the third floor. She went inside and up the stairs.

Through the door, she heard Alexander sighing loudly.

"Leah, she's fine. I'm sure it was just an extra job that had Jacob working all night."

"She never does this, Alexander. She always tells me what job she's got. She always checks in first. Cora wasn't dressed for a resurrection tonight. She was wearing his second best!"

Cora opened the door, and silence befell the apartment. In the kitchen, Alexander was smoking an early-morning pipe in front of the smoldering kitchen fire. At the sight of her, Leah snatched her apron to her face and cried with relief.

"I'm fine," Cora said, her voice raspy with tiredness and too much imbibing. "I only fell asleep after I had a little too much to drink. Everything is fine."

"Fell asleep? More like fell down drunk! I can smell your liquor stink from where I stand! Where were you? Who were you with?" Leah barked, after she'd mopped her face clean of tears.

"I was with Theodore Flint."

"Your makeup! It's all gone! He must have seen—he must have noticed."

"Oh, Leah, he was a nazy cove—he didn't notice at all."

"Nazy cove! You were just as drunk! Your breath smells like the Old Brewery! I'm the only one who drinks in this house, and I drink enough for both of us!"

"Well, that's true," Cora said, chuckling.

"Enough," Alexander said, silencing them both. "How could you let your guard down like that, Cora?"

"But I was Jacob, not Cora!"

"It matters less, but it still matters," Alexander said. "Charlotte would be furious if she knew the risk you just took. Don't ruin the sacrifices she made for you. You mustn't forget what's at stake. Not now, not ever."

"I know what's at stake." Cora had let her voice rise to her normal pitch, and took her hat off, mussed her hair, and unbuttoned her top collar. "I made a mistake. But nothing untoward happened, and I came out with a deal with Theodore."

"You're calling him Theodore now?" Alexander said, eyes even.

"Is that a crime?" Leah said. "She might get married someday. Have a family. He's going to be a doctor, and they do well enough. They might move away, and she'd have a new name."

How odd. Leah never, ever seemed much interested in having Cora married off, and now twice in two days she'd raised the topic. Oh, why had Cora spoken Flint's given name aloud? Tiredness, no doubt.

"Flint," she corrected herself. "Leah, let's have no more matchmaking when there's work to be done. Coffee, please."

Leah stomped to the kitchen hearth and poured a cup of boiled black liquid, and set it before Cora alongside a warm, sweet loaf speckled with raisins. Cora took a ravenous bite, followed by the bitter brew.

"It was worth it. We've a deal to work on the next several resurrections, and I've found out some information about Hitchcock."

"Hitchcock? The fellow you dug up a few days ago?" Alexander waved at Leah. "My goodness, Leah. Stop ruffling your feathers, and eat with us." He stood up to pour her a small glass of port, despite it being nine o'clock in the morning, and pulled out a chair. Leah sat down with a thump.

Cora explained the findings of the dissection, and also the disappearance of Ruby with the tail. Alexander and Leah listened gravely. Cora saved the worst for last.

"Flint spoke of rumors of another unique specimen to be had. There have been murmurs of a girl with two hearts. From Frederick Duncan himself."

Leah and Alexander both went still, Leah with her port in hand and Alexander with bun halfway to his mouth.

"Are you sure?" Alexander said.

"Yes. Flint was drunk when he said it, which is why I believe it. He'd been holding it back."

Leah's hand trembled. "But he didn't—he didn't—"

"No, Leah. He gave no sign whatsoever that I was the girl. He said it was too hard to believe. But if enough people repeat an unlikely rumor, it becomes real."

"I haven't heard the curator mention it once. This must be very new." Alexander looked out the window, where the sun had disappeared behind a haze of smoke from a bonfire down the street. "We knew that Dr. Grier continued to speak of you after we left Gowanus. He may have spoken to many physicians in New York." He looked Cora straight in the eye. "Maybe you should take advantage of what you know. Leave New York. Go to Philadelphia, or west, to Ohio or Iowa."

"I could," Cora admitted. "And yet, these last five years, I've made connections I'm loath to leave. I have skills that make good money now."

"Which you're short on. Rent is due in two days, Cora," Leah reminded her. "And by the end of the hour, I'll piss away the last few drops of port." She looked forlornly at the empty bottle.

"I can pay your rent," Alexander said.

"No. You've already done so much for us, Alexander." Cora stood, smoothing down Jacob's wrinkled shirt. "I know it's been a dry last few weeks, but there's more work ahead. We'll finish our next few jobs. Tighten our belts. And then I'll leave New York and start over. Perhaps become a teacher somewhere. Leah, you'll find better-paying work without me."

"I'll not leave you, Cora. I shan't." The words were sweet, but there was something in Leah's eyes that betrayed her. Cora understood the temptation. She could be the maid for a wealthier family that actually owned a house. When Leah followed Charlotte into poverty years ago, it was because she loved Charlotte, almost like her own child. But being poor wears on a person, even with bountiful supplies of love.

"Your plan sounds reasonable," Alexander said. "If all goes well, you might leave New York in one month's time. Well before those rumors lead to anything."

She nodded and yawned. Leah pushed an envelope toward her.

"Don't forget about these."

Cora withdrew two poisonously hued orange tickets.

Castle Garden Theatre
Jenny Lind, September 11, 1850

Oh. This was *the* Jenny Lind, the marvelous singer whom P. T. Barnum had wooed from across the ocean for a reported $150,000. The "Swedish Nightingale" had created a mania everywhere. New York was awash in Jenny Lind snuffboxes, gloves, fans, paper dolls, and other items in the stores along Chatham Street.

She'd almost forgotten she'd purchased the tickets. Unlike a Philharmonic Society event, or at the scandalous Astor Opera House, still reeling from the riot there a year ago, this concert would bring in not only the best of society but those who would normally stay at home. It was a concert not to be missed.

"I'd nearly forgotten. Leah, would you like to come? Or Alexander?"

"I don't have the stomach for the theater these days," Alexander said. "Perhaps Leah can go with you."

Leah nodded with a grin. She loved the theater, when she had a chance to go. Castle Garden was one of Cora's favorite places. She would attend regularly to scout out ailments, occasionally before the persons themselves even knew they were sick. She didn't always want to wait for the good doctors to bring her cases. She'd found one gentleman who had an oddly tall stature and elongated fingers that had escaped his own doctor's notice, and a woman with a cancer eating through her cheek; she'd attended in her regular theater box nearly half-asleep on laudanum.

But even as Cora looked forward to the opportunity to scout for new specimens, she wondered if others were scouting for her. Had Flint felt her extra beating heart beneath his hand last night? Did he suspect she was the phantom girl with two hearts?

Even more frightening was that she had the terrible urge to tell him her secret—which made no sense at all.

CHAPTER 9

Cora wore an evening dress of cream and pale-green silk, her wig parted down the middle, its poufs secured with matching green ribbons. Leah dressed in a sober black satin, her best. The driver took them down Broadway toward Castle Garden, just beyond the Battery, where scores of onlookers stared at the bulwarks and vast rigs of ships from China and England. Theatergoers were already in lines along the narrow bridge connecting Castle Garden to the rest of Manhattan, as if the round building were too fine to touch the commonplace island. Leah gaped as they found the line for orange ticket holders.

"They said there would be thousands of tickets sold," Leah said. "Look at all of us!"

"Yes," Cora said, not really listening. She was already scouting the crowd, assessing the bodies as if she could see through their vestments. This one had a limp and a cane, likely a result of some rheumatism—common enough. That one had a facial palsy, hidden cleverly with a black lace veil. Another had a skin color that was not quite right—rather jaundiced. Could be too much drinking and a sick liver, or else a tumor. She recognized another member in their group—a Mr. Ellington, whose dropsy had been cured by a healthy bloodletting last winter.

"Cora, let's go into another line. This one is altogether too long." Leah impatiently danced from one foot to another, a telltale sign of discomfort that Cora recognized. Perhaps her garters were too tight.

Cora frowned. "This is the line for the orange ticket holders, Leah. We must stay here. And I see a fellow with a very odd limp and gait. I ought to seek out his name. The family is close by."

"I don't like the way this crowd stares at you, or me. Let's move off to the side, just for a while."

Staring? Who was staring? Cora carefully looked about. Usually, she was the one staring, and as she did so, people often felt her gaze and drew away. Something about her foreign features and her imperturbable stare gifted her with a slightly otherworldly air. Cora had a booted toe halfway in the world of the dead, after all.

That shadow gaze heralded a finite end that she feared herself but had never felt. Until now. So, when Cora searched the crowds being slowly inhaled by the open doors of Castle Garden, she searched for a steady pair of eyes preying upon her person, looking for a physical sign that betrayed her secret. But those weren't the kind of eyes she found.

Instead, she found the blonde woman. The very one from the Grand Anatomical Museum. Once again, she was accompanied by the Schermerhorn gent. They were in a line full of green ticket holders, and when the line advanced, the woman remained fixed in place, staring with open hostility at Cora and Leah.

"Who is that lady?" Cora asked.

"I don't know," Leah said. "I don't like the way she looks at you. We should leave."

But the lines began to move more quickly, and soon the woman was forced to advance until she was lost in the crowd before them.

The concert itself was something of a disappointment. Barnum had been touting the brilliance of Jenny Lind to the point where people thought she might be a celestial being on earth. Nearly thirty thousand had welcomed her when she disembarked her steamship. So, when Jenny Lind opened her mouth to sing, Cora was expecting music in the form of transcendent fairy dust to spew forth—but it was nothing of the like. Very good singing, and that was all. It gave her more leave to use her brass opera glasses to observe the patrons for signs of morbid illness. There was always a treasure hiding among the healthy.

It wasn't until intermission that she had the opportunity for an introduction, though it was not with whom she expected. As Leah complained over the cost of a punch and Cora silently cursed the choice to wear her most painful pair of heeled slippers, someone touched her elbow.

Cora turned. It was the woman from the museum—but not the blonde one, the one who'd been arguing with Drs. Tilton and Goossens. Dr. Blackwell, wasn't that her name? She was accompanied by another woman as modestly dressed as herself, albeit in richer fabrics of silk poplin and garnishes of ribbon.

Now that Cora could really examine Dr. Blackwell, she found that the woman possessed a mix of qualities that didn't stir well together, like vinegar and butter. She was slight of stature, only five feet tall, but with keen, dark eyes. However, the telltale nonparallel gaze revealed one of her eyes to be artificial. Her clothes were dun in color and simple, and she was practically throttled in wool, she was so modestly dressed. Poufs of hair fell against her smiling cheeks, but her smile was as sharp as a blade.

"Hello there. I confess, I don't know many people in this city as yet, but I know you!" Her voice was comforting and low, without being syrupy. "I saw you at the museum the other day, did I not?"

"You did," Cora said, caught off guard by the abrupt and somewhat improper introduction.

"I am Dr. Elizabeth Blackwell."

"I am Cora Lee, and this is Leah O'Toole." She looked left, but Leah had disappeared in pursuit of a refreshment. She loved that punch a little too much. "Ah. Well, that *was* Leah. Please forgive me, but is it quite true? You are a doctor?"

"I am, indeed. Newly graduated from Geneva Medical School upstate."

"And did you study anatomy? To its fullest extent?" Anybody could call themselves a doctor after paying for a few classes. A true physician, however, took the pains and paid the price to study anatomy from a cadaver.

"I have. Goodness, the head and neck anatomy was most challenging. The genioglossus! Styloglossus! Hyoglossus! Do you enjoy the anatomic arts? I believe they let ladies into the lectures these days."

Palatoglossus, Cora added silently. "I do," she said aloud, warming up to the woman.

"Well, I am searching for a position, and the dispensaries won't speak to me. I have already opened up a practice on Union Square."

"Oh! I haven't seen your sign as yet."

"The landlady refuses to let me hang out my shingle. Says that it's disgraceful. She seems to think that a woman doctor's office is akin to a brothel." Dr. Blackwell laughed at this, but "Mmm" was all Cora could manage. A woman doctor *was* an anomaly.

"And what do you do?" Dr. Blackwell asked imperiously.

"I beg your pardon?" Cora said.

"You seem sharp enough." Which was a compliment, because Cora had hardly said anything as yet. "Have you had a proper education? Have you a profession? You know those physicians, I dare say. Are you an apothecary?"

"Goodness, no," Cora said. "Certainly, I've had an education, but . . ."

"Oh, come now. Foxglove. Do you know what it is? What it's used for?"

"Dropsy," Cora said, without thinking. Oh, she should have said the wrong thing. But her mouth continued to speak, almost without her permission. "But it's not always so useful. It's a poison, if you give too much."

"You do know a bit! Now, see that fellow there. He has dropsy." Dr. Blackwell nodded in the direction of a man whose legs looked like tree trunks, tightly encased in plaid wool pants. "Pale face, jugular vein bulging at the neck. He needs my help, but I have no introduction, so I shan't foist myself upon him."

Dropsy. So ordinary. That one wasn't worth her time. Cora made a small pfft sound before she realized it.

Dr. Blackwell arched a dark eyebrow. "Do you find this dull?"

"Oh! No, I just . . . I ought to find Leah. Intermission is nearly finished."

"Ah! Hello!" Dr. Blackwell waved her arm in an alarmingly vivid fashion to someone behind Cora. "We meet again. This is a small town! You meet two people in two days, and thence again you see them at the most popular concert of the year!"

Cora turned and came face-to-face with the blonde woman. The very one who couldn't keep her malignant stare away. In such close proximity, the lady hardly had time to change her expression from embarrassment (over Dr. Blackwell's flagging her down) to cold anger (at seeing Cora).

"It appears that for once, I am allowed the introductions. This is—"

"I know who she is," the lady said abruptly. "Cora Lee, is it not? Now I know for sure. I recognized your maid."

Cora's mouth went utterly dry. "Leah? I don't understand."

"You appear to be in excellent health, Miss Lee." She said this as if it were a crime. Such public words about her health made Cora flush. What was this woman talking about?

Dr. Blackwell's eyebrows drew together. "Oh. Miss Lee, have you not been well?"

"No . . . I mean yes, I am well, thank you," Cora stammered.

Dr. Blackwell's bonhomie disappeared in the presence of the other woman's dour attitude. "Then I see you've met Miss Cutter before."

That name. An electric shock ran through her. The name that Cora ought to wield, if she had taken her family name through her mother. She looked at the blonde woman more piercingly. The lady appeared the same age as herself. Charlotte had once mentioned a sister-in-law who'd given birth just after Cora's mother. What was the name of the child? It sounded like scissors. It was French—

"Suzette?" Daniel Schermerhorn appeared at her side. "The bells are ringing. Intermission is over. Shall we?"

"Yes, Daniel." Suzette Cutter turned on her heel without a curtsy and left the group.

Dr. Blackwell shook her head. "I do apologize. I had no idea there was a history between the two of you."

"Not a history, exactly," Cora said. She fanned her face.

"I supposed you've had a rift?"

"Not at all." How can we have a rift, Cora thought, if I've never met her? If I'm not even supposed to exist, since Jacob Lee is the only child of Elizabeth Cutter? And Suzette somehow knew Cora was a girl! And had inquired about her health. Her health, of all things! None of it made sense.

Leah reappeared, and Cora introduced her to Dr. Blackwell.

"Did you say you're a doctor?" Leah, her eyes agog, said, not noticing that Cora was still blank faced with shock. "Why on earth would a woman become a doctor?"

Dr. Blackwell simply took a deep breath. No doubt it was a tiresome and repeated exclamation.

"Because a woman can take care of the sick as well as a man can. If only I'd helped that fellow this morning. Do you know, I was outside of the Sixth Ward dispensary inquiring about a position when a poor man was brought in, insensate. He'd been garroted, but his porte-monnaie hadn't been stolen. They'd held his neck long enough that he'd fainted, but held on too long, alas. And the dispensary wouldn't let me examine or treat him! It was a shame. He died on the spot, and I might have helped."

"How awful," Cora said.

"Yes. I'll never forget him. Had an enormous port-wine stain covering half his face. I've never seen one so large before."

Cora went silent. There was a man she'd been following for more than a year. William Timothy. He had an enormous port-wine stain on his face, but he was also reported to have six fingers on his right hand, which he kept covered with a large ill-fitting glove. But Timothy was otherwise healthy and robust and rarely checked in with his doctor over on Delancey. Cora had no hope he'd die from an early death unless there was an accident.

Or something more nefarious than an accident.

William, Cora thought, what happened to you? Where are you now?

"When—" Her voice cracked, and she cleared her throat. "When did this happen?" she asked.

"Why, only this morning."

The bells signaling the end of intermission rang. Bodies rustling in silk and satin poured back into the theater, encompassed by murmurs of merriment. Dr. Blackwell waved a cheerful goodbye and rejoined her small party, and Cora and Leah were soon left alone in the salon outside the theater doors.

"He came from a good family," Cora whispered to Leah. "He'll be buried tomorrow, and I don't know which cemetery it will be."

"But that's tomorrow," Leah complained. "We paid good money for these tickets. We ought to watch the rest of the performance."

"Not with that woman in there," Cora said bitterly.

"Dr. Blackwell? Agreed!"

"I don't mean Dr. Blackwell. I mean Suzette Cutter. My cousin. Who seems to know who you and I both are."

Leah's face went from red, to white, to pasty green before her eyes rolled up in her head and she fainted dead away.

Well. It looked like they'd be missing the second half of the performance after all.

WILLIAM TIMOTHY

I ought not to be dead.

When you're garroted, you're not supposed to die. I've seen the victims myself many times, and there's the right way to do it, you see. I believe for me, it was done entirely wrong.

I had been accepting bags of rags brought in by street children, who'd likely stolen them from the rotting piers near Fulton Ferry. The rags, you see, make good paper, and our paper business has been doing so well that we were on the verge of purchasing our own home near Stuyvesant Square.

Usually, Robby or Irvin comes with the largest bags, but they were drunk or recovering or some such, and instead, the little kinchin had come straight to me to sell their wares. What a state they were in. The bedraggled Irish, only weeks off the boat, now sending their children by the hundreds and thousands into the street to pickpocket, beg, skim sugar, or gather rags. At least the rag children are doing somewhat honest work.

So, a half morning of bargaining had done me in, and I called to Sarah, my wife, to lock the door. I would meet some fellows who promised to secure a good sale to the *Tribune* if I'd entertain them with a hearty meal.

My establishment is swept free of the filth that piles against the doorways nearby, but walking Pike Street is a trial. A small dead pig lay in a shallow, mud-filled indentation in the road, and the crows were plucking its eyes out, while the kinchin were throwing stones at the crows.

I made a wide berth around the spectacle, close to the alleyway between a grogshop and pawnbroker. An arm shot out from the shadows, encircling my throat and pressing hard upon my windpipe, until I couldn't attempt a cough, or yell. The fellow kicked my right knee from behind, and my body sagged as I lost my footing.

Several passersby saw my predicament. I am used to the world staring at the birthmark splashed like currant jam across my face, but this time, no one pointed or laughed; they all averted their eyes.

I knew about garroting. It was common enough, and I understood that in the next moment, a ragtag child would rifle through my pockets—quickly, effortlessly, stealing any moneys I possessed.

But none of the ambushing party went through my pockets.

A smaller man, with the top hat and gaudy plaid of a b'hoy, laughed loudly. "Aw, Roy, you nimenog, too much lap again, eh? We'll deliver yeh, tangle-foot as yeh are."

I wasn't drunk, though. And I wasn't Roy. He took out a small bottle of liquor and splashed it all over my person, so I'd smell as drunk as the criminals painted me.

I knew this game; we've all heard about the games these men play, the counterfeiters, the pickpockets. Now that they'd had their fun, made me look like a drunken fool amongst friends, they'd take my portemonnaie and free me. I'd go back home, penniless, and endure my wife's worry over what could have been. It could be worse.

And then it was.

"Hemp the flat!" whispered the b'hoy. I knew not what he meant, until the large oaf encircling my neck began to squeeze. The other lifted my ankles, and together they drew me deeper into the darkness of the alleyway. Now I could see my assailant. His ears were terrible knobs of flesh, as if they'd swollen into fists of bread dough. Ears I would never forget, if I'd been given the time in life to remember.

"Apologies to this swell. May God receive yeh," he said, before choking me in earnest. My face felt like it would burst, and my heart thumped hard in my chest, and I struggled and struck out, but they had me firmly. I couldn't draw breath to scream, and the cry died behind my lips as everything went black within a minute.

They took my lifeless body and carried me through the alley to Rutgers Street, then westward, the destination of which confounded me. But they were interrupted by a police officer.

"What are you doing with this man?" he demanded, his clothes plain but a copper star shining dully from his breast.

"This Sam's a nazy cove, sir. Too much of the sky-blue. Delivering him home."

"He's not drunk. Look at him. He's purple as a flag," the policeman said, touching my cheek, still warm but not for much longer. "Bring him to the hospital. Or better yet, there's a dispensary right here, across the street."

The two men stared at each other. Clearly, I was destined for another place, but they had no choice but to deposit me in the dispensary, from where my wife was called for and where she found me, dead as can be.

And all I had wanted was lunch.

CHAPTER 10

Cora had sent out several notes to the physicians who knew the dead man, as well as her boys, asking if they knew anything of William Timothy's burial site. Her little messenger boy had been fairly flying all over town with her notes in tow. Leah made herself busy with sponging and pressing Cora's dress, which had gotten dusty on the walk near the Battery.

The rest of the evening, Cora's thoughts were consumed with Suzette Cutter. "How could she know about me? I thought they'd been told I was a boy."

"I don't know," Leah said. She shuffled from her left to right foot as she sponged the dress. Her nervous dance again.

"Why would she care about my health? Does she know about my . . . condition?"

"Perhaps Charlotte spoke to her and didn't tell us," Leah said.

"I suppose I could ask Miss Cutter myself," Cora said, thinking out loud.

"Oh, fie, dear! That's a mistake, it is!" Leah set down her iron. "Don't encourage her. We're not to speak to them!"

Cora didn't say anything further, but she turned the problem over and over in her mind. There was one way to find out why Suzette Cutter had such animosity toward her, and how she even knew Cora existed. That worried her more than the woman's anger. But neither today nor tomorrow was the day to do so.

The next morning, she readied herself in her mourning clothes. But she was anxious; anxious about the unexpected nature of his death, and that she hadn't received a single response about where William Timothy was to be buried. There were too many cemeteries on the island for her to visit each one. She needed more details.

Finally, when the clock on the mantel chimed nine, there was a knock on the door. Leah rushed to open it. Cora was pinning on her hat as she descended the stairs.

Alexander stood in the doorway. He held a parcel that smelled of sugar and bread.

"Good morning! I've brought breakfast, and a message for you," he said.

"Oh! From my boys?" Cora asked, snatching her reticule as Leah went outside to search for a hackney cab.

"What? No. I mean Duncan. He wonders if you received his note the other day. Says he wished to meet with you for tea tomorrow but didn't receive a response. Oh. It appears as if you're leaving."

Just then, a scrap of a child, dirty from head to toe, ran to the door.

"Oy, for Miss Lee! Two pence!"

Alexander took out the pennies, and the little scamp was off, but not before Alexander took the bit of paper and gave it to Cora.

The words were barely legible. She recognized Otto the Cat's scribble.

11 st cimitary, downt now wich

Eleventh Street. There were three cemeteries there, the two belonging to Saint Mark's and the Eleventh Street Catholic Cemetery. But the Catholic cemetery had stopped doing interments two years ago.

"Thank you, Alexander. I won't be able to stay for your lovely breakfast. I'm off to do my scouting. Perhaps we can meet at the museum tomorrow, then?"

Alexander looked disappointed. "Of course. Until then."

Cora nodded, but she felt wretched anyway. She hadn't seen Alexander very often lately. There was a time when he came to dinner three times a week, and breakfast every Sunday. She had been so busy, she'd neglected her uncle. She knew that he missed Charlotte's friendship. They often talked of her—her sayings, her love of books, her love of Cora.

"I'll tell you what," Cora said. "You may bring me to the tea, and we'll talk more then." She had an idea of setting him upon Suzette to find out what she knew. That might throw him in the direction of other ladies who might appreciate his artistic talent.

"Very well," he said.

She kissed him on the cheek. "I'll be there."

Alexander went inside to deposit his package of sweet buns. Leah had flagged down a hack, one of the nicer ones, and Cora stepped in, but before the driver shut the door, she remembered.

"Leah, I'm short on money. Can you—"

Leah's eyes widened. "The crock is empty, miss. We need this one. We need it very badly. I thought you still had five dollars from our last job?"

"I spent it the other night, with Flint."

"No money? No ride. Don't care how fine you look," the driver growled, and instead of shutting the door, he opened it wider. He cursed as she got out, then jumped into his carriage and whipped the horses away.

Not good. She liked to show up at the cemetery in a nice hack, with her nice clothes. The uppertens didn't walk to the cemetery, even if it was rather close to Irving Place.

"Well then. I'd better be off now, empty purse and all."

"Yes. Go and do your work and get us a good thirty dollars! And be careful!"

Cora hurried, without trying to look too hurried, down Second Avenue to Saint Mark's Church, its spire lofty and ever graceful. There were underground vaults on the east and west sides of the yard. Across the street was a larger plot where the slightly less well-to-do were interred. Here was where Cora found a small gathering of family, already leaving the graveside where a coffin lay waiting to be settled beneath the earth. She unobtrusively joined the back of the small crowd of bowed heads, dabbing her eyes and hearing the words of the Episcopalian priest.

". . . So cruelly taken from us, into the bosom of God . . . By the grace of the Timothy family . . ."

She stared at the casket. She wondered if William missed his family already. It was cruel; he was too young to die. Normally, the bodies she scouted had succumbed to nature's own timetable, as everyone had. But for William—this was bitterly unfair. Her eyes smarted, and she dabbed them with her handkerchief. She never cried at funerals. Never. Her sentiment was irritatingly in the way. Enough, Cora, she thought. Do your work.

A young gentleman stood near to her. When the lady on his other side turned to a different mourner, she spoke low.

"Poor souls of our Father. I hope William rests in peace and isn't disturbed by those . . . those . . ." She raised a handkerchief to her dripping nose, the words seemingly too horrifying to be uttered.

"No doubt he will." The gentleman lifted his eyebrows. "Bloody thieves. Luckily, the coffin is locked."

Cora put a hand over her heart and exhaled in dramatic gratefulness. The crowd soon dispersed, several following a carriage festooned in mourning drapery that took the principal family away. Cora peeled off from the group, removed her black shawl, and walked briskly west as soon as she'd turned the corner. She wiped her face one last time.

Enough sadness. William Timothy no longer suffered, and neither should she.

So, there would be a locked coffin. They would need different tools, but locks had not kept Jacob away from his prizes. Tonight, they would retrieve poor William, and Cora could worry a mite less about the kitchen crock empty of coins.

She went home to eat, then sent a message to her crew to pick up Jacob with the wagon and tools at eleven o'clock. But as she dressed that evening, she realized she'd forgotten to alert Flint. Now, there wasn't time. It was a relief, though. The memory of waking in his bed, his hand across her ribs, was still too fresh.

Otto the Cat, the Duke, and Friar Tom showed up at the appointed hour. Now that it was dark, Cora was in her element, ready to dig a ten-foot trench if need be. Right when the wheels of the wagon began to turn, Puck ran up to the wagon, panting.

"Late, sorry, here," he said between breaths. He vaulted into the seat next to Otto. "Where's the goosecap?"

He meant Flint. Yes, Flint was very silly. Though, less of a goosecap now in Cora's mind.

"Not here tonight," she said.

"He's made inquiries, you know," the Duke said. "To other resurrectionists, about doing some digging farther north on the island, or in Green-Wood. He's got a fire in his belly."

"He'll burn quickly, then," Cora said, lying in the back of the cart next to two shovels and using her entwined hands as a pillow. "He doesn't know what he's doing."

"He was asking the right questions, from what I heard," said Tom. "I like him. And he ate almost as much as me." Which for Tom was apparently a sign of good character.

"Stow your wid," Cora said, and they accordingly went silent. She wasn't in the mood to hear good things about Flint. "Anyway, I've made a deal with him. Next three bodies, he gets a cut as long as we deliver to either his school or to the Grand Anatomical Museum." The men all began to protest, but Cora held up a hand. "Your pay will be the same; only my share is cut. Got it?"

Her team murmured assent. She regretted the deal, now that it had been made. But it kept her in the game, in case Flint found a body before her—and after all, she'd made the deal so Flint would tell her about the dissection of Hitchcock. That bizarre green tongue . . . She needed to find out why he'd died the way he did. Had he been poisoned as Flint said? She also needed to find out where Ruby Benningfield had gotten to. For that matter, it was strange that William Timothy had been garroted. Murders for money happened often enough, and yet— now there were three people from her watch list, dead or disappeared when they shouldn't have been.

Their party continued down the street, which was quieting rapidly as midnight approached. The inhabitants of this part of town appreciated their sleep. When they arrived at the cemetery, the gate was unlocked, and there was no guard. No doubt the family rested well, assured that the locked coffin would suffice to repel night visitors.

They'd just begun to quietly pick up their shovels and crowbars when Puck jumped out of the wagon and whistled.

"Oh. This one. I'm a goosecap myself. Forgot I have to be elsewhere. G'night."

Cora started. None of her men ever abandoned a job after they'd already shown up. They either came, or they didn't, and on the rare occasions they didn't, it was from a near-death case of cholera.

"Puck," she growled, "you leave, and you don't work for me anymore."

"Aye, and that's the way I'll have it. I've no time for secondhand jobs."

Cora cursed. Puck whirled around and punched the end of the wagon so hard, it jerked forward and the horse neighed with alarm.

"You're late! Too late! I already got my pay, and better than what you give, with your crumbs and sour brandy." For a second, he looked like he might come and tackle Jacob directly; Cora had already reached around her back to curl her fist around her dagger. But Puck backed away and smiled a rotten-toothed smile. The last they heard was his crooked whistle as he walked away.

"I made a mistake bringing him that first night," the Duke said quietly. "Better that he's gone."

"Aye, better," Cora agreed, but Puck's words unsettled her. What had he meant, he already got his pay?

"Come," Otto said, his arms full of shovel and burlap. "Moon's risen!"

It was two hours of hard labor before they discovered what Puck had meant.

"This box has been picked. It's unlocked." Even in the light of a quarter moon, Cora could see that the Duke, their expert lock picker, was frowning. He lay down flush against the ground and pulled at the coffin's lid. It opened wide, letting the thin moonlight illuminate what Cora dreaded to know.

The coffin was empty except for a pair of shoes and a fine suit of brown wool.

"We've been beat," Cora said, pushing back to sit on her knees.

Otto took off his hat and threw it on the ground.

"Well now. That would explain why Puck was off in a hurry when he saw the job," the Duke said, scratching his head.

"Puck stole this body earlier this evening. That's why," Cora said flatly. "He's working a second gang. And they beat us." The others cursed aloud.

"All that work, and no money to be had!" wailed Otto.

Puck and his men must have come only just after dusk, a dangerous time, but they'd been fast, neat, and efficient, and hadn't left a trace.

The robbers had just been robbed.

CHAPTER 11

"Are you quite sure?" Alexander asked.

"Yes," Cora said. "Not only was William Timothy murdered, but Puck and another gang took his body before we could. We've never been outmaneuvered. Everyone knows who we are, and how we work." She shook her head. "Alexander, I think Puck may have killed this man, just to steal his body."

"From what you've said, he doesn't seem to have the intelligence for such a plan."

"I don't know, Alexander."

The round cobblestones beneath her feet weren't the only reasons she felt unsteady. What if Puck had also killed Ruby, who was still missing? And Hitchcock? What if he heard rumors about the two-hearted girl, and came after her too? She tried not to think of it. True, Puck didn't seem keen enough for such machinations. And how was he finding out about these people? She'd never told her boys of her special list.

Alexander patted Cora's hand on his arm. They were walking to Grand Street to meet Frederick Duncan. Cora hadn't slept well after the previous evening's disappointment. Leah had gone to the pawn-broker to see what money she could get for some crockery they didn't need, as well as the fine amethyst-hued paste parure, including necklace, earrings, and bracelet, that Charlotte had given Cora on her fifteenth birthday. She dreaded seeing it go. At breakfast, there were only two leftover sweet buns. Leah's eyes glistened with hunger at the plate, so Cora had pushed them to her, claiming she wasn't hungry.

Just then, her stomach rumbled. Alexander looked at her.

"Are you well? Did you eat?"

"Yes," she lied. "Anyway, let me know if you hear anything at the museum, or elsewhere. Anything at all."

"I have to go to Philadelphia in a day or so. It will be a quick trip, but I'll tell you if I observe anything before or after. But, Cora," Alexander said, with an added sigh, "you promised only a few more of these, and already things are getting complicated."

"It's only for a little while longer, Alexander."

He sighed again. As they strolled downtown, she watched her uncle, whose face was lined with worry. He was looking older than usual, more careworn. It upset her that he didn't glance at the pretty ladies who walked past them. Nothing would give Cora more delight than to hear that he'd found someone to marry. It was time for him to put the memory of her aunt to rest. Alexander's energy in caring for her and Leah ought to be spent on building his own future.

As she leaned on his arm, a waft of lilac essence issued from his sleeve. Perhaps it was from a passing woman, but she smelled it again after several more steps.

"Why, Alexander. I smell perfume on you. Have you been in the company of another woman today?" Cora teased.

She was surprised to see her perpetually composed uncle blushing. Blushing!

"Don't be silly. The woman next to me on the omnibus was bathed in scent. I'm sure it saturated my clothes." But he was still ruddy in the cheek.

Cora's hearts expanded at the thought of her lonely uncle finding love. And yet, a yawning emptiness lived there too. Her mind flashed to Theodore Flint, and to the sensation of his hand resting on her chest.

Oh, Cora. Don't think such things.

They arrived at the tea shop. Inside, patrons were enjoying plates of sugar cakes, tiny pies both savory and sweet, and cheesecakes on elevated platters. The scents of coffee and tea rose into the air. Cora spotted the curator at a table reading the *Herald* and smoking a cigar. Tea was at the ready, steaming on the table. He stood to welcome them.

"Ah, the beautiful Miss Lee! And Alexander. How kind of you to escort her. And escort her I would—look at that figure! I shouldn't let her out of my sight if I were her uncle either!" Leah had tightened her corset an extra inch, at Cora's request. It had the desired effect.

"Mr. Duncan, how good of you to invite me to tea. We have much to discuss."

"Indeed! Alexander, feel free to leave us. We'll only be a half hour at most, and I should like my acquaintances to gossip about having a tête-à-tête with a beautiful, unattached lady."

Alexander nodded, but Cora noticed the muscle on his jawline ripple. Apparently, the curator irked him as much as he disgusted Cora. As Alexander turned, he leaned toward her.

"I can stay, if you need me," he said.

Cora shook her head. "No, I'm fine. I shall catch the omnibus home after we're finished here."

Alexander didn't appear any more reassured, and yet he acquiesced. Cora wasn't worried about being alone with the curator. They were in public, and there was little harm that he could inflict upon her. Words were only words, after all. She sat down primly, smoothing her dress.

"I'm delighted to see you again, Mr. Duncan."

"Please, call me Frederick. I was so happy that you've come. My, but you're a luscious thing. They should serve you, instead of plum cakes." He was eyeing the swell of her breasts rather than her face. Cora's stomach churned, but she managed a smile as Duncan poured tea into their gilt china cups. "I've heard a rumor about you, you know," he said.

Cora's silver spoon clinked awkwardly against the china. She could feel her heart against her corset, like a fist punching the whalebones. On her right side, a tiny echo thumped, as if both her hearts were warning her.

Run.

He knows.

Cora restored the smile to her face. "Most rumors are nothing but smoke and shadows, dear Mr. Duncan. To which rumor are you referring?"

"The rumor that you are unlike any other woman I have ever known." He leaned in closer, and the steam from the tea rose and curled around the sides of his beard, as if he were the devil hovering above a conflagration. He crooked his finger, coaxing her closer. "You . . . are a resurrectionist. A *woman* resurrectionist. I know all your secrets now."

Cora leaned back, a sigh of relief cresting under her rib cage, so enormous that she nearly let it out.

"Ah. And where did you hear this rumor?"

"I have been asking about who might help me find the best specimens for my museum. Yours is a name whispered, not spoken aloud, Miss Lee. I have been assured in the dark corners of this island that your work is some of the best."

She sipped her tea slowly, deliberately. He had no choice but to wait for her lips to release the cup's rim. She smiled. "They speak the truth. I am the best."

"How? You're nothing like the usual species of digger that swarms over the graveyards. How could someone as beautiful and fine as you become such a . . . creature?"

She considered the word, *creature*. Creatures could be ordinary or magical or rather horrific. She didn't like the word at all.

"Why I do what I do is my business." Cora hesitated. For a moment, she had no wish to bring bodies to Duncan. She felt a possessiveness, nay, an almost protectiveness over the people she'd been watching. But she shushed her conscience. She needed the work, so she continued. "But understand, I am more than willing to help make the Grand Anatomical Museum more money, and by extension, your pockets full."

"And instead of warming a bed at night, you work, Miss Lee?"

"My brother, Jacob, does the night work."

"Ah, then you will be free to join me for supper, after the theater, won't you?"

Cora only smiled, but her hand curled into a fist under the table. "Of course not, my dear Mr. Duncan. Why, just having this repartee with you now is exhausting as it is, what with you and your charm!"

"Oh, I could exhaust you in more ways than you could imagine," he said, and pursed his lips. Lord, the licentiousness in his eye. She'd rather watch a pile of maggots. "I won't stop trying, you know. I have a habit of procuring whatever I should like to have." He leaned in closer. "Pray tell me, what specimens can you foresee bringing to my museum?"

"What are you wishing to receive?"

Cora sat back in her chair, and the curator only smiled. A waiter brought over a plate of small pies—oyster, egg, and ham. She'd cram them in, if she were Jacob right now. But the conversation had taken away her appetite. Duncan had no such qualms. He stabbed the oyster pie, then the ham one, and ate heartily.

"I can tell you what I already have," he said. "Alexander is working on a wax anatomical Venus. But I would like to complement it with more preserved specimens. I have heard of a fellow named Mütter in Philadelphia, a surgeon I believe, who has amassed a collection like no other. If he were to erect a museum, all of New York would flock to its doors, and I cannot have that. As it is, I must contend with Barnum's American Museum, and that quack Jordan with his Museum of Anatomy. It seems that every medical establishment must have its own galleries and cabinet and try to compete with me.

"I have skulls from the servants of King Henry the Eighth, and impressions of feet from Pompeii. But the museum is missing breadth. I have but one club foot, several worm infections from Africa—oh, this is ridiculous. You can fill in the rest. Oh! And we have been fortunate to receive a beautiful new specimen. A fantastic port-wine stain. I don't know if the specimen will preserve well, but we shall try."

Cora stopped breathing for a moment. "Port-wine stain, you say? Who procured the body?"

"I can't tell you all my secrets, now can I? I received it just this morning. It was worth every penny."

Cora frowned. It must have been Puck. But whom else was he working with?

"Would you prefer I contact you next time?" the curator said. Another order of miniature pies had landed on the table, these being treacle, cheese, and crab apple jelly.

Cora lifted her fork. "Of course. We are the best team, after all."

"Yes. They say Jacob Lee has a knack for knowing where and when the strangest cases meet their end. Or perhaps that was you, all this time."

Cora bowed her head in assent.

"Aha! Then you already know that this gentleman was six-fingered?" he said.

"Yes," Cora said, easing the crab apple pie onto her plate.

"And the other lady in town who had a horn growing out of her cheek?"

"Yes." She took a bite of the pie, but it was horribly sour. "That lady went to Europe, however. She shall be back in about two months, I believe. I also know about a lady coughing up hair, and one poor gentleman with a jaw disfigurement, a matchmaker. There was a girl with a tail that I'd been following, but I don't know what happened to her. She disappeared."

"Oh, she didn't disappear, Miss Lee." The curator procured an ivory toothpick from his inner pocket and began cleaning his teeth before her. "Her tail and backbone are safely preserved in the basement of the museum as we speak."

Cora's mouth went dry, and the rest of the pie was forgotten.

How? How could a second body escape her notice and be in his possession? That was nearly a twenty-dollar profit, gone. And it cannot have been a natural death. Not after such a disappearance.

"Is that so? And how did she make her way into your midst, may I ask?" She tried not to sound perturbed, though her heart rate began to rise and her quickened pulse swooshed in her eardrums.

He threaded his fingers together and placed his elbows on the table. So uncouth. "For that information, you must dine with me, Miss Lee."

She smiled back. "We are together now, my dear Mr. Duncan. Why don't you tell me?"

"A happy accident, is all," he finally admitted. "An acquaintance found her in an alleyway near Stewart's and brought her to me. Must have slipped on the refuse and hit her head."

"Not such a happy accident. That girl ought to have lived a long life. Does her family know?"

"Why on earth would I know that? Tell me, Miss Lee, are you growing a conscience in regard to the dead? They're still dead. Peace of mind is just that, in the mind. Not on earth, with earthly problems like why the waiter won't refill our teapot." He clanked his china down with a sharp note. "I must go. We'll continue to discuss our business over dinner, Miss Lee. Oh, and keep an open eye. I've a list of the specimens I should like to have." He handed her a folded paper. "I'm handing them out to all the resurrectionists. Did you enjoy the hothouse flowers I sent? For that, you owe me at least a kiss."

They stood, and the curator leaned in for a kiss, but Cora only held his hands in her gloved ones, with a grip so strong it cracked one of his knuckles and made him gasp. This way, she was able to keep her distance and affect an air kiss, without actually touching skin.

He hastily withdrew his hand from hers. "Good God, what a grip," he said.

"Years of pianoforte lessons!" she lied. "Thank you for the tea, and the list."

"It was my pleasure," he said, still rubbing his sore knuckle. "I shall see you off, as I've another meeting here in a minute." He showed her to the door of the restaurant, his hand on the small of her back. If only she could smack it away. As he returned to the restaurant, relief filled her.

"Well. You took long enough."

Cora squinted up through the sun's glare at the speaker. Theodore Flint, of all people! She was momentarily surprised into silence.

"Did you eat my share of the food too?" Flint said, more acid in his tone than she'd heard before. He peered left and right along the sidewalk, but wouldn't look her in the eye.

"You? You're the person meeting with the curator in there?" Cora said.

"Am I not allowed? You don't own him."

She stepped up to him, narrowing her eyes. "It was you. You stole that body last night!"

"What are you talking about?" Flint said.

"You took that fellow, Timothy. He was gone when Jacob arrived. Coffin empty."

"I didn't take him," he replied, irritated. Patrons entering the tea shop stared curiously at both of them. "Let's talk over here."

He led her into a small alleyway next to the restaurant, where two cats were battling over a pile of kitchen scraps.

"It wasn't me," Flint said, defensive. "I don't know who took the body."

Cora studied him. He had removed his hat, and his hair was mussed and sweaty. He smelled like earth, like the good smell that arose from the grist mills on Gowanus Creek when she was a child. He bore a scent of honesty.

"Very well. I believe you. The curator would have said so, in any case."

"So, Jacob was digging up a body last night? Why didn't he tell me?"

"There wasn't time," Cora said. There wasn't money to send a messenger, now that she thought of it.

"I thought we had an agreement," Flint said. "I thought Jacob told you."

She turned. "Yes. I know. He did."

"Then why did your team go to that cemetery without me?"

"It doesn't matter. The body wasn't there."

"That's not the point! Was Jacob too drunk to remember that we promised to split the next three bodies?"

Cora stayed silent.

"If I'd learned of a new body and didn't tell you," Theodore said, "would it anger you?"

Of course it would. Her face softened with remorse. "I'm sorry. I'll have Jacob fetch you next time I hear news." She sighed and leaned against the brick. "I apologize for doubting you."

"And I apologize just the same. I guess we're both feeling a little desperate for the next sale."

"Yes. Business hasn't been . . . good. And now, two bodies have been taken without me. Without us. It's strange, Theodore. Death is usually such a predictable affair, and these have been anything but."

"I'll tell you what's odd. You called me Theodore." His mouth turned up in a smile, a very small one.

"Oh, I'm sorry. Mr. Flint, I mean."

"No, that's not what I mean. All my friends call me Theo. Only my mother called me Theodore, and only when she was cross."

"Was?"

"She died in the last yellow fever epidemic a few years ago. My father too."

Cora touched her gloved hand to her lips. "Why, my aunt died then too."

"And your parents?"

"I haven't known my parents since I was born," she admitted. She was so inured to this fact that there wasn't a trace of sadness in her words. But Theo seemed shaken.

"So, we're both orphans. We ought to be a little more civil to each other, don't you think?"

"Well, we can start with this." She pulled the strings of her reticule. "Here. The curator gave me a list of specimens he'd like to procure. I expect he'll give you a similar one." She hadn't read it yet, but handed it to Flint.

"Is this normal, for your anatomists and such to ask for specific bodies?"

"No. But the curator is not an anatomist, and he's looking for a spectacle worthy of attraction."

Theo opened the neat piece of paper and read the fine handwriting. He turned sideways, so their arms touched and they could read it together.

> *I have examples enough of normal anatomy, but the other museums begin to outnumber me with their grotesques. If you could come across the following, I shall pay up to one hundred dollars apiece. See pricing below.*
>
> *Siamese twins, any portion thereof showing connections ($400)*
>
> *Scrofula, large size, minimum 10 cm ($70)*
> *The effects of tight lacing, maximum 33 cm ($60)*
> *A pair of Mandarin feet ($100)*

> *Articulated skeleton of abnormally small or large male ($100)*
>
> *Articulated skeleton of abnormally small or large female ($100)*
>
> *Afflictions of the eye, spine, or other parts as a result of self-abuse ($50)*
>
> *Fish-tailed girl ($300)*
>
> *Six-toed foot ($10)*
>
> *Webbed hands or feet ($100)*
>
> *Tumor of the nose or cheek or eye ($80)*
>
> *Young woman with two hearts ($500)*

Theo handed the slip of paper back to Cora, whose mouth had gone dry. He was speaking, but his voice seemed muffled and far away. She felt unbearably hot, the alley suddenly much too narrow, too confined. Unsteady, she began to walk toward the street. Theo babbled on and on.

"Can you believe . . . fish-tailed girl? Does he think this is some mystical shopping list of sorts? I cannot imagine . . . Grotesques! He goes too far. These are people, after all. I cannot abide by the baseness of these museums sometimes. At least the anatomists aim to learn . . ."

Cora's ears began to thump with her heartbeat, and for a moment she wanted to laugh. *I have a heartbeat in my ears too.* She looked down and thought it odd that the sidewalk seemed tilted.

"Goodness. Are you quite all right, Miss Lee?" Theo asked.

Cora shook her head once, before a swirl of nausea and coal-black tar consumed her vision. Her hands darted forward, grabbing at nothing, and everything in her existence winked out.

CHAPTER 12

Cora's first thought when she woke was, My, this bed is hard as a rock and smells of swine.

Her second thought was, Why are all these people in my bedroom staring at me?

At which she realized, That is blue sky next to Theo's head, and I'm lying on the street.

Oh dear.

"Are you all right?" Theo asked anxiously. His palm was cradling her head—and she was suddenly terrified that he might feel her wig moving.

"I'm fine," she said, sitting up.

"I very much doubt that. You fainted."

"So I did. But I'm very well now." A lie, because she still felt vaguely nauseated, and an unnatural torpor consumed her limbs. The sight of so many strangers staring at her was even more sickening.

The crowd around Theo broke up with a wave of his hand. "Please, give the lady room for fresh air." His eyes went back to Cora. "Didn't you have anything to eat in there?"

"Not much," she admitted. "Please. Make them go away. I'm quite all right now."

The ladies and gentlemen in the crowd were thrilled to see a prostrate woman on Grand Street—how very dramatic. Theo waved them away, and soon she was standing and leaning on Theo's arm. Something fluttered away from her gloved arm—the note from the curator.

"Oh! We need that!" Cora said, remembering that the last thing she'd seen before she'd fainted was a line from that very note.

Young woman with two hearts

A passerby plucked the paper from the gutter and handed it to her. She thanked him, and Theo wrapped his arm around her waist.

"I'll take you home. You need to rest."

Theo waved down the omnibus that approached, keeping Cora clear of the four horses stamping their feet and paying the fare for them both. He kept his hand around her waist while they sat, though there was no fear that she would fall again.

Near to Irving Place, the omnibus rattled to a stop, and Cora leaned on Theo's arm until they reached home. Leah opened the door, her face blanching at the sight of them.

"Oh! What's happened, Cora? Are you ill?"

"Fainted," Theo said. "She needs some hot beef tea and rest."

Leah ushered them inside, and immediately put her sturdy arms around Cora's waist. Theo held her arm on the right, and they went upstairs.

"My room is this way," Cora said, feeling nauseated again.

"No!" Leah said, giving her a frightened look. Oh. Of course. Jacob's clothes were probably already set out on the bed for tonight. "No, ah, I'm in the middle of airing your bedding. You'll stay in my room for now."

So, into Leah's room they went. It was smaller and plainer than Cora's, with a narrow but comfortable mattress. On a shelf above the fireplace, Leah had propped up a small cross, a Bible, and a piece of knitted lace that had belonged to her mother back in Ireland. A wooden box held her hairpins and ribbons for Sunday Mass. There was a miniature of Cora's mother, Elizabeth, and that was all in the way of decoration.

Leah shooed Theo out the door and ordered him to wait in the small sitting room downstairs. She locked the door with a key and began undressing Cora.

"I knew this corset was too tight!" Leah said. "You have to be kinder to yourself, Cora."

"It was hot for a September day, that's all. And I hadn't eaten enough. I'll be fine."

"Being Jacob takes you out of practice of being a lady and being accustomed to wearing your stays. I'm certainly glad that that young Flint could help you. I owe him one of my best cream cakes," she said.

"Yes, he was very kind," Cora admitted.

"Well, then perhaps you might pay him back with some attention. He looks at you like *you're* a piece of cake, let me tell you."

"Stop it, Leah. Now is not the time. Why don't you just bother Alexander instead of me?"

"He doesn't listen to that kind of talk. Nor does he want children."

"Then get married yourself," Cora said, not unkindly. "And adopt one of those poor creatures selling rags on the street. I would never stop you."

But Leah didn't seem particularly keen to discuss her own matrimonial hopes. She tucked the sheets around Cora so tightly, they felt like a corset made of bed linen.

"I'll get you some broth and send that Mr. Flint on his way. You'd better compose a thank-you letter soon," she said.

"Oh, Leah," Cora said, closing her eyes.

Leah marched out and returned in a minute with the portable writing table that had belonged to Charlotte. Cora preferred to write in the sitting room downstairs.

"There you go. I'll be by in a few minutes with a hot drink. And you can write later. It's the ladylike thing to do. Write somethin' romantic!"

After a few minutes, Leah returned with a hearty beef tea and a few soda crackers. Charlotte's jewelry had fetched enough at the pawnbroker's to provide food for a week or so, as long as they were tight on spending elsewhere. When Leah gathered the tray, she kept the door open with her elbow.

"Mr. Flint would like to say goodbye."

"I thought he'd already left!"

"He refused, until he saw that you were better and did not need to call for the doctor."

Cora's eyes widened. "Goodness, we don't want that. Send him in."

She propped herself up in bed and smoothed her wig. Theo entered, hat in hand.

"You do look better," he said, relief relaxing his face.

"I don't really need to be in bed. But what Leah says, goes, in this household. At least when it comes to invalids."

"You should listen to her advice, then," he said, kindly. He handed her Duncan's list. "Here. You should keep this."

Cora nodded but didn't unfold it. Theo laughed.

"Can you believe this list? As if we can snap our fingers and procure these items at a market for him. Fish girl! Does he mean a mermaid? He'd be better off asking your wax-figure-maker friend to create such a myth."

"Yes," Cora said, trying to keep her voice light. "Ridiculous."

"And then again, with this two-hearted girl. It's too fantastic to believe."

Cora couldn't hide her frown, but she nodded anyway. "But you mentioned it—her—before. Jacob told me you had. Where did you hear of the notion? It's not possible, after all." She tucked her trembling hands beneath the bedsheets.

"Duncan brought it up, but he wasn't the first. Said he'd heard or read of a small-time doctor in Brooklyn—Grier, I think the name was. Apparently, he claimed to have examined the girl. Some exotic heritage, to explain the finding. Chinese? Maybe I was dreaming." Theo smiled, a little too brightly. He looked elsewhere, as if trying to bring Cora's attention to the wall, or the mantel.

"I should rest," she said, curtly.

This time Theo nodded. "Should I send for Jacob? Is he sleeping in this house somewhere?"

"No," she lied. "He's out today. I don't know where."

"Well, perhaps I'll see him tonight. Goodbye, Miss Lee."

"Goodbye . . . Theo." She wanted to say, And you may call me Cora. But she couldn't. Not yet. Not now. There were shadows chasing her, and now was not the time to lower her guard.

⟿

Cora slept the rest of the day and night. She didn't realize how tired her body had been until the next morning, when she awoke close to noon. She felt restored, and was immediately keen on doing some rounds at the cemeteries to scout for new bodies. Even if she couldn't procure one with a particularly interesting finding worthy of the Grand Anatomical Museum, the university still needed bodies for dissection and would likely want to increase the number of articulated skeletons for study. The school was young, and it was matriculating more students than ever. She'd tended to focus on the strange, as they brought in the most money, but now was not the time to be particular. She had no more jewels she could sell without looking inappropriate at events.

Resting on the edge of the bed was Leah's writing desk. Perhaps she ought to send Theo a letter asking that they write or speak at least once a day, to check in if there was any news. And to thank him, of course, for helping her.

She reached for the wooden desk. It was cleverly made, with holes in the top for the ink bottle, pounce pot, and pen, plus a hinged top that concealed paper, a few cheap envelopes, a penknife, extra ink, string, and sealing wax. Cora lifted the lid and found that it was nearly empty of paper already. But Leah had been saving old bits of sealing wax, to melt down and reuse, thrifty as she was. A few old seals were broken into pieces, crowding a small well, and she picked up one fragment. It was ruby wax, stamped with the impression of a rose.

A rose. Odd. She couldn't remember receiving any letters with roses on the seal. She rifled through the other pieces and found another that fitted the fragment. And another. Soon, she had one full seal that had been broken cleanly into four bits. The image was of a shield with a rose above it.

It was the seal of her mother's family, the Cutters.

Charlotte hadn't corresponded with them since before they moved to the island. She looked at the seal. It didn't seem aged or crumbling enough to be that old.

Cora pushed the desk aside and crept out of bed, testing herself first to make sure she wasn't dizzy. She looked about Leah's room. There was nothing unusual that she could see. A wooden comb with two broken teeth; a pitcher and ewer, cracked but serviceable. One dress hung off a nail, awaiting mending while she wore the other. Only her nicest black dress was hung behind a curtain. An extra hat and gloves perched atop a lidded basket full of underthings and folded muslin petticoats.

Cora delved into the basket: nothing out of the ordinary. She checked under the edge of the thin mattress, and there a ridge of papers scraped against her fingertips. She lifted the bedding to find a package of papers bound with a cord.

They were letters, all in the same hand, and all addressed to Leah. The seals had been torn off—the very ones in the writing box, with the same shade of ruby wax. She opened the top envelope.

August 1, 1850

Miss O'Toole,

    Enclosed please find the funds you have requested. Again, I should very much like one of our personal physicians to examine Miss Lee, seeing how gravely ill she seems, so that she may receive the proper care. To be sure, the examination would be absolutely private and discreet. No doubt her condition is unusual in nature, but I believe many of the physicians below Fulton Street to be quacks. Father is not inclined to send more money until she is properly evaluated. I should be concerned if she refuses, as your letters have not been forthright with her own explanation of the symptoms.

    Sincerely,

    Suzette Cutter

Cora couldn't breathe. She couldn't move.

Leah, of all people, had contacted the family after all this time, after their cruelty toward Charlotte and her mother, after everything Charlotte had done to keep them away from Cora.

Cora's anger was so fulminant, she couldn't speak. She could hardly breathe. She went to the chair by her dressing table and picked it up, raised it above her head, ready to throw it against the wall.

They knew.

Leah. How could you?

Cora tried to grasp control of her anger. She slammed the chair down instead of through the window, and grunted in anguish. Faintly, she heard Leah exclaim at the noise from the kitchen downstairs.

Suzette Cutter! That was the very lady Cora had formally met at Castle Garden. The one who'd been staring at her at the museum, who seemed angry with her. Well, it all made sense now. Leah had been begging for money, on Cora's behalf. But where had the money disappeared to? How could Leah have done such a horrific thing, to expose her so? The worst of it was the humiliation. Charlotte had explicitly begged Leah and Cora never to contact the Cutters, after being cast off.

Cora didn't bother to dress herself, just snatched the letters in her hand and flew down the stairs barefoot. Leah was in the kitchen, scrubbing a pot with sand and a touch of lye, her hands bright pink from the causticity.

"What was that noise?" she asked, looking up with surprise. Her eyes lit upon the bundle of letters in Cora's hand, and she dropped the pot. It clanged to the floor. "Oh, Cora." She covered her face with her hands. "Oh no."

"What is this, Leah? How could you have written to them without my consent? How could you?" Her hand holding the letters shook. It took every effort not to shout and let her neighbors hear her words. "They know I'm not Jacob, then. And you lied to me. I trusted you, Leah. All these years, I trusted you!"

Leah opened her eyes; they were pink rimmed. She put down the pot and wiped her hands on her apron.

"I had to! We had some money put by, from Charlotte, but it ran out last year. What you bring in doesn't make up for it. We needed it for food. For your dresses, for the hacks."

"Why didn't you tell me? I'd looked at the books in the last few months. It was tight, I know, but was it really so bad? I could have tried to double up on jobs, scouted the other cemeteries farther north."

"You were already working so hard, miss."

"But to speak to that family? After they cast us off—"

"Aye, cast us off, but always with money. It was Charlotte's wish to move here so we could raise you as a proper lady, away from that Dr. Grier. But that meant no more Cutter money. And now Charlotte ain't here, ain't she? And you, being proud, and not accepting help from Alexander either. It was that, or I quit, and I won't quit."

Cora reached for a nearby chair and pulled herself into it. She needed her strength to think. She took in Leah's words, letting them reside within her for several minutes. Finally, she looked at Leah, who hadn't moved from where she stood, eyes cast down.

"Leah, what did you say about me? About why I was ill?"

Leah again covered her face with her hands. But Cora needed to hear her say it. She simply waited, until Leah finally inhaled enough courage and said it so quietly, only God and Cora might hear.

"I told them the truth."

CHAPTER 13

Her family knew.

"They believed you?" Cora asked.

"No, they didn't. Because Charlotte never mentioned it. I told them Charlotte said you were a boy so they couldn't find you someday—'twas done out of anger and resentment. So I . . . Oh, forgive me, miss. But I found your birth records. Dr. Grier had kept diaries with all his work. It took me more than a year to find out where they were. I wasn't allowed to take the diaries, of course, but I told them where it was writ down. Before that, they'd sent a little money, but after the diaries proved you had a true ailment . . . they sent more."

"Where are these diaries of Dr. Grier? They need to be destroyed," Cora said, standing. "Help me get dressed. I need to find them, now."

Leah followed her upstairs to her room, where she pulled off her nightgown and put on a chemise, and Leah bustled about, gathering her petticoats and corset.

"At the University of the City of New York. His family had a connection there, and they promised to keep them in their library after he died."

The diaries might be difficult to find. The school was packing and moving to its new building. They might be lost; they might not. But if she could destroy the proof, it would be easier to dispel the rumor Dr. Grier had been spreading all these years. And lately, with those possessed of curious anomalies dying unexpected deaths, and Duncan's horrific wish list, it was absolutely necessary to obliterate the rumor. Which meant two visits today.

Once her wig was on, her dress perfectly buttoned in place, and a decent meal in her stomach so she wouldn't repeat the catastrophe of yesterday morning, she was ready.

"Where are you going? To the medical school? They wouldn't allow me inside, miss. I had to pay to even ask about the papers. They won't let a lady in such a place!"

"Yes, they will," Cora said, heading out the door.

But before she stepped a toe into the archives, she needed to ask for a favor.

━━━◆━━━

It was late afternoon when she approached the boardinghouse that Jacob had left only a few mornings ago. The street was noisy with day workers spilling from the buildings, ravenous for beef and beer. Cora stood before the front door, swelled her breath, and knocked.

The landlady answered, looking like a wizened grandmother. She gathered a shawl over her shoulders.

Cora curtsied. "May I speak to Theodore Flint, please?"

"I'll ring him for you. No ladies allowed in the boardinghouse, I'm afraid."

Cora nodded.

The landlady shut the door, and a few minutes later, Theo opened it. His face lit with astonishment and a smile. The landlady craned her neck, trying to listen to them. Theo stepped outside and closed the door so they could speak on the sidewalk.

"Miss Lee! What are you doing here? How are you feeling?" He must have just washed up; his hair was wetly slicked back, and he smelled of store-bought soap.

"I'm very well, thank you. I just needed a meal, and some rest. And the curator—he talked on so, I hardly had a moment to eat."

"Ah, so I can blame him for your malady. Excellent." His smile softened. "I am very glad you are better."

"I am," Cora said. "But I am here to ask a favor. Seeing that you are almost a doctor, would you . . . could you be so kind as to provide an attestation to this fact?"

Theo leaned against the door. "I don't understand. A note? To say that you're healthy?"

"Yes. You see, I have some relations who believe I am unwell." Cora was overgesticulating, so she threaded her fingers together and held them down. "They know nothing of me. They think I spend my days lying abed, drinking drafts all the while." She smiled as charmingly as she could. "They want to foist a doctor upon me, and it's quite unnecessary. But if you could write a note to say that I am quite healthy—I would be most grateful."

"Of course. I should be happy to write an attestation. But I'm not yet a physician—"

"Oh, they shan't know the difference."

"I suppose I can sign my name, and the institution, without the degree. That might suffice."

"Yes. That might do," Cora said.

Theodore frowned. "But I have to examine you. I won't lie and say I have if I haven't. And I do not mean to take advantage of your situation. If you are healthy, it will be only a moment of your time."

"And this is where the favor comes in, Mr. Flint. We are colleagues, you see. I cannot have you examine me. It would be improper."

Another frown. "Then why don't you ask another doctor? A real doctor, with a real degree?"

"I know most of the physicians on this island. I don't really wish to have any one of them examine me."

"You could see that new female physician. Did you hear about her? She must be a little mad."

"Oh. I hadn't even considered it. By the way, her name is Elizabeth Blackwell, and she is perfectly sane. I've met her myself. However," she said, thinking it over, "if that's everyone's response to a female physician, then it won't help my situation, will it?"

"Then go to a regular physician," Theo said.

"With my line of work, I simply cannot. It's too . . . personal."

"The practice of medicine is necessarily personal," Theo said, not unkindly. He sighed, and looked beyond her to where the sky above the shops grew streaky with orange and rose. Storekeepers were lowering their awnings and shutting their doors for the evening. A voice yelled a friendly hello to Theo from far down the street; he waved cheerfully back, and for a moment, Cora was jealous. Perhaps Theo did have friends.

Cora clutched her reticule and smiled brightly. Her sanguine artifice began to weigh on her. This was more difficult than she'd hoped. "I understand. Thank you anyway. Good day. Good evening, rather. I mean, good afternoon." She turned and walked quickly up the street. She couldn't walk fast enough. What a terrible idea. Now he would be more than curious about why she needed a letter, or refused an examination.

A hand grabbed hers. She turned, to find Theo there. He had trotted to catch up, and his hand was warm and gentle in hers. She could pull away with very little effort, if she wished.

"If I may," he said. She didn't understand what he was asking. But then his hand slipped about hers, until his fingertip lay against the inner, soft aspect of her wrist. He was checking her pulse. Here, an exam of sorts, in public, on Broadway. She caught her breath, hoping her two hearts would behave, would not skip or play an erratic rhythm in the rivers of blood beneath her skin. Her cheeks warmed.

"There. Strong and steady as can be. If that's all I can do, then it's good enough for me. I spent enough time with you to recognize a healthy bloom on your cheeks, and to know that as long as you eat your breakfast, you're well enough."

"So, you'll write my letter?"

"Better yet. I'll tell them myself."

"Oh," Cora said. She was about to tell him how unnecessary it was, when she realized—this was a better idea. Anyone could read a letter and doubt its legitimacy. It would be harder to dispel the truth if given in person by a man of authority. She'd seen time and time again that an emphatic male voice was hard to disagree with. "Oh," Cora said again. "That would be wonderful."

"Where are these mysterious relatives of yours? When shall we go?"

"Now would be perfect," she said.

"Now?" Theo looked down, and he seemed embarrassed by his plain trousers and smudged shirt. "I don't really look the part."

"I can fix that. You seem the correct height." She took a slow walk around him as she regarded the width of his shoulders, and the narrowness of his waist. She liked the way his hair was trimmed so that the brown strands on his neck tapered to a point. "You'll do."

"Will I? I feel like I'm about to be traded for a horse."

"Something like that," Cora said, smiling. "Come with me. We can pay our visit by early evening if we hurry."

"Where?"

"You'll see."

They stood before the Grand Anatomical Museum. The front door was firmly shut for the evening, and many of the stores on the street were shutting up for the night.

"What are we doing here?" Theo asked.

"Looking for Alexander. He lives here, next to his new studio. But I've never visited him here."

"But elsewhere?"

"Yes," Cora said. "He used to do the wax works for Barnum's Museum, but Duncan offered him more. His old studio is down near Henry Street."

"Henry Street. That part of town." Theo crinkled his nose a little. "Does he know we're coming?" he asked.

"Of course not. Come," Cora said. On the left side of the museum was a narrow alleyway crowded with spent billets and boxes of trash. Cora had to pick up her skirts to navigate the piles of refuse, and on occasion Theo held out a hand so she could jump over a muddy puddle that stank of piss and sour porter.

In the back of the building was a tiny lot shared by the building on Duane Street. Not that there was much to share—it, too, was crowded with discarded boxes, broken glass, a large decaying cabinet in pieces, and more refuse.

But there was a door here, down a few well-swept steps.

Cora rapped her knuckles on the door.

After a minute, Alexander opened it, wiping his paint-covered hands on an apron.

"Cora! What on earth are you doing here?" Alexander's gray eyes landed on Theo. "What is he doing here?" And there was an unspoken question in his eyes, leveled at Cora: Why are you with this boy?

"We need some good toggery, Alexander," Cora explained.

"Clothes? Pardon me?"

"I'll explain it to you. May we come inside?"

Alexander nodded, and stepped back to let them inside. The entrance-way was dark. He led them forward, and they saw a room on the left full of pieces from the museum that were not currently on display—wax figurines of a gentleman's face riddled with smallpox, a rather small taxidermied zebra, shelves and shelves of large illustrated tomes, glass cloches both empty and full of shells and dried pieces of vegetation and insects preserved in lifelike, occasionally menacing positions.

On the right, there was a windowless room lit by an oil lamp. Here were several pieces of work draped in linen, and a fireplace with a sizable cauldron for melting plentiful amounts of beeswax. Blocks of yellowish-brown wax were piled upon a large worktable, and Cora saw some of the familiar items she'd remembered from his last studio—a vise that held ceramic eyeballs that needed their irises painted and glass corneas attached; a cabinet full of human hair in different hues. On another table, an enormous tome of Vesalius's anatomical drawings was open, showing a man with his internal organs on display.

"Amazing, look at that hand! It's so lifelike." Theo pointed at a wax hand that appeared to be dissected down to the ligaments.

"You're not here for a tour," Cora whispered when Alexander frowned at Theo's comment.

The next room was small, containing a clean and orderly apartment, with a hearth and a rough but neat table and two chairs. Alexander ushered them inside and brought with him the lamp from the other room. A large rat scurried past, and he stomped at it. It ran behind the table and disappeared.

"I'm so sorry. They eat the wax in my studio. I must set some more traps soon."

He set down the lamp and crossed his arms. "What does he need to borrow? And why?"

"Will you excuse us for a moment, Theo?" Cora said.

"Theo?" Alexander repeated, eyebrows raised. He looked at Cora seriously, then at Theo, and back at Cora.

"Of course," Theo said, and hastily backed out into the corridor. Cora closed the door behind him.

She explained, as quickly as she could, about Leah, and the letters, and the Cutter family, and the plan. Alexander sat down on a wooden chair by the fire and rested his forehead on his hand.

"Oh, Leah. If I had known, Cora, I would have stopped her. What an absolutely atrocious mess."

"Yes. And now I have to clean up her mess, and Theo is going to help."

"You're sure he doesn't know about your condition?"

"Absolutely."

"What if Miss Cutter mentions it?"

"I'll interrupt her before she can say the words. Dr. Grier made it clear that such a person couldn't survive, and here I am. I'll battle that issue with Theo if it comes up."

"Is he really going to be believable as a physician? He's so young, Cora."

"It will work." She touched Alexander's hand, and he put his on top of hers.

"But then," he said, "you'll owe him a debt. Jacob owing him is one thing, but you—I don't like it."

"I don't either. But I can pay him back in what I've learned, and that's valuable. It will be all right."

"Very well," Alexander said. He was always so complacent when it came to Cora putting her foot down on what mattered. Like when she decided she would follow in Charlotte's footsteps and scout the cemeteries for bodies to unearth. Then, too, he had agreed to her plan even though both he and Leah thought it was an abominable idea they'd hoped would stop after Charlotte died. Alexander stood up. "What would you like me to do?"

"Make him look respectable, please," Cora asked, and Alexander laughed.

"I'm a sculptor and a painter, not a haberdashery clerk."

She smiled warmly. "You know how to look handsome, Alexander. I'm sure ladies do appreciate it when you step out."

He waved his hand. "Never mind that. Send him in."

Cora opened the door and told Theo to step inside.

"He's all yours," Cora said, and shut the door.

About ten minutes later, the door opened. Theo stood next to Alexander, smoothing down the lapels of his coat. Not quite a splendid fit, but he and Alexander were close enough in size that the illusion worked. Theo's unruly brown hair had been slicked with a touch of grease, the curls now in better-behaving waves. A crisp shirt of broadcloth under a simple but elegant gray silk vest showed under a long jacket of neatly brushed brown wool, with trousers to match. There was a gold fob hanging from his vest pocket, and his shoes were polished.

Alexander was fastidious about the details. Theo looked like a gentleman—not too rich, but good enough to be earning an excellent income. Good enough to look like a successful physician. This would work.

"You've done it, Alexander! We'll return the clothing tomorrow, without a single snag. Thank you."

Theo went out the door, nervously scratching where his collar rubbed under his chin.

When he was out of earshot, Cora whispered, "Be honest, Alexander. Did you threaten him?"

"Like any good uncle, I told him that if he crossed you or hurt you in any way, I'd find a way to put a thick layer of boiling hot wax on him and he'd end up as Frederick Duncan's newest, latest exhibition."

"You didn't!" Cora stifled a laugh.

"Well, I was tempted." Alexander smiled. "You know, Cora, I believe he genuinely cares for you."

"Oh. Well. Oh."

"Just be careful."

"I will." She stood on her tiptoes and kissed him on the cheek. "Wish us luck."

Alexander nodded, and they were off. They didn't speak for the entire time that they rode the omnibus up to Fifth Avenue and Eighteenth Street, where Leah had been sending her letters. When Cora had brought up her family, Charlotte would say, *We don't speak of the Cutters. They aren't our family anymore.* And Cora would go outside and catch frogs instead, all the while repeating Charlotte's words to herself. She learned to say the words with disdain and detachment, as if remarking, We don't have elephants here. They aren't our pets.

Cora's thoughts drifted to the only Chinese woman she'd ever heard of or seen (at least in drawings)—Afong Moy, a Chinese woman who toured the country years ago. At exhibitions, people would gawk at her bound feet, her silken clothing, the decorative objects of porcelain and jade about her. But in her imaginings, Cora would ignore all these things. She would take Afong's small hand in her own, and nestle next to her on a carved ebony chair, to ask, "Tell me about who you are. Tell me who I am." But she knew that such a conversation could not happen, nor would it reveal what she truly wanted to know. Her identity was not so easily discerned. It was up to her to decide who she would be.

⟞⟝

The omnibus would go no farther than Fourteenth Street, so they left and walked the rest of the way. As they approached the correct address, Cora regarded the row of stately new mansions. Marble-clad Italian facades lived beside rich French châteaux styles and Gothic-like miniature castles, each politely calling for attention at an appropriate distance. No simple, quiet Federal houses here. With every decade, a wave of conspicuous wealth crept upward into the wooded and occasionally boggy land of New York City. Where it would end, Cora had no idea.

"Here it is," Cora said. The building was one of the more austere on Fifth Avenue, but larger than the others, with Corinthian columns and marble aplenty, three stories tall and taking up half the block. In front of the mansion, Cora readied herself.

"Nervous?" Theo said, pulling again at his collar.

"A bit. Here, allow me." She straightened his collar and smoothed the curls that had bounced back on his head. He looked young, and nervous, and together they didn't look altogether very confident. This would not do. "Remember," she said. "You know more medicine than anyone in this house."

"And you're healthier than a horse," Theo said, smiling nervously. "And probably smarter than anyone in this house too."

Cora tried not to beam from the compliment. "Be on your best behavior," she whispered.

"I'm always on my best behavior." Theo winked.

She turned to the grand double doors, burnished in perfectly stained chestnut. The large brass knocker was so heavy, it nearly made her gasp. When it dropped, it thundered so loudly that she and Theo both shuddered.

Now, all Cora could do was wait.

CHAPTER 14

Footsteps approached the door, and it opened silently on well-oiled hinges.

A maid stood there, taller than Cora, and looking even richer than she, despite the fact that one wore livery of crisp black and white and the other, her best burgundy silk dress, only three years old.

"Yes?" the servant asked. "May I help you?"

Cora blinked at her accent. Good God, they'd even imported a maid from England.

"My name is Cora Lee, and I am here to see Miss Suzette Cutter. This is Dr. Flint, from the University of the City of New York. We have a matter to discuss."

"Is she expecting you?" the maid asked.

"Yes," Cora lied.

The maid stepped back and allowed them inside. Cora tried not to gawk at the ebony entrance table inlaid with ivory, or the lilies in a Chinese vase set in the center. Italian moldings decorated the walls, and a small crystal chandelier lit the foyer. The oil paintings on either side of the hall were enormous—nearly six feet tall—and of country-sides she'd never seen, abloom in poppies and wheat. A staircase with scrolled handrails on both sides stood before them in carved mahogany and crimson carpeting nailed down with polished brass rivets and bars.

Cora sniffed the air. It smelled of beeswax polish and clean linen, and faintly of the gaslights in their small wall-mounted lamps.

"Please wait here," the maid said, and they stared at their surroundings, attempting to keep their mouths from dropping open.

"You're related to these people?" Theo whispered.

Cora nodded, not wanting to speak out loud.

Down the hallway, voices murmured behind closed paneled doors. One voice went higher than the other, and there was a light thumping sound, as if a book had been dropped onto a table. The pocket doors opened, and the servant emerged, her face red.

She curtsied before Cora and Theo. "My apologies. Miss Cutter is unable to speak to you tonight as she is otherwise engaged with guests. If you would be so kind as to leave your card, I will be sure she receives it."

Cora and Theo looked at each other.

"I suppose we could return tomorrow . . . ," Theo began.

"Miss Cutter," the maid said, unsmilingly, "made it clear that she will be occupied all day tomorrow."

"Thursday, then," Cora said.

"I'm afraid that won't be possible." The servant's pressed lips made it clear—they would not be seen. Not now, not ever.

Cora narrowed her eyes, and her hearts thumped an extra, irreverent beat. "Well, that just won't do, will it?" Cora said. She stepped aside and marched down the hallway to the doors that the servant had recently left.

"Miss! You cannot—I cannot allow this—you must leave now—"

But Cora was not to be stopped. Theo, too, followed her but tried to grab her elbow. Cora threw his hand off.

"If I cannot speak to them, it will be the end of me, and I cannot have that," she said, more fiercely than she had intended. She gripped the polished brass handles of the pocket doors.

The doors slid away, revealing a beautiful, lush salon, complete with fireplace, enormous marble mantel, velvet chairs, and two extremely surprised Cutters. A lamp fringed with dewdrop crystals graced a nearby table. Several books were piled neatly upon it: *The Mysteries of Udolpho*, *The Castle of Otranto*, *The Old English Baron*. Someone here had a taste for macabre reading.

Suzette was there, along with another woman, an older and heavier version of Suzette. Presumably her mother. Charlotte had only one other sibling, Charles—Suzette's father—but he had died some years ago from a fever. And Cora's mother, Elizabeth, had been Charlotte and Charles's only cousin. The two women were dressed in silk and enough lace to make Cora itch from a distance. They both stood. Even though they entertained no one, Suzette wore a costly parure of garnet, and her mother wore pearls. Cora doubted the mother was the consumer of those scandalous novels.

The elder Cutter bore down on Cora immediately. "What is the meaning of this? Jane, can you not do as you're told? We will suffer no visitors tonight, especially not *her*."

Cora bristled. She could have said *it* and had the same effect. "I beg your pardon, but I must have my say, and I will say it."

"And what is that?" Suzette asked. She straightened her tall figure to full effect, and stared at Cora with an icy imperiousness. "Do you wish to repay the money you have stolen from us, harassing us for scraps all these months? She said you needed it for medicines, and doctor's visits, and to keep quiet. Clearly you haven't needed them, and you certainly have not kept out of society."

"I have come," Cora said, taking a moment to steady herself, "to apologize."

Suzette's mouth closed, and she immediately looked at her mother.

Mrs. Cutter set her brown eyes piercingly upon Cora. "Very well. Have your say and be off."

"I want to apologize for my maid's letters, soliciting funds on my behalf. They were written without my consent or knowledge. If you have records of the funds sent, then I shall be happy to repay them, down to the penny, as soon as I am able."

The Cutter ladies again glanced at each other.

"Then . . . this was all your maid's doing? Leah?"

"Correct," Cora said. Her heart was calming now.

"You are, in fact, the daughter of my cousin-in-law, Elizabeth Cutter?" Mrs. Cutter asked. She moved her head slightly, as if seeing something in Cora's visage that she had not noticed before.

"I am, but I do not carry her name, nor do I intend to publicize the connection in any way."

"And so . . . you aren't ill?" Mrs. Cutter said.

"As you can see, I'm quite well. In fact, may I please introduce Mr. . . . Dr. Theodore Flint, of the University of the City of New York. I considered having him write a letter on my behalf, but I feared you might destroy it before it was read."

"Indeed, I would have! You were supposedly very ill, indeed!" Suzette said, but her mother hushed her with a single glance.

"Good evening, ladies," Theodore began. "I am here to attest to the fact that I have known Miss Lee now for some time, and she is in very good health. Whatever her maid may have said, as you can see, it's quite false."

"But there were records," Suzette said. "We wouldn't have given the money without proof, and we had it. How can this be? How can you survive with such a condition?"

Cora raised her hand. She didn't want Theo to know what they spoke of, and she must tread carefully.

"It was a misstatement, even in writing. I have no such affliction, and I wish for it to be known that the doctor in question was a drunkard and a liar. He fabricated this story to extort money from my aunt Charlotte for unnecessary doctor's visits. Any talk of my poor health ought to end, here and now. In that way, any stain upon your family, similarly, shall be quelled. You know how rumors spread."

Mrs. Cutter, twice the breadth of her daughter, walked forward and leaned her ring-encrusted hand upon a chair back. "Upon my word, you make demands as if you have a right."

"My life and my body are mine, madam. I may say anything I like about them."

Suzette actually smiled at this, and when Cora saw it, her lips twitched. Mrs. Cutter turned quickly, and in a flash, Suzette's smile melted into a thin line.

Cora spoke once more. "I thank you for your time. I make no apologies for the actions of my mother, or my aunt, but I will apologize on behalf of my servant. She will be appropriately punished, and neither of us shall bother this family again. It will be as if you don't know me, and I shall return the favor."

"We don't speak of you, to be sure," Mrs. Cutter said coldly. She snorted. "A bastard child of some foreign sailor, with no claims to this family? Jane, show them out."

Cora's body flushed warmly, and Theo stared at her as if he had not really seen her before. She never revealed her dual heritage, and now Theo, of all people, would know. He might put it together—the two-hearted girl with Chinese ancestry. After she had done so well and carried out the conversation without an actual mention of her affliction!

Outside, in the cool evening air and the quiet among the uptown residences, Cora finally exhaled as if she'd been holding her breath this whole time.

"Well. I suppose that went well?" Theo said.

"Yes. It did. You did splendidly, Theo. I'm very grateful." They began walking down toward Union Square.

"I had no idea you were related to the Cutter family. They might as well be the Beekmans or the Schermerhorns or the Astors. And they've cast you off?"

"Yes," Cora said simply.

"So, your father's not exactly a Schermerhorn himself," Theo said, and Cora stopped walking.

"Oh. You heard that."

"How could I not?" Theo asked, curious. "Who's your father? Where is he from?"

He had stopped walking, and turned to face her. "I thought you looked different. What kind of—"

Cora held up a hand. That word, *what*. Not asking about a person, but a thing. "Does it matter, if he were not a lofty Schermerhorn?" Cora asked. "If he were black? Would you stop speaking to me? Would you be a blackbirder, and sell me into slavery even though I'm free?"

Theo held up his hands. "I only asked."

Cora spoke slowly. "My blood runs as red as yours, Theodore Flint. You of all people should know that, after all your dissections. I am no less than any other woman on this island, including the high-and-mighty Suzette Cutter."

"Then who is your father?"

If he had been closer, Cora would have slapped him. His curiosity was an intrusion. The park was dark, but there was light enough from the moon to see his face. She'd seen his expression before on the nameless faces that stared at her when she walked around the city. A confusion—as if Cora were out of place and they didn't know where she belonged. They wanted her categorized like an insect.

"I don't know who my father was."

He cocked his head at her. "The fairy tale. The girl with the two hearts. She was said to be half-Chinese."

Cora's body stiffened. "Does that make her not wholly human?"

Theo went silent.

"It's not me," Cora said quickly, snuffing out her small rebellion.

"What affliction did they think you had, Cora?"

"It was nothing. A . . . a breathing ailment." The lie sounded just like that, a lie.

"Was your father a Chinese sailor?" he persisted. "And Jacob? Is he . . ."

"We are twins, so yes, we share the same father. And as I said, I'm not sure who my father was. Are you satisfied, Mr. Flint? Are you done solving the puzzle of me? Have you finished sorting me like a coin to learn my worth?"

Flint ran his hand through his hair. Mussed, it clashed with his fine clothes, and he, too, looked unclassifiable. "Why didn't you tell me before?"

"Why was it relevant?" Cora demanded. "Am I different now?"

"Of course you're different. It's in your blood."

"What is? My inferiority?"

"Well . . . no . . . I mean, some would say yes, but—"

"Stop. I understand. Good night, and thank you for your services. Please return your clothes to Alexander as soon as you can. Jacob shall be in touch if another body comes into our midst."

She began to walk hurriedly through the park, when a shrill female voice rang out behind her.

"Miss Lee! Wait a moment! I wish to speak to you."

She turned, as did Theo, who was still standing there. They saw Suzette tripping toward them, a fine wool shawl hastily wrapped about her shoulders.

"I had to leave through the servants' entrance," she gasped, "to escape Mother."

Cora said nothing; she had nothing left to say to either Suzette or Theo.

Suzette tried to catch her breath. "I need to speak to you. Alone." She looked pointedly at Theo.

"As I am very much unwanted here anyway, I shall leave. Good night. Miss Cutter, the pleasure was mine," Theo said, though he looked hardly pleased. He gave Cora a bitter glance, before walking away. When he was out of hearing, she turned to Suzette.

"Yes?" Cora said. "What is it? I thought I made myself rather clear."

"That fellow you brought, Mr. Flint?"

"Dr. Flint," Cora corrected her.

"He's no doctor, you know," Suzette said, eyebrows raised.

"Pardon me?"

"I went down to the archives at the university, only ten days ago. I read Dr. Grier's diary entries myself."

Cora's hearts thumped in quick succession. "Oh. You . . . read them?"

"I did. A family friend allowed me in, as a favor. His papers were not written by the hand of a drunken gentleman. They were lucid, and professional. And when I was in the Stuyvesant Institute, Mr. Flint was there too. He was in a line of new students. I saw him, plain as day. Taller than the rest, handsome with that dimple on his left cheek. That's why I remembered him. He is no professor. You cannot believe him, if he says you're healthy. You ought to see a real physician, Miss Lee. He's fooled Mother well enough, but not me."

"And this is why you've run out here to tell me?" Cora shook her head. "You hated me so only half an hour ago."

"Before a few days ago, Leah's letters were enough to convince us of your ailment. She knew the date of your birth, information about Charlotte and Elizabeth. I thought—I thought I recognized you at the museum. There is a portrait of Elizabeth in our attic storage. You look a bit like her—the same figure, the same nose. A certain enigmatic air. And then I was certain at Jenny Lind's performance, when I saw you with your maid. You looked so well, and it angered me to see you in your nice dresses. I was convinced the whole thing had been a hoax and that you were abusing my family terribly—two hundred fifty dollars since August. But I decided to find out for myself."

There were several benches around the oval green of Union Square, and Cora sought one out and sat down. This was too much. She had come here to cut off ties and convince them she was well, and here was Suzette telling her that none of it had worked. And on top of everything, there was an enormous debt to pay. How would she ever be able to pay back even half the sum and still put bread on her table? It was far more than they'd ever needed for daily living expenses. What on earth had Leah spent it on?

"Why are you telling me this?" Cora asked. "Why are you being kind to me?"

"By telling you the truth? Most people would find that's an unkindness," she said, laughing, like a bell in the night. She sobered. "To be honest, I don't know." She stared out into the darkness and sat down next to Cora. "No, I do know. I have a brother in Europe who's ten years older than I am, and I hardly know him. I have no other cousins, no sisters. Mother says I ought to spend more time with real people, instead of burying my head in books about murders and phantoms!"

"Oh. You're the reader of those books I saw?"

"I am," she said. "I love them. Have you read *The Castle of Otranto*? Oh, the church trysts! Isabella stabbed! Do you know it?"

"I confess, I do not," Cora said, smiling. How strange to see such a lovely creature so enraptured by the macabre. And then she silently laughed at herself.

"I do love secrets. But your servant's is far less salacious than those in the books. Lying servants are not terribly dramatic. Now that I know you have good intentions, I do not wish you any harm. I fear that Mr. Flint is telling you falsehoods, and you may be in danger."

Flint was the last person she could imagine who would hurt her. She still remembered the sting of her knuckles when Jacob punched him with beautiful accuracy last week. But this truth was more deadly than anything.

"Miss Cutter, may I ask a question?" Cora asked.

"You may call me Suzette. I suppose you can ask, but I'm not sure I can do anything."

"Those diaries of Dr. Grier—where were they located? At the Stuyvesant Institute, or the new building?"

"Oh. The new building. On the upper floor. They were quite difficult about allowing me in, being a woman, and of course I wasn't a student. My mother's physician had to escort me. They'll never let you in, Cousin."

Cora nodded. Well, perhaps Jacob would have no trouble. He would do the job of destroying the diaries, and then Grier's legacy and rumors would have a better chance of disappearing for good.

Suzette stood. "I must go. I'll never be allowed out of the house again if Mother knows I've spoken to you."

"Thank you." Cora reached over and squeezed Suzette's cold, soft hand in hers. She shook her head. "I am so grateful, you have no idea."

"You're welcome, Cousin Cora." She laughed lightly. "You know, if you'd stayed in our family, they might have named you Allene. There's always an Allene in every other generation. Mother was obstinate about naming me Suzette." She smiled. "It's nice to have a cousin after all this time."

With that, Suzette trotted the two blocks back to her house in the moonlight.

Cora was now quite alone. Tonight, she had hoped for so much. She had gained a debt, gained a cousin, and lost Theodore Flint. After the way he looked at her, any friendship between them had disintegrated. They would work in the same circles, until Cora earned enough money to pay back the Cutters and finally leave the city, for somewhere no one had ever heard of a girl with two hearts—or a girl with at least one broken one.

IDA DIFFORD

There are many things in the world that God will not let me understand. He keeps his hand hovering over the reasons, just out of view. He will not explain to me why, for example, he's chosen to have this boil growing upon my neck. A chaotic collection of teeth and bone and hair. The good doctor has said that he has even seen "nervous tissue," whatever that might mean. I do not understand his language.

But it grew and grew until wrapping it deftly in lace or silk could conceal it no longer. It opened and drained, a foul-smelling odor like ripened cheese emanating from it, vile and abominable to my husband, and to me. It is as if God has stored the worst sins of the world beneath my skin.

I could not stand it any longer, particularly when the coughing began. Coughing and coughing, the sensation of tickling threads deep within me, until I'd cough up a tendril of dark, silky hair. And then another, and sometimes a clump. The devil himself was growing within me, I knew it. But on the day of surgery, something felt so very strange.

Agatha, my servant, had come in from the market and brought me a new batch of tea—a very good China tea. And in making it, she steeped it too long. It was terribly bitter, and I asked her to be more careful with the temperature of the water next time. I am loath to waste tea that has come halfway across the ocean for me, so I drank it all.

But soon, my jaw felt tight, and I could not prevent myself from clenching my teeth and tightening my body in the most peculiar and uncomfortable ways. But the surgery was to happen that morning, and so I went, hoping to tell the doctor about my predicament. My dear husband accompanied me and begged me not to squeeze his arthritic hands so hard. But I could not help myself.

It was nerves, and only that, the surgeon reassured me. My gown was changed, the drapery placed over my body, and the chloroform dripped dutifully onto cotton wool placed over my face.

I was clenching my teeth so hard that I could barely speak. Every muscle in my body was on fire, alighted with a tension of a thousand Samsons pulling down a thousand temples. Only there were no temples, only me. Only a body made of sinew and meat and nails and teeth, all tearing asunder, and there was naught I could do to stop it.

I was dead before the good doctor ever picked up his blade.

There are murmurs that they are coming for me. My body goes to God one way or another; I know this now. Have at it, you beasts. You are the ones rotting from within, not I.

Not anymore.

CHAPTER 15

The next morning, Cora dressed herself in Jacob's finest clothes and came down to breakfast. She didn't want to go out as Jacob in broad daylight, but she had no choice. Leah was making baked eggs, and hot tea was already on the table.

"You were home late last night," Leah said. "Was that nice fellow Mr. Flint with you?"

"Not so nice, but yes." Cora sipped her tea and looked around the kitchen. The cutlery was the same as they'd had since Charlotte was alive; the crockery the same, too, save for a broken dish or two that had not been replaced. Cora always turned in the monthly rent herself. It had risen modestly by a dollar or two each year.

"There's a letter for you this morning." Leah handed it to Cora, who put it down, not wanting to be distracted.

"Leah," Cora asked, "what became of the money you took from the Cutters?"

"The money?"

"Yes. Two hundred fifty dollars. We've had lean times this last month, I know, but such a sum! Surely we can send most of it back."

"Oh." Leah went quiet for nearly a minute, but Cora waited. Finally, with no place to hide, Leah frowned with guilt. "I spent it. Every penny."

"On what?"

Leah started to breathe a little heavier. "I don't know."

"How could you not know?" Cora demanded.

"I just . . . I lost it."

"Lost it? How?"

Cora stared her down, not blinking once as Leah squirmed. Sometimes her stares were as loud as screams.

"I . . . lost it betting on Hy Claremont's dog and rat fights."

Cora looked at the ceiling. "Leah! Are you *mad*? You know Hy Claremont only plays a skinning game! Why would you do such a thing?"

"I'd heard that May, that silly whore of a cook next door, had won ten dollars on a bet. It only cost fifty cents, and I had a little extra dibs that week. So, she put fifty cents for me, and I won! Fifteen dollars. So next time, I bet five dollars and lost it, but I didn't have it, and so they charged me interest, but I thought I could get even, and an eight-dollar bet would take care of it, but then I lost that one."

"Oh, Leah! That's how they rope in every new gambler." Cora slouched in the chair, defeated. "Why didn't you tell me? We could have squared your bill and been done with it."

"Well, I would have, but then I won again, this time a half eagle! So, I kept going and . . . I'm so sorry. I couldn't stop! The devil took me. I wrote to the Cutter family, thinking it wouldn't ever reach your ears. I felt like they owed us. And when Miss Cutter came here, I showed her how poorly we lived—"

"Oh good God, Leah! You let her in the house? Here? Did you let her into my room?"

"Well, only for a moment—"

"Leah!" Cora pounded the table so hard, the cutlery fell clattering to the floor. "She could have seen Jacob's clothes. She could have seen my ledger, with all the people I've been tracking. If she spoke to the police, I could be arrested!"

"I'm sorry! It was only a little while ago, and it won't happen again. I thought it would help get more money. But it only angered her more. Irving Place was too nice, and she thought it a rich place for us. I promise I won't let her back here again."

"Oh, Leah. What a mess we're in now. The whole city knows there's a girl with two hearts running about, and Frederick Duncan is eager to have my chest flayed open on a silver platter in his museum!"

"No, no, it won't come to that! I've paid off my debt!"

"But now I shall have to pay the debt to the Cutters," Cora said. "This is what I'll do. After our next job, I shall send the Cutter family five dollars—not much, but enough to show that I keep my word."

"And I'll help," Leah said. "I could sell rags or do some extra piecework with the tailor upstairs."

"For seventy-five cents a week? It won't be worth it. I need more work, is all."

"Then this should help," Leah said, pointing to the letter she'd handed to Cora before.

It was from Dr. Goossens. One of his patients had died overnight—Ida Difford, the lady with the large tumor in her neck who was coughing up bits of hair. The tumor had opened a little, and the doctor had seen what seemed like teeth and even nerves growing in a chaotic array. The note read that the mass had grown to the point where it was time to operate. She had died in surgery.

Unexpected, wrote Goossens in his note. *She was a robust, healthy woman before this, but her heart must have been weak. After a small dose of chloroform, her body grew rigid, almost like a tetanus case. She stopped breathing.*

Cora put a hand over her mouth, frowning deeply. The poor woman. It could not have been easy, having her body rebelling in terrible, nonsensical ways—oozing tumors and coughing up hair. And hoping for a cure, while encountering the opposite. Cora had cared far less when receiving the news of a death in the past—she had been so focused on her connections, on the money. But lately, she could imagine with far more clarity what their lives were like. The shame, the discomfort, the search for a treatment. The despair.

And her death was . . . odd. Tetanus didn't happen so quickly, and she had not heard of patients getting it from a surgery with such immediacy. Especially with Dr. Goossens, whose assistant had a habit of cleaning his instruments between each surgery.

Cora noted the time and place of the upcoming funeral. She sat down at the writing desk in her room and wrote a note to her graveyard boys to gather around at six o'clock, just barely after sunset. This time, they would be the first at the grave. This time, they would not have their profit taken from their very hands. Ida would end up in the hands of a capable anatomist. Her death would help someone, someday. Wouldn't it?

Cora now had the day to address yet another item that begged her attention. She knocked on a door down the street, a shabbier but still nice building on Irving. It was filled to the brim with a family of nine children. The father was yet another tailor whose family members each did piecework for the shirts and wool clothing sold in Pearson's Store on Broadway. But one of the children, George, a ten-year-old with snapping black eyes, ran Jacob and Cora's letters when she needed a swift delivery.

One of the raven-haired daughters answered, clad in a large apron, with pins and needles stabbing a pincushion tied to her wrist. She smiled brightly.

"Oh. Hello, Jacob. You look nice, and it isn't even Sunday! How is Cora?"

"Very well," Cora answered in Jacob's deep voice. Stella was always trying to flirt with him. "Is George here? I need a message delivered quickly."

"Yes, one moment." She turned and called inside. The boy came to the door, wiping jam stains from his mouth.

"Send this to Friar Tom. You know where." She deposited a few coppers into the boy's sticky hand. "And I've another job for you, if you're able."

"I can do it," George said. "If Ma says I may."

"Can you tell me when Leah comes and leaves? And can you follow her, just long enough to see what direction she's going?"

"Yes. I can go all the way, if I have money for the omnibus or the horse car."

"Excellent. Keep yourself hidden." She deposited a half dime into his hand. "Off you go."

They shook hands, and Stella waved an enthusiastic farewell while George put on his cap and ran out the door, heading for Tom's house on Suffolk. Cora kept her face shadowed under her hat and walked down to the new University of the City of New York building on Fourteenth Street. It was a plain but respectable building—three stories tall, with a bright new railing running up the steps and a side yard enclosed by a fence. Dr. Grier's records must be here.

She opened the door and found a gentleman sitting at a desk. Inside, several workmen were still painting some of the trim, but it looked like most of the rooms were nearly done.

"Good day," Cora said, removing her hat and carefully using her uppertens gentleman's voice. "I am an assistant to Dr. Goossens, and he has sent me here on a commission. He is researching a curious case of his, and believes that one of his deceased colleagues, Dr. Grier, had cared for a similar patient. We were told Dr. Grier's diaries were entrusted to the archives here."

"That I do not know. Only half the archives have moved at this point. Upstairs, second floor to the left. Mr. Bell is putting the books away, I believe, and can help you."

Cora thanked him. Upstairs, she passed open doors to an empty amphitheater that was still having wax rubbed dutifully into its banisters. Farther down, she found lecture rooms and the library. A frail older gentleman was checking off books on a list and shelving them one by one.

"Hello," Cora interrupted. She once again explained her purpose, and the older man frowned.

"Ah. I shelved those books some time ago. I'm on the *T*s now. The diaries are not allowed to leave the premises, and you must sign our register."

Cora nodded. She looked at the register and signed a name—*Jack Ketch*—a position—*Asst. to Dr. Scribble*—and the date. *Jack Ketch* was flash for *hangman*. As she finished signing, she looked up the names and dates of previous visitors. Lo and behold, there was Suzette Cutter, from ten days ago, as she had said. Most of the other names were physicians or students. But flipping to the current page, she ran her finger quickly down the list.

Theodore Flint, Yr 1, September 14, 1850

Well. It looked like Flint had been doing some studying as well. Only yesterday, in fact.

And then, a few lines before, on the tenth—

Frederick Duncan, curator, GAM.

Cora stared at the names. Another one, even more recent, caught her eye, from this very morning—

Davey Swell.

Cora tried not to laugh. The name was flash for *gentleman witness*, like in a court proceeding. There was nothing written next to it where it asked for position, or institution. Likely a jokester student—though, based on her time with Theo, medical students never seemed to know flash all that well.

"Excuse me, sir? Do you keep a record of what documents your visitors read?" Cora asked.

"Ah, that we do not. Only if they are removed, but while we've been transferring our collection, we haven't allowed that."

Cora went to look around in the *G* section. On the lowest shelf, there they were. Four books. She pulled out the first one. It was leather bound, the pages within not too yellowed, but clearly well thumbed. It was small enough to steal, by stuffing down the back waistband of her trousers. And then any evidence of the two-hearted girl would be gone forever.

Cora took out the first book. On the first page inside, it read, "The Journals of Thomas Grier, MD ～ Vol I, 1807–1817." The second was 1818–1830. So, Cora's birth should be documented in the third. She pulled it out and opened it. The pages felt loose from the binding, and she flipped to the first page.

It was blank.

The next page was blank as well.

Cora lifted the entire interior of the book, and it came clean away from the binding. She replaced it on the shelf, and took out the last volume, which might still have some musings about Cora and her hearts. This one, too, had been replaced with an entire book filled with blank pages.

Someone had beaten Cora to the job and stolen away the proof that she and her hearts existed. Whoever took them—they knew what they were doing. In fact, the false books were exactly the same size and breadth as the original journals, as if they'd been made exactly for that purpose.

The original journals had been here ten days ago when Suzette visited. And now they were gone. It would have been easy for Frederick

Duncan to measure the journals, and return under a fake name and steal the interiors.

Davey Swell, indeed.

What was more—it could have been Theo. He and Duncan had visited within days of each other. In fact, Theo had visited the very morning before they'd spoken to Suzette at her home. But he'd said nothing about it that night. Nothing at all.

As much as she loathed the idea, she had to invite Theo to tonight's resurrection. She would have to endure his rude stares and comments about her inglorious birth. And what was more—Cora's team would hear about it, and what would they think? It could break up their group, if things went the wrong way.

But she could ask Theo about Grier's journals as well.

Tonight was going to be a disaster. Cora had no choice but to embrace the disaster and prepare for her world to explode.

She left the building and walked back home, hoping for some rest and a comfortable lunch. Lost in thought, she turned the corner on Third Avenue, when a large man bumped her shoulder.

"Pardon."

"It's nothing," Cora said, and walked past. He grabbed her arm, rather suddenly, gripping her so hard, it hurt.

"I think you're lost, Jacob Lee," he said.

She jerked her arm away and stared at him, hard. She had never worked with him, nor did she remember his face from evenings near the Five Points. The man was far taller than she was, even with Jacob's shoe lifts on. The man's neck was the width of his head. Wide-set eyes of pale blue peered at her. She noticed a yellow jacket with tails, and a pair of garish blue-and-black striped pants. A cheap stovepipe hat. Another greasy Bowery b'hoy.

Cora looked about. No one else walked nearby. A pile of large crates concealed them from busy Fourteenth Street.

"And who are you?" she said, after spitting on the ground between them.

"That won't matter, will it?" He took a step forward. He was backing her into a wall of crates.

Cora pivoted to run, but the man shot out a large, meaty hand—a hand so big, it covered her nose and mouth. With brute strength, he bent her neck back as his other arm swept around her waist, carrying her off her feet. Strong as she was, she was slight in stature, and she loathed the disadvantage right now. He pulled her kicking and punching into an alleyway. He was quick and quiet, and she'd not even been able to holler a cry.

Within seconds, Cora had been pulled halfway between the avenues; between the buildings were heaps of rotting cabbage leaves, broken bottles, and empty crates and barrels. Cora kicked hard, and her boot contacted a brick wall, which threw off the balance of her assailant.

"Stop that, now, old boy. Stop it. Can't have you make a ruckus."

Cora suddenly went limp. To her attacker, it felt like giving in. For her, it was a feint. Cora didn't have time for attacks, or robbery, or common everyday murder. She needed to eliminate this problem now.

Or rather, Jacob must.

There was a blade in her boot. Now that she had stopped struggling, her assailant reached for his own waistband, probably for his own knife. Cora pointed to her vest pocket, pointed with agitation, as if she had something there to offer.

"What's this?" He reached for the vest and felt coins there, and in patting her other pockets (idiot—a better murderer would search after she was dead), she had the moment she needed.

Cora quickly bent her knee, grasped her dagger, and sliced it across the face of her assailant. He yelped and released her, and Cora spun around, holding the knife between them. The b'hoy cried and blubbered, his hands covering a gash across his nose and cheek. Blood dribbled down his face and off his chin, staining his hands with scarlet ribbons. It was a good, deep cut. She stepped closer and touched the knife to his chin, and he held his hands up, crying.

"D-don't!" he blubbered.

"That's better," she said. "Good Lord, you stink like curdled swill milk." He moved his hand ever closer to the sheathed knife at his waist, and she tsked. "Don't do that now. If I cut here"—she slid the blade to the front of his neck, pressing—"you'll never speak again." His small eyes grew white around the edges as she pressed the blade into his tender flesh. "So, while you can speak, tell me. What's your business? What's your game?"

"I've no game! Just . . . needed some brass . . ." He suddenly shot out his hand, attempting to slap away Cora's hand and the knife, but she dodged backward quickly, swooped her hand down and out, and brought the knife across his face in a neat arc. Now an X-shaped gash covered his entire face; the tip of his nose was one slice away from hitting the cobblestones.

"Speak!" Cora hissed. "Why do you know my name?"

He held his hands up again as his hat tumbled off into a muddy puddle of filth. "I was . . . dead set on you. I jus' wanted the prize on Duncan's list. Five hundred cans! Everyone says you and that sister of yours'll clink the whole list o' innocents before a body can try! You've a caravan enough!"

Cora pressed the knife in deeper, causing him to blubber for real. So, he'd targeted Jacob for a kill. And *caravan enough*? She wanted to laugh at the idea. As if Cora and Jacob were fat and rich from resurrections. So that was what people thought, that Duncan's list of wanted corpses already as good as belonged to the Lees. Jacob and Cora were competition that needed to be eliminated.

She twisted her knife in the groove between his jugular vein and carotid artery.

"I could ketch you now. You'd bleed like a pig at the butcher's. And I could sell you to the university for only five dollars. That's all I'd earn."

The man closed his eyes, and tears dripped down his face, making clear paths in the bloody smears and dirt.

"What's your name?" Cora asked.

"Ewan. Ewan Gerry," he blubbered.

"Ewan Gerry. You tell every jinglebrain out there that Duncan's list is as bogus as a clay coin. The five hundred for the girl with two hearts won't happen. There's no such person, and Duncan's a fool to offer a dollar on her. And any bene cove who attacks me or Cora Lee will end up sliced and ottomised by yours truly. You're Catholic, aren't you? Irish?"

He nodded.

"You know the ottomised never get to heaven. You understand?" Personally, she didn't believe in heaven or hell. An earthly life was hell enough, and heaven appeared in the ephemera of every day, like dust motes sparkling in a quiet sunrise, or a warm handshake on a frigid day. Stolen gifts. But she had no problem using other people's godly fear when it was handy.

Cora pressed her knife a little deeper, and a drop of blood clung to her blade edge.

"Don't stifle me like the other stiff 'uns!" he cried.

Cora squinted at him. "Stifle?"

"Haven't yeh?" He was crying hard now, sniffling between words. "Hushed 'em for coin?"

"My sister and I don't kill people. Who told you that?"

"I jus' heard it, here and there."

"We get our quaroons the natural way. You tell people. And stay away from us." She motioned her knife tip left and right just half an inch from Ewan's face. "Or I'll make dog-paste of your mug."

"Yes sir!"

She stood back and let her arm fall. When Ewan didn't move, she raised her eyebrows.

"Go!" she roared.

And Ewan fairly fled for his life.

CHAPTER 16

Leah was beside herself when Cora arrived home. She helped Cora bathe carefully, and fed her an extra-buttery gruel. She fussed and mussed until Cora smacked her hands away and shut the bedroom door so she could "rest." She needed to think.

Cora was in shock herself. It never occurred to her that she and Jacob would be targeted by their competition. Worse, rumors were out that they were killers themselves. She wondered, Had her work created an opportunity for others to hurt people like herself, where they might be targeted before their time? Perhaps she was at fault. But I'm evening the odds, she thought. All those poor, dug up. The rich should suffer too. Shouldn't they?

But she also knew she didn't need a complication like police in her life right now.

Cora couldn't give the appearance of being intimidated, and she couldn't afford to lay off work. She had other things to think about too. When Leah stepped out to buy some liniment for Cora's bruised skin, she dressed as Jacob and visited little George, who reported that Leah had never left the house.

Good.

Alexander had sent a letter, mailed from Philadelphia. Oh, she'd forgotten he had mentioned he had a trip planned. He would be livid when he found out about the attack. He went to Philadelphia occasionally, to peruse the extraordinary anatomical collection at Jefferson Medical College, sketch the items afterward, and present them to Duncan as possible new pieces. He would stay one more day before returning.

"You should stay home tonight," Leah said, worried.

"I can't. I have work."

"But even Jacob isn't safe!"

"We have a job, Leah," Cora sighed. "I have to go."

After more arguing, Leah gave up. She could not bear to sit at home and worry, so she would spend the rest of the evening with the upstairs maid, whose tailor family was going out to see a show at Vauxhall Gardens Theater.

Just before sunset, Cora, as Jacob, met with her boys down the street on the southeast corner of Union Square. Theo, Friar Tom, the Duke, and Otto the Cat were all ready to go with their equipment hidden under burlap. Puck, as expected, hadn't resurfaced, but Cora braced herself for a possible row if he did show up, either here or at the cemetery.

She decided to say nothing of the attack. She needed more time to gather her thoughts, about what happened, and why Theo had gone to read Dr. Grier's diaries—and whether he had stolen them.

"Trinity Church?" Otto said from his perch, holding the reins to his placid horse.

"Yes," Cora said.

"By Wall Street, or up on One Hundred Fifty-Fifth?"

"One Hundred Fifty-Fifth. No more interments by the church these days." Cora hadn't looked Theo in the eye yet; she was loath to reveal her foul mood at just seeing him. And Theo hadn't looked Jacob in the eye yet either. Very well. She just wondered when, and how, the inevitable eruption would occur.

"And afterward, I'll be buying the body," Theo said. "I've sixty dollars for this one." He clapped his hand on Cora's back, which was such a surprise that she nearly choked on her spit. "Even you can't say that's a bad deal. I worked a generous contribution from Dr. Wood, who wishes to keep it for the anatomical cabinet he is planning at the school."

They all jumped into the wagon, but Theo kept chatting, as if the discussion with Cora last night had never occurred.

"We ought to have a clear night ahead," he said. "Don't you think so, Jacob? Once the cloud cover leaves, it'll be moonlight all the way. And I have extra money for any guards."

Cora hadn't had time to scout the gravesite today for guards. She was sure there wasn't a mort house at this cemetery, but there might be other deterrents. She grunted, hoping it would stop the talking.

"We should get more oysters tonight, after. Though less rum this time, if that's all right," he said, patting his stomach.

"Och, you're a baby! Can't handle a brusher of rum, eh?" Tom said, laughing.

"No. Last time Jacob and I drank, we were as numb as a peg leg. Weren't we?"

Cora cracked a smile. Theo's cheer was wearing her bad mood away. "You don't even remember me leaving, do you?"

"Oh, I do," Theo said, winking. "I'm just a polite drunk."

Cora's brief smile disappeared. Had he really been awake? If so, had he remembered laying his hand on Cora's second heart? But Theo was now laughing over a joke of the Duke's, and they had their arms around each other's shoulders, whispering and laughing quietly, as if they'd been friends since the womb.

As the wagon rolled and clonked up Fourth Avenue, Otto quietly gnawed on a corner of hardtack. Meanwhile, Tom had joined in on the Duke and Theo's discussion.

"I'm telling you, I've given her flowers, I've brought chickens. And she still won't give me her time," the Duke said. "Still angry."

"Ignore her," Tom said. "That's what all wives want, for their husbands to give them money and then pay them no more attention! Or you could bake a good pudding. Puddings always make mine happy." Tom brought food into every single conversation. About God ("I don't go to church, because you can't eat oysters in church"), about smelly feet ("Now, a good cheese might smell as good as bad feet, you know").

They laughed harder. The Duke poked Theo in the ribs. "I know who you like. Jacob's sister. I've heard you talk about her."

"She's not available to the likes of you," Cora said, trying not to snarl.

"See? Miss Lee will pay you more attention if you're dead in a grave than alive and well. I've never seen her interested in a man," said the Duke.

"Ah, maybe all she needs is someone with a fat purse, and she'll be out of this business. I'm surprised she hasn't already caught herself a husband," Theo said. "'Tis a sad business, ours is, though it makes us wages well enough."

"No one speaks for my sister, except my sister," Cora said, taking out her knife as she often did when the subject came up. She wiped it thoughtfully on her sleeve and sheathed it.

"If anyone did, they'd end up . . . how do you say it?" Theo grinned. "'Scragged, sliced, soaked in a knock-me-down, and ogled in a glass jar!'"

"Well said!" Otto said, laughing.

Cora smiled despite herself.

Driving up Fifth Avenue, they passed the imposing Egyptian-style reservoir for that good, crisp Croton water. The cobblestones disappeared and were replaced by hard-packed dirt. They passed the Deaf and Dumb Asylum, into the Nineteenth Ward, and eventually passed the massive double receiving reservoirs. Here, the bustle of the city dwindled to expanses of trees and small farms. Otto whipped his horse to hurry them along.

At Hamilton Square, they turned west past the bone mill and turned again northward, past Leake & Watt's Orphan Asylum and the Lunatic Asylum. This was where the unwanted were hidden, far away from the sizzling bright gaslights of downtown. The city only wanted food, and pulsing bodies, and water; it spit out its unwanted and dead to the periphery of its heart.

Cora watched Theo out of the corner of her eye, wondering if he had Dr. Grier's journals tucked away in his room somewhere. Wondering if he was planning on killing her, once he realized who she was. Well, perhaps tonight if she was able to get Theo drunk again, she could rifle through his belongings, find them, and destroy them. Of course, if it was the curator who had the diaries, well, it would take more than just a bottle of gin to get them back.

Finally, they arrived at Trinity Cemetery. It was dark as ship's pitch, with the moon still behind the clouds. The cemetery was enormous, spanning two whole avenues all the way to the Hudson railway line by the river's edge.

"How will we find the grave in the dark?" Tom complained. "I wish Miss Lee had scouted this place out beforehand. Too busy slapping her callers, I'm sure."

"Or too busy wanting to slap other people; that's a fact," Cora said, loudly enough that Theo could hear.

"I'm sure if she did, they deserved it," he said quietly. Cora looked at him quickly in surprise.

"There! There's the spot. I can see a smudge on the greenery. New soil turned over that ridge," Otto said. He was higher in his driver's seat and could see better.

They drove closer, and finding the site quiet and devoid of any guards, went to work quickly. The grave was unattended, but up here, such a long drive from the medical schools, it was no surprise that new interments would go unnoticed. There was no headstone as it would be another week until the mason finished his work. Each of them took turns digging, until they hit the coffin with a hollow knock.

"Ay, there's the eternity box," Otto said.

Using a wedge, they pried the casket open and found a woman in her forties or fifties, wearing a silk dress of dark blue, bedecked in silk around her throat and wrists. Several layers of bandage and muslin were wrapped about her neck, which was misshapen and protuberant on the left side. But the group all covered their mouths in surprise.

Her body, still in the throes of rigor mortis, was bent and curved, her belly thrust upward toward the top of the casket. Only her shoulders and heels touched the bottom of the casket. Her arms were stiffly drawn toward her chest, fists clenched, and even in death her face was a fierce grimace of pain.

"Why does she look like that?" the Duke said, scratching his head.

"Looks like tetanus," Theo said. "But she was well-to-do. Not a laborer working in dirty conditions with a traumatic wound. That's odd."

Cora would have clutched her own chest at the sight of Ida, but she composed herself. "It's not odd; it's unnatural," Cora said. "Look at her face. Her hands. I've seen this before, once, a few years back. It's not tetanus. It's strychnine poisoning."

"How can you be so sure?"

"I can't," she said. "There's no way to prove it by dissection. But there was a boy who lived near our cottage who would poison rats with strychnine. He'd a dark heart, that one. One day, he gave it to his grandmother after she beat him with a switch for stealing sugar. He was angry, but thought it killed rats, not people. He'd hoped she would receive a stomachache in return for the whipping. When my aunt found her, she looked the same. Stiff, like all her muscles had been stretched tight. Fists in balls, teeth clenched . . . It happens faster than tetanus." She threw down her shovel. "Anyway, back to work before someone sees us."

It was back to business, but not for Cora. Another body, dead before death was ready. She was so chilled by the regularity of these bodies turning up conveniently and unnaturally that her hands trembled as they gripped the knife that sliced away at the woman's silk gown.

In her head, she apologized to Ida over and over again, which made no sense. Cora hadn't killed her. But the people being killed were on *her* list. The apologies didn't prevent her hands from shaking, though. She could no longer ignore this pattern. She thought of who was next in her ledger. Of course—Conall Culligan, the gentleman with an abnormally tall stature. She would send him a note to warn him to be careful. Cora would have to be vague because everyone on her list so far had died of disparate causes.

Soon, they had Ida undressed and out of the coffin. Cora helped the others heave the body onto a cloth and roll her up tightly. The cloth-covered corpse was bent like a half-opened parentheses, with the other side encasing the answer, missing. Cora gently laid her head down when they placed her in the wagon.

"That tumor is a piece of work, Flint," the Duke said, closing the casket. The rest of the team began replacing the soil. "But for the strychnine, we should charge another ten. If you can't pay it, we can see if Duncan will."

"No, I'll pay it. It's worth it. I've the money," he said.

After cleaning up the grave site as well as possible, they took the long journey 144 streets back through the darkened city to the new university building, where Cora had been only twelve hours ago looking for Dr. Grier's journals.

They took the body around the back of the building, and into a rear room where it would be prepared for dissection tomorrow. Theo handed over the seventy dollars, and Cora quickly counted out ten each to Otto, Tom, and the Duke. She split the remainder and gave fifteen dollars to Theo.

"And now? We drink?" the Duke said.

"As soon as you put your horses away. It's time for some flickering and a slap-bang."

They all gave one another hearty claps on the back, but Cora didn't share in their rejoicing. She quietly said her goodbyes to Ida. Down to the Bowery they went, and by two o'clock in the morning, they had eaten their way through four platters of fried oysters and drunk three rounds of porter. The Duke and Tom were having a row over which pugilist would win at the match tomorrow. The Duke stumbled home, and Otto left to find a square game at the gambling house next door, tucking his tail carefully into his rear pocket after it had gotten stained from oyster grease.

"I'm not ready to go home. I've no lectures tomorrow. Come, Jacob. There's a billiard saloon down the street. Shall we?" Theo asked, clapping him hard on the back.

"I don't like billiards," Cora said. Despite her four drinks, she was feeling wary, and because of her four drinks, she was swaying slightly. "Or bowling. Not tonight."

"Come now. You're better company than my empty boardinghouse. At least you go home to Leah when you go home," Theo said, staring at the wall. "And Cora."

"Leah snores" was all that Cora could say, before she remembered. Theo's loneliness had a way of materializing at the edges of scenes, behind words and gestures, hidden under neat stacks of textbooks in his bedroom. She remembered that his parents had died of yellow fever. "Haven't you any other family?" she asked.

"No." He shrugged.

"Well, you should do what Leah says I should do. Get married."

"I've no money. No one wants to marry me."

"No one would want to marry me either," Cora said, grimacing into her empty glass.

"We should marry each other, then."

Cora turned in surprise, and Theo was grinning. "I'm not a bugger," Cora said. "Not my taste, is all."

"Still, you wonder. Who cares, as long as someone is there to come home to every night? I'd like that. I'd like that very much. Wouldn't matter what they looked like, or where they came from. Would it?"

Cora blinked, and her hearts hardened. "You don't mean that." She looked away. This was the same Theo who had demanded that Cora reveal who she was, or rather, what she was. Was he just trying to sweeten up her brother, to get into Cora's good graces again?

"I don't always know what I'm talking about," Theo said hollowly. "Sometimes when I say things out loud, I realize how stupid and wrong I am." After a long silence, he said, "Let's just go home. After one more drink." He waved his hand, and another round of tumblers were refilled with water, instead of the night's deep scarlet porter. Cora was slightly surprised. Apparently, Theo didn't want to repeat the other night of thorough drunkenness.

They paid for their drinks and went out into the night. Here, the Common Council didn't bother to pay for gaslights, as the people were considered below the worth of a gas line and good lamps. It was a good ten blocks before they could see the street enough, when the clouds loosened their fist, releasing the milky half-moon again.

It was a long walk home, as the omnibuses had stopped running at midnight. Theo was drunker than Cora had first thought—he stumbled over some loose cobblestones and twisted his ankle. Cora helped Theo drape his arm over her shoulders, and she kept her hand firmly around his waist. She hadn't been this close to a man since falling asleep in Theo's bed only days ago. This time, she would not make the same mistake.

And yet, she kept finding herself glancing at Theo's silhouette, faintly lit from the shy moonlight. After a time, Theo wasn't limping nearly so bad, but he didn't withdraw his arm from her shoulders. It was strange and sweet to feel the warmth of another human being, borrowed as it was.

Cora wished they had another ten streets to walk, but they had already reached Theo's boardinghouse.

"She'll be so angry with me, when she opens that door," Theo said, finally unhooking his arm from Cora. The left side of Cora's body was suddenly chilled in the night. For someone who'd seemed so disgusted by Cora's parentage last night, Theo didn't seem bothered by it now, with Jacob.

"Well, good night," Cora said lightly.

"Good night," Theo said. He hesitated awkwardly by the door, unwilling, for some reason, to go inside.

"Good night," Cora said again, and still, Theo didn't knock on the door.

"May I . . . Can I tell you something?" he asked, his face sober all of a sudden.

"I suppose so. You've told me your sad tale of woe already, so I'm ready for more."

"Well, all right. Here." He pulled Cora's sleeve, and they ventured to the alleyway by the boardinghouse. Crickets chirped in the tufts of weed growing nearby. Theo leaned in closer. Maybe he was going to tell her about Grier's journals. Or about a new body to procure. Oddly, she didn't care. She was strangely happy to have another few minutes with her competition, who drove her a little mad at times, who was now swaying a bit closer than expected. He didn't smell like oyster pie or wine, just like smoky September night air. A scent that promised impossible things, like the idea that the coming winter would bring nothing to fear.

"What is it?" Cora asked. "Are you mauled? You going to be sick?"

Theo blinked, furrowed his eyebrows, and leaned in to kiss her.

CHAPTER 17

Cora didn't know what to think.

She didn't know how to act, or what to do. Thoughts intruded in lightning-fast streaks while Theodore Flint went on kissing Jacob Lee's mouth for far more seconds than zero, which was what Jacob ought to have allowed.

When it seemed both too soon and too late, Cora pushed Theo away. They were both panting slightly, and Theo immediately began to shake his head.

"I'm sorry. I'm so sorry, I shouldn't have done that," he said in a waterfall of words.

"You shouldn't have done that," Cora said, wiping her mouth with her sleeve. "I guess that answers the questions as to whether you were courting my sister, after all. I never pegged you as a bugger."

"I'm not." Theo spun halfway to the right and leaned against the brick wall of the boardinghouse, looking up at the moon because he wouldn't look at her. "I'm no bugger, Cora."

There was a long silence. Cora covered her mouth, afraid to utter a word. Maybe he was drunk still; maybe the words were a simple mistake.

"I didn't misspeak, Cora." His head turned to look at her. "I know who you are. I know you're one woman playing two people. I've known for days now."

Cora shook her head. She'd fooled her entire team of diggers, she'd fooled the entire island of Manhattan, and parts of Brooklyn, and— oh—how could she not have fooled Theo? How could she have been so stupid as to let him close enough to discover the truth? How could she do anything now, knowing that her one protection was gone?

"You can't tell anyone!" she whispered. She felt the blood drain from her face, her stomach sinking low in her belly, as if it might drop down to the wet soil of the island. She had stopped disguising her voice, and even for Cora, it was a terrifyingly strange thing, speaking in her feminine voice in her rough, grave-digging clothing outside of her home. "You cannot. Oh God. How did I let this happen?"

"Come inside with me," Theo said. "Come with me. We'll talk. I want to know. And I want to apologize for what I said the other night. I can't stop thinking about it. I was wrong, and I was treating you like some sort of horse breeder. I'm so sorry."

Cora shook her head. But Theo stayed immutably silent for several minutes. Finally, he said, "I'll tell you what I know. And you can tell me what I don't."

She wanted to bolt, but sooner or later, she had to know how he'd seen beneath the ruse, learn how she should have done better. And she had to know whether he'd taken Dr. Grier's journals, whether he planned to expose not just one of her secrets, but all of them. She had to know. So, when Theo went to the boardinghouse door and knocked, she allowed it. The matron of the house had thrown on a haphazard shawl and let them in. Theo murmured something about his cousin staying over, and that was that. Upstairs, he locked his door behind them. Cora leaned against the door and waited, staring at her boots.

She wished to run, run, run all the way to Irving Place, but she knew running wouldn't erase the fact that Theodore Flint knew. So, she didn't move her booted feet, only listened, frozen as wide-eyed as a rabbit in the tall grass when a shadow passes. Only, this shadow wasn't flitting away. It weighed her down, like a tombstone.

"I haven't spoken my thoughts to anyone," Theo said. "I guessed that Alexander knows, and your maid, of course. And no one else. Because I noticed, the first time I met you as a lady, that you wore wigs. I could always see that little line between your forehead and the hair. My mother wore them, so I used to think of it as a game—to see which women wore switches and such. And last week—you wiped your face makeup with your hand. I'll bet you never let anyone close enough to notice, but I did."

Cora couldn't help it. She pushed away from the door and tried to walk away, but he grasped her hand gently and didn't let go. He pulled her close and held her upper arms, still talking. Cora looked at the floor, at the ceiling, at the papered walls, anywhere but Theo's face.

"You and your brother, you never were in the same place at the same time. And your boots—Jacob's boots—they always looked odd. The heels were too big and blocky. They make you taller when you aren't. And when we went to visit your cousin yesterday, neither of you said a word about Jacob. Because he doesn't exist."

"Good God, Theo. Just say it," Cora said miserably.

"Say what?"

"Say what you haven't been saying."

He let go of her hand, and his fingertips brushed the fabric of her jacket, just above her right ribs. She shivered and shut her eyes tighter.

"I know about your second heart."

With that, Cora sank to her knees and covered her face.

He knew. He knew everything. And it was her stupidity, her carelessness, that had brought this truth into their midst. Her desperation to earn more money had forced her into Theo's world, a world that pulled him so close that he could smell that she wasn't a man, see that her hair wasn't real, feel that her second heart was always there, beating incessantly and irreverently where it oughtn't.

Cora didn't cry, because Cora never cried. But she kneeled there for a minute, just dissolving in her mistakes. The alcohol had nearly dissipated from her body, and everything was sober and blank and raw. Theo simply waited. And when he grew tired of standing, he sat beside her on the floor, nary an inch away, and folded his arms on his knees. The moonlight shone in two rectangles on the floor, and as time passed and the angle of the light changed, still Theo said nothing.

It must have been around four o'clock in the morning when Cora fell asleep. She awoke an hour or so later, feeling warmth against her cheek, a cramping in her spine. Her eyes fluttered open, and she found that Theo had wrapped his arm around her back, and she had used his broad shoulder as a pillow.

He wasn't cursing out this strange girl with stranger parents and her eccentric insides. He wasn't running to Frederick Duncan to sell her body. He had stayed.

Oh God, they had kissed. What would Leah think? What would Alexander say? Leah would be elated, and Alexander? Theo had made a horrible first impression. She could imagine Alexander and Leah fighting while Cora covered her ears, embarrassed. She wanted to laugh, but she remembered her life was currently a tragedy, and that Theo was now part of her tragedy as well.

Her back cramped a little, and she was forced to sit up. Theo glanced down at her face. Her short hair was falling slightly into her eyes, and he brushed it to the side so he could see her better in the predawn darkness.

She thought about kissing him. In her mind, she imagined it— leaning forward, turning her face upward, breathing his exhalations and letting their lips touch. But she couldn't. She couldn't.

And just as she decided that she would not, in fact, kiss Theodore Flint again, and that she should get up, go home, and go sleep in her own bed while she figured out what on earth had happened tonight, Theo spoke.

"Hello there."

"Hello," she said, not knowing what else to say. Because there wasn't much that could be said when you faced a person who knew everything you didn't want him to know. When you felt the explosive combustion of utter relief and anxiety at the same time, and when the person who seemed to recoil at who you were a day ago now cradled you on his shoulder.

"Have you forgiven me yet?" he asked.

"I can't really think straight, to be honest."

"I can wait." He went silent after that. For a very long time.

And in the absence of saying anything, she had to *do* something.

So, Cora leaned in a fraction. She closed her eyes. And she kissed him.

It was different from the first kiss.

The first had been nothing but shock. It had been abrupt and strange and terrifying.

This was slower. Warmer. Just as Cora thought, *I ought not to be doing this,* Theo slipped his hand around her neck and threaded his fingers into the short hair above her nape.

He was gentle, and he was patient. It was just a kiss, but all the rum and spirits had long since dissolved away, and it was only them. Theo was patient, unlike his usual self, always with a toe inching toward the future, trying to stay ahead of Cora. Theo wasn't running right now, and Cora had stopped fleeing. The stillness in her mind was alien and dizzying.

After what seemed like an hour, but was only moments later, Cora broke the kiss.

"Is that what it's like?" she asked, blinking.

"Yes."

"And how many girls have you kissed before, Theo?"

"Not many. You're the first person I've ever kissed who wasn't wearing a dress, for that matter."

"Oh." Cora had stopped listening and had leaned in to kiss him again. Before long, she had let him unbutton the top of her shirt and see her underclothes, padded with leather to bulk herself up. He didn't exclaim in surprise; he didn't remark upon the painstaking efforts of her deceit. In the thin darkness, because Cora could not have tolerated light in this moment, she allowed him to pull her boots off, unfasten her trousers, unwind the covering around her breasts. He brought her to his narrow bed and shed his clothes. Cora covered her face with overlapping hands, but she peeked through the apertures of her fingers and watched him as he lay next to her and pulled her waist closer.

Not once did he ask about her heart.

Not once did he search for it, unasked.

They had an hour before dawn, and they spent it without saying a word, without needing to.

CHAPTER 18

As soon as dawn broke, the spell was also rent.

Theo and Cora still hadn't spoken about what Cora was building up in her mind as the all-encompassing *why*—why she had played two lives and lied all these years. She took her head off his shoulder, which had been her pillow for the last half hour, and he kissed the top of her head.

"I must go," she said, and he nodded. "Turn to the wall."

Theo obeyed, and Cora quickly dressed. She was sitting in a chair and tying her boots on, when Theo turned around and propped himself against the wall, his bedsheet tangled around his waist and legs.

"When shall I see you again?" Theo asked.

"Soon." She didn't know what to say. The less the better.

"That's not soon enough." He began dressing, and Cora turned around to face the door, wishing she could watch but not letting herself. She listened to fabric rustling, shoes being put on, and the steps behind her. Theo slipped his hands around her waist and kissed her cheek. "I have two lectures this morning at the university. Come with me."

"What about the dissection? The lady we just dug up?"

"This afternoon. Do you want to go?" Theo asked.

Cora wrapped her hands around her arms and shivered. "No, I don't. But I have work too. I have to go home and change."

"Don't. Come with me. And then in the afternoon, you can go home and work. I'll tell my schoolmates you're looking to enroll."

"I can't."

"It'll be safer for you not to be alone," Theo said. He rubbed his stubbly cheek against her soft one. "I could keep you company for a little while." He gently bit the cartilage of her ear instead, and she laughed and laughed, and finally rumpled his hair.

"All right! You win. I'll come."

And so they left. Even though the sun had barely risen, the street was already awake, with people opening up their storefronts and sweeping the dirty sidewalks. But to Cora, the whole city was somehow brighter, fresher.

As the boardinghouse keeper hadn't yet begun cooking breakfast, they paid a few pennies for a crusty loaf of bread, tore it in half, and chewed on it all the way to the new university building. Students were already spilling through the doors, and at the sight of the light-colored building, Cora stopped.

"Do I look all right?" she asked him, adjusting the hat on her cropped hair. "I've no makeup on to hide my face."

"It's all right. You just look younger; that's all. Very boyish. I'd kiss you to show that I meant it, but that wouldn't go over well, would it?"

Cora hid a smile, but then frowned. "I saw your name," she said, forcing down her last swallow of bread. "In the library there."

"Yes, I was there a few days ago."

"What were you looking up?" she asked.

"Dr. Grier's journals. Duncan's claim about the woman with two hearts seemed so outlandish, I had to know if it was true, or a rumor. I mean, maybe Dr. Grier's assessment was wrong, but it's there. He saw what he saw."

"You weren't the only person looking," Cora said. "Frederick Duncan's name was in that log too."

"But he's been there several times," Theo said. He waved her forward, and they went inside to the upstairs operating theater. "He sometimes has books taken out so his artists can copy the drawings for his displays. It doesn't mean he was looking at Dr. Grier's journals."

"I suppose so." She paused. "Is there a student or doctor here with the surname Swell?"

"Not that I know of. Why?" Theo asked.

"I saw it in the books. It's not a real name. Did you write it?"

"Goodness, no."

Cora paused. There was another question she had to ask. There was no putting it off.

"Theo. You said some things to me, that night we went to see my family."

Theo's face went white, and he looked at his shoes. "I said and asked things that were ungentlemanly. Cruel. You aren't inferior, and I didn't mean to imply that I agreed with those who think so. I don't. Your parentage has nothing to do with the fact that you are a superior creature to me in every way, Cora Lee."

Contrition and sincerity weighed on his shoulders, but she felt light, lighter than a speck of ash rising into the sky. There was so much relief, more than she'd felt in ages. "Let's go in. I forgive you, Theodore Flint. If you forgive me for lying to you about who I've been."

Theo beamed. Nearly all the students had gone in, while they were speaking in the corner of the hallway. They entered the surgical theater. Once again, they took the highest seats. Two of Theo's fellow students, Strawtick and Snout, recognized Jacob. They curled their nostrils at the sight of him and turned pointedly away. As Cora and Theo sat watching the operation (a poor fellow who needed a walnut-sized bladder stone removed), they whispered to each other about the lithotomy position, and whether the surgeon would work anterior or posterior to the perineal muscle, and all the while Theo kept surreptitiously finding Cora's hand and covering it with his own.

One lecture on arm anatomy later (Cora fell asleep until Professor Draper slapped his pointer stick against his table before him—she wasn't the only one who had fallen asleep), they were off to walk the short few blocks to Cora's house at Irving Place.

Leah was perched on the front steps, her face red as a fresh cow's liver from the butcher.

Cora would have been happier to see a starving grizzly bear.

"No note! Another night out! With him? Were you with him again?" she hollered.

"Shhh! For God's sake, Leah. Get inside. I have to change."

"With him?" She pointed at Theo. "And will Mr. Flint be watchin' yeh?"

Pedestrians on the street turned around to stare, and little George peeped out from his window next door to yell.

"Oi! Jacob! I sent two messages. Don't let Leah burn them before you read them!"

Cora nodded to him and turned to Theo.

"You'd better wait outside. I'll be . . . Cora will be out in half an hour."

Theo opened his mouth to say something, but Leah's face had not lost its livery color, so he wisely shut it and began pacing up and down the block instead.

Door closed, Leah let open a tirade that would have made Charlotte proud.

"Where were yeh?"

"I fell asleep at Mr. Flint's house again. After our work yesterday night." She dug the money out of her pocket, saving five dollars for Suzette. "Here. Enough for part of the rent, and groceries."

Leah took the money and shoved it into the crock above the kitchen fireplace, before spinning around. "That's two times! Never have you ever stayed out the whole night! And are you mad, talking about changing into Cora, in the light of day, for him to hear? Are you drunk?"

"No."

"Did you have carnal relations with that boy?" Leah demanded.

Cora rolled her eyes and looked up at the ceiling. "Oh, Leah."

"Answer me! I'm as good as your mother, and I ought to know."

After a long silence, Cora finally nodded. "Yes."

Leah took a rag from the worktable and threw it against the wall. "Well then. You're engaged. No more going about as Jacob. You can pay your men like you have before, and collect your money, but no more digging. You could be with child, for all we know!"

"I'm not engaged. And I won't be with child," Cora said as patiently as she could. She walked over to the small cupboard where they kept their ipecac and bitters and opium syrup. She took out a brown jar stuffed with a musty-smelling herb. "I have this."

Leah put her hand on her chest, and her cheeks went a pasty-yellow color. "How do you know about that?"

"This tea? The tea you make every month, after you've been shopping a little too long at Hiram's grocery?"

Leah went silent. Cora had never mentioned the affair, because it didn't hurt anyone, and Leah deserved some companionship all these lonely years with just Cora. The tea was some combination of Queen Anne's lace, pennyroyal, and something else. It was bitter, and acrid, and Leah had never been with child.

"Make me a cup, will you, Leah? I need to bathe and get dressed." She exited the kitchen, but Leah followed.

"But what about Flint?"

"What about him?" Cora said, turning at the bottom of the stairs.

"Will you marry him?" She shook the anger off her face and sighed. "Will you? Because I think it would be a good thing for you to settle. To have a child." She shook the tea. "Maybe . . . you don't want this tea after all, Miss Cora."

"I have other things to worry about," Cora said. Like survival. "Make the tea, Leah, and let that be the end of it."

Cora sponge bathed as quickly as she could, before putting on her undergarments. Leah helped with the rest after bringing her a steaming cup of the tea, which was far less bitter than she'd anticipated. Cora took a moment to write a letter to Suzette, enclosing five dollars, and asked Leah to post it. And she wrote a letter to Conall Culligan too. Warning him that his life was in danger, to watch his food, his back. She did not sign it, of course. Before long, Cora was pinching her cheeks and reaching for the doorknob.

"Oh! Your other letters!" Leah handed them to Cora. "And we ought to send Alexander an invite for supper or breakfast when he gets back this afternoon."

Cora nodded absently, tearing open the envelopes.

She flipped over the first envelope. One was from Suzette. Already!

> *Miss Lee,*
> *I should like to apologize for our family's behavior two nights ago. I confess, this is all very strange and new, and I did not expect for you to so willingly undo the unsavory and deceitful actions of your servant.*
> *I should like to see you again, soon. Perhaps luncheon, or a walk along the Battery?*
> *Warmly,*
> *Suzette*

It was unexpectedly friendly. Nay, almost . . . lonesome.

She opened the second letter, but it was somewhat mangled by the post. Part of the bottom was ripped.

> *Miss Lee,*
> *Another one for you. Some type of fit, perhaps. Slated for a burial at Calvary Cemetery tonight. Conall Culligan, the extremely tall fellow. There are nearly twenty burials there today alone, so I wish you luck on locating the correct one.*
> *Yours,*

Here, the paper was torn. But still, it must be from Dr. Blake—he had been the one seeing Mr. Culligan for symptoms of dropsy and regular bleedings.

But for a long moment, Cora's breath wouldn't come, and she covered her mouth to stifle a sob. She still had in her hand the letter of warning to Conall—all but too late. She cursed herself. She should have found him in person! But would it have mattered?

Garroted? Killed? Another unnatural death. Alive a few days ago, and not alive today. A wink of time in history. Her mind went to dark places, thinking of Conall, whether he was at peace, or savagely furious at his circumstance. Whether he was furious at Cora. She wished she could speak to him. He was the last name on her ledger; she was sure of it. What if Cora was the next on the list now?

Cora breathed again, before she became dizzy. But she was alive now, and work would keep her alive a little longer, long enough to exit this city. She would have to take the Twenty-Third Street ferry over the river, to find the right burial area. Twenty burials today! At least it wasn't fifty. But she knew this fellow. She'd seen him once—nearly six and a half feet, with spidery fingers and a long face. He was Irish, like so many buried at Calvary, a Catholic cemetery. Culligan's family had built a small empire in running goods up the Erie.

Surely, he'd have family of similar stature. She bid goodbye to Leah, who was still frowning hard enough to make vinegar cry, and went outside, where Theo was waiting.

"Well! There you are. And here I am."

"And here we must part," Cora said hurriedly. She showed Theo the letter. "We have more work. It's a stellar find, and we must know whether Duncan is willing to pay more, or your Dr. Wood, for his anatomical cabinet."

"Wood may be willing, though so many in a week may overtax even his funds. I'll go and meet with him. Be careful around Duncan."

"I always am." She accepted a kiss on the cheek. "I will see you tonight, in any case. We can meet at the ferry at five o'clock."

"Do you regret last night?" Theo asked.

"Not yet, I don't," Cora said, with a tiny smile.

"Well, I guess I'll have to make sure that you don't." He grinned.

They parted, and Cora headed for the avenue to take the omnibus down to the Grand Anatomical Museum. She heard, from very far away, a man, shouting at the top of his voice.

"I kissed a lady!"

A few hoots and hollers sounded afterward. A woman crowed at him to quiet down. Cora covered a smile with her gloved hand. She was rather sure the voice had been Theodore Flint's.

At the museum, she spoke to the man at the ticket booth.

"I have a business meeting with Frederick Duncan."

The man, mustachioed and red eyed, looked down a sheet of paper. "I don't see an appointment here, but your name is on a list to be let in, without question. There you go, ma'am." He waved to the other man gathering tickets from the crowd lined up to see the *New Exhibition of the Wondrous Tailed Lady*. Before she left, she asked, "Is Alexander Trice back in his studio yet? I am his niece."

"Oh. Yes, been there all day today."

"Oh! Good, he must have come back early." Cora pushed back from the booth. "Thank you."

Alexander was likely getting to know Philadelphia well, with his visits to Jefferson Medical College and spying on the anatomical collection belonging to Dr. Mütter, the one Duncan worried might open a museum that would outclass his own. Perhaps that would be where she made her home. She wondered if Theo could imagine a life in Philadelphia too.

Inside, she was directed to Frederick Duncan's office on the second floor, overlooking Broadway. Cora knocked briefly, and a gruff voice commanded, "Come in."

She entered. The first thing that surprised her was the enormous snarling lion's head mounted upon the wall, fierce and frozen and dead. The second thing was that Duncan was not alone.

"Miss Lee! I am entranced! Come in, come in. Why, I am inundated with ladies this morning. Two of you in my midst, doling out the fates of the living and dead! If my wife were to see me, she would think I was running a scandalous establishment!" The lady stood up from the chair in front of Duncan's enormous carved desk. She turned and bowed coldly.

It was Elizabeth Blackwell, seething with fury.

CONALL CULLIGAN

I have had the most unfortunate luck in stature.

My mother was only five feet and found the opposite of herself in my six-and-a-half-foot father. One from Cork, one from Dublin, they met on the boat to New York harbor amidst whispers of despair that Ireland was not worth staying for.

They dodged the Nativists unscathed and built their shipping business when the Erie Canal opened up. Then I was born, a thin, long baby that my mother called "a string of a child like his father."

And like my father, I grew and grew, fingers like harvestmen among the wooden blocks I played with. Ma fed me watered-down milk in the hope that I would not grow as much as Da, but it was all for naught. I outgrew my father by two inches, or so they said, because Da died the day my wee sister was born. They said that she caused such pain for my mother to bring into the world that it tore my father's heart in two, for that is what he complained of before he died at her side—a renting of his insides.

I am now a year shy of his age when he died, and every day I would walk about with my hand inside my vest, asking my heart if today it might tear apart, or if a young, pretty girl like Anne O'Brien might ruin it instead. I'd feel the strangeness of my rib cage that wasn't like the other lads' who swam in the river in the hot summers. Mine peaked like a low roof in the middle, curiously pointed instead of flat.

Alas, Anne didn't have a chance to ruin my life; someone else did. I went to the shipping yards to make note of the boxes of saltpeter being sent off to Virginia. I was bending over when I felt a ligature about my throat.

Not hands, nor fingers, but something fine and hard. It was so thin, this wire, that I could not grasp it or pull it away. I struggled, and with my height I was able to twist, but when I tried to holler for aid, my assailant pulled mercilessly, and the wire sliced through my windpipe with a whoosh of air. I fell to the dock.

Father had his short bit of time. His body was a clock wound only halfway. But I—I had even less. That stranger took something from me. There is no peace in this otherworldly sleep I possess now.

I will wrestle the discontent within my grave. Woe be it to anyone who hears my anguish in their dreams.

CHAPTER 19

"Dr. Blackwell," Cora said, attempting to keep the surprise from her voice.

"Ah, you know each other? Even better!" Duncan clapped his hands together, and toured around the women like they were marble statues. "Do you know that Miss Blackwell—"

"*Dr.* Blackwell," Dr. Blackwell interrupted. Her English accent became so very pronounced when she was ruffled.

"Is soliciting our venue for a set of educational lectures on health? For ladies?" He clapped again and laughed. "It's brilliant! And a terrible waste of our space! You'd be better off discussing the mating rituals of Asiatic beetles!"

Dr. Blackwell's murderous expression seemed fitting. She wasn't furious at Cora; she was furious at Duncan. He was hardly even treating her like a proper lady.

"And you! Did you know, Miss Blackwell, that this lovely creature before you, Miss Lee, is a treasure who finds me treasure? I'd like her in my cabinet, I would. A doll of my own, so very unusual! So, Miss Lee, have you a new specimen to discuss?"

"Specimen?" Dr. Blackwell asked, eyebrows raised.

"Indeed, I do," Cora said. "But perhaps we can discuss it after your visit with Dr. Blackwell."

Just then, the door opened, and one of the museum attendants appeared. "There's a problem with the shipping books. We need you to take a look, sir."

"Now? I'm busy."

"The teamster wants a word. Says we underpaid, and he won't go away until you look at the numbers with him."

Duncan pouted beneath his well-curled and well-waxed mustache. "Very well. One moment, ladies."

After he'd left, Dr. Blackwell examined Cora with her good eye. "It is good to see you again, Miss Lee. I don't believe I realized that you had a profession that brought you within this museum's footprint."

"Indeed, I do." Cora was normally shy about discussing her trade with anyone, but Dr. Blackwell seemed determined to make a career in the city as a physician. She might become a source of new specimens. "I have been helping the museums and medical schools procure cadavers for study."

Dr. Blackwell took a step closer. "For study? Or for entertainment?"

"Pardon me?"

"I am grateful to the cadaver that I studied at medical school. He helped me help others, by educating me. But there is a fine line between the education of the public as a means to better society as a whole, and base amusement. We ought not to laugh at the hand dealt to another human being, something they have little control over."

"I sell to the universities, and to museums, for educating the public," Cora said.

"Are you so careful?" Dr. Blackwell asked.

"I try to be. But there is a demand. As such, I supply that need."

"I see. It is interesting how, on occasion, supply and demand have a way of flourishing beyond our control."

Cora frowned. Surely, her work did not increase the demand. She had not noticed more requests for her work. But the names in her ledger flashed in her mind. Randolph. Ruby. William. Ida. Conall. It didn't make sense. Perhaps it was all just bad luck. People had all manner of private dramas that ended in tragedy, did they not? But her reasoning did not settle well with her. Dr. Blackwell kept speaking.

"And where do you find these subjects?" Dr. Blackwell asked. "Do you visit the potter's fields in all your finery?"

"Goodness, no. My brother works in that vein. But we do not scour the potter's fields. I choose not to subject the poor, or pilfer the burial grounds of black people. They have been served their share of disadvantages since birth, and made their wishes clear with the Doctor's Riot more than fifty years ago. They needn't worry about me."

"Ah!" She narrowed her eyes. "So, you are a fell Robin Hood, then, are you not?"

Cora said nothing. She was not enjoying this conversation, and her own discomfort was worse than anything.

Dr. Blackwell finally softened her severe expression. "I apologize. Your reasons for what you do are you own, of course. Far be it from me to tell a woman what she can and cannot do. As for the future physicians who need cadavers for study, there is no question of that necessity. I don't approve of grave robbing, and yet it is possible I have benefited from it. I do hope that someday the medical establishment will find a better way. Dr. Draper at the university proposes a law to take bodies from the poorhouse. I disagree. The poor should be given as much respect as anybody."

Dr. Blackwell walked to the cabinet behind Duncan's desk. It was crowded with stuffed exotic birds of brilliant scarlet and emerald, chunks of pyrite, and skulls of various animal creatures, including human. A waxen head, splayed open to show the intricacies of the muscle, sat nestled at the end of a shelf.

"Look at this," Dr. Blackwell said. She gingerly picked up the waxen head. "Orbicularis oculi," she said quietly, pointing to the circular muscles about the mouth. "Zygomaticus major, and minor," she murmured, now pointing to the chin.

"No, that is the depressor labii," Cora said, gesturing to her own chin before circling her left eye with her forefinger. "This is the orbicularis oculi."

Dr. Blackwell shot her a sharp glance. "Very good, Miss Lee. Very good. I was hoping you'd correct me. It is a shame that your anatomic skills aren't helping the living."

Frederick Duncan opened the door and mopped some sweat from his forehead. Dr. Blackwell smiled and held out her hand.

"Mr. Duncan. I shall be on my way."

Duncan kissed her hand, and as Dr. Blackwell left, she surreptitiously wiped her hand on her skirt. She smiled kindly at Cora.

"Goodbye, Miss Lee. If you ever need a consultation, you may see me in my offices off Union Square."

Cora curtsied, and Duncan bowed. After she left, Cora was alone with Duncan, who mopped his face with his handkerchief. "Can you believe her? Wanting to do a series of medical lectures. For ladies! For both unmarried and married ladies. It's absurd. No one will have her. We certainly shan't. There is nothing more disobliging than discussion of bills, Miss Lee. I apologize that they took me away from you."

"Oh, I—"

"With your face, you ought never to have to worry about money. Never."

The compliment gave Cora the urge to wash her ears out. With lye.

"I have come to discuss a new case," she said. "The University of the City of New York is settling on a price as we speak. A gentleman, six and a half feet tall, age thirty, with abnormally long limbs and fingers." An intrusive image appeared in her mind—a note she'd written on the side of her ledger: *Walks in the gardens by the Crystal Palace. Enjoys flowers.*

No, Cora, she thought. Do your job. "I believe we shall find multiple anomalies within—apparently it is an inherited trait, and his father dropped stone dead at the same young age."

"Ah!" Duncan's eyes lit up. "Ah, yes! Wonderful!" He looked like a child receiving a gift he'd already been expecting. "And this could be something preserved, or used as an open auditorium-style dissection?"

"Absolutely. He would be a perfect inclusion in the university's anatomical cabinet, however." But behind Cora's bright smile was a leechlike attachment to her insides that spoke quietly. I don't want to do this anymore.

"I see." Duncan came closer to Cora, but just as she began to lean backward to avoid him—she had a terrible fear that he might actually try to kiss her—the door opened again.

Duncan growled. "Oh good God, can a man not have a private moment in his office?"

This time, it wasn't a museum assistant but two children who pushed their way in, in a flurry of red cheeks and sticky fingers and bouncing curls. A girl and boy—twins by the look of their similar heights and amber hair color—dressed smartly in fine brown wool with velvet trim. Conall Culligan had two children too. The twins' minder, a tired-looking older woman, stood at the doorway.

"Father! We got pink candy and yellow and green candy!" said the little girl.

The boy chimed in, "Can we bring Mortimer to the museum tomorrow?"

Duncan stooped down. "No, little Frederick, we cannot bring the pug to the museum. He'll try to eat my stuffed tigers!" Duncan curled his fingers and growled.

Cora smiled.

"Miss Lee, my children. Frederick the third, and little Pearl, my jewel. Pearl will no doubt marry a scamp, and Frederick will waste away all his inheritance, but what is a father to do?" He smiled. But Cora was repulsed that he could be fatherly one moment, salacious the next.

"Indeed. They have stolen more than your heart, I believe."

"Yes. Children, out. Bertha, take them away. Out, out."

The lady ushered the children away, and Duncan stood.

"I'll tell you what, Miss Lee. I shall give ten dollars over and above whatever the university bids on this case."

"I see," Cora said. She turned to the door, happy to be leaving. "I'll think on your offer. If we deliver the body, we'll have a deal."

"Very well." As he opened the door, he put his hand on her waist. "Everything I do, Miss Lee, I do for my children. And my wife. But I do believe that you and I could be a great pairing, in this profession."

"Pairing," Cora said tonelessly. As she said it, his hand crept up her waist, over the stiff basque of her dress. His fingertips were only inches away from the underside of her breasts. She opened the door but saw that his children were still quite nearby. Cora did not want to startle them with a harsh word or movement.

"Yes," Duncan said. "You see, I believe a man has many hearts. A heart for his children, a heart for his wife. A heart for God, and, if he be as generous as I, a heart for other beautiful specimens." He squeezed her bodice ever so slightly, and it was so near to her second heart that she had to step away quickly. Her face went scarlet. "And a heart for work, as you see." He smiled at her.

Cora was silent. Why all the allusions to several hearts? Was he trying to tell her he knew? She should tell him that the rumors of the two-hearted girl were untrue; the journals of Dr. Grier gone. But what if he had seen them? What if he was the one who had taken them and he was even now trying to trap her in a confession?

"Consider my offer," Duncan said. "We can discuss it further at our next meeting, I am sure."

"I am sure we will," Cora said, loudly enough that his children and their caretaker could hear. "But know, Mr. Duncan, that I do not possess an occupation simply because I am unmarried, or begging for matrimony. I possess the occupation for myself, and myself alone." She leaned closer to whisper. "So, you see, you may keep your hearts to yourself." She glanced at little Ruby and Frederick, and smiled charmingly. "You have more than enough loves to keep them occupied. Good day, and ready your men tonight for the delivery."

She left, but instead of worrying what Duncan knew, she found herself turning over Dr. Blackwell's words.

It is a shame your anatomic skills aren't helping the living.

❖

The dig was a terrible one.

They suffered through a brief ride, three cents a person and an extra five for the wagon. It was Cora's second of the day after her initial scouting trip, during which she cried at the funeral—true tears, as if something inside that had been quietly patched over so many times finally rent and no longer held. Her eyes were still puffed, but no one noticed between Otto the Cat vomiting into the river, and Friar Tom being upset over the nervous horse. While they drove to the cemetery, Tom elbowed Cora.

"Someone handed me this last night," he said. He gave a slip of paper to Cora, who read it.

It was Duncan's wish list.

"All the ragtag resurrectionists know about Duncan. He's been receiving more bodies every night, more than he needs."

"I see," Cora said. Theo gave her a worried glance.

"Mermaids! And girls with two hearts," Otto said, swinging his tail. "Although I hear that's no rumor; she's real. She's from China! Or some such."

Cora wanted to vomit herself. Theo said, "It's all nonsense. All lies. Duncan is trying to get attention, that's all."

"Attention that's boiling over on the fireplace. Everyone's speaking of it."

"Enough," Cora said. "We need to be quiet. And get to work."

They arrived at the cemetery and began their work. A fence enclosed the family plot, and the wagon was left at the bottom of the hill. Hours in, they stood around the pale white body that lay on the newly turned earth. Cora's conscience picked and gnawed mercilessly at her emotions while she stripped the body. All along the way, images of Conall's life invaded her mind: How he must have grieved over his own father's death. How frightened he must have been, facing death. To make things worse, Dr. Blackwell's words had been like a splinter in her ankle, digging itself deeper the more she tried to ignore it.

"Wot's that?" Otto pointed at Conall's neck.

Theo waved her close to inspect the body. "Jacob. Take a look."

Conall's body was lying on his back, but his neck was nearly half-way severed by a thin cut. This was no ordinary garroting. Cora felt the blood drain from her face.

No. No, no.

The Duke started rolling up the body in the sheet they'd brought. "Poor lad."

Theo helped him. Together, they hoisted the body, with the Friar carrying three spades and a leather bag of tools.

"I say we bring him to the university," Cora said. Her eyes were smarting again. Thank goodness it was dark.

"We'd lose ten dollars' profit!" Otto said, already huffing.

"I can do the arithmetic, I know," Cora said. She thought back to how excited Duncan had seemed when she told him about this body. And to the frenzy he'd apparently started with his list. "I just . . . I think Duncan had something to do with it. The man was murdered, plain as day. Anyone who wanted to rob him didn't need to cut his neck almost in half. And Duncan seems to want new bodies so badly."

"You think he's having these people killed?" Theo said, his face upset.

"The lady with the tail is now on display there. Didn't you see? No one dies naturally of having a vestigial tail. And he told me he had her body brought straight to him; she wasn't even buried first. He wanted her for his collection. Oh good God," she said when her hands slipped, and she had to rehoist Conall's feet onto her hip. "I'm sorry!" she said to Conall, more to anyone else. Soon, the body was in the wagon, and they were headed back to the ferry.

"If we're selling to him, they'll start to think we had something to do with it, you know," the Duke said. "That would be the end of us. You'd all go to the Tombs, and I'd get scragged at the gallows."

"If you die, we'd all die with you," Cora said.

The Duke snorted. "That doesn't make me feel better. How about none of us die?"

"I like that option," Theo said.

They laughed. By the time they made it to the university, they were all quiet from tiredness. Theo paid them their brass, and the men dispersed home, too tired to share a round of rum before dawn. Theo looked at Cora.

"I suppose we ought to say good night," she said rather unconvincingly. She felt awful, after the night. And a quiet room alone sounded less pleasing than falling into a frozen river.

"I suppose so." Theo rumpled her short hair. "Stay with me, then."

"Your cot is too small."

Theo reached for her waist. "I doubt that Leah will approve when she sees me in the morning."

"Leah already knows." Cora shrugged. "She shall have a fit, but then it will be over."

Theo said nothing more, his silence and smile an assent. They walked back to Irving Place, and Theo carefully followed Cora upstairs. Theo either did not see, or chose not to comment, on the moisture in

Cora's eyes. Her grief over Conall's death had worn her to the bone, and reaching for Theo lessened the gnawing discomfort. She needed this oblivion, this audacity of being very much alive.

They were painstakingly quiet throughout. Very quiet, though not completely silent. Not that it mattered. In the room next door, Leah's thunderous snores concealed every floorboard and bedstead creak they created.

CHAPTER 20

Cora awoke just after dawn. She wanted to avoid Leah walking in to discover a tangled mess of bare limbs and bosoms in the bed.

"Wake up," Cora whispered, nudging Theo's ribs.

"Mm. No. Not yet," he murmured, and pulled her closer. He slid his hands around her waist and against her rib cage. Cora was suddenly aware that one of his palms covered her second heart, and she stiffened reflexively.

"I'm sorry." Theo pulled his hand away. His voice was warm and husky from sleep. "Does it bother you? Does it hurt?"

"No. It doesn't hurt." She closed her eyes and forced herself to relax a little, then pulled Theo's hand back up to her right ribs. "There it is. The thorn in my side."

For a minute, Theo let his fingertips touch the little hollow between her ribs where he could feel her second heart pulsating. He put his other hand on her wrist and felt the simultaneous beats, like a symphony of small drumbeats.

"It's beautiful."

"Yes, and it's going to be the death of me," Cora said. She pulled away and snatched a muslin petticoat lying on the floor. She covered herself, and stood up, twirling her hand to tell Theo to turn his back to her.

"You know, I've seen a lot of naked women." He grinned.

"But they were all dead. And this one is not, so turn around."

"Point taken." He flipped over onto his stomach, laying his cheek on his folded arms, facing the wall. "What could happen? Dropsy? A heart infection?"

Cora dressed quickly, as well as she could without Leah. "I've never had dropsy. But when I was a child, I had an apoplectic attack. I thought I'd be an invalid for life, but it went away after a day."

"Still, you're quite well now," he reasoned.

"So was the girl with the tail, and the gentleman with the red mark on his face. But they all died before they were ready. Someone is hunting people with medical ailments, Theo. I could be next."

Now mostly dressed, she turned around, and she listened to the rustle of fabrics as Theo dressed.

"The gossip about the girl with two hearts will stop eventually. You've never seen a doctor for this. And that's the one thing all those other deaths had in common. A physician who knew, and likely told more than just you about the person." She heard him fumbling with his boots. "You may turn around."

Theo stood in her bedroom, hair rumpled, shirt rumpled, but to Cora's eyes he was like a newly wrapped present. He looked at her sweetly, shyly. Unlike the rash and overconfident boy who'd yelled at her at their first meeting—*Cora Lee, I think I love you!* He held out his hand, and she took it. They kissed quickly, and he touched her hair again.

"I like it short. But don't forget your wig."

"Oh. Yes." She went to one of the two on the wicker head forms in her armoire and tugged it into place.

"I think I like you better dressed as Jacob. And then I don't have to be so careful around your fine lace and your fine hair."

"You will now. Leah is downstairs, I can hear the pots clanging. Let's shock her as gently as possible."

But Leah was not in the kitchen. Instead, Alexander stood at the stove, putting slices of roasted ham and bread onto three plates. He looked up at them blandly, and said, "Sit. Eat."

Theo muttered a halting hello, but it sounded as if he'd been inexplicably afflicted with a stutter. He cleared his throat two times, before attempting to speak again.

"Mr.—Mr. Trice. Good morning. I—I—"

"Not really a good morning. Not at all. Eat first, and we'll talk later. I heard you two whispering, so I sent Leah on some errands. If she saw you two come down the stairs, she would have probably committed murder right here and now."

Cora descended to a seat at the table, her eyes large and her face white.

"Oh. Thank you for breakfast, Alexander. I . . . well . . . Leah does know already. About Theo and me."

"Not the same as having you two spending the night in the next room." Alexander pushed a steaming cup of tea toward Cora. "This is for you. You're to drink it three times a day, not once." He stared hard at her. "You should be more careful. About everything. I heard about your attack, and now this." He pointed to the tea. "Leah is no druggist. Her herbs were years old, and she's probably barren, which is why they seemed to work. She diluted the crock with regular tea, did you know that?"

Cora stopped drinking, and Theo cleared his throat again. He heard Alexander's words, understanding the tea's purpose.

"Why would she do that?" Theo asked.

"And you're going to be a doctor? You don't have much in the way of deduction, do you?" Alexander wiped his hands down, poured himself and Theo coffee black as mud, and began sipping. "She wants very much for you to be with child, Cora."

"Why?" Cora said.

"She wishes for you to be married. To stop all this resurrection business. She wants to live a steadier life as a maid in a household with a doctor earning a good income." Alexander stuck out his fifth finger at Theo. "That's you."

"Well, I am not ready for that," Cora said, now drinking her tea more earnestly.

"Why not?" Theo asked. He put his coffee down. "I haven't asked you, Cora, but . . . well, why not get married? I'll graduate in only one year. I might even become a professor at the university. Dr. Draper and Dr. Pattison have already mentioned that there would be a surgical position for me, with all I'm doing to help with the anatomical collection with Dr. Wood. You could stop working. No more digging, no more Jacob."

Cora stared at him. Alexander seemed somewhat pleased at Theo's burst of ideas.

"I am not ready for a domestic life," Cora said quietly. "I can't live here in New York for much longer. The rumors about me—they're growing so fast. I can't help but worry that after Conall Culligan, I'm next."

"Who's Conall?" Theo asked.

"The bloke we dug up last night! Good God, he had a name!" Cora said, her voice so sharp that Theo balked. Alexander put a hand on her arm, and she calmed herself. "People actually believe I exist, Theo. I'll have to leave soon."

"I'm already building a reputation here in New York. It's where I want to settle," Theo said, raising his voice. "And we're trying to get rid of the rumors. We can, I'm sure. Like you said, you've never seen a doctor about it."

"I've seen you," Cora said. "You know."

"And I won't tell a soul!"

"You already told someone!" Cora hissed. "When I was Jacob, before you knew I was the girl with the affliction! Remember? When you were drunk, only last week? You told me about the girl with two hearts. And those terrible wish lists of Duncan's—they've already gotten me nearly killed!"

Theo stood up. "I apologized. What else would you have me say? I already said I would help make these rumors go away, but you can't let go of my mistakes." He went to the door. "This is really remarkable, these words issuing from a person who pretends to be two people and lies to everyone she meets." He put his coat on and turned to Alexander. "Thank you for breakfast. I'm off to my lectures. Good day."

Cora didn't rise, nor did Alexander. They heard the door slam, and about a minute later Leah came in through the back door with a basket of apples, a small sack of flour, and a dead chicken yet to be dressed. Her meaty fist had its headless body by its feet, feathered neck stained with drained blood.

"Was that the Flint boy walking out the front door?" Leah asked, color rising to her cheeks. "Was it?"

Alexander nodded, and Cora covered her face, already wanting this day to be over. But Leah had barely begun. She hollered at Cora for bringing a man over, for threatening their very home (the landlord might force them to leave if they knew Cora was having gentlemen over, something Cora hadn't considered). She yelled at her thoughtlessness, her licentiousness, and for not "consulting her," which made Cora roll her eyes. And then Leah began hollering at Alexander.

"And you! You call yourself her uncle, and you're never here! You're gone all the time; you never break bread with us anymore! You should have counseled Cora to stay away from that Flint boy. She doesn't listen to me!"

"Because you are not my mother," Cora said, standing up.

"No, indeed, I am not! Your mother found a lowly Chinese tar—a sailor, of all trades! And she couldn't keep her thighs closed, and now here's her daughter doin' the same! These Cutter women, always getting themselves into trouble!"

"You're the one who wants me to marry him!" Cora spat.

"Then *marry* him!" Leah said, shaking the dead chicken at her.

"In the meantime, Leah, would you please stop adding regular tea to Cora's medicinal tea? Even that sly trick is beneath you. She doesn't want a child."

Leah's face suffused red. "Well then. She can buy it herself, if she don't trust me."

"I think my work here is done," Alexander said, draining his coffee. "I'm off to my studio." Hand on the door, he paused when Cora stopped him.

"Wait. Leah's right. We haven't seen much of you lately. I had a worry that you're going to leave us and move to Philadelphia when we're not looking!"

He raised his eyebrows. "I'll be honest; I've considered it. I dislike working for Duncan. He's horrid. He has several large-sized projects I'm working on." He sighed and reached out with his other hand to pat her shoulder. "I will take care of you, and if you and Leah move to Philadelphia, or Boston, or England, I will come." He leaned forward to kiss her forehead. "Just remember. The Cutters cast you off, and Theodore Flint ran away when the subject of marriage elicited a discussion instead of obedience. Sometimes, blood is not at all thicker than water."

Alexander left the kitchen. Cora had to endure another fifteen minutes of Leah's tongue-lashing. It was only the arrival of a few letters that spared her. Cora excused herself to her bedroom while Leah angrily plucked the chicken in the kitchen, as angrily and loudly as one can pluck a chicken.

The first letter was from Frederick Duncan. He was livid. He had seen that no body had been delivered last night, and he raged about not being taken seriously. He wished to discuss it directly with Cora today and demanded that she not refuse him.

The second letter was from Dr. Henrickson. He was a physician that Cora hadn't checked upon in some time, one that had been taking care of two patients she'd been interested in. Dr. Henrickson was unfortunately a drunkard, and he often sipped gin between appointments at his home on Franklin Street. But patients liked him, as he tended to accept bottles of wine or rum instead of monetary payment.

The hand was unsteady, but he wrote that a certain gentleman, Jonathan Fuller, had finally succumbed to a bout of indigestion so terrible, it killed him. Cora recalled this patient—she had even followed him one day to see the severity of his affliction. His gout was disfiguring. Large tophi—solid chunks of uric acid that had crystallized under his skin—protruded from his ears, toes, and knuckles, to the point where he was nearly homebound. She had seen him walking in Tompkins Square once, watching a game of rounders, before demanding that the family member accompanying him bring him back home. Fresh air never agreed with him.

Well. That was another piece of good luck. He was much older, and a bout of dysentery or typhus was an ordinary way to die. It seemed like she and Leah would have good money coming in. After such a drought! Three bodies, in three days. But then her uneasiness kicked in again. Too much death, in such a period of time. Yet this one seemed innocuous enough—surely, Duncan wouldn't bother arranging murder for a mere case of gout.

She read the rest of the letter.

Will be interred tomorrow, according to the family, at the new Evergreens Cemetery, but apparently fear grave robbers, and will have a locked coffin and a guard for one week's time.

I am confounded, however. He ought not to have died from eating a bad roast. His family was quite well, in comparison, after eating the same meal.

Miss Lee, there are murmurs amongst my colleagues that your brother may be burking these sick patients. I cannot abide by such practices, you know.

He thought Jacob was burking the victims?

Cora had heard of Burke and Hare, the Scottish murderers who smothered victims and sold them to an anatomist, Robert Knox, who had no knowledge that they'd been murdered. It had all happened about twenty years ago. She had always drawn a line against doing anything that hastened death. Did Dr. Henrickson not know that Jacob would never commit such an atrocity? This was a dangerous rumor, one she'd have to stamp out at their next meeting.

She went to where she kept her ledger and all the correspondence with her doctors on a small table, amongst a few piles of anatomic textbooks and other letters.

The ledger was a wide, flat book, containing a neat list of patients, doctors, and ailments, along with home addresses and notes about when Cora had last checked in with the physicians. Along the edges, Cora had added other items too: Names of their children. How Conall owned two spaniels and loved those flowery walks. How Jonathan disliked the oyster saloons, but drank huge quantities of his favorite port. The prices she'd secured for various ailments were listed on a separate page.

But the ledger was gone.

With the flurry of deaths recently, she hadn't had a chance to open the book and write down the sales numbers and details. She couldn't remember the last time she'd looked at it—perhaps two weeks ago? She tried to recall the names she'd added most recently. Randolph Hitchcock. Ruby Benningfield. William Timothy. Ida Difford. Conall

Culligan. But this one, with the gout, Jonathan Fuller, was added long before.

What did it mean that most were dying in the order that she had written in her ledger? Of course, there was one person who belonged on that ledger but was absent. Herself, of course.

"I am no different, and no better," she said, as if speaking directly to Ida or Ruby or Conall. Yet oddly all these years, she had not said such a thing aloud.

And now the ledger was gone.

Who had access to this room? Leah, of course. But so did Theo—only this morning, in fact. And he'd been in the house before, the day she fell ill. And then she remembered—had Suzette Cutter not come to her room on the occasion she'd visited Leah? Cora thought back to when that would have been. Had she seen the journal since then? She didn't think so. But what on earth would Suzette want with a list of the sick and the dead?

Cora readied herself and asked Leah about the ledger.

"I don't know. I don't touch your table, messy as it is. I never have, I promise."

Leah was a nervous liar, and in this case, Cora felt certain that she was telling the truth.

As Cora walked to the Grand Anatomical Museum, her mind ached with unease. Her world was a cautiously curated fabric of secrecy, information acquisition, and quietly executed resurrections. And the fabric was fraying on all sides—the bodies being stolen out from under her, people turning up murdered—the exact same people on her list, which was now missing. And there were Grier's missing diaries. She had yet to discover who'd taken them, and why. Was someone trying to expose her? Perhaps the danger wasn't due to her two hearts. Perhaps she and Jacob had become too successful to live. How ironic that the very vocation she picked up to protect herself placed her in danger, for different reasons altogether.

Her confusion didn't lessen once she met with Duncan. He ranted and raved about her betrayal.

"I'm going to have a word. You'll see, I'm going to have a word. Shoddy work! Shoddy work, indeed!" Duncan yelled, at the walls, it seemed, while Cora stood before him. He turned to her and addressed her. "And you! I promised you above and beyond—ten dollars! What business do you have saying no when we agreed on the price?"

Cora sighed. "I said I would think on it, Mr. Duncan. There is no agreement until Jacob delivers a body."

"But it was my body! We discussed it!"

"True, and I apologize for that misunderstanding. But you see, this gentleman, Mr. Culligan, whom we had discussed for delivery—we believe he was murdered. Strangled with a wire, it appeared."

Duncan's eyes bulged. "In what way should that matter? That is none of my business!"

"Jacob thought it would be a better case for the students. The university can handle receiving bodies of such abused quality, because they receive any quality, from the worst to the extraordinary. Your museum cannot handle that kind of . . . insinuation." She chose her words carefully. "A reputation is a delicate thing. Would you want anyone to link you to a murder, for profit?"

"I am no killer," Duncan said. He'd said it a little too vehemently, a little too quickly.

"Of course! Which is why we steered that taint away from your good institution."

Duncan went to the window, watching the line outside his museum. It was always shorter than Barnum's. He took out his handkerchief and wiped his face.

"It doesn't matter; it doesn't matter. I'll soon have an exhibit that will leave Barnum salivating at my feet. So, they have that little General Tom Thumb and taxidermied elephants. We will have better! Just wait and see."

"What exhibit?" Cora asked.

"In time, you'll see. In the meantime, I have my eye on another exhibit. A personal one. Alexander is commissioned for the work."

"Yes, Alexander said he's been quite busy with several works. I should like to see them when they're on display."

"Oh no. They're very small personal projects," he said. He cocked his head slightly, as if trying to make out Cora's eye color, or whether she had a stray piece of down stuck on her cheek. "Yes, small ones." He looked down at his desk. "I'm about to ask him to do another Venus for me, only a foot long. A recumbent one, similar to the European wax masters, with the face of an angel. I don't like the British style—too real. Patrons like a little romance, even in anatomy." He smiled. "I would be delighted if you let me give you a personal tour sometime."

Cora had stopped listening. She wondered if these personal projects added to Alexander's dissatisfaction with wax work.

"Miss Lee?"

"I'm sorry. I apologize, what did you say?"

"A personal tour?"

"Oh. I have another engagement shortly. Perhaps another time."

"You should keep an eye on that Alexander. He's never here when I want him!"

Cora raised her eyebrows. "What do you mean?"

"Do you know where he goes? I do. You ought not to put so much dependence on such a family member. You need a better benefactor. Don't you think?"

"I do very well, thank you, with or without the support of Mr. Trice. Not every woman needs a man to take care of her," Cora said.

"Like Elizabeth Blackwell?"

It wasn't the first name she'd considered, but she nodded. Why not? Why not be like her? Cora knew anatomy as well as or better than any student at the university. She might learn the practice of medicine similarly.

"Miss Blackwell is a pariah in this town. I imagine her practice on Union Square is failing miserably. Do you know—they made her rent an entire floor of the building, because no renters would stand to be in her tainted proximity?" He laughed aloud. "Take my word, Miss Lee. I may be married, but I am in a place to be your very good friend. Remember that."

Staring at his mustache, and his gaudy green-and-yellow-striped trousers, Cora felt her breakfast and tea working their way up her esophagus. She held them down.

"I appreciate the offer. In any case, I shall be in touch with other specimens, Mr. Duncan."

He came forward to kiss her hand, leaving a wet mark. She could have sworn that she felt his tongue against her skin during the brief kiss. When Cora left, she considered purchasing a barrel of whiskey to pour over her hand to wash away Duncan's polluted touch.

By the time she had left the building, she realized that Duncan never actually denied having anything to do with Conall Culligan's murder.

And . . . she'd completely forgotten to ask him about Grier's missing diaries.

CHAPTER 21

Alexander was not in his studio. Cora went there directly after her visit with Duncan. But the door was locked, and the front guard said that Alexander had left early in the day.

Her mind was a confusing jumble. Her fight with Theo. Her need to drink her midday dose of tea soon. Wanting to scrub Duncan's kiss off her hand, down to the bone. The resurrection they must do tomorrow night, for the gouty old man, and her escalating distaste for doing any resurrections ever again.

At the center of this chaos were her original intentions. She must pay back the Cutters, and before the gossip of the two-hearted girl bloomed into a riot of noise, she must leave New York. Which meant leaving Theo.

It was that last thought that made her clutch at her chest, frowning. After their row, the stink of bitterness rose above her like a halo that refused to be cleansed away. He'd assumed she'd fall in line to marry him. He didn't know her. He didn't know her at all. She began to walk back home, when a newsie on the corner thrust a paper almost in her face. He had a stack of small newspapers and was yelling at the top of his lungs.

"Get your daily news! One penny, only one penny! Jenny Lind to perform her sixth concert! Eighteenth Ward watchman assaulted with ax will live!"

Cora was about to pass by, when he yelped, "New York's Two-Hearted Maiden soon to be on display at the Grand *Anatomical Museum!*"

Cora tripped over her own feet. She grew light-headed and forced herself to breathe. She pivoted to the newsie—a little smudge-faced boy no older than eight, his arms waving the papers at everyone who passed by within a few feet.

"Let me see that," she said.

"One cent," he said. Cora hesitated, and he reasoned, "Only one cent! *Herald* charges two pence!" Cora fished the coin from her reticule and handed it to him.

She took the small newspaper and walked across and up the street, to the gated quiet of New York Hospital. There were several benches on the manicured lawns, and she sat down and closed her eyes.

This could not be happening. It couldn't. It was only gossip. It must be a mistake.

When she had caught her breath and the dizziness had settled, she began to read. The article was the third on the front page in the upper right where the local news was listed, and very tiny at that.

Two-Hearted Girl Sought for the Grand Anatomical Museum

Frederick Duncan, curator and proprietor of the Grand Anatomical Museum at 300 Broadway, is seeking to obtain a specimen for his exhibit, a young woman famed for owning not one but two beating hearts.

Duncan is confident that they will obtain the specimen soon, and will be selling tickets once the details are confirmed. "There will be nothing like it in New York, or any great city in the world," he stated. "It will be a once-in-a-lifetime finding—a Venus like no other."

Visitors now can view The Wondrous Tailed Lady, The Anatomic Venus, The Womb's Miracles, *and* The Tin Whistlers Show *at only twenty cents per visitor. The museum is open Monday through Saturday.*

The single sheet of newsprint was trembling in her fingers. She crumpled it on her lap and closed her eyes. How could this be? How could Duncan be so bold to say that he would have the exhibit, before he knew who she was? Even if he'd stolen Grier's journals, he didn't have a name of the girl. He couldn't be absolutely sure she existed. Could he? Only Alexander, Leah, and Theo knew.

Unless Theo had told him.

No.

Duncan gave no indication that he knew about Cora's secret. The newspaper article simply must be a boastful way of getting attention. These penny papers were always trying to print the scandalous bits and pieces of New York life.

But it would only fuel the rumors and the competition among resurrectionists to find this girl. And if the rumors spread enough to associate a name with the two-hearted girl . . .

Cora shivered. Her first instinct was to discuss this with Theo, but she couldn't. She was too proud to go back and apologize; and she had nothing to apologize for, she thought defiantly. She might go home to Leah, but Leah would only fuss over her.

Alexander wasn't in his studio. But perhaps she could find him. She knew he often went to Market Slip—it was where his favored paint and dye company brought in the goods he often used for his sculptures. She would go there.

Cora uncrumpled the newspaper and folded it neatly into her reticule, and left the hospital grounds. She surreptitiously looked over to the corner where the newsboy was still selling his penny papers to eager passersby. Were the buyers glancing toward her? Could they know that she was *that* girl? But no, no one was looking. She hurried down Broadway, oblivious to the cacophony of the street noise.

At that moment, Cora saw Alexander. He was exiting an omnibus two streets away from the Anatomical Museum. Several debarking passengers obscured her view of him. She wouldn't call for him, or wave her arms. Now was not the time to bring attention to herself. If only she could transform instantly into Jacob. She wanted to hide in him, immerse herself in his safety.

So, she walked at a ladylike pace, perhaps thirty feet behind Alexander, watching him and others threading their way past the lines outside the museum. Alexander took a sharp right after the entrance, down the alleyway that led to his door. Just then, another gentleman also took a sharp right down the alley, only ten steps behind Alexander.

Cora halted. She knew of the various techniques that the city's unsavory might use to take advantage of others. There were countless ways to pickpocket a gentleman, and countless more to earn a dishonest dollar. Clever ways, as when women robbed men they'd lured into their room for a tryst. Alexander was smart, though, and unlikely to be fooled. But then again, he hadn't once looked behind him.

Cora quickened her pace until she reached the building's corner. She caught a glimpse of the man as he rounded the rear of the building. He wore the scruffy clothing of a dockworker. She had seen a nape of dark-colored hair, and a hunched appearance, as if the stranger did not want to be seen.

From afar, she heard a door shut. Cora followed quietly down the narrow alley. As she clutched the twisted strings of her reticule, she realized that she was unarmed. If this man was attacking Alexander, what could she do but scream? She could fight, but with four layers of petticoats and a corset, she'd be at a grave disadvantage.

She rounded the building and faced the cast-off furniture and refuse behind the museum. There was that one cabinet whose glass front was broken, the shards of glass dusty and forgotten in its interior. Cora bent over, grasped a sharp piece, and wrapped the end of it in the fabric of her purse. If she must, she could use it for a quick upward thrust under the rib cage. It would be enough to give Alexander and her time to flee and seek help. She gripped the shard behind her skirts as she crept down the stairs to the doorway.

She listened. Inside, it was quiet. But then she heard voices—male voices, talking hurriedly, and then a thump. What was that? There was another thump, and a grunt of pain.

"No," someone had muttered. "Don't."

Cora suddenly panicked. What if someone had realized that she was the two-hearted girl? What if they had tracked Alexander down to get to her? Then she should run. She should run, now, and quickly.

But there was Alexander, on the other side of this door. She had to help him, after all he had done. She could not leave him like this. Alexander was no fighter, but Jacob was. Her femininity might fool the attacker, and one sharp wound to the neck would end all of this.

Cora touched the doorknob and found it unlocked. She opened the door and heard more bumps and thumps, another exclamation, and the sound of something like earthenware hitting the floor and shattering.

Cora walked quickly down the corridor, past the wax works in the studio and ghostly covered sculptures in the storage room. There was a faint light coming from the tiny room that held Alexander's small kitchen hearth and bed.

A groan issued from his room, followed by a sigh.

Cora stopped. It wasn't the sigh of someone meeting his untimely fate. She knew this sigh. She had been the creator of such a sigh only last night when Theo had bitten her neck and driven his body against hers.

Cora was suddenly uncertain of what to do. She held her breath and decided to tiptoe forward. The light from the room cast a thin golden sliver upon the wooden floor, and she leaned her fingertips against the doorjamb to peek inside.

She had trouble understanding what her eyes were witnessing. The two men were standing against the rough-hewn table upon which rested a dirty spoon and plate. A ceramic bowl was shattered on the floor where it had fallen.

Alexander's back was to Cora, and he had pinned his assailant against the table from behind. But it wasn't a struggle, but something else. A rhythmic shoving match, and with every shove, Alexander was grunting, and the man in front of him was grunting, too, and occasionally letting out a soft cry of pleasure. Cora could see now that Alexander's trousers had loosened over his hips, and the man he'd pinned to the table had his trousers down around his thighs.

Cora inhaled quickly, and her shock was loud enough to draw the men's attention.

Alexander turned, and the instant he met Cora's eye, she fled. Behind her, she heard his plaintive cry.

"Cora!"

But Cora couldn't flee fast enough. She recalled smelling lilacs on him, assuming he'd been with a woman! He'd probably told the truth, that it was a scent from a random passenger on the omnibus. She thought about Alexander always gently rebuffing Cora and Leah's wish that he marry and settle down. All those times he'd made sure he knew where Jacob would be at night—it wasn't so that he could tryst with the female prostitutes and *filles de rue* who loitered outside theaters under the gaslights; it was so that Cora might not see that they were men, not women.

"Cora!" Alexander yelled again. She was already gathering her skirts to exit the studio, but just as she reached the door, Alexander caught up with her, still shoving the front of his shirt into his trousers. "Don't leave. Please. Let me explain."

Cora dropped the glass shard to the floor, where it cracked in half, and she put her hand on the door.

"Please. Don't leave," he said.

She hesitated. She had seen men together in some of the upstairs lounges Jacob frequented, finding a room for themselves in the back parlors; she had been to some of the dances in the Five Points, where certain women had unshaven chests peeking above poorly fitting bodices, their beards already grown past a clean shaving hours earlier, and the men who chose them for a dance knew full well they weren't really women. None of this had bothered Cora. *People do as they please, as they have for centuries,* Alexander had once told her, and she had heartily agreed—but he hadn't told her *this.*

"Go to my studio," Alexander ordered. "I'll be there in a moment."

Cora nodded. He deserved to be heard. She entered the studio and sat on a stool near where Alexander created some of his soft-wax sculptures. This one he was currently working on was of a man suffering from a tuberculous growth on his cheek, based on two sketches pinned to the plaster wall.

Murmurs came from the hallway. The other gentleman wore a hat low over his forehead, obscuring his face. But as he walked past the studio door, Cora's discerning eye saw that he was young. Perhaps only eighteen. He was of slight build, but wore bulky, ill-fitting clothing to make him seem larger. He didn't make eye contact, only rubbed his mouth as he passed Cora.

Alexander came and stood in the doorway. He wrestled his hand through his hair and closed his eyes.

"I am sorry you saw that," he said quietly. "I should have told you."

"There's nothing to tell. You don't owe me an apology," Cora said.

The studio was sunken into the ground, several steps down from the corridor, and Alexander sat upon the steps. "I guess you and I both have been hiding our other lives for a little while, haven't we?"

Cora nodded. She had to force a smile, because it occurred to her—she had felt like Alexander was leaving her behind to make his own family. She looked up. "How long has it been going on?"

"A few months," he said.

"Is that why you lied about how long you were in Philadelphia?" she asked as gently as she could.

"Yes," he said simply. "I came back early. Sometimes we meet here, and there's a room we get sometimes, at Madame Beck's."

"You could have told me. I would have wanted to know. I would have had you both over for supper." She tried not to frown too hard. "I'm so sorry I intruded," Cora said. "I thought he was a pickpocket! He looked like it."

"So do you, when you're Jacob," Alexander noted.

"Except I'm not picking pockets; I'm picking graves," she said, smirking. But then she sobered. It wasn't funny, and she regretted the joke immediately. "Here I am concerned about myself, and I haven't once thought about you, and your life. You worry too much about us, Alexander. We're holding you back." It was hard to keep the jealousy out of her voice. Alexander had a love in his life; Cora did not. Cora had nothing of the sort anymore.

"Nonsense," he said, waving his hand.

Cora's hand rested on her reticule. The glass shard had torn a small hole on the side, and she saw the newspaper inside. She thought of not saying anything, but Alexander worked here. He might know more about what Duncan was thinking.

"And once again, I need to talk of myself." She pulled out the penny paper and handed it to him. She pointed to the corner, where the tiny article was.

He read it with a deep frown, before going to his large fireplace and lighting a long taper. He touched it to the end of the paper, which burnt bright and quick, before dropping it into the fireplace. They watched the flames until nothing remained but curled black ash, like a shrunken, malformed ghost.

Alexander turned to her, his eyes still on the smoke wisping upward from the ash.

"I think it's time," he said slowly, "that you left New York. Forever."

CHAPTER 22

"I can't leave New York," Cora said. "Not yet."

Alexander looked at her. "Why not?"

"If we move, I only have enough money to provide for Leah and me for a week at the most. It's not enough. And I owe the Cutter family."

"I can pay for that," Alexander said.

He was offering to pay for everything. Even with his own personal life, as she'd seen.

"Two hundred fifty dollars?"

Alexander paled. "That much? I couldn't provide half that." He thumped his fist on the wall. "I should have known to keep a closer eye on Leah."

"It was her transgression, not ours," Cora reminded him. "But that's only part of the problem. The secret is out," she said, leaning over and stabbing the ashes of the newspaper with an iron poker.

"Then we can find out the sources of the rumors and eliminate them."

That sounded oddly like a threat of some kind. "What do you mean?"

"I mean," Alexander said with a measured voice, "we can convince people it isn't true. At this point, who knows? Leah, you, and me, of course. Suzette Cutter—"

"She knows I exist, but she doesn't know my hearts are real. But she's not the problem. Word has gotten out in the Five Points. Duncan's list has convinced people that this girl—me—is a prize worth killing for. Or at least, taking Jacob and me out of the business. It's too big to contain, Alexander."

"You shouldn't speak to Suzette Cutter, at least," Alexander said.

"I think she considers me family," Cora said. "I don't think she would try to harm me."

"Does it occur to you," Alexander said, "that you're another Cutter heir? That you're competition?"

Cora sputtered out a laugh. "Don't be ridiculous! They can rewrite their entailments to exclude me. I haven't been part of that family since even before I was born!"

"But if the legacy is written in such a way . . . it's possible it could be entitled in a manner that is not changeable. It happens, often enough, in the older families, and the Cutter family has a lineage going back to estates in England. And Suzette would get nothing, if she's younger than you. Is she?"

"She is only a little younger than I am, by a few months. I never thought of it," Cora admitted. "Apparently there are many things I haven't considered. I'm sorry, Alexander."

"Stop apologizing. I should have made sure the door was locked, is all. It's not every day that your family walks in on your trysts and embarrasses you utterly."

They laughed together, and the dissonance in Cora's heart abated.

"I can meet with Duncan, to find out what he really knows about this, after the article," Alexander said. He raised a single eyebrow. "And have you spoken to Theodore Flint about this?"

She fiddled with the tear in her reticule. "I'm not sure Theo and I will see each other anymore."

"Good. Keep it that way. The less you talk, the better. He's in the business, and he's not to be trusted."

Cora opened her mouth to protest, but found that she couldn't. She rose to leave, and exhaustion suddenly threaded through her limbs and weighed her down. In her mind, she was running, running, running away. Even now, so near to Alexander, she felt unsafe because only two stories up, Frederick Duncan was wishing she was dead and splayed open in an amphitheater. She shivered.

As she walked out, her dress brushed against the linen draped on a piece of unfinished work, sending it fluttering to the ground. She stooped to pick up the sheet and cover the piece, when her breath caught.

It was a miniature waxen figure, about ten inches tall, but with a noticeable crack through its middle. Wearing a Grecian robe, the figurine had black tresses that curled over its bare ivory shoulder. But the face had a Far Eastern flair to it. Rosy lips, with dark eyes drawn out just slightly to the temples.

It looked like Cora.

"What is this?" she asked coldly.

Alexander quickly snatched the linen out of her hand and draped it over the broken figure.

"I'm sorry you had to see that. It's a commission. From Duncan. He's had me work on a few pieces for his private collection, but I didn't realize until after I'd completed it that—that he—"

"It's me, isn't it?" Cora whispered.

"He didn't say so," Alexander said, looking miserable. "Not out loud. But he kept visiting and asking me to change it this way and that way. And once I realized what he'd done, I pretended I'd broken it and had to start over again." Alexander took the piece, snapped it in half where the crack had begun, and set both parts in a large cauldron that hung over the fire. "I'll melt it down now, but he's still going to want it. The last time he visited, he said, 'It doesn't have her eyes, not yet.' And I asked to whom he was referring, and he laughed. 'You should know your own family!' And then I really knew."

"It makes sense," Cora said. "He just mentioned to me that he was having you work on some personal pieces. And the way he looks at me . . ." She stared vacantly into the fire, watching the feet of the Cora statuette turn into a gooey mass against the cauldron's bottom. "Like he wants to roast me for dinner and spend eternity dining." She shook her head. "Very well. I don't need him to make myself a salary. I need not see him ever again. And if you can keep 'breaking' my likenesses, then maybe . . . maybe he'll forgo his obsession once and for all."

Alexander smiled helpfully, but there was no hope in his eyes. "Maybe."

The stretch of days that followed was a blur of tedium and frustration. Cora stayed home, afraid to even set foot in the late-September sunlight. She drank herbal tea three times a day, and meanwhile Leah watched her as if she were always on the verge of escaping. Her boys pilfered the grave of Jonathan Fuller, but they were able to sell the body for only ten dollars, as his death wasn't unusual—he was simply quite old—and his gout was sadly crippling yet ordinary. After turning down two more resurrection runs with her team (they were for pilfering ordinary bodies at Potter's Field on Fourth Avenue near Fiftieth Street, but Cora refused, as did Jacob, leaving them to handle the small sales on their own), Cora was growing increasingly restless. She rarely spent a whole day indoors, and now it had been well over a week.

She wanted to take up Suzette's offer to meet, so she sent another letter with a payment, agreeing to meet but knowing that Suzette's ability to escape her mother was the limiting impediment. That had been three days ago. When Leah came home from the grocer, she held an envelope. Cora tore it open quickly.

"What does it say?" Leah asked.

"Suzette has invited me to go with her to see a . . . Oh! It's a lecture by that woman doctor you met at Castle Garden, Dr. Blackwell! She did find a venue for her lectures. How surprising. It's in the basement of Hope Chapel."

Leah's nose flared. "What would a woman doctor lecture on?"

"'The Laws of Life with Special Reference to the Physical Education of Girls.'" Cora shrugged.

"Well, you ought to let me go with you. Or have Alexander chaperone you there."

"No doubt Suzette will have a chaperone herself," Cora said. After all these days at home, the thought of extra accompaniment felt smothering.

"I shall go, if she doesn't have a chaperone."

"Oh, Leah. If something were to happen, I'm more than capable of handling it. You could throw your butcher knife, but that won't do to carry it about in public, now would it?"

"Very well," Leah huffed.

The lecture was for the next day, late in the afternoon. Cora waited, nervous as she'd never been. She wore her second best in gray poplin with blue ruffles and embroidery, but kept fussing with the trim nervously. Leah scolded her.

"She's only a person, like you, and no better." Leah seemed still a little burnt by knowing that the Cutters considered her a dishonest maid who deserved a scolding, or worse, to be let go. But Cora had forgiven her. Mistakes are common as pigs, and Cora had to give Leah allowances for being weak minded at times.

At the sound of the small brass knocker against the front door, Leah opened it to find a servant whose hair was grizzled with gray. He bowed and asked for Miss Lee. Suzette waved her arm through the window of a fine barouche on the street.

"I shall be back before supper," Cora told Leah.

"Be careful," Leah said.

Suzette nodded to Leah, but her smile for Cora had vanished at the sight of the maid. The door closed behind them.

"I am surprised you haven't dismissed her," Suzette said as Cora was helped into the Cutters' stylish barouche, with two matching Morgan horses calmly waiting.

"She's like family. She's known me since I was a child. I have to forgive her."

"I see," Suzette said. They said nothing more for a few minutes. Suzette was rearranging some mussed curls against her cheek. Her dress, a beautiful tiered green-and-black silk, took over the whole inside of the barouche.

"So, are you to be married soon?" Cora said.

Suzette blushed and put her hands in her lap. "Why on earth would you ask that?"

"You're speaking to me, first of all. And we're going to a lecture by the only lady doctor on this entire continent," Cora said, trying to hide a smile. "They're the actions of a woman who shall soon have her own castle and a husband consuming her time."

"Oh."

"Also, you're wearing a new ring," Cora said.

They looked at Suzette's ungloved hand. It was true. She wore a new gold ring on her fourth finger, in the shape of a snake with a rose-cut ruby in the serpent's head.

"I did get engaged. Only just a few days ago." Suzette didn't smile. "Daniel says that Queen Victoria had an engagement ring just like this, only with an emerald."

"Daniel Schermerhorn?"

She nodded. He was everything Cora wasn't—wealthy, powerful, connected to all the uppertens worth knowing.

"Do you love him?" she asked.

"That's a very forward question," Suzette snapped. She covered her mouth. "Oh. Mother says I ought not to speak my mind like that. I apologize."

"It's all right. I've a habit of speaking my mind as well." Cora smiled.

Suzette relaxed a little. "Well, Mother says love happens eventually. Though I wish I could just marry a companion. I've a friend, Anne White, whom I've known for ever so long. You'll meet her someday. Ladies spend more time with friends than husbands anyway!" She suddenly blushed hard at her words, and waved a hand away. "As for Daniel, well. He's not terribly happy about marrying me, I suppose. Your existence has changed things quite a bit."

"Indeed?" Cora asked, her second heart thumping in parallel to her other.

"You do realize that half my inheritance is yours? Which means that Daniel's family is a little upset at the news. The smaller inheritance has diminished my consequence, I suppose." She put her hand on Cora's arm. "Please don't think I'm upset. I'm rather happier that you're around. Being the only young Cutter in the family, it's . . . it's something. They spend more time worrying after you now, and that's honestly a relief."

"They worry about me?" Cora asked. "What do they say?"

"Oh, they talk about your maid, and how terrible that was—you'd be surprised how many times they can repeat this fact for entertainment." She frowned. "They worry that you'll enter society and make things difficult for the family."

"Difficult," Cora said, cringing at the word. "Do they know you were going to see me today?" Cora said.

Peter coughed and leaned forward to maneuver the reins in his hands. Suzette drew closer. "I told my mother I needed to see about some gloves and a new pelisse before the weather turns colder. She will let me go to a shop or two by myself, as long as old Peter keeps close by."

"Your secret is safe with me," Cora said. "Speaking of secrets . . . or rather, of nonexistent ones . . . may I ask a favor?"

"I suppose so," Suzette said. "What is it?"

"I would be grateful if you and your mother never mentioned anything about Dr. Grier, or the lies about my hearts, to Daniel, or to anyone. As I have said before, it's all untrue."

"Why?" Suzette's eyes were wide open and unseeing.

"Have you ever been to Barnum's American Museum?" Cora asked.

"Oh yes. It's incredible! And the Grand Anatomical Museum. I saw you there one day."

"You remember the anatomical subjects, then."

"Of course. But they were all waxen, or drawings. Daniel thought they were barbaric, but I confess, I thought them extraordinary, and rather dramatic."

"Well, I'm not extraordinary, Suzette," she said, lying easily. "But someone might think those rumors Dr. Grier spread are true and wish my body on display on a shelf in the museum."

Suzette actually laughed, before she frowned. "You're not in jest? You can't possibly mean . . . They wouldn't . . ."

"They would, Suzette. It has happened to others. The museums are very lucrative. They're always looking for new displays to bring in more money."

"Oh." Suzette covered her mouth with her fingertips. "Oh!" She looked at Cora. Her eyes shone, as if dawn had alighted on her irises. "How horrifying! It's just like from a story!"

"I can see why you love those books of yours at your home. Like *The Mysteries of Udolpho*?"

Suzette blushed. "Mother is always furious with me for reading them. But I suppose it puts me in a good position to help you. I'm not afraid of such things—skeletons and dark castles. Secrets. I'll keep yours; you don't have to worry."

The barouche stopped in front of 718 Broadway, where the very plain and forgettable Hope Church sat tightly between a hat shop and a grocer. Suzette and Cora were helped off the barouche, and they purchased tickets for two dollars inside the doorway from a sober-looking old man. Cora tried not to balk at the price. Down in the basement, about ten women were clustered in groups of wooden chairs set up in the small room.

Dr. Blackwell soon emerged from a side door and began her lecture. The ladies were rapt and listened to her thoughts on healthful diets and exercise. For the entire hour, Cora thought to herself, I could do this. And even charge two dollars a ticket. She just made twenty-four dollars! The same as Cora's profits from one good resurrection. Before she could give it more consideration, the lecture was over. Dr. Blackwell saw Suzette and Cora, and waved them over.

"What a delight to see you both!" She turned to Suzette. "You're the only ladies here who aren't friends of Dr. Warrington, a very kind gentleman who has always encouraged my career."

"A male doctor approves of your career?" Suzette said. "That is impressive, indeed."

Dr. Blackwell smiled, and her pink cheeks were merry against her plainer, dark dress. "Yes, it is. And here I am, despite Mr. Duncan turning me away from his own establishment. There is a lesson there, somewhere, do you not think, Miss Lee?"

Cora smiled only a little. "There are lessons everywhere, Dr. Blackwell. Whether we choose to listen to them depends on our own good sense."

"Is that Aristotle?"

"No, it's Cora Lee." She smiled. "Thank you for the lecture, Dr. Blackwell."

Outside, Peter waited by the barouche. The ladies from the lecture exited the church, in their Quaker-style dark dresses. The fading twilight made the plain white fichus about their necks look like flying birds.

"Oh, let's walk back. I want the evening to last a little longer. That lecture went by too quickly," Suzette said.

"That sounds lovely," Cora said. "But what about your driver?"

"Peter, follow us from a distance," she ordered. "That will satisfy Mother, I'm sure," she said. Peter touched his cap and went up into the barouche to follow at a slow pace.

Suzette hooked her arm into Cora's, and they strolled along the sidewalk. It was an odd feeling, walking arm in arm with a lady, with family. Even with Charlotte alive, Cora never had the opportunity. She'd dressed as Jacob until her body began to change. On their few outings dressed as a young lady, Cora had stood in discomfort and awe of her beautiful aunt, who was busy scanning faces for untoward glances at her niece.

What would Charlotte think, Cora wondered, if she knew I was walking with the very family that had cast her off? She wondered if Charlotte would think it was smart, or a betrayal, or just dangerous. Charlotte would say, Be on your guard, Cora. At all times.

Always. Because they will come for you, when given the chance.

"Oh! Look at that ribbon! I've wanted it for so long. The perfect grosgrain, in that shade of green. Look, Cora!"

Cora looked in the window, and smiled, but ribbons were never anything she cared for. Leah fussed over how many tucks were in her dress, or whether the trimming was rich enough, but not too rich to gather too much attention. The store owner was locking the door, when he saw Suzette, and he offered to reopen if she wished to look. She turned around to make eye contact with Peter—goodness, she couldn't even cough without a chaperone's approval—and stepped inside the store.

"Come, Cora! I'll only be a moment. I've wanted to trim my hat with this color for ages."

"I'll stay here," Cora said, smiling. "I like the cool air."

"But look! They're so beautiful! Just a minute!"

Cora laughed and shook her head. "I'll wait here for you. Take as much time as you wish."

She heard Suzette point out several different ribbons, and through the window, Cora could see her perusing the shades of emerald.

She turned to watch the passersby while she waited, and saw a man across the street staring at her. He was medium height, with brown hair and brown clothes and a stovepipe hat. Unlike the others on the street, pausing by the shop fronts, he stared at her, only her. She quickly looked away, walked a few steps southward away from the store to the front of a glove shop, and looked again.

He had matched her steps and walked a parallel ten steps just as she had.

Surely, he couldn't be following her. She looked up the street, and back. There were no other women walking alone, only Cora. A group of men, boisterously arguing over the Whigs' most recent split at the Syracuse convention, strolled just ahead. Cora matched steps with them, hiding slightly behind their mass for another street, until they turned the corner and left her behind.

And still, the stranger was across the street.

Not again. She couldn't endure another attack. Suzette was so close by, and Cora was unarmed. She would go back to the barouche and stay with Peter by the shop, and likely her pursuer would retreat. She turned and hurried back to the store, but found the owner closing it yet again.

The barouche was gone, and so was Suzette.

"Suzette!" Cora called out. "Suzette!" She looked uptown and saw from a distance that the barouche had left without her and was turning the corner at Twelfth Street. Suzette must have thought that she had grown weary of waiting, and knowing how close Cora's home was, left on her own.

Cora looked to the other side of the street. The man was now crossing toward her, dashing ahead of oncoming wagons and carriages. In seconds, he'd be across Broadway.

He was coming for her.

CHAPTER 23

Doing the only thing that made sense, Cora began to walk as quickly as possible uptown. If she stayed amongst the men and women on the sidewalk, she would be safe. In only ten minutes, she could be home, behind a locked door.

She saw no watchman nearby to call to for help. No policeman either. She turned to see whether the man was still following, but she saw only ordinary pedestrians chattering about supper or the upcoming evening's festivities . . . There. A glimpse of a dirty brown shirt and—

"Cora!"

It was Suzette, her head poking out of the closed barouche, coming down the other side of Broadway. Peter yanked on the horses' reins to bring them to a halt.

Cora paused to scan the crowds again.

The man was gone.

"Suzette!" Cora smiled, but Suzette's matching smile was quickly replaced by concern.

"Are you all right? You look positively white. I thought you'd left and we circled the block looking for you and . . . Goodness, are you ill?"

Cora waved her concern away, and several passersby made room for her to cross to the barouche.

"A little indigestion," Cora said simply. "But I'm fine now."

"Are you sure? Should we call for a doctor?" The words tumbled out so quickly that Suzette could hardly catch her breath. Oddly, she looked lit from within, as if this were the most exciting thing to happen to her in ages. "You look a fright. We'll bring you home immediately. You mustn't run off like that again!"

No, thought Cora. I can't run.

She couldn't run away. Because as long as she dared to live, she was either competition or she was a prize. Looking at Suzette, whose worries amounted to finding the right color of ribbon and trembling over the vicissitudes of normal life, Cora felt impossibly far away. All her life, she'd been at a distance to normalcy. She didn't realize how exhausted she was.

She had to put an end to this, to the running, to the distance that separated her from the living. Unfortunately, that meant speaking to Theo again.

CHAPTER 24

Leah was in a state when Cora came home, her complexion pale and her hands shaking.

"I'm all right," Cora said as Leah fussed, helping her remove her gown and wig.

"You're not all right. That was too close. From now on, you ought only to go out as Jacob. I can tell people that Cora is ill."

"That won't work. People suspect that Jacob has been killing people for our business. He's a target because that terrible list of Duncan's has convinced every mug and looby in the Five Points he can make five hundred dollars digging up graves."

Leah stopped gathering up Cora's petticoats and dress. Cora stood in her muslin underclothes, attending to her wig, which needed some grooming.

"What?" Leah said. "They think you and Jacob are burking victims?"

"Yes. Even Dr. Henrickson mentioned it in a letter. And that fellow who attacked me." The idea still made Cora queasy. She was no murderess and never could be. She held her stomach, just thinking about it.

"Are you well, Cora?" Leah watched her suspiciously.

"I am." She straightened up and made herself look well.

"I'll make your tea and draw you a bath."

"No. I don't need a bath. I'm going out. As Jacob. I need to find Theodore Flint."

"Flint! Why?"

"Never mind why. I need to speak to him."

"But after what you said about Jacob? It's not safe. You shouldn't."

"I must. The center of all of this is the rumors about me. Dr. Grier may be gone, but as long as his diaries are out there, his voice is louder than mine, and I can't speak. Theo will tell me if Duncan's added any more details to the rumors."

"That old pickle Duncan won't tell the truth," Leah reasoned.

"He may not tell Theo he stole the diaries, but he might reveal details—for example, if Dr. Grier wrote down Charlotte's name, or my mother's. Those details can be traced to me, and Jacob."

Leah stood by the door, as if waiting for Cora to change her mind. But seeing Cora pulling on a grubby pair of trousers and one of her stained shirts, Leah sighed and closed the door.

Cora had heard that sigh so many times before. The sigh of knowing that Cora would do as Cora wanted. That this was not the life that Cora was meant to live, all these years after her infant voice protested the cruelty of winter's cold, and she lustily breathed her first breaths in defiance of everyone who wished she didn't exist.

—◆—

Cora, dressed as her brother, waited across the street from Flint's boardinghouse and watched the yellow glow of his room window. There was a gauzy curtain drawn there, and she could see a single shadow pass back and forth. Not two, which gave some comfort.

Not that she cared. Anything between the two of them had long since left. He hadn't tried to contact her, nor had she sent him any messages. A match had been lit after their argument, and any gentle feeling left was now in cinders.

The light in Flint's room winked out, and Cora took a breath, receding into the shadow of the building's corner. Flint exited his boardinghouse, looked up and down Broadway, and then began walking briskly downtown. The gaslights hissed at Cora as she passed by each iron light, following Flint from fifty paces behind him. The only women to be seen were enticing customers into the gambling houses and rum cellars.

Flint paused at Grand Street, and entered Madame Mary Beck's house, an establishment that Cora knew from her evenings dressed as Jacob. Cora tipped her hat forward a little to cover her eyes, and stepped into the doorway. Piano music played by a well-dressed black man filled the air, and luxe furniture filled the room. Drinks were served by the fine-looking ladies of the house, who swarmed over patrons and invited them to private rooms upstairs. Inside, Cora was offered a drink and accepted, waving away the few girls who approached Jacob, their scarlet stockings showing above brightly laced boots decorated with tassels and bells.

Flint was not in the front room, so Cora carefully slid into the next room and pretended to be interested in a dice game by the back wall. Out of the corner of her eye, she saw him. Flint was in a far corner, hardly noticing the mabs with their corsets tight on their ribs beneath their bare breasts. The women ran their fingers along his shoulders, tweaking his hat, and offering him more of the same if he'd only pay for an upstairs room for several dollars. But he wasn't paying attention to any of them. He was talking heatedly with a man sitting on a chair, surrounded by women plying him with icing-covered cakes and liquor.

It was Duncan.

They talked quietly, so Cora couldn't hear a word, but Flint seemed perturbed, and Duncan placid. A staircase curled around this scene, rising to a second story filled with room after room that issued the same odor—of stinking sweat, the sticky leftovers of couplings, opium smoke, spilled liquor, and cheap perfumes. Flint and Duncan simultaneously turned their heads to watch a woman descend the steps.

The girl looked like Cora's twin.

She wasn't, of course. But she had the same build, breadth, and height. Her eyes were carefully smudged with kohl to make them appear more narrow and drawn out, like Cora's. She wore a very obvious wig that matched Cora's color exactly, and some carefully applied makeup had darkened her eyebrows to match.

Flint's mouth dropped open a touch, and his mind suddenly seemed devoid of sense. Duncan, however, grinned.

"There she is! Come here, come here. I've a lap for you, and more if you'd like."

The Cora look-alike shook her head. Duncan reached for her hand, and before she could escape, he captured it and drew her closer. She smiled—a terribly fake smile; her teeth were more crooked than Cora's—and turned her head away, to avoid his hoary breath on her neck. After a few murmurings, she was released, and she walked to the bar near to where Cora stood watching the dice game. Flint was watching her too, and Cora had to turn her back so as not to be noticed.

"Duncan wants more brandy," the look-alike told the barmaid, who reached behind her to open a new bottle.

"He's paying well tonight. Keep it going," the barmaid said, grimacing. "Swine. He's keeping the ladies away from other paying customers."

"Can I speak to you? I'll pay you for your time," Cora said suddenly, moving to her side.

The look-alike wouldn't even meet her eye. She kept those brown irises on filling the brandy glass in front of her.

"Talk? Well, well," the barmaid said. "Audrey is occupied. Try another."

"I want her," Cora said, keeping her voice low. "Audrey." She kept her head down, afraid that her doppelgänger might recognize her disguise, though they'd never met. She dug into her pocket and let the coins click invitingly.

"No," the look-alike said without smiling. She eyeballed Cora head to toe. "I only have one patron, and he's particular about what I do, and who I do it with." She looked over her shoulder to where Duncan and Flint were still talking closely. "Only one."

"Aye, he pays her well to be a lady bird." The barmaid winked. "Very well. We could buy the building next door if we had as many situations like hers."

"Anyway, you could be my brother; you look enough like me," Audrey said, somewhat coldly but kindly at the same time. "And I wouldn't wish to speak to my brother about my work."

Cora looked over her shoulder. Flint stood up to shake Duncan's hand, then leave. Cora ducked her head down, but this was normal behavior. Houses like this were full of dark culleys, as they were called, the ones with wives uptown who visited their mistresses in the evening and needed their business quiet and well kept.

"Hello, Audrey," Flint said from somewhere very close to the back of Cora's head.

"Hello, Teddy," Audrey said, a little too sweetly. "Not staying?"

"Not tonight. Be careful if you step out at night."

Cora heard her pat Theo's cheek affectionately. "You're sweet."

Now was the moment she should talk to him, ask him more about Duncan and the diaries. But his ease here in the bawdy house and with Duncan—it unsettled her. How many times had he spoken to Duncan and not told her? Perhaps he'd spent nights here in Madame Beck's, or other bawdy houses. He seemed too comfortable here. Maybe he'd gone behind her back on other occasions.

In a moment, Flint was gone. His familiar scent trailed behind him, and for a second, Cora was strangely homesick. She wished she could be back in his room, away from Leah, away from the cemeteries, Theo's hand casually on her ribs and not caring at all what beat beneath them.

But then Duncan's voice called out loudly again for his brandy, and she shed all thoughts of Flint.

The look-alike took two glasses of brandy back to Duncan, who sipped his and tried to paw the girl at the same time, but she whispered in his ear and soon went back upstairs. Duncan did not follow her, but then again, he still had a wealth of unfinished food before him. Cora drained the last drops of rum, ordered another, and steeled herself. Her internal argument told her she would not need Flint as a go-between. She walked over to Duncan's table.

"I'm Jacob Lee. Cora's brother," she said rather abruptly and rudely, but she was Jacob, after all.

Duncan squinted at Cora-as-Jacob. "Ah, I've heard much of you. What a sister! What figure! You look like twins, almost. I see you're a man of good tastes. Madame Beck has the most beautiful girls, and certainly the most obliging."

"Anyone is obliging, for the right price," Cora said evenly. A girl nearby approached, and began rubbing her breasts against Cora's shoulder. Cora gently pushed her away. In the corner, two men were cozily sitting with their arms about each other, chatting over tumblers of whiskey. A twinge of jealousy plucked at Cora, seeing their warmth and closeness. She looked away, back at Duncan. "I'm to have a word with Mr. Duncan, if you please. Buy yourself a drink," she said, and handed the girl a few coins. She kissed Cora on the cheek and turned away. Cora wiped her cheek discreetly.

"Ah, so you're not so hungered by the servings here, are you?" Duncan observed, sipping his brandy. His right hand was comfortably situated over the breast of a flame-haired mab on his right knee.

"I'm more hungered by a penny earned, Duncan, as you are." She sipped her drink. "What did Flint want?"

"Nothing that concerns you," he said. He smiled instead at someone past his head and waved. "Look at that beauty!"

Cora ignored his attempt to distract her. "I read about the two-hearted girl in the paper. Is it true? You have a bead on this girl?"

Duncan sat back a little and sighed. "Well, I've a bead, all right, but the target keeps moving." He spoke to the redheaded girl. "A plate of oysters, fried. And be generous with the pepper." She got up, and he smacked her bottom as she left. Duncan leaned in closer to Jacob. "If you know anything, I'll pay for that information. And I'll pay more if you bring her in."

Cora threaded her fingers together, knuckles appropriately stained. "As I'm sure Flint said he would."

Duncan shrugged. "Flint has a keen interest in that prize. He seemed even keener to find out who else is competing. This call for specimens was the best idea I've ever had. It's not up to me how it happens, but it shall happen."

Cora pointed her finger at the floor. "You put up five hundred, and you're asking for that girl to be murdered before her time."

"I'm not asking any such thing," Duncan said coldly. "It's a museum, boy. Not a gallows. I don't fund killing, and I never have." He said the last words loud enough for half the room to hear. "And I'll say the same to the watchmen, if they ask me. I don't wish to make the Tombs my home, and I won't wish to replace my armchair for a cold one in Sing Sing. I'm a businessman, that's all."

Cora tried not to smile. "So, you don't know who she is? Who her relatives are?"

"No," Duncan said, and he seemed rather perturbed by the admission.

"And Flint? Does he pretend to know? Because I've heard many a boast from him that means naught."

"As have I. He's a young cuss who wants in on the game. He says he's searching for the items on my list. Didn't have any, but I can read a face. He was fairly bursting with a secret. If I flatter him enough, he'll tell me all about it. I've seen it happen, time and time again."

Cora swallowed, trying to look nonchalant, but she believed Duncan. Flint was a breath away from telling her secret, or cashing his chips. "And what do you know of the girl?"

"So many questions. Let me ask you one. Do you know her?" Duncan said. He smoothed his mustache downward.

"No," Cora said flatly.

"And that lovely sister of yours?"

"She doesn't know either."

"Are you so sure? She seems to know an awful lot about all the strangest cases in town. I heard she talks to the fine doctors of this island and searches for the best bodies."

"That she does. Like a clerk for the reaper himself." There was a time when she'd be proud to boast, but it gave her no pleasure any longer. She would be out of the game soon. Very soon.

Duncan smiled. "She's clever, she is."

"Yes. Too clever for you," Cora said, nearly growling. "You keep your eyes off my sister, or I'd be happy to pluck one of them out. Gallus Meg doesn't have a jar of pickled eyes in her establishment, but I could get her started."

The redheaded mab returned with a steaming plate of oysters, dotted with black pepper, and the scent of it caused Cora to reel with nausea.

And she froze.

Cora loved oysters, as much as all her boys did. Never before had she felt so repulsed by a fresh plate of cooked shellfish. Her hand went to her stomach, and she thought to herself:

No. Oh no.

It can't be.

Involuntarily, she closed her eyes.

"Smells that good, eh?" Duncan said, himself closing his eyes and sniffing the platter. He took a two-tined fork and skewered two in a row, like jiggly beads on a string, and stuffed them into his mouth. The oyster juice dripped off his beard, and Cora felt bile rising onto the back of her tongue. She stood abruptly.

"I've got work," she said hastily.

Duncan wiped his mouth with a handkerchief, before standing and pulling Cora's collar, closing the distance between them.

He whispered, "Listen. I've had an offer. Someone who knows they can get close enough to the girl to poison her, maybe smother her, in a way that her body would still be in pristine shape for a public dissection. I did not respond. I'll not be linked to such a person, but . . . it could happen. If not me, someone else will pay. And if she dies, I want her." Duncan's hot, briny oyster breath washed over Cora, and she tried hard not to gag. But something about his words didn't seem fervently innocent enough. They came too easily, as if he were prepared to have the right things to say—*I'll not be linked to such a person. It's a museum, not a gallows.*

"Aye. I understand. And who's offering?" she asked.

"I don't know. I've received two such letters, and it was enough to make me wonder if it will happen soon."

"You know it will happen soon," Cora pressed him.

"I do not. But if it isn't real—" He corrected himself. "If she isn't real—and it is rather unlikely she is—I'll make her. I'll have your uncle make me a fine wax figure, or have Flint sew together two hearts in a pretty corpse. It ought to be easy enough to fool the public. But she'll need to be young, and pretty at that. A striking beauty would be best."

Cora nodded, and tried to pull away. She was ready to leave Duncan and his oysters and the half-drunk tumblers of brandy, whose scent seemed to resemble spoiled fruit rather than fine spirits. Duncan wasn't quite ready to let her leave, however. He pinched her collar tighter and drew her closer for a final word.

"I like you, Jacob. And your sister. You feel like family to me."

Cora could smell his sweat, his breath, his mustache wax. Nausea rose again, and she concealed her discomfort with a raised eyebrow. He smiled and released Cora's collar. She gratefully inhaled air that didn't stink of Frederick Duncan. The women had regathered around him and were vulturing about the plate of oysters.

"I'd give this all up for a good woman," Duncan said, waving his arm about.

"You have a good woman. You're married," Cora reminded him.

Duncan sat and refilled his tumbler. "She's tired of me, and my bed, since the children were born. If she wanted, I'd give her a divorce and a fine retirement upstate. I could do with a fresher partner in life. One who understood my business, perhaps added to it." He leaned back. "Consider it, Jacob. I could care for your sister. I could give her a life that wasn't about bargaining over the dead. She could live with the living. She could be with me."

"I'll consider it," Cora said, because she needed to end the conversation so she could bolt out of the bawdy house. Duncan shook her hand, and Cora simply nodded and left. Out of the corner of her eye, she saw Audrey watching from the top of the stairs.

As soon as she rounded the corner outside of Madame Beck's, Cora ran to the gutter and pitched forth her stomach's contents, then wiped her mouth with the back of her hand.

It wasn't Duncan that had made her sick. Duncan, his greed for her two hearts, and his horrendous and philandering offer of marriage were suddenly the least of her worries.

Cora was with child; she was certain of it.

CHAPTER 25

When Cora reached home, the house was dark. She quietly unlocked the door and crept inside, so as not to wake Leah. Upstairs, Leah murmured in her sleep. Cora removed Jacob's hat, unbuttoned her shirt and slipped a hand against her chest, then untightened the garment that bound her breasts. She threw the fabric to the floor and rubbed off the darkening makeup on her face.

Cora lit a tallow candle, then went into the kitchen and found the crock that contained the herbal tea. She sniffed it deeply, then went to the tin that contained the regular tea.

She sniffed it.

They were identical.

Both were tea, though the herbal container still had trace scents of pennyroyal and Queen Anne's lace. Leah was still adulterating her medicine, even after being confronted about it. And now Cora faced the consequences.

In the silence and darkness, she wished for Charlotte. If she were here, there would be advice and comfort, and even forgiveness for her mistakes. There would be a shake of the head and a laugh over committing what other Cutter women had been brash enough to do. She'd followed her hearts, her faulty hearts, and fallen for a man when it was the last thing she ought to have done.

Cora slid down against the cabinet and encircled her knees with her hands. She would not cry. There was no room for weeping, though she ached for release. She had allowed this tiny flame of life to be lit inside her belly, and now it would be extinguished before it had even begun, if she couldn't outrun the shadows clawing after her.

Theo—Flint—had been asking Duncan about the girl. But Duncan himself didn't even seem to know if she was real, and meanwhile he was receiving offers for her death. Requesting it, demanding it. Who would do such a thing? Dr. Wood, who was building his anatomical cabinet? No, it couldn't be. He was in competition with Duncan. He wouldn't be asking for help with killing her.

Upstairs, Leah's voice grew louder all of a sudden. She must be having a nightmare, as she occasionally did. But this was different. She seemed to be arguing with herself.

Cora narrowed her eyes and moved to the door to listen more carefully. No; Leah was arguing with someone. Cora grabbed a knife from the kitchen. The front door had been locked when she came home, but she had no idea whether the back door had been broken through. Thieves were not above going northward to the wealthier neighborhoods, and one of the homes nearby had been robbed of its silver last week.

Cora didn't hesitate, didn't bother with the candle, just ran up the stairs, two at a time, and threw her shoulder against the door as she turned the knob.

Inside, Leah was fully dressed, complete with travel cloak and a brand-new carpetbag Cora had never seen. On seeing Cora, she dropped the bag to the floor in astonishment. But what was more astonishing was Theodore Flint standing at the foot of her bed, his hand fisted with several sheets of paper.

"Cora!" Theo said.

We are with child, you and I.

It was the first thought that crashed through her mind, but she bit her tongue.

"What are you doing here?" Cora asked coldly. And then to Leah: "Why on earth are you dressed for travel, Leah? Where are we going?"

"It's Leah," Theo said, taking the papers in his hand and slamming them down on the woolen bedcovers. "She's the one. She's been asking Duncan, and my professor, Dr. Wood, for a bidder to kill you. She's been shopping you around like a side of beef."

Cora's stomach churned, and she felt her head go light like tissue paper in a fireplace. She bore down, forcing herself not to get more light-headed.

"What are you talking about?" Cora asked.

"These. Dr. Wood gave me these letters he'd received. Leah admitted they were from her. They asked for a minimum bid of five hundred dollars for your body, delivered to the university. She was going to up the bid to seven hundred dollars if you became with child."

Leah stood motionless, just clutching her hands together. Her face was stone, not sad, not guilty, not giddy at the relief of revealing herself.

"We ought to leave," Leah said, somewhat hoarsely. "Because this man—" She pointed to Theo. "This man is threatenin' to kill us both! I was hurrying to pack your bags, and he came at me, waving these letters, like a madman."

"Leah. You've continued to change out my herbal medicines. I've noticed" was all Cora seemed able to say at the moment.

"Because I thought it would help yeh get married!" She brought her hands to her face, digging her fingers into her eyes, as she did when she was tearful. "I wanted yeh to stop your job. I thought this . . . this man, he'd make a good husband. And I'd get more brass, in a regular way. But he wants you dead, Cora! He's got the arsenic in his room. He tol' me. He wants me to help, because he cannot do it himself."

Cora looked at Theo, whose face was livid.

"She is lying, Cora. The letters are hers. Don't you recognize her handwriting?" He thrust the papers into her hands.

Cora took the letters. She read a line.

> . . . *And I wuld like a sum of five hundred dollars for payment if the body be delivered* . . .

Cora frowned. Leah always misspelled the word *would*. Also, Cora recognized the paper from the portable writing desk in Leah's room, and the words sounded like Leah's spoken ones.

"Oh, Leah." Cora let the letters fall to the floor. "Leah. How could you?"

Leah hadn't moved. She looked at Theo, then Cora, the despair in her face disappearing rather quickly, replaced by a stubborn expression. But Theo stayed resolutely silent, and Cora did too. Leah always spoke in a silence, as if quietness were too painful to endure.

"How could I?" she finally blurted out. "The doctor said yeh wouldn't live this long. He said you should've died years ago. All I've ever done is patiently wait. But you never make enough money, not enough for this life. Everything I've put into yeh, I ought to get something back. What do they call it, those mutual—what is it called? In that grand building on Wall Street. Life insurance. Back pay, for what I'm owed."

"Owed? Owed?" Cora could barely stutter the words out. "If we hadn't paid you enough, then you should have left me and Charlotte!"

"I loved Charlotte, as if she were my own! But she said that you'd take care of me, and the money would come steady-like, with your work. But it weren't never enough. Why else might I work for a mongrel?"

"I am not a dog, for God's sake!" Cora hissed.

But Leah didn't hear her. "That cousin of yours would have kept paying, if she hadn't talked to yeh. 'Twas all ruined." She wiped her mouth with her sleeve, because she'd been spitting out her words. "And if you'd had a babe in your belly, I'd have made an extra two hundred. That's what the university doctor told me."

Cora stared at her, the words seeming as if they'd been spoken by someone else. Leah—her Leah—had been prepping her for a slaughter all this time. Her Leah had never cared for her. She'd cared for her body, and those two lumps of throbbing meat in her chest. She had been a job, from the day she was born. She thought back to moments when Leah tenderly cooked and fed her gruel when she had the grippe, or sewed a beautiful new gown for her. Every single moment, false.

"Leah, please tell me you didn't reveal my name."

Leah said nothing.

Her silence was worse than a brickbat hurled at her face. Cora folded the letters carefully, and put them on Leah's bed.

"I thought you wanted me to marry him," she said, unable to say Theo's name.

"Aye, so you'd get pregnant and fetch a good price."

Theo was dumbstruck, as was Cora. She couldn't move a limb.

"Get out," Cora whispered, not looking up. When Leah hadn't moved, she raised her face, her eyes feeling like she'd dropped thistles beneath her lids. "Get out," she seethed, trying not to scream.

Picking up her carpetbag, Leah lifted her chin and pushed her shoulders back. She walked to the bedroom door. Without turning around, she said, "He offered to kill yeh, you know. Your Dr. Flint, here. He was ready to sell yeh off, neat as can be. He made a whore out of you and planned to skin you alive. You ask him!"

Cora heard her footsteps going down the stairs. The bedroom door shuddered with the draft from the force of the slamming front door.

Leah was gone.

"She's lying," Theo said, his face reddening.

Cora said nothing.

"She's lied to you before, hasn't she?" Theo said. He drew closer to Cora, but she flinched at his proximity.

"Did you talk to her about wanting to kill me?" Cora said.

Theo sighed. "I did. But it was only to bait her. I suspected she was trying. She'd said things to me before that I couldn't understand, that one time I brought you home after you'd fainted. How you would be good for my career, one way or another. I thought she meant marriage. And then I realized maybe she didn't. I had to find out . . ."

"Who else did you tell about me, Theo?" Cora turned around and looked at him. He looked different than the quiet, cold, and confident Flint at the bawdy house with Frederick Duncan. He looked directionless.

"I didn't tell Duncan," Theo said.

"That isn't what I asked. Who else did you tell?"

Theo sighed, and this time he sat on the chair by the door. "I told Professor Wood and Professor Draper. I asked if it was truly possible for someone like you to exist, but I didn't say your name, or who you were. And they both said no, it wasn't possible."

Cora shook her head. "But you had more to tell them, didn't you? Didn't you? You couldn't help but say what you knew. That you felt two hearts in my chest. You examined me when I was asleep, didn't you?"

"It wasn't on purpose. But—"

"But you told them! Oh God, and Leah told them my name!"

Theo sighed again. "I did. But I swear, I never told Duncan. He doesn't know who you are."

"It doesn't matter. Everyone is looking for me. Between Leah and you, and Dr. Grier . . . the rumor is larger than the both of us. A woman with two hearts, with one Chinese parent. It's only a matter of time before someone takes me, like they took the girl with the tail. And the tall man. They're coming for me, Theo." She started pacing the room, like a trapped thing. "And you told them I was real. You promised you wouldn't tell anyone. And you even told Leah you would kill me? With arsenic?"

Cora held her belly—a reflexive gesture that Theo wouldn't understand. What if this child had two hearts too? Her problems would start all over again. They would find her and her child in Philadelphia. They would find them in Virginia. There would be no end to her fear.

Unless . . . there was no more rumor to be afraid of.

Unless there was no more Cora.

"You need to leave," she said. "Now."

"Cora, I'm sorry! I only said these things to draw out Leah. To make her tell the truth. And I have found the truth. And Leah's gone now! It's over."

"It's not over. I've been followed, and Jacob has been attacked—because of me. It's never going to be over, until I'm dead." She went to the door to open it. "You have to go."

Theo stood there, fixed, while Cora's head swirled with a thousand anguished things she couldn't say. Finally, he headed for the stairs.

Mechanically, she went down after, locked the front door behind him, and then went to the window to be sure it was secured. She checked the kitchen door at the back of the building, then looked about the kitchen like a lost child, barely registering that several items—Leah's favorite cookery tools—were missing.

Oh. The crock.

Cora went to the crock above the kitchen hearth, where they kept their money. The most recent resurrections had left a pile of coins there—eagles and half eagles, dollars and half dollars. It was empty. All the money Cora had now was in her vest pocket—five dollars, forty-two cents.

For all she knew, Leah still made plans for her death. Cora looked around. This wasn't a home to her anymore. She gathered a blanket from her room, dragged it downstairs, and sat in front of the locked front door with a chair propped up under the doorknob. She wore every knife she owned—all four—and closed her eyes with her fist wrapped around the largest one.

And still, she didn't sleep.

Someone was knocking on the door.

"Jacob! Miss Cora!"

It was a child's voice. George, the neighbor boy. Cora's hand was still gripped around the knife, and she sheathed it at her waist as she pushed herself off the floor. Glancing through the window in the parlor, she saw indeed that it was George, and only George.

She opened the door a tiny sliver.

"Two letters. Have you any for me?" George asked.

"No," Cora said, her voice coarse and gravelly to match the clothes she still wore as Jacob. She fished out a few coins from her vest and handed them to the boy.

"Also, someone came by this morning. A man. He was looking through the windows."

Cora tried not to groan. It was probably Theo, looking to make amends.

"Did he have brown hair? About this tall?" She held her hand a few inches above her own head.

"No ma'am. Looked like one from those gangs. I can't remember the name. Dead Rabbits? Swamp Angels? It was odd to see one of them so far uptown. My sister and I were outside playing rounders, so he asked us who lived here."

Oh no. Please, tell me you said nothing, Cora thought.

"And what did you say?" Cora asked.

"He said he had a gift for the pretty young lady, the one with Chinese blood in her. I said that the only pretty young lady on this whole street was Miss Cora, and that she had dark hair and dark eyes. So, I said I'd take it, but he wanted to talk directly to Miss Cora. But then he cussed and went away."

No, no, no.

They were looking for her. A girl with two hearts, with the right heritage. A five-hundred-dollar prize was worth knocking on doors, to search her out. And now they'd guessed her abode.

"George, I want you to tell any strangers who come here that we've left. Because we're leaving, forever. Leah is already gone."

"Leah's gone! Where are you going?"

"Paris," Cora lied. "We have relatives in France. We're leaving on the next boat tomorrow night, and we're staying at the hotel on Eighty-Fourth Street."

"So far away?"

"Yes." She reached into her pocket and pulled out a quarter-dollar coin, a week's worth of pay for the little boy. "Here you go. Thank you for being such a good postman, George." She smiled sadly and closed the door, sitting back down on the floor after she'd relocked it.

Cora was stiff and bone weary. The night had passed wretchedly, but she had things she needed to do—speak with Alexander, for one. Much as she loathed the idea, she would have to borrow money in order to flee New York. She would have to tell Suzette that she could not pay her back, at least not for a few months until she could get settled. But these thoughts did anything but soothe her. The rumors would still follow her.

Cora opened up the envelopes George had given her. They were from two physicians, Dr. Neville and Dr. Orford. Both had patients she had been following, a gentleman who'd contracted elephantiasis after traveling in Africa, and another patient with leprosy of the face. She opened the first letter.

My Dear Miss Lee,
I have been informed recently of a rumor that you have
a cardiovascular ailment that might be of some concern.
Several physicians and I invite you, with the utmost
respect, to our amphitheater at the College of Physicians
and Surgeons for an examination. Our most preeminent
physician in our department, Dr. Willard Parker, would
waive his fee of five dollars for a thorough evaluation. I
only wish you had confided in me earlier, as I would have
discouraged the overexertion through your line of work—

Cora crumpled the letter. She went to the hearth and immediately set the letter aflame with a taper. She peeked at the other letter, and this one only gave an update on the lady with leprosy. As if her job mattered anymore. Cora's identity was out in the world. Everything that Charlotte and Alexander had done to protect her was for nothing.

There wasn't much to do here. She drank down the last of the coffee (she wondered if the little bean inside her belly liked coffee). And then she ate some stale bread from the bread crock, but it was drier than hard tack. It managed to soothe her stomach enough that she could wash up, dress in another set of clothes as Jacob, and leave through the back door.

As she walked southward, she didn't feel like Jacob anymore. He felt like a cheap costume, too transparent, and her brother's persona was no longer one she could comfortably own. Cora seemed to catch the eye of every man she passed by. With Jacob's dirty cap and stubble, she knew that she wasn't much to look at. But now that her identity was no longer a secret, it seemed like the whole world had its acid gaze on her.

She must be brutally careful with every step from here on out. Saving her coins, she eschewed the omnibus, walking as quickly as she could. But when her pace picked up, a wave of nausea came upon her, and she had to slow again. The little parasite inside her was already dictating its wishes to her, she thought ruefully, patting her stomach again.

"Not your fault for being a dictator," she murmured.

Finally reaching the museum, she surreptitiously slipped down the alley to Alexander's studio, but it was locked. She knocked, and no one answered; then she peered through the lone cellar window. There were no lights on past the storage room. Where could he be? She walked back to the sidewalk, considering checking the shops she knew he frequented. But just then, Alexander emerged from a store down the block with several wrapped parcels under his arm.

When Alexander saw Jacob, his face lit with surprise and a smile. Cora couldn't return the smile—she was too anxious to tell him everything. That she had no home. That Leah was gone. Oh, everything. She walked toward him, passing a rum shop where several drunken men and a woman were perched on upended barrels, laughing over a joke. A wagon carrying a dead horse rolled by, and children chased it, throwing stones at the head, the animal's tongue lolling over the wagon's edge. But as she dodged the crowds on the sidewalk, she stumbled against a man walking in the opposite direction.

"Jacob. Jacob Lee. That's you, init?"

Cora stepped back quickly. It was Puck. The cheese-eared resurrectionist who stole William Timothy's body and abruptly left her and the gang that night weeks ago. In the bright light of day, he was even uglier than she'd realized. His eyes were small and curranty, mouth wide with yellow teeth like a dried corncob. He was with another man, shorter, thinner, but with a sparse black beard and a missing eye. His eyelid sagged over the empty socket, the edge of his eyelashes raw and red.

"I've no business with you," Cora said roughly. "I hear you're doing fine without us." She tried to veer around them, but Puck stepped to the side and blocked her. Her pulse quickened, and suddenly she thought, *I'm with child. I can't risk a physical altercation.* Her panic made her think slightly less clearly—if she could just dash down the alleyway, she could escape. So, she moved toward the alley.

It was the wrong direction.

"A word," Puck said, and hooked Cora's arm hard, pulling her easily into the dark corridor. Cora yanked her arm free and pivoted back toward the street, but Puck threw his meaty hand out and caught Cora's cheek hard. She heard the crunch of her cheek splitting against her molars and tasted the salty tang of blood in her mouth. A hand encircled her throat, then a second. Puck was choking her, only just enough so she couldn't escape. She kicked his groin, hard, and kicked it again, but Puck simply spun her around and instead locked his elbow around Cora's throat. His hand rummaged around the inside of her jacket, finding the pockets, the small collection of money there, but after throwing the handful of coins to the ground, the meaty hand had kept rummaging.

"You like your sister, then? You got some extra thumpers in here for sale? They say a girl who looks like her'll fetch five hundred dollars. And I don't know another girl, young, with the China look about her, like yours. She must have the two hearts, eh? You're so ugly, you'll only get half that, but it's still worth it, init?"

"Let him go." Alexander stood in the entrance of the alleyway, a tall shadow that darkened the scene further. His clothing showed that he was a tradesman, and a reasonably well-to-do one. Puck thrust his chin out.

"Go on. You're not wanted here. I don't work for that museum anymore! I make my own way now."

"Release him," Alexander said. A vein throbbed at the side of his temple, and he put his parcels down. Puck tightened his stranglehold on Cora's neck, and she could feel her eyes bulge. She kept forcing her elbows backward to hit his ribs, over and over again, and then thought, You silly goose, get your knife. So, she reached for the only one within grasp, but it was gone.

"Looking for this?" the smaller man said, holding up her blade. He'd pickpocketed it when they'd bumped into her. An old, old, trick, and yet she had been too distracted to notice. Distraction was the thief's best friend, and it might be the end of her.

"I told you to release him," Alexander said. "I've already alerted the watchman."

"What? That useless old nut?" the smaller man laughed, his voice high and raspy. "He's half-drunk all the time. You'd best be off."

Alexander stepped forward, and the small man turned away, as if to ignore him and help Puck. But quickly, the small man spun back and jabbed forward with Cora's knife in hand. Alexander dodged it far more quickly than Cora would have expected. With a surprising agility, Alexander snatched a broken piece of wood leaning against the alley wall, expertly sweeping it in an upward arc and catching the man in the chin. Next, he swung it down, the stick cracking over the apex of the man's skull. As he fell, Alexander thrust the end hard into his belly. Just like that, Puck's companion was unconscious and bleeding from the mouth along the gutter.

"Release him," Alexander said again, wiping the perspiration from his forehead with his other hand.

"Old man, you should step aside," Puck said. Cora's eyes pleaded with Alexander.

Don't. Leave. Run.

But Alexander simply swished his stick leftward and down, and proceeded forward. Cora was so winded from being choked that Puck simply threw her against the wall, and her head clonked against the brick. She panted for air, coughing and rasping. Between gasps, she saw Alexander strike Puck across the shoulder—so hard that the smacking sound reverberated against the alley walls.

Puck only smiled. Alexander recoiled, and raised his stick again, and smashed it against Puck's arm. Again, Puck only smiled. Blood saturated his shirt where the stick had split the skin underneath. On the third swing, Puck caught the stick as it flew toward his face and wrenched it away. Alexander, who staggered back across the uneven landscape of the refuse-strewn alley, raised an arm to protect himself when Puck struck his right arm, then his right knee, buckling Alexander to the ground. Puck lunged forward, crushing Alexander's right forearm under his boot.

Not once did Alexander scream or yell, but one last kick to the head and he was unconscious. Cora, finally able to breathe, scrambled forward and grabbed her knife from the thin man, and held it up as Puck turned and barreled toward her. She ducked, and with an efficient movement, brought it down double fisted on Puck's booted foot.

He roared in pain, and just as he lunged downward to grab at Cora, she pushed her entire body weight onto the hilt of the knife, sinking it straight through his boot and hearing bones crack beneath the blade as she pinned his foot to the packed dirt between the cobblestones.

Puck screamed. He reached down to punch Cora in the head, and she swiftly removed another knife from her boot and sliced at his swinging arms. Red blood dripped across both his forearms.

The smaller assailant at the end of the alley began to wake up. He saw Cora and Puck, who was pinned to the ground and howling in pain.

"No more scouting, Puck. We've jammed enough for innocents!" And then he ran out of the alley and was gone.

The words brought clarity to Cora's eyes. *We've killed enough for bodies.* So, resurrecting hadn't been enough. Now she had an explanation for all the people on her ledger ending up dead before their time.

"You. You're the one who killed them, aren't you?" Cora hissed.

Puck only yelled, and Cora stood up enough to land a hard kick to Puck's chest. He fell backward, foot still tethered to the ground. The fall made him howl as the knife sliced partway through his foot. She raised her other fist, and for good measure, stabbed him in his other thigh. A fresh scream shook the alleyway.

"The blonde woman with the tail! Did you kill her?" Cora yelled at him.

Puck lay on the ground, howling at the blood gushing through the dirty leather of his boot, and the new rivulet that stained his trouser leg.

"Yes," he gasped. "They told me to use her ribbon and fix her neck tight."

"Who told you?"

"I got a message from the museum, that they'd pay to kill her. But they wanted me to leave the body by Stewart's, a gammy idea. I brought it straight to that Duncan fellow, and got paid extra."

"Who else did you kill?"

"The fellow with the berry stain on his face. Owwww—"

William Timothy.

"That's why you left our resurrection that night—you realized you'd already taken him?" Cora asked, pushing harder on the knife.

"Aye." He blubbered. "Let go of my foot! I'm sorry, Jacob, by God I'm sorry—the price on your sister's head is so big, I thought you'd be worth a try too."

"Did you give strychnine to that old woman with the neck tumor? Did you kill that fellow, Hitchcock?"

"Who? What's that? Na, I didn't!"

He looked utterly confused, so she believed him. Why some, and not all, dead at Puck's hand? Were the others only coincidence? A crowd had gathered around the entrance to the alley, and the watchman suddenly appeared, hollering for help. Cora let go of the knife, and Puck whimpered, hyperventilating like a trapped rabbit.

"This one," Cora said, running to Alexander's prone body. She cradled Alexander's unconscious head. A large welt was raised over his left eyebrow, growing even as she held him. "He's hurt badly."

"We'll take him to the dispensary; it's only a few streets away."

"Thank you."

"The coppers will need to talk to you for questioning. Did you do that?" He pointed to Puck, who was blubbering over his impaled foot.

"Yes. He tried to rob me, and my uncle here."

Just then, Alexander stirred. He looked dimly up at Cora, whose eyes were wide.

"Go away, Jacob," Alexander said. "I'll find you someday. Go far away. Now."

Cora's eyes watered as she held his head, but another wave of unconsciousness swept over him, and he sagged in her arms. She felt his pulse—it was quick and strong. He'd only swooned; he'd improve with rest and medicine.

She gently laid him down on the filthy dirt-packed alley. While the watchman's attention was elsewhere, she slipped through the crowd of onlookers.

There was no hiding anymore. There was only one way to bring this relentless chase to a satisfying, inevitable end. Cora had to die. But death wasn't a foe; it had provided for her all these years. It had whispered secrets under casket tops, and told her stories while wrapped in shrouds. There were many ways to die.

And Cora would, in fact, die—but on her own terms.

CHAPTER 26

There was only one other place to go for help. Maybe two.

Within the hour, after nearly running all the way there, Cora—with Puck's blood on her hands and still dressed as Jacob—raised the great brass knocker at Eighteenth Street.

The door opened, and the maid, clad in her proper black livery with a crisp white apron, answered. Her mouth dropped open at the sight of Cora.

"May . . . I help you?" she asked, recoiling.

"Please, I need a word with your young mistress, Miss Cutter."

The maid's eyebrows went up when Cora used her normal, feminine voice instead of Jacob's.

"And you are?"

"I am . . ." Cora cleared her throat. There was no hiding now. "I am . . . Miss Cora Lee. I've been in the most unfortunate accident—" She tried to wipe the blood off her hands, but it was dry now and too late to hide. "Please. I need to speak to her."

"Absolutely not!" The maid began to shut the door.

A voice called out from beyond the door. Suzette's voice. "Who is at the door, Jane?"

"A vagrant."

"Suzette!" Cora cried out, holding the door open before it shut completely. "It's Cora!"

"Oh!"

Cora heard a patter of slippers on polished marble, and Suzette pushed her maid out of the way. Her eyes were enormous when she saw Cora in her men's clothing, her hair dirty and shorn short.

"Goodness gracious me!" Suzette exclaimed. She simply stared, mouth agape like her maid's, for quite some time. "Why are you dressed in such a fashion?"

"It's a story," Cora said. "A very long one. I have to leave New York, but I need your help."

"Is that . . . blood?"

"Yes, but it's not mine." Cora realized too late that her comment didn't improve the situation at all.

Suzette waved away the maid, hissing a quick warning, "Don't you dare tell Mother or I'll have you out of this house quicker than you can blink"; then she ushered Cora inside. Suzette brought her into the drawing room, and sat her down. She ordered tea and food, but Cora could barely eat.

"Thank goodness Mother isn't home. Why on earth are you wearing men's clothing? What happened to your hair?" She was an equal mix of shock and excitement as she reached over and touched the shorn hair that lay flat and sweaty against Cora's forehead.

"How much time do we have before your mother comes home?"

"A few hours. Mother is attending a Ladies' Aid Society meeting."

"That's what I need, then. A few hours. And a bath. And maybe . . . a dress."

"A dress!" Suzette sat back. "Well, that's the easiest part, I'll allow. Tell me everything."

So, Cora did. It was as fantastical a story as could be imagined, except that it wasn't imagined. Perhaps the novels Suzette read helped temper her shock over the macabre subject matter. Suzette, to her credit, didn't leave, or turn Cora out of the mansion, but asked pointed questions here and there.

"So, it was true, all this time. About your two hearts."

"Yes," Cora said, misery drawing her mouth down. She pointed to the right side of her chest, below her breast. Her shirt was crinkled and stained there. "It's here. I feel it beating when I'm tired. And it runs fast when I run too. And there are people out there who would rather have it in a glass jar, on a shelf, than in my chest." She let her hands fall limply into her lap. "I had to lie to you, Suzette. About all of this. It was the only way to be safe. And now I need your help."

"I don't understand," Suzette said.

"I need to leave this life behind. I need to leave my name, and my body, and even that inheritance that we share. I don't want any of it."

"How?"

"Somehow, I need to make the world think that I've died. Without dying."

"That's ridiculous. Just leave town! Surely the rumors will abate."

"I would, Suzette. But look at me. I can't change the way I look. I can't presume to disappear into a city of people who know at a glance that I'm different. The rumors will spread to Boston, and Philadelphia. They'll follow me. And even if they don't, there will never be peace. So, I'm going to make my own peace, and kill this life."

Suzette stood. She paced about the parlor, her silk skirt rustling behind her as she turned and turned again. "Well. If you're going to die, why, we need to get you to a doctor, don't we?"

The suggestion made Cora stiffen with fear, until Suzette explained herself.

Yes. Of course they needed a doctor.

But first, Cora had to be subjected to a very long scrubbing in a bathtub with the help of the maid, who admonished Cora for her dirty fingernails. Afterward, Suzette gave her one of her older dresses to wear—a lovely pearl-gray silk, with pink lace and pearl buttons on the bodice and puffed sleeves—and except for being a tad long, it fit well. As for the hair, there was nothing to be done. Cora refused to go back home to get her wig, and Suzette proposed using the explanation that it had been shaved due to a fever recently—doctor's orders. Suzette found a lovely piece of white ribbon to grace her short hair and tied a bow just above her left ear. The maid exclaimed that it was *"charmant,"* and Suzette agreed, it would do.

As Suzette called for the barouche to take them out, she looked over at Cora. "Don't worry. You'll be the prettiest corpse this town has ever seen."

Cora winced. "Pretty is less important. Corpselike is more important."

"Well then, I have some excellent powder you can use, to pale your skin. And I've some other ideas as well, but first, we must go. Quickly."

As the barouche made the short trip to Fourteenth Street, Cora wondered if Alexander had been taken care of at one of the dispensaries, or even taken to the hospital at the Bellevue Establishment, or New York Hospital. When she had gotten out far enough from town, she would send a letter to let him know she was well. But her intent was not to allow Alexander to follow her. He had his own life to live; perhaps their separation was a blessing cloaked as a tragedy.

Who knew where Leah was. Likely on a stagecoach bound for gold country, or elsewhere. If all went well, she would never see Leah again. Perhaps, Cora thought, she really ought to go to Paris. Leah hated all things French, and Cora had always wished to learn more of the language. The only foreign language that Charlotte had taught her, really, was flash, and that didn't exactly count.

The barouche stopped suddenly. "Here we are," Suzette said. "I hope she's in."

Cora nodded, and they stepped out of the carriage. She had to be extra careful of her dress—it might be the last one she wore, if things didn't quite go as expected. There was no sign outside, as Dr. Blackwell had said, and so they went inside and upstairs to the second floor. The wooden floor and plainly plastered walls were scrupulously clean, and on only one of the doors was a sign:

ELIZABETH BLACKWELL, MD

Suzette and Cora looked at each other.

"You do realize," Suzette said, trying and failing to hide a grin, "that this is the most absurd thing that I have ever done, or will do. It's like I'm inside one of those novels I read all the time."

"It is like a terrible dream," Cora said, then frowned. "Though I am sad that we won't have more absurd adventures in the future."

"Perhaps not. Perhaps," Suzette said. She turned back to the door, and rapped with her knuckles. The door opened, and Dr. Blackwell appeared, in her usual plain dark dress that covered her properly from neck to wrist.

"Well! Miss Cutter! And Miss Lee! To what do I owe this visit? Goodness, what has happened to your hair, Miss Lee?"

"I'm afraid my cousin here is ill," Suzette said, and they were ushered inside. "Very ill, indeed."

"I see! Or rather, I do not. Excepting your hair, my dear—I don't see that you look ill, except that you are a touch pale."

"We have a very peculiar problem, Dr. Blackwell," Cora said as she sat down next to Suzette in front of the table where Dr. Blackwell sat. "You see, I have a physical ailment that has drawn unwanted interest. It would be easier to show you than tell you."

Dr. Blackwell folded her hands together on the table. "Very well."

She ushered Cora into another room, where Cora disrobed and put on a long white shift. On the other side of a partition, she sat on a slim table covered with clean linen. Dr. Blackwell brought out what looked like a tiny trumpet attached to a flexible tube. "It's a Golding Bird. The latest in stethoscopes."

Dr. Blackwell listened to her upper heart and both lungs, then palpated her stomach. She listened with the Golding Bird, and then examined her again. She looked at Cora's eyes, her throat, her skin, her pulses by her ankles, wrist, neck. She noticed how her hands were thick from hard work, and her neck bruised, though she didn't ask why.

"You seem normal enough, and healthy," Dr. Blackwell said finally.

"Here," Cora said, pointing. "Put your stethoscope here."

Dr. Blackwell knitted her eyebrows together, then pressed the bell-like end of the stethoscope over her right ribs. Her eyes widened, and she lifted the bell and listened again.

"It sounds like a . . ." But she wouldn't finish her sentence. She lifted her hand and raised it just above the skin of her ribs. "May I?"

Cora nodded. Dr. Blackwell laid her calm, warm, and dry fingertips over Cora's second heart. And then she listened to her hearts again, and listened some more. She had her lie down, then stand up, all the while listening.

"I don't quite know what to say. It's just beneath the rib cage. Same pulsations as your heart. I can't understand how the vasculature could support . . . There wasn't a distinct systolic and diastolic phase, but perhaps the valves are malformed. I can't imagine how the connection to the inferior vena cava would look . . . or if it's simply an accessory heart . . ."

"I can tell you, it's not just a benign accessory organ," Cora told her. "I've had a severe apoplectic attack in the past."

"At your age?" she said, surprised.

"Yes. As a child." Cora slipped off the examining table and went behind the screen to change again. Suzette helped her with her corset and to tie on her petticoats.

Once they were seated again at the table, Dr. Blackwell began writing on a piece of paper, dipping her quill.

"I should think that gentle exercise in addition to a cardiac tonic would suffice. Stagnation is your enemy, Miss Lee, so I would recommend an occasional bleeding—"

"Oh," Cora interrupted. "I don't need medicine to get better. I need medicine to get worse."

"Pardon me? I believe I misheard you." Dr. Blackwell's smile faltered.

"You know of my line of work?" Cora said.

"Yes. A shame that you should have to take up such a position."

"Well, I took the position on purpose, to know if and when I might become a very wanted specimen for the anatomical museums and cabinets in this city. And that time has come."

"Oh!" Dr. Blackwell put her pen down. "But surely, you don't mean . . . Who would ever . . ."

"I have been followed, propositioned, and attacked. Twice, now that I can admit that Jacob is me," Cora said. "And I don't know if I'll be lucky enough to survive the next assault. This is why I need your help."

"What exactly do you need?"

"I need to die, Dr. Blackwell."

———◆———

Before Cora and Suzette left, Dr. Blackwell wrote down directions for the druggist. Cora hoped the drugs would not affect the baby. But so far, she had not miscarried after her attacks. It was a strong little creature. She had decided not to tell either Dr. Blackwell or Suzette, for she couldn't take the chance that either of them would stop her plan. Her child wouldn't be born without a price on its head.

Dr. Blackwell handed over the directions and said, "I hope to see you again someday, Cora. Alive, well, and unfettered by your fear."

"One can only hope to outlive fear," Cora said.

"And one can hope to live outside the shadow of death."

Cora nodded. If she survived this, there would never be any resurrection work for her. Never again.

Suzette and Cora walked quickly to the nearest druggist's shop, only two streets away. The shelves were stacked with dark brown bottles of various sizes and shapes. Behind the counter was a wall of glass jars filled with herbs and powders. Ceramic jars were beautifully labeled with blue glaze: mumia, or ground Egyptian mummy, smelling of bitterness and earth; leeches, with air holes in the lid; opium, aloes, and nux vomica. The odor of earth and herbs and illness permeated every corner.

Cora handed the slip of paper to the elderly man behind the counter.

"Foxglove," he read out. "Hawthorn. Skullcap. Tincture of belladonna, and opium." He read the note critically and looked up at Cora. "Is this for you?"

"No, indeed. My father. He has dropsy. A weak heart," she said.

"You're not to give these to him all at once," the druggist said, his face wearing a severe expression of worry.

"I understand. He's been taking these for some time, depending on his symptoms. We didn't like Greene's Apothecary," Cora said. "They cheated us," she added, repeating an oft-heard complaint of said store.

"And that shall never happen here!" The druggist busied himself measuring out the medicines, and Suzette waited, looking nervous. To several paper packets, he added a small bottle of tincture of belladonna, another of tincture of opium, and handed the packages to Cora. Suzette slid money across the counter. And then they left.

"Where will we buy the ice?" Cora asked, entering the barouche.

"I'll send Jane out for it. There is an ice house several blocks west of our home. They deliver to us when we're making sorbet in the summer."

Back at the mansion, the maids seemed relieved that Cora hadn't somehow reverted to her bloodstained men's clothes. Suzette looked at the large clock in the foyer and frowned.

"We don't have much time. I don't know if this is going to work. Are you sure there is no other way?"

"No," Cora said.

"Can you not just go far away?" Suzette said.

"I can't. I won't have to look over my shoulder all the time, and I can make a new life for myself. I can become a maid somewhere, and maybe a governess. Or a teacher."

"Or a doctor," Suzette said, not smirking at all.

Cora sighed. New careers were for those who had the luxury of calm wonderings. "We should do this. Now. We're wasting time."

Suzette nodded but frowned. She called a maid into the salon and asked for tea.

"Leave the tea aside—we would like to steep it ourselves," she instructed her. "And order ice. Twice the usual amount."

The maid curtsied and went on her way. Within ten minutes, she had brought out a large pot of boiled water in a warmed teapot, cups, milk, sugar, and a small dish of tea leaves. When the maid went away, Suzette took the tea and wet it with a splash of water, and Cora withdrew the medicines from her reticule. She sprinkled the foxglove, hawthorn, and skullcap herbs into the steaming pot. The steeping water turned brown and smelled absolutely medicinal. Cora's nose flared over the pot.

"Well. This won't be pleasant."

Suzette poured two dark cups of the infusion, then dumped the rest out in the side of the fireplace, scooping any sign of the herbs into the fire, where the wetted clump hissed and smoked. She then added the wet tea leaves to the empty pot.

"How will they work again?" Suzette asked.

Cora sipped the first cup as quickly as the temperature allowed, grimacing as she swallowed the bitter liquid. She paused before picking up the second cup.

"The foxglove, hawthorn, and skullcap will slow my pulse. Hopefully to the point that anyone looking at my neck or touching my wrist won't feel a heartbeat." She started sipping the second cup. "The opium tincture will sedate me and slow my breathing. And the belladonna drops, you have to put into my eyes. They'll counteract the opium, which would constrict my pupils, and instead make them look large."

"Why?" Suzette asked, confused.

"People's pupils are very large when they are freshly dead," Cora said.

"I would say I'm impressed that you know these things, except they're horrid," Suzette said.

"A skill I'll be leaving behind shortly." The tea made her queasy, and for a moment, she held her belly, hoping her child wouldn't mind. She had no choice—she would be chased to the grave if she didn't do this, and they would both perish. She took the brown bottle of opium tincture and measured out the drops into her now-empty cup.

Before lifting the cup, she held her chest. Her hearts began to thump erratically. They skipped beats here and there, sped up a touch, then followed with more yawning gaps, as if a drunkard were knocking on a door while succumbing to sleep.

"I can feel the effects already," Cora said.

Suzette reached out and touched her hand. "Are you ready?"

"Yes," Cora said. "Remember, run the ice bath first. As soon as I'm in it, send all but the last letter out, and be sure your servant delivers them personally." Suzette had finished writing the letters. They were addressed to three physicians that Cora often worked with, as well as Dr. Blackwell—who promised to do the final assessment and keep the other doctors from touching her body beyond the very minimum. There were also letters to Frederick Duncan and Theodore Flint, so they could pay their final visit, and only one unsigned note by Cora herself, addressed to Alexander. She promised she would contact him later, and that she was safe, but said nothing else. Someday, she would send a more thorough explanation.

The last letter was for her graveyard boys, sent to the Duke, whom she trusted the most. They would not find out about her death until well after the fact, for she did not want them at the graveyard to guard an empty casket and risk their lives. And she also did not want to know if they would try to sell her body. Cora would be heartbroken if they did. She would rather not give them the opportunity to even consider it.

There would be no funeral. There would be no graveyard service. Suzette would demand that Cora be quietly and inconspicuously buried in the family plot at the Evergreens, and that a guard be posted to prevent any disturbance of the casket. If anyone did open the casket, they would discover several handfuls of soil Suzette had taken from the ferns decorating her room, as well as an old dress and torn undergarments— the exact contents of a pillaged casket. It would appear as if another resurrection team had beaten whoever chose to dig her up.

But Cora would not be inside. She would be recovering, hidden, in Suzette's bedroom for as long as Suzette could hide her. When Cora was fit enough to walk, she would take a small bag of clothes and a tiny cache of money, and catch a stagecoach to Philadelphia, or Baltimore. From there, she would write to Suzette, who would somehow procure another bit of money. Her name would change, and Cora would no longer be Cora. After the second letter to prove she was safe, Cora would never write to Suzette again.

Cora put her cup of opium down. "I don't know how to thank you, Suzette. I shall be losing you all over again. I was never so happy to have family back in my life until we met."

"Or rather after that," Suzette said, laughing softly. "I hated you when we first met."

"Yes, you did." Cora's smile vanished. "I do hope you find happiness with your husband. Or your friends! I don't know if I shall ever marry. I'd be too afraid."

"So, you're sure to leave that young doctor behind? Mr. Flint?"

Cora nodded. She thought of how he had talked about the race to claim her body with Duncan, at Madame Beck's, and their last fight. If Flint wanted to be her lover, or even her friend, he had failed miserably. She thought back to their first meeting—how brash and confident and wickedly naive he was. She missed that Theo.

A toast to you, Theo, she thought, picking up her teacup. No broken hearts for you to sell to the highest bidder.

Before she drank the last of the opium tincture, she said, "Remember to tell the maid the ice is to soothe my fever. Don't let them touch me and see that I'm not warm. Run the ice bath, send off the letters, and set the extra ice in the bed for me to lie on, when the visitors come."

Suzette nodded.

Cora drank the alcoholic, bitter tincture down to the last brown drop, then set the cup delicately in the saucer, and handed the two brown bottles back to Suzette, who hid them in a fold of her dress. Suzette plucked a small bell from the edge of the table and rang it.

The maid came in momentarily.

"Jane, I'm afraid Miss Lee is not feeling well. She has a fever. Please run a cold bath for her, and bring the ice upstairs. All of it."

"Do you wish to call for the doctor?" Jane asked, her eyes wide at seeing Cora resting her forehead against her hand, slightly slumped over in her chair.

"In time. We'll try the bath first."

Jane curtsied and quickly exited the room. Suzette looked anxiously at Cora. "Cora, dear. How are you feeling?"

Cora looked up at her, eyelids already drooping.

"Horrible."

CHAPTER 27

Cora ought to have been shocked at how quickly the medicines were taking effect, but she was too drowsy to be shocked about anything.

A treaclelike heaviness had spread over her limbs, and her head swam with dizziness. She checked her pulse and found she had trouble locating it on her wrist. It was becoming too slow and weak. She was nauseated but fought the urge to vomit. She needed to keep the medicine in her stomach. Dimly, she was aware that the light outside the window was waning. Twilight had come. Or was it her vision that was dimming? Her mouth was dry, as if she'd drunk sawdust shavings instead of tea, and she blinked sleepily at Suzette. Her cousin's voice seemed to be coming from a tunnel.

"Cora? Cora?" Suzette said, but her lips didn't match the words. Cora thought maybe she was saying, "More, more," as if Cora needed to take more medicine. Cora reached for her cup, but it was empty. She knew that. How odd that she would reach for it. She did anyway, and hooked the teacup with a feeble finger, but it slipped off and shattered on the floor.

"Jane!" Suzette cried. "We need to get her upstairs. To the bath. Quickly."

The opium had worked so quickly. But of course, she had not eaten a thing all day except a few stale crumbs at her home. Which was not her home any longer. Leah was gone, Leah who had raised her to sell her. Like a pig. Worth more if she was a pregnant sow, which she was.

"Sow!" Cora exclaimed suddenly, and Suzette looked at her with a troubled expression. Why didn't Suzette understand the joke?

"All right, Cora. We'll go upstairs." She raised her voice for the sake of anyone who could hear her. "You're burning up with a fever. Come now." She came over to Cora and offered her a hand. Cora was too tired to lift her hand, so Suzette slipped an arm around her waist, hoisting her up off the chair.

"We are going, goooooinnng," Cora slurred.

"Yes, we are. Upstairs to the bath. Remember?" Suzette whispered. Her face was all concern with a hint of panic, but her voice was quiet and steady. "The ice bath."

Suzette was gesturing to the maids, who were bringing fresh linens up the grand staircase outside the salon. Cora saw the polished mahogany railing, the rich Persian carpets on the floor, and the gilt medallions decorating the walls. Maids were carrying buckets of water upstairs for the bath. Another brought a sheet gathered up in the corners, containing something wet and dripping, with chunky edges. The ice.

In the washroom upstairs—everything was white and shining and scrubbed and polished—a large porcelain bath lay next to a pedestal holding a ewer and basin, along with an ebony shelf full of bath salts and soaps. One of the maids approached Cora with an eye to undressing her, and Cora stretched out her arms, Christlike.

"No," Suzette said, shooing the maid away. "I'll undress her myself. Leave the towels. I'll be out in a bit."

Cora could barely stand. Her head swam with wooziness, and darkness bled into the edges of her vision. She put her hand on her chest and found that her gown was already gone, and she stood only in her petticoats and one of Suzette's old corsets that didn't quite fit. Soon Cora stood shivering in only a loose chemise and long pantaloons, Suzette drew her to the bath.

"It's ice cold," Suzette said. "As you said it should be."

Cora nodded, and while holding on to Suzette's steady arm, she slipped into the bath. The water knifed up her calves and thighs, and when she sat down, she couldn't suppress a cry. Immediately, her skin erupted everywhere in gooseflesh, and she shivered violently. The cold seemed to awaken her from her opium stupor. She shook her head and put her hands on the edge of the bath, as if trying to pull herself out again.

"You have to go lower," Suzette told her. "You need to cover your shoulders too."

Cora's teeth already chattered, a clanging that echoed in her skull. "I can't. Suzette, I can't."

"You must," she said soothingly, almost too persuasively. "This is the plan. Your plan, remember?"

"What if . . . ," Cora said through chattering teeth, "What if-f-f this k-k-kills me?"

"It won't. You won't die."

But Suzette's words seemed hollow. A dull voice of alarm swirled in the recesses of Cora's mind. Alexander's voice: *Does it occur to you that you're another Cutter heir? That you're competition?*

Panic widened Cora's eyes. She looked up at her cousin who was pushing, pushing, pushing her back into the water. Soon, the iciness enveloped her to her neck.

"I think you need more opium," Suzette said, almost to herself. "Yes. She's too awake."

"I s-s-suppose I should d-d-die with my eyes c-c-closed," Cora chattered.

"You should, yes. I'll be right back."

Cora watched as Suzette whisked out of the room and closed the door. She heard the doorknob make a slinking sound. Suzette had locked the door so the maids wouldn't interfere.

As she waited in the bath, her shivering began to slowly subside. Maybe, she thought, I should get out for a while. But when she attempted to clench the sides of the slippery porcelain bath, her fingers were too numb to comply. She put her finger in her mouth and found her tongue felt hot against her fingertip.

I must lower my temperature more, she thought, and closed her eyes to sink deeper into the tub. The floating chunks of ice clanked around the bath's edges and her knees as she sank down to allow the water to cover her mouth. The iciness in the center of her body squeezed, tight and painful, until it transformed to a quizzical, dull warmth. Almost pleasant.

Cora didn't realize that she had fallen asleep until Suzette unlocked the door. Cora opened her eyes in tiny crescents to see Suzette carrying the bottles of medicine in her hand, and another great enamel basin of ice chunks balanced on her hip. One by one, so as not to make noise or a splash, she put the great pieces of ice in the water to replace what had melted; they floated like grand uncut diamonds. She looked at Cora just as Cora's eyes slid closed again.

"Cora!" Suzette said.

Cora could not answer her.

"Cora!" Her voice sounded more forceful, but not frightened. Cora felt a hot hand on her forehead, and the same hand slipped under the surface of the water to shake her shoulder.

Cora's own hand rested lightly against her chest, just over her left heart. Stubbornly, it thumped against her palm. Faint, but there.

Thump.

Thump, thump.

Thump.

Thump.

Thump.

The beats were erratic, with very slow pauses between them. The herbs were doing their work. Cora forced open her eyes and saw Suzette working on the medicine droppers. She realized she had fallen unconscious for several moments.

"I sent the letters out," Suzette said. "You've been in the bath for almost an hour now. Your lips are positively blue. It's time for the belladonna," she said. "I'm sure it will sting. I'm sorry, Cousin." For a lady of the gilded uppertens, she possessed a startling comfort with the medicines, the ice, the plan.

Suzette leaned over and pulled Cora's right eyelid up. Cora saw the brown glass dropper loom closer, closer, like a stick ready to pierce her very skull. Something blazing hot and painful hit her eye. She winced and wanted to cry out, but her mouth was still beneath the surface of the water. Suzette lifted the other eyelid, and an explosion of searing pain hit the other eye.

"I don't know how long the drops will last. I may have to put them in again, before the doctors arrive. But, Cora," she said, putting the medicines back on the shelf, "you mustn't react to me, or to Dr. Blackwell, or the other physicians, when they come to see you. You can't move. You can't breathe. You can't snore. If they pinch you, you can't react. Do you understand?"

"More . . . ," Cora rasped, her throat so dry. "More . . . opium."

"All right." After several moments, she felt Suzette lower her bottom lip. A dreadful bitterness spread over her tongue. "And now, we should get you out of this bath and into the bedroom. You are cold as death, so we've done that well enough. I brought two extra slabs of ice and put them in the bed, and extinguished the fire. I kept only one small lamp lit, so it's quite dim."

Suzette did her best to try to get Cora out of the bath, but eventually she had to call the maids for help. Cora was now truly ill enough that there was no lying necessary to show how incapacitated she had become. She didn't have to be considered officially dead until the "guests" arrived.

With the maids' help, Suzette put her into a long nightgown, dried her hair, and lifted her onto Suzette's bed. The nausea in her belly was overwhelming. She wanted terribly to vomit, but again, she swallowed down the bile in her throat and willed her stomach to be still.

A maid whispered, "Is she dead?"

"She looks it. She was well just a few hours ago!" said another.

"I don't know. She had a swoon, but perhaps it was a fit. She's had them before, but this is the worst one yet. I think it was brought on by an ague of some sort." It was as if Suzette were feeding the lines directly from Dr. Blackwell herself, who had prepared her for questions they might encounter.

One of the maids sniffed. "What kind of life she had been living, I can't imagine. Those clothes she was wearing!"

"Yes, and she wasn't in good health to begin with," Suzette said. "Fevers can take people so quickly sometimes. We must call for her family." She dabbed her eyes with a handkerchief, despite the lack of tears.

Inside the room, viewed from Cora's barely opened eye, there was a canopy bed, festooned with thick gold damask and silk fringe. Everything seemed to appear now in duplicate, and oddly washed in a glaze of jaundiced yellow. Cora was laid atop hard, cloth-covered slabs of ice. But she was already too cold to care about any discomfort.

"It's the fashion now," one of the maids whispered, while arranging the bedcovers. "There's a man who can make the corpse look so real. He keeps them on ice until the interment."

"She's not dead yet!" another maid whispered.

"If she isn't, it shan't be long," the first maid replied.

Suzette shooed away the maids again and went to a table with a large mirror before it. She took a box of face powder and brought it over to Cora. She carefully added the whitish makeup to her entire face, her hands, and her upper chest, whisking away the extra powder so the finish was more natural.

"You are as dead as I can make you, Cousin," Suzette declared quietly. "There is nothing more to do but wait."

CHAPTER 28

Before she slipped into unconsciousness, Cora recognized that she was numbingly cold, and her back was damp from the melting ice. A few times, Suzette came in to make sure the bed had towels nearby to keep the ice from soaking the linens and conspicuously dripping to the floor. But when she touched Cora's stiffened hand, or face, she nodded with satisfaction. Cora must be cold enough that anyone who felt her would assume she had been dead for hours.

Her mind was a whirling, confusing storm of images, interchanging with voids where time and distance tangled with the present. She'd note that Suzette was touching her cheek, or changing a pad of bed linens nearby; and then she would be at home in her old, decrepit cottage on Gowanus Bay, twelve years go. Cora would be dressed in a little boy's clothes, chasing dragonflies that alighted on the mud chinking of the cottage walls. Leah would be scolding little Jacob for being outside too long, while Charlotte wrote another letter, asking for more funds. And somewhere in the background, there was Alexander, with a precious pair of dead fowl, doing his best to supplement the meager supplies of the house.

Vaguely, she noted that Charlotte stood up to greet someone. It was Dr. Tilton, whom she had seen only a few weeks ago. But she couldn't see him. She just knew it was he, from his voice at her side.

"I cannot believe it. She was the one with the two hearts? And all this time, she concealed it from everyone. It's unbelievable."

"I didn't know whom to tell," Suzette said. "Miss Lee had mentioned your name—I thought you were a family friend."

There was silence as she felt his warm fingers on her cold hand, but it left just as quickly. There was a creak of a door, and new voices murmuring quietly. She could hear footsteps on the soft carpet beneath the bed.

"Mr. Flint," Suzette said. There was a pause. "Dr. Blackwell. And Mr. Duncan. I apologize for the shocking news. She was well earlier today, but there had been a fever. She seemed terribly overtaxed—her constitution must have been weakened."

"A fit, did you say?" Theo said. His voice was hoarse.

More silence. Suzette must be nodding. There was sniffling, and a rustle of handkerchiefs.

"Where will she be buried?" Theo asked. Something in Cora's hearts seemed to knock, then go silent, like the wind dislodging a chestnut from its branch and falling, falling.

Calm, Cora tried to tell herself. Be calm.

"Evergreens Cemetery," Suzette said. "I've spoken to Mother. She'll be laid in the new family plot we've purchased. It's only right."

"Who else knows?" Theo asked again. His voice was strangely unemotional.

"You, and the doctors she once worked with. I believe that gentleman she called her uncle is still in the hospital?" she said.

"Alexander is in the hospital? Why?"

"He was attacked on Murray Street. We sent a message to him, but he hasn't replied."

Cora's eyes smarted. She remembered how Alexander had fallen in and out of consciousness. What if his wounds were worse than she realized? What if he had died?

There were more murmurs. The maids came in and out, and then Mrs. Cutter came in to briefly greet and say goodbye to the visitors. Whispers were quickly doused by the matriarch of the house.

Cora fell back into brackish, frozen slumber again and again, her body made so inert by the medicines and ice that she felt tied with ship ropes to the very core of the earth.

And every time the specks and slivers of wakefulness arrived, her thoughts were too disjointed for her to even wonder whether she'd survive this. She recalled several words being said around her.

Shocked

It's true

Heart

Hearts

Heart

Hearts

How

She wanted to string the words together like beads on a silk cord and finger them like a rosary, as if each one had the power to erase all her past sins, every misstep.

At some point, she seemed to awaken long enough to hear two voices just outside the door.

"Let the servants take care of it, Suzette. My God, you've spent almost every moment in there since it happened. You've done what you can."

"I won't leave her," Suzette was saying.

"There is nothing left to do. The burial will be in hours. Your mother doesn't want her in this house for longer than necessary. Anyone of importance who knew her has already seen her."

"I won't leave her," Suzette repeated, the stubbornness in her voice rising.

"Drink this."

"What is it?" Suzette paused. It sounded like she was sniffing something.

"Wine. You need to calm yourself. This is a shock to you, I understand. But remember—this is a blessing. It's better she is out of our life. It was a disgrace, what her mother and aunt—your aunt—brought into this family. It will all be laid to rest now."

Suzette sputtered and coughed. "This isn't just wine. What did you put in here?"

"Something to calm you."

"What was it?" Suzette said, her voice rising. "A soporific?"

"Laudanum. Quite a bit too. I'd like to see you rest. This amount of excitement must be addressed." There were low murmurs, and Suzette's voice began to crack. She was crying now.

"I have to be in the room with her," she insisted.

"I forbid it. The plans are already in motion for your cousin's burial. You need not attend to the details." He paused, and his voice lowered. "Your fixation is unhealthy, Suzette, and unbecoming. Too much time with those terrible novels, I'm sure, and that will have to change. I understand you grew fond of your cousin, but enough. It's up to God now to hear your prayers."

The door was shut vehemently, and there was a click of the lock.

Cora tried to open her eyes, but her face somehow didn't obey her. With a herculean effort, she raised her arms but found that only one arm moved. Her right. And only a tiny twitch of her finger. Her left side was completely numb, immobile. And she was still cold, so cold. The back of her body was soaked from the melted ice, and her head swam with dizziness. Since the room was empty, she tried to speak.

Nothing issued from her throat.

She tried to open her eyes again, but she could not. Another wave of dizziness came, the now familiar treaclelike tentacles of unconsciousness pulling her down. She should not have asked Suzette to give her the extra dose of the opium. She might have died. Perhaps she was dying. She would laugh at the irony if she were not too drugged to do so.

She'd been asleep for some time, when she realized her body was moving. But not by her own volition. Warm hands, gentle hands, were on her body.

They were undressing her.

"We'll put her in the same gown that Miss Cutter lent her," the maid, Jane, was saying. "The missus says so."

"And what did the miss have to say about that? The way she acted, she didn't want anyone in here but her."

"She didn't have much to say about it," Jane said. There was a slightly smug sound to her voice. "Mr. Schermerhorn fed her laudanum, and she's sound asleep in the upstairs guest room! I suppose that's one way to silence your wife-to-be."

The other maid's hands had grabbed Cora's hip and shoulder, and she was now in the process of turning her over; her arms flopped, doll-like, according to the law of gravity. She could feel the air on her wet back, and a towel drying her off.

"Goodness, she's soaked through with this ice. I suppose they wanted to preserve her for a while. Did they call to have a daguerreotype picture?"

"No. I don't believe so." Cora was rolled, left and right, and there was a tugging on her arm. "Never mind with the corsets, Minny. Just put on the chemise and bloomers, and lots of perfume along the way. Her hair, we'll just comb it and put in a fresh ribbon." Jane paused. "Pity. I heard she used to go to cemeteries to find dead people for the resurrection men."

"No! She did? A Cutter woman?" Minny whistled. "No wonder the elder missus wants her buried and out of the house! I heard that the fiancé wasn't the least pleased that Miss Cutter might have to share her inheritance. Perhaps Miss Cutter gave her poison! She reads those terrible novels all the time, about ghosts and murders."

"I shouldn't be surprised if half the uppertens had used some inheritance powder to get their gold. But this one was ill anyway," Jane said, poking Cora's chest.

"Mmm. Ugh, she's awful cold. Lot of good that ice did to banish the fever."

There was more rustling of sheets and garments, flopping of Cora's body this way and that way, as careful as the maids tried to be. Inside, she thought to say something.

You shouldn't dress me. I'll do it later.

I'm not really dead, you know.

I'm so sleepy. So very sleepy.

"Did you see that?" Jane said.

"What?" Minny stopped touching her. "What is it?"

"I swear, I saw her breathing."

"No, that can't be. Three doctors said she was dead. They said she had no pulse. She's dead as a day-old fish."

"Watch her."

For an eternity, Cora didn't breathe. It was rather easy—she was already breathing so slowly.

"Fetch that mirror, Minny," Jane said. Cora felt a cold piece of metal on her upper lip. They were looking for the steam of a breath issuing from her nostrils. Cora didn't breathe, and a knot of discomfort began to tighten in her chest.

"Nothing. She's dead." The mirror was withdrawn, and Cora was unceremoniously flopped over onto her stomach as they buttoned the back of her gown. Facedown, she could breathe a little without being noticed, though her face was compressed into the linens on the bed. There was more primping of her body, and in the process, Cora fell asleep again.

When she awoke later—perhaps a few minutes later, perhaps a few hours—she was no longer soaking in the wet, cold sheets. In fact, the feather mattress felt harder, and the air reeked of perfume. Oh. It must be the lily of the valley perfume they put on her when they changed her clothing.

She heard voices, but they were muffled, strange, and masculine. The sounds were oddly distant and near at the same time. Cora tried to move her fingers, and she jerked a little when she realized her fingers were threaded into a cold, lifeless hand.

She wiggled her fingers free from the dead one, but for some reason, the left side of her body did not respond at all to her commands. She tried to lift it, to move her hands and toes.

Only the right side of her body responded.

She attempted to open her eyes, which was enormously difficult as they felt pasted together. But slowly, they opened. Her left eyelid felt so sluggish compared to the right. Everything was dark. She shifted as best she could, just her right hand pushing against the bed. Her wrist hit wood nearby, perhaps a chair. The sound of her wrist hitting the hard surface made a quiet, cottony sound that seemed everywhere at once, as if the walls had drawn closer.

She tried to speak. Perhaps Suzette was nearby now.

"Errrruuuuuuh" was all that issued from her throat. Her tongue pushed uselessly against one side of her mouth, unable to form words. This couldn't just be the herbs she'd taken, or the laudanum. Something was wrong.

Oh no.

She was having another apoplectic attack.

It was almost too ridiculous—she and Suzette had lied about an attack and a bout of fever, and here she was having a genuine fit. She tried to speak, but once again her vocal cords didn't comply. Only a louder hissing noise issued from her throat.

Cora moved her right hand again, and this time reaching out, she felt a solid panel of wood. She lifted her arm, and her knuckles bounced against a hard plane, only a foot above her.

No.

No, this couldn't be.

No.

Cora opened her eyes as wide as she could, but it was dark around her, darker than a moonless night. Her hand began to wildly knock and thump against the wood, and she began to breathe, faster and faster, until she realized she had to be calm. After all, she was supposed to be dead.

But she wasn't supposed to be in a coffin, nailed firmly shut.

Not now.

Not yet.

CHAPTER 29

A strange voice outside the coffin hollered.

"Off, be yeh. Evergreens. Quick like. There'll be no family waitin'."

Her body lurched, and she felt movement. Gravel crunched underneath turning wheels. Hooves clonking against cobblestone, and a whinny. She was in a wagon, no longer inside the Cutter residence.

They were going to bury her.

She wanted to scream, but she couldn't. And she couldn't bear to keep her eyes open, lest they adjust to the dark. If she saw the reality of a coffin lid only inches away, she would go mad.

Cora had to get out, without letting anyone know she was still alive. Somewhere out there, Suzette must know. Or did she? Her confused mind remembered Suzette's fiancé giving her laudanum to sleep—or was that a dream? Suzette was supposed to hide her in the room, placing only her torn clothes and handfuls of soil inside the coffin.

She let her working hand explore the wooden walls, while the wagon jiggled and bumped along a road she could not see. There was soft cloth padding beneath her. The wooden planks were relatively smooth. She scraped one with a fingernail, and could tell from the sound that the wood was thick, too, not like the cheap, thin pine boxes that the poor could purchase, knot-filled and barely sanded.

A small amount of light peeped in through the edges of the lid. Hopefully, that meant air enough to let her breathe. But once she was under the ground, it wouldn't matter. She would suffocate.

Cora still felt dizzy, even lying down. Being unable to use the left side of her body was a problem. A vast problem. What if the effects of her fit were permanent? Even if she could open this coffin, she couldn't escape because she was now an invalid. Someone must help her. Suzette must help her.

Cora drooled a little, a disgusting feeling and so infuriating. She couldn't close her mouth properly, and saliva dripped freely down her cheek and neck.

Her right hand moved to her lower belly; she wondered whether the tiny thing inside her there was still alive, or whether it, too, was a victim of her apoplexy. She didn't think she'd had a miscarriage. She wasn't bleeding; that much she knew. Keep me alive, and there's a chance for us both, she thought.

But she might die, and very soon. She thought of Alexander, hopefully not acquiring a case of typhus at one of the city hospitals, and of Theo. This was his opportunity. He was the only resurrectionist who knew of her death right now. He could dig her up and claim Duncan's bounty. How would he feel, when she was splayed open to the world, to find out that he'd been the agent of the death of his own future child?

The very thought of it brought on a sob. Cora never cried, and yet the tears fell in thin rivulets down both surfaces of her cheeks. At least there was one part of her body that still worked on both sides.

Small mercies.

The thud jarred her awake.

Her spine bounced against the bottom of the coffin, and she inhaled in surprise as her eyes opened to darkness. She had fallen asleep again.

The wheels of the wagon had stopped turning, and the horse's hooves no longer clacked on the street. There must have been a ferry ride, but she'd slept through it.

Her left hand twitched, and her fingers reached, too, though she was unable to completely lift her left arm. It tingled with a strange sensation, as if a thousand ants were biting her arm.

Her left arm was working a little! But where was she?

A rain of soil and pebbles hitting the casket answered her question. Another shovelful brought on fresh panic.

No one would come for her.

No one would save her.

Her plan had gone wrong, and the fierce instinct to stay quiet, to hide, to hide behind a false death, was swallowed whole by the realization that the men burying her were her only salvation now.

"Heeeeooo," she croaked. Her good hand slapped the coffin's side, and she tried to pound on the lid, but there was no room to pull back her arm to hit any harder. "Stahh . . . sthop," she lisped. "Stop!"

The only thing that answered her was another shovelful of soil and rocks. Soon, the sound became more muffled. Already, there must be an inch of dirt atop her.

"Ssstop!" she cried, her hand thumping the side of her tomb over and over again. "Help. Help. Please, help." But her voice sounded small even in her own ears.

"Help!" Cora cried.

But no one answered her.

There were no birds singing.

There were no crickets calling.

There was nothing but the sound of Cora's breathing and cries, and the silence of being forgotten deep within the earth.

Because she had been so ill from the herbs, Cora had no idea how much time she had lost while bobbing in and out of consciousness. She didn't know if she'd been buried first thing at dawn, or late at night. What she did know was that soon, the news would spread that the girl with two hearts, the impossible girl, was dead now and ripe for the taking by whichever resurrectionist found her first.

But they'd have to locate her and wait for dark. It might be hours before she was dug up.

Even another five minutes was insufferable.

From sheer panic, Cora kicked and screamed, her knees bouncing against the lid, her weakened left side awakening slowly only to be limited by her confined space. But very quickly, she realized she would use up what bit of fresh air she had in the casket, and calmed down. The worms cared not for her screams.

She found that she was hungry, as it had now been well over a day since she'd eaten. Her mouth stank, and her tongue was both dry and pasty. Her bladder, which had been functionless from the side effects of the medicines, was now filled to brimming. During a fit of crying, she couldn't contain her body's overwhelming urge to relieve itself, and she urinated in a pool over herself and her gown, which sopped up the liquid and left her legs and back damp and reeking of ammonia.

"I'm going to die here," Cora said, happy to hear she was enunciating words again, but the despair answered her in silence.

No one can hear you.

No one.

Her own team would not even know she had died until tomorrow, when they received Suzette's note, well after her grave might already be pillaged. She grew sleepier and sleepier. Suffocation ought not to be so comfortable, she thought. In her exhaustion, her mind began to create the impossible—crickets spoke to her with Irish accents asking if she wanted to buy a loaf of bread; a leech discussed bleeding her to dry out her corpse more efficiently. The medicines had lost their potency, but now something terrible replaced them: the degradation of her own self and mind. And yet she was growing too stupefied to care.

She heard a scraping but few sounds of voices, and she thought, The crickets and worms and the creatures of the earth are coming to get me. And she had some satisfaction that she would be consumed by the wild creatures of the earth, instead of the uncivil creatures of man.

The scraping grew louder, and she wondered, for a moment, whether the flesh was being peeled from her bones. This ought to hurt more, she considered.

Suddenly, there was a cracking noise, accompanied by the squeak of nails being pulled from new, unseasoned wood. Dirt fell softly onto her face and her dry lips.

This was the strangest dream she'd ever had. A nightmare, and yet she felt so pleasant, like she was taking a warm bath after a night of working in the bitterest cold.

Male voices spoke, their words swirling around her tangibly, as if she could touch them.

"There she is, boys."

"I can't believe it. The poor lass! After all she did for us."

Someone blew their nose, and a splat of phlegm hit the side of the casket.

"It's a good thing we found her early. Let's have a moment, boys. Then we'll get her into the wagon and rebury her in the woods, a good seven feet deep so no one ever finds her."

It was quiet for some time. Someone sniffled, and there was a muffled, very masculine sob, and then a *thud-thud-thud,* as if someone were patting someone else's back. The dirt on Cora's lips dusted her tongue and melted to the back of her throat, irritating it. She coughed. She opened her eyes, coughed again, and squinted into a night sky partially lit by a scythe moon.

"Is it time for work?" she mumbled.

"Jesus, Mary, and Joseph, she's alive!" someone yelled.

With eyes so wide that whites ringed their irises, Friar Tom, Otto the Cat, and the Duke stood staring at her.

"How in the devil did you get in there, Miss Cora?" the Duke said, stooping down to touch her hand.

"Where's Jacob?" Cora muttered. "Who are you?"

Tom threw his shovel aside and turned to look at the Duke, who looked at Otto.

"She's delirious," Otto said. "And she smells like a privy. Come on, let's get her out of there."

Otto lowered himself into the grave and began to gather Cora up in his arms. The Duke came down to wrap her gown around her legs so they could extricate her.

"Light as a feather," Otto said, hoisting up her torso while the Friar lifted her legs.

"Where is Jacob?" Cora repeated.

"She can't remember that she's Jacob," the Duke said.

"I can't believe she was Jacob all this time," Otto said, pulling her onto the grass as the Duke hoisted himself out of the grave. "And I can't believe that I had no idea until you told me an hour ago. I'm a right idiot, I am."

"I was fooled too," Tom said, tucking his shirt in around his rounded belly. "Are you saying you knew all along?" he asked the Duke.

"It was plain as day, but then again, I've always been able to tell the difference between a man and woman, not being married to the gin bottle like you two."

"You knew?" Cora whispered. She tried to focus, and soon she recognized the Duke's grizzled black-and-gray hair. His face shone, and his eyes were warm with safety.

"I did, Miss Cora. I always knew," the Duke said, "but it wasn't up to me to say so. Things were working out fine as it was."

Cora smiled weakly and sagged back onto the ground. She retched once, then again, but nothing came up.

"She looks bad, Duke."

"She does. Looks like someone poisoned her. Maybe her hearts aren't strong enough. My wife will help me nurse her until she's better. After that, she can disappear wherever she wishes. It was a bad decision, to hide from the living this way, but with hundreds of dollars on her head, perhaps it was easier than running."

The Duke gently wrapped a cloth around her body to keep her warm and enticed her to drink some water. Half of it slipped down her trachea, and she coughed violently, closing her eyes.

"Oy, who's that?" Tom stood suddenly from where he had been wrapping their digging instruments up in a heavy cloth.

Cora stiffened. She wouldn't have lifted her head to look, even if she could. Anyone else had to believe she was dead, so she kept her eyes closed and her breathing slow. She heard footsteps approach, boots quietly falling onto the grass.

"That's ours," a voice said.

"She's not anyone's. She's going back into the grave. Her family hired us to make sure she sleeps long and sound. So, there's nothing to fight over, you see," the Duke said coolly.

But Cora recognized the discomfiture in his voice. She blinked and looked up to see her boys surrounding her limp body, legs like stout pillars around her.

"You shouldn't talk. I'll bet you've escaped your owner, haven't you?"

"I'm a free man," the Duke said, but his voice was even tighter than before.

"Free as a dog that's slipped the rope."

There was a click, and a shot like a slap in the dark. Tom shouted and leaped over her body. She heard fists hitting skin, a tussle. Someone hit the ground, and the air went whooshing out of their lungs. A boot kicked her face as someone tripped over her body, and legs twisted and squirmed above her torso. The blow to her head shook some of the grogginess from her. Two men were fighting half on her body, half on the ground. There was a cry, and she heard someone fall nearby—into the grave. Something hard hit bony flesh—like a spade against a skull.

The Duke was moaning, and nothing was to be heard from Tom, or Otto. Cora wanted to open her eyes, and she wanted to fight, but after being stiff in the coffin for so long after her apoplexy, she could still barely move her left side.

"That didn't take long," a voice said, the same one that had first interrupted her boys. She wanted to cry inside—what had become of them? Who had been shot? Were they dead too?

"What will we do with the innocents? Throw them in the grave?" another voice said.

Bodies? No! her hearts screamed. They couldn't be dead. Her boys. They couldn't be.

"We should sell them. University would take them, five apiece."

"No. Not tonight. Let the stiff 'uns rot here."

She heard them walk over to her, and someone seemed to be hovering closely.

Don't cry, Cora thought, praying that her eyes would obey. Don't cry. Don't breathe.

She had to pretend to be dead. If she didn't, they might kill her, and then there would be no hope at all. She held her breath and stayed as limp as possible. A hand touched her face and pulled her lower lip down.

"No gold here," the voice said, and the hand traveled over her neck, her bosoms, and then her waist, where it began tugging at the laces of her dress. There was a grunt of disgust. "She stinks like a barn." More tugging at her dress.

"No!" the other voice said, the one with authority, the one that likely shot the Duke. "They said not to undress the body. Leave it on."

"That's no fun, ain't it?"

"Shut your mouth and do as I say. Roll her up in that cloth and load her on the wagon."

There was a quiet assent as she was dragged several feet. A rough, stiffened cloth was tucked around her arms, pinning them to her body, and she was rolled like a pastry until the cloth nearly smothered her face. But there was enough room to breathe. She was pulled off the ground and laid down on a hard surface, likely the wagon.

"That one's still breathing," one of the men said.

"He'll be dead before morning. I've no more bullets to waste tonight." She heard reins and a horse's hooves stamping. "We've a delivery to make, gentlemen. Let's go."

CHAPTER 30

Everything was muffled. All Cora could do was concentrate on breathing against the dirty, stiff fabric wrapped about her. Her filthy dress was squeezed tight around her body, and every joint creaked from stiffness. The left side of her body was no longer numbed, but now it spasmed from disuse. And all the while, Cora toiled with the crushing ache in her hearts. Were her boys dead? Who would bury them and watch over them?

Cora would, if she could. It would not be fair, if their bodies were pillaged heartlessly. She imagined someone laughing at Tom's bare head with that fringe of hair, Otto's cat tail being heartlessly thrown into the dirt, the Duke's insensate body being tossed into a cart. She blamed herself. Why shouldn't they receive the same fate as those they'd made their living from? Hadn't she always thought that a body had best be used for something worthwhile, as the dead didn't need it?

But the thought of the Duke being dug up, or Tom, or Otto—it was too much. It wasn't fair.

Good God. What lies had she been telling herself all these years?

A hard boot came down on her shoulder as one of the resurrection men rested his leg on her. And then all she could think was, What will they do when they realize I'm not dead?

They traveled for some time, over the ferry again back into Manhattan. Everything was relatively quiet, so it must be deep into the night. There were no other sounds of horses or carriages, no omnibus drivers angrily yelling.

The resurrection men were quiet, as they should be. Cora lifted her chin a little, which allowed her to keep the cloth away from her nose and mouth. The wagon stopped, pitching this way and that way as the men jumped off. The cloth around her legs was tugged hard, and she was pulled from the wagon and carried some distance.

There were murmurs, and a door opening. A door shutting. Opening again, and more murmurs. She was carried downward, somewhere. She couldn't smell much, but there was a distinct scent of something slightly sweet—like flowers. Her body was laid on something rather soft.

Was she at the university? Would Theo be shocked to find that he'd purchased a live body? Or perhaps she was in some part of the basement at the Anatomical Museum. She would not be surprised if Duncan insisted on seeing her naked, before her dissection. And weak as she was, it would be too easy for him to smother her once her true state was known.

Doors closed again, and it was quiet. She heard footsteps, and very gently, her wrappings were slowly peeled away. Finally, her body flopped with finality, open to the air and free of her covering.

A hand touched her face, then her neck, against her left carotid artery. She couldn't possibly hide that she was alive anymore, but she was terrified to open her eyes, so she didn't. The hand traveled down her arm and pressed against her inner wrist, feeling her pulse.

"Cora?" a voice spoke quietly.

She knew that voice.

Her eyes opened. Alexander sat on the edge of a thin pallet bed. A large bruise shone over his left eyebrow, a remnant of Puck's attack. His eyes were wide, and he was shaking.

"Alexander!" Cora cried out, and she reached for him. Her right arm shot forward, and her left, still weakened, flailed limply.

"My God! You're alive!" he said, and embraced her. "I can't believe you're alive."

———※———

It took some time for Cora to explain what Alexander didn't know. Her letter had said almost nothing, only that she'd contact him later. She told him how she'd decided to fake her death. The ruse had worked too well—and Suzette's inability to stay at her side resulted in her accidental burial. She told him about Otto, and Tom, and the Duke, and cried fresh tears.

"They tried to save me, and they're dead. Or as good as dead," Cora said through disjointed breaths.

"I'll go there as soon as you're taken care of and see if they need help."

"We should go now!" she said, clutching his arm.

"I need to care for you first, Cora." He closed his eyes. "I thought you were dead. I went to your house, and that little boy, George, said word had spread that you'd been struck with brain fever. We found out you were going to the Evergreens, so I hired the resurrection men to get your body. I told them to make absolutely sure no one else touched you. I had no idea that your crew would be there. I'm so sorry. I just . . ." He ran his good hand through his silver-and-dark hair. "I cannot believe that you're alive."

"I can't either," Cora said, grimacing. She lifted her left arm again, and the movement made her head swim. She made a timid fist. "I feel wretched. I had another apoplectic attack, but it doesn't seem permanent so far." She finally looked around her. She'd assumed she was in Alexander's room, below the Grand Anatomical Museum, but this was a different room—smaller, darker. There was the low sleeping pallet, covered in a few blankets, and a small table nearby. An oil lamp glowed against the roughly plastered wall. "Where are we?"

"My old studio." Alexander stood up. "Duncan wouldn't let me work on anything that didn't end up in his museum, or his own cabinet, so any side work I've done has been here."

"Oh, yes, I remember." Cora hardly recognized it, the room was so bare. But she knew there were two other rooms here—one with storage, and one where he did his sculpting. She'd never liked it, though—it was in the basement of a building near the Five Points, on Henry Street. Cheap as far as rent went, but because so much of the Five Points used to be a wet pond, it was always damp underground, with the wood rotting too early and plaster disintegrating before its time. There were no windows.

Alexander stood and pointed to a basin and ewer on the stand behind him, plus a stack of clean cloths. "Here are some things so you can bathe. I have a dress that was used for a commissioned portrait years ago, but only one, and it's a bit ridiculous. It will have to do until we can get more clothes for you. I've an old nightshirt you may wear while you rest."

Cora sat up weakly. "I ought to write to Suzette and let her know that I'm all right."

"In time. Right now, everyone thinks you're dead, and it's safer that way." Alexander winced a little when he turned to leave.

"I didn't even ask if you're all right! I heard you were in the hospital."

"Yes. My head—they said I had a severe concussion of the brain. But I'll be fine," he said. "All that matters is you're all right. Now, you need to clean up, and eat, and rest."

Cora's eyes watered. She needed all of those things, and the offering of them was such a blessed relief that she released the breath she'd been holding—seemingly for days. Now, she could leave New York and not worry that shadows would be following her. She was safe. Finally.

Alexander had provided a cotton nightshirt that was far too large for her, and after bathing, she lay back down. There was no bleeding, so perhaps the baby inside her had survived the onslaught of medicines and the physical strain. An absolute miracle. She said nothing to Alexander, though, when he brought her some nourishing broth, a biscuit, and some tea. She couldn't see telling anyone for a while. Something in her felt that it was not a secret to be revealed lightly, and not right now.

After she had taken several sips and swallows, Cora's head ceased feeling like it was detached from her neck. She filled Alexander in on what had happened since they parted in the aftermath of Puck's attack.

"So, all the physicians now believe you are dead. That's all that matters." He gathered the soiled dishes, and Cora lay on the blanket-covered pallet. Alexander blew out the lamp. It was so very dark, almost as dark as the interior of the coffin had been. Cora's hand clutched the rough wool beneath her. She feared sleep but wouldn't say it aloud. Alexander stood at the doorway, dishes clinking lightly in his one arm.

"You're safe, Cora. Finally, safe."

"Alexander, please do see if you can find out whether the Duke is all right. Please."

"Of course I will. I promise. Try to get some sleep."

And with that, he closed the door, and Cora shut her eyes. Her life could begin again now. But there would be no more Suzette, no more Leah, no more Theodore. No more Otto, or Tom, and maybe no more of the Duke.

She wondered whether the cost was worth it.

——❖——

When Cora awoke, her body was still aching and stiff, but she felt the clean bed linens under her hands, the clean cotton gown around her body. She was safe. She was warm. She wiggled her fingertips, right, then left, delighted that she could move them nearly equally. She rolled her left ankle and stretched her toes, a delicious sensation after such frightening weakness.

The room was dark, but she could see some shadows and shapes. A three-legged stool nearby held the extinguished lamp. She could stand, gingerly, though she listed very slightly to the left. She carefully limped to the door but found that it was locked.

She knocked gently.

"Alexander," she called. All was quiet. "Alexander!" she called out louder, rapping her knuckles hard on the thick oak door.

Nothing.

He must have locked the door to be safe. Perhaps the front door was not secure for some reason. After all, her existence was a secret. She felt for the doorknob, and her fingers located a tiny keyhole beneath. She felt carefully along the walls, and found the table against the wall that held the ewer and basin. Below it was another shelf, which held two books. Not knowing what they said in the dark, she tore out several pages and silently promised Alexander she would sew the pages back in, or use a good paste to repair them.

Cora slipped a piece of paper under the door, then two more, until she'd covered the span of floor just outside the door. She tore another small piece of paper and rolled it up tight and thin, and carefully poked it into the keyhole. She felt the key on the other side dislodge, then fall with a clank to the floor. One by one, she pulled each piece of paper back into the room. Hopefully the key had landed on one of them. And it had.

She unlocked the door. Outside of the tiny bedroom, the basement of the building was dark. There was one room across the way—a tiny kitchen—and at one end of the hallway a storage room with cloth-covered armatures, mounds of wax, and tiny pots of paint. Reds, ochres, and bright greens.

"Alexander?" she called.

She walked down the hallway and felt the air open up to a larger space. The studio. The warm scent of beeswax met her, along with the smokiness of fireplace ash and dampness seeping through the walls. She made her way to a table where Alexander's sculpting tools were laid out: Thin clay paddles and shapers, some as thin as lancets. A thin wire bound to two short sticks, for cutting through large slabs of clay and blocks of wax. She groped her way to the fireplace and found a box of matches. Atop the mantel was a candlestick with a waxy stub within it. She lit the match, and soon the candle began to burn brightly.

A dark shadow scurried past her. A rat. She shivered and held the candle aloft.

The studio had several wax figurines, but many of them were in pieces, either in the process of being made or destroyed; it was hard to tell. Cora drew closer to a piece lying prone on a long wooden slab. She pulled the cloth away and held her candle aloft.

It was a woman's figure, lying down with her hands clasped together between her bosoms. It was most certainly wax, which was strange. Alexander said he did mostly his clay and marble sculpting here. The figure was entirely naked, not unlike a statue she might see on display at the Vauxhall Gardens, like a dryad with flowers crowning her hair. But this was no Greek statue. The hair was black, for one thing, and very short—short like a boy's.

Short like Cora's. Her hearts thumped erratically, either in warning or as a sequela of the medicinals still lingering in her system. She leaned over to look at the face.

Dark eyes only half-open, as if the figure were waking up, falling asleep, or in ecstasy. The short hair was beautifully painted, with rich brown highlights against the sooty black, as if the sun were reflecting against the strands. The eyes were slightly narrow, with black eyelashes painstakingly embedded into the lids to mimic reality. Cora touched the hair on the figure's head. She was wrong—it wasn't painted. It was real human hair, each strand embedded separately and carefully cut to look exactly like Cora's.

The likeness nauseated her.

"Duncan must have ordered it," Cora murmured, and shuddered at her own mention of his name. Though why Alexander would work on it here, as opposed to his studio at the museum, she had no idea. This nearly naked version was the same size as Cora and looked far too real, as opposed to the tiny doll-like figurine. A real linen cloth had been artfully twisted to cover its upper thighs, twisting prettily between its breasts and over its shoulder. She wondered that Alexander hadn't destroyed it like the others.

Nearby, there was another figure covered in cloth, and she gently tugged at the fabric. Underneath was yet another likeness of Cora. Same short blackish-brown hair, same stature, but this one was completely unlike the poetic figure of the other sculpture, which swooned almost romantically, in the fashion of the European wax artists.

This one was in the style of the English wax artists—shockingly realistic, with all the grotesque allure of the truth. The figure was lying on its back, feet parted and splayed. Bruises lined its neck like a collarette of blue flowers, and its eyes were only half-closed, staring into the nothingness of the air above. Its breasts lay small across its chest, and more bruises purpled its rib cage. There was no poetry in this figure.

As with the other, it appeared that the hair was real human hair. Cora reached down to touch it, and it felt sticky. She took her hand away, holding the candle to her fingertips.

A reddish hue smeared across her fingertips.

"Paint," Cora said to herself, and she wiped her fingers on her gown, leaving a rust-colored blur. She touched the figure's cheek, wondering how Alexander had been able to make the skin look so very real. It even sprang back with an unexpected elasticity.

Because this wasn't hard, sculpted wax.

It was dead flesh.

AUDREY MARCH

He was a man with particular tastes.

Working for Madame Beck was thorny drudgery. Every night, a different swell, wearing a fine suit and owning a mouth like a backed-up gutter. Every night, more rum to make it all a little less terrible. But I had a warm bed under a roof, and the bread was good. Madame liked us well fed—no slamkins, scraggly mabs, nor cows in her house. No stargazing for me, walking the streets looking for work.

"A man doesn't want to hold a dog bone," she'd say.

And then one day, Madame Beck called me into her parlor. She situated herself like a queen in the armchair trimmed with gold and emerald velvet.

"I've a new one for you, Audrey," she'd said. "A good prospect for the both of us."

"Then send him in," I said, but she said no.

"From now on, he's your only swell. The only one. You go with him to his house, when he wants. But he wants no one but you. And he's very strict about it. Said he'd have you followed to be sure you're exclusive."

"How much?" I asked. For this kind of work, to be a lady bird—a woman who sells herself exclusively to one man—it must be worth it.

"More than enough for your bed and bread, and for you to please him whenever he wishes." She put a pipe in her mouth and lit a match, inhaling and letting the smoke form a screen before her face. "There's another thing. He wants you to wear this, half the time." She took a bundle of fabric and tossed it at me. I separated the pieces of clothing, and held them up one by one.

A pair of men's boots. Trousers, old and stained. A brown shirt and cap. And a long piece of cloth.

"That," Madame Beck said, "is to bind your bosoms when you wear these clothes."

"Eh! He's a bugger! You ought to ask Pretty John instead."

"No. Not a bugger at all. The customer didn't want John. He wanted you. He knows you're as female as they come. And you're never to speak to him during any of the meetings. Never. You follow him to where he goes, keep your squeaks quiet, and go on your way. Understand?"

I didn't, but money was money. Madame Beck said I was to cut my biscuit-hued hair, and keep it colored dark by adding a rinse of crushed black walnut hulls after my baths. She gave me a crayon of waxy black to make my eyebrows dark and eyelids longer.

So, for more than two years, I met him. Sometimes at his dark dungeon of a place on Henry Street, where he had me wear a blue silk dress and raised the hem to do his business on his flat bed, by a starving example of a fireplace. I always ignored the cloth-covered things in the larger room there. Once I'd ventured to peek beneath one, and the swell had hit me so hard that I'd bitten my tongue. I never looked again.

Sometimes, he had me come uptown to the Grand Anatomical Museum where he made wax images of all sorts of dead limbs and such, but he didn't care that I saw those. He just pushed me against the wall, pushed my boy's clothes down, and pushed himself inside me.

He rarely spoke to me. Only a word here and there.

Go home.

You're late.

Be quiet.

Hush.

The money was worth it. Always worth it. Except for the one strike against me, he seemed nice. Honest, I thought. He paid Madame regular like, and I got to eat an iced cake every week because she was happy with the money.

He was nice, until he wasn't.

He'd asked me to visit, only this time it was a letter he'd written to me directly, not to Madame Beck. A time, a date. And his studio, on Henry Street. There would be twenty dollars waiting for me. So, I went.

I didn't say anything to Madame Beck. Why should I? This was money without any skimming for the house, and I was happy to oblige. So, I came, and he had me take off my clothes, and I did, though he'd never asked me to remove my garments before. And he'd said, "What's your name?"

He'd never asked. I always assumed he knew, but I suppose he didn't.

"Audrey," I said. "What's yours?"

He didn't answer. He seemed disappointed at hearing my name. Or my voice, I'm not sure. I reached to unbutton his blouse, but then he hit me, hard, across the temple. It hurt so much that I doubled over, and before I could hold out an arm to ward off another blow, his hands were around my neck.

No words.

Not even a grunt of pleasure or displeasure.

I was seeing stars within a few seconds. I fought, but he pitched me backward and sat on my rib cage as he subdued the life in me. And then I was gone. I've been here on this cool slab of wood for nearly two days. My body has yet to bloat, but it's no longer stiff, and I'm less here than I was before. The sunlight has grown dimmer; the dark is yet darker. Then someone takes the sheet off me, and there's this girl staring,

staring, staring. Why, she looks just like me. And when she touches my cheek, I think—oh.

Oh.

I understand now.

She probably knows, now, what kind of creature he is. I don't even need to be alive to say to her, Be quick, girl. Run.

Because she does.

CHAPTER 31

Cora opened her mouth to scream.

She began to breathe so hard, so fast, she felt dizzy. Her hand holding the candle shook, so that scalding wax dripped off the edge and spilled onto her skin, though she hardly noted the pain.

It was a body. A real body. A girl, so very human, and who looked so very much like Cora. She clamped her free hand over her mouth. She had to be quiet. She didn't exist anymore, did she? What if someone blamed her for the death of this girl?

Who was she? Had Alexander brought her here? Had he killed her?

The questions were too horrid to ask. But Cora had to know. She leaned forward. And then she placed one of her hands about the girl's neck. Her hands were too small to cover the bruises around her neck—someone with larger hands, man's hands, had strangled her.

Cora cocked her head and looked at the girl again. She was so very familiar, but with the facial bruises and swelling, she was hard to place. Cora stooped to look beneath the bench, and saw several items of clothing bunched up.

Trousers, torn. A dirty shirt that was too damaged to wear. Galluses. A long, winding piece of thin gauze. So very ordinary, and familiar. They were clothes that she might have worn as Jacob. And then recognition widened her eyes. She knew this shirt, these trousers. They were exactly the ones worn by the young man that Alexander had trysted with.

And then, as if the tumblers of a finely oiled lock had suddenly turned into place, she understood.

It wasn't a boy whom Alexander had been having relations with, or who he'd admitted was his lover. It was the girl, Audrey, whom she'd spoken to at Madame Beck's.

I only have one patron, and he's very particular about what I do, and who I do it with.

Not Duncan. Alexander.

And Alexander didn't have trysts with men; he had trysts with a fake Jacob. Possibly a fake Cora, too, if this girl had put on a dress and a wig.

He'd been lusting for something that was at his fingertips all this time.

"I have to leave," Cora said, backing away from the corpse. But to where? Her house on Irving Place was no longer a sanctuary. She couldn't go to Suzette—the rest of the family thought she was dead, and all her efforts to conceal herself would become worthless. She'd nearly died to disappear—she refused to sacrifice what she'd earned for herself.

"I have to leave," Cora repeated, as if her voice knew better what needed to be done. She made her way through the dark passage to the front door. It was thick and riveted with brass. And it was locked.

She padded quickly down the corridor back to the tiny room where she had slept. Inside the room, she looked for her old dress, but it was nowhere. She couldn't wear Audrey's clothes—they were too torn to be wearable. Another dress hung from a peg on the wall behind a curtain. The gown was beautiful, short sleeved and oddly out of fashion. It was an ice-blue silk, with a high waist under the bust, and festooned with yellowing lace and real pearl buttons dotted about the neckline and trim. Something Empress Josephine would have worn. She pulled it on, unable to fully button it without Leah behind her.

She didn't even know where she would go. She only knew she had to leave this place. If Alexander had a reason for this, he could explain it in the light of day. Cora's borrowed slippers from Suzette were missing, but there were the men's boots under the bench where Audrey's corpse lay. She laced them on quickly. Her dress would hide them in public.

Cora went to the thick front door. Like the bedroom door, it had a keyhole for the lock, but this time she could see through the keyhole that the key was missing. No doubt Alexander had it, but sometimes there were duplicates. She went back to the bedroom, searching under the thin mattress and rummaging along the few objects that sat on the little table. As she turned quickly, her skirts knocked over the table, and Cora saw a stack of ledgers that had been slipped beneath it. The thin ledger on top looked familiar. She picked it up and flipped through the pages. She saw her own handwriting, her list of anomalies. But several of the names had been crossed out. And scribbled along with them were notes she had not written.

> ~~Randolph Hitchcock III / Dr. Smyth / abdominal aortic~~ ~~aneurysm~~
> > ~~40 Waverly Place~~
> > ~~Work: 21 Broad Street~~
> > ~~Last check with Dr. Smyth, July 30. Note sent August~~ ~~10 with reply August 15, no new symptoms. (Always~~ ~~wears red vests; dislikes opera; prefers plays)~~
> > Supper 6–8 p.m. in Trent's Oyster Café/Marsden's Eating House/Mercer Dining Saloon/Wilson Oyster Saloon
> > Frequents Madame Emeraude's Tuesday, Thursday, Saturday, after supper (Belle is the favorite, ofttimes Mary or Victoria)

Cora flipped the page.

> > ~~Ruby Benningfield/Dr. Goossens / vestigial tail~~
> > ~~28 Greenwich Lane~~

Letter sent March 18, no new symptoms. Unlikely to progress. (Likes ices; favorite colors are pink, peach, and orange.)

Home most days. Occ visit Stewart's, walks at the Battery. Always accompanied. No dining out. No visitors.

"Ruby," Cora said, and touched the ink struck through her name. She turned the pages, speaking the names aloud, as if in prayer. "William Timothy. Ida Difford. Conall Culligan." There was Jonathan Fuller—several pages back in the ledger, and unmarked. But all the others were struck through, with notes in Alexander's hand regarding the places they frequented for food and for pleasure, and whether they were often accompanied.

Alexander.

There was yet another journal beneath her ledger, and she pulled this one out too. The inside bindings had come loose, and the pages fell to the floor.

On the first page was written:

The Journals of Thomas Grier ~ Vol. III, 1831–1840.

Alexander had taken the diaries. He was the person who'd signed the register with the false name, Davey Swell, flash for "a gentleman witness." Of course. The proper gentleman who saw all the crimes being committed, only he was committing them himself. Had he taken the diaries with the same goal as hers—to protect her identity? But then, why not tell her so? That bothered her less than her stolen ledger, and the names crossed out. Only Fuller had died naturally, and his hadn't matched the pattern of deaths. She grabbed the candle and went to the studio, assessing it in a way she hadn't when she'd first emerged from the room.

There were lengths of ribbon sitting in a box at one of the work-tables. She remembered that occasionally Alexander's work might have a piece of real ribbon around the neck of a sculpture, to add more realism. But she'd never considered that a ribbon might be used as a weapon. Could it have killed someone like Ruby? There was the clay wire, and she recalled how Conall Culligan's neck had nearly been severed with something thin and fine. Had he given these to Puck? She went to the other side of the room and examined the paints. The green one was capped, and she read the side.

Paris Green

It had the same hue as Hitchcock's tongue. On the other side of the bottle was a skull and crossbones symbol. Poison. How much had he put into the food that Randolph Hitchcock had eaten? Enough to dye his tongue and stomach bright emerald green. And to kill him quickly. And after another half hour of searching, Cora found two small bottles, one empty, one half-full in the kitchen.

Battle's Rat Poison
Poison!
Best Strychnine Formula
Quick and Easy

The rats. There were always rats in the studio, eating the wax, or so Alexander had mentioned.

Everything he'd need to strangle or poison someone was here in his studio. Her ledger . . . It was a sort of macabre wish list, wasn't it? But her targets hadn't been dying fast enough, and Alexander knew she needed the money. And she steadfastly refused to accept money from Alexander himself. It made sense. She had known for some time these men and women had died from causes not directly attributable to their ailments. And right when she needed the money more than ever, the bodies started showing up. Murdered, conveniently so.

Behind her, the doorknob to the street rattled. She felt the air shift, and the door open, then close. Cora ran back to her room, quietly shut the door, pushed the books hastily back underneath the table, and sat down on the narrow bed. She hid her booted feet under the dress—if he saw them, he'd know she'd found Audrey's body.

In a minute, she heard footsteps approach, and Alexander's tall, spare form filled the doorway. He'd lit a lamp and held it low, where it cast warped shadows above his eyelids and nose. His silvering hair looked like silk and wire mixed together, and his clothes were ever so slightly nicer than before. Broadcloth trousers, well fitted, and a fine muslin shirt beneath a dark jacket. He smiled. It was odd to see Alexander smile so readily.

"Well! You're up. And I see you've found the dress."

Cora smiled. She made a decision not to say a thing about the body, or the two journals. She would wait to see how Alexander reacted—and if she could steal away without him knowing. In her weakened state, she would be unlikely to overpower him. Much of Jacob's strength had diminished with only one bout of being ill.

"Yes. I only just woke up and put it on." Cora adopted a sweet smile. "I can't thank you enough for helping me, Alexander. I'd be dead if it weren't for you."

"I know."

"Did you find out anything about the Duke?"

"What?" He seemed confused for a moment, then added quickly, "I couldn't find him. No word. I'm sorry, he must have died as well." He produced a package from inside his jacket and handed it to her. Several plain buns from the bakery. "I brought you something to eat."

Cora nodded, but nausea began to overwhelm her. She was an excellent actress, but the little child within her cared not for such things. An empty stomach and all the physical trials of the last two days were taking their toll. She bit into one of the soft-crusted buns. Alexander's eyes glittered, watching her.

"I ought to write to Suzette," Cora said, trying to keep her voice reasonably bright. She had a bad habit of talking and eating, born from being Jacob all the time.

"I already wrote her," Alexander said. He sat down next to Cora but hesitated. "I told her you had died. That we were too late, retrieving you from the casket."

Cora swallowed and tried to keep her voice even. "I wanted to tell her I was all right. Why would you say that?"

"To keep up the ruse, of course. It's best for now that everyone thinks you're dead. And then later, when all is safe, you can write to Suzette again. But now, we cannot, not for years."

She cringed, inadvertently, at the word *we*. And then just as quickly, she purged the evidence of her disgust from her face.

Alexander blinked, as if he'd lost sight of Cora for a second, then seemed to recover. "Anyway, I should be on my way. I have work to do."

"I'll need new dresses," Cora said. "Perhaps I could visit the dress-maker when you're out. I can wear a bonnet to disguise my hair."

"No!" Alexander yelled. It was shot in the dark, so loudly and so vehemently that even Cora shook on the bed where she sat.

"It'll be all right," Cora said. She put a hand on his sleeve, and he calmed. She had never had to calm Alexander before—it made her feel as if she had entered a foreign land. "At some point, we'll have to leave this studio, and when it happens, I'll need a disguise."

"Of course you will. But let me take care of that. You can't take the chance of leaving now."

She smiled. "Of course. I understand." Alexander stood. As he exited the room, he touched the doorknob and paused.

Oh no. The key. It was still on the inside of the door. He carefully pulled the key out, turned it over in his hand, and looked at her.

"Oh, that. I let myself out," Cora said with a light laugh. "I was looking for a chamber pot."

Alexander frowned and glanced at the corner of the room, where a chamber pot lived rather obviously.

"I meant . . . I was looking for . . . the . . ."

Alexander didn't even wait to hear the rest of her second lie. His booted feet strode quickly and purposefully down the hallway, into the studio, where the body of the mab, Audrey, was lying exposed, her shroud in a pile on the floor because Cora had forgotten to replace it. Holding his lamp aloft, Alexander turned from the corpse to Cora, who stood in the doorway of the studio.

Silence stretched between them, so tight and thin that Cora thought it might snap and make her bleed. She had to say something. If she could leave this place, it wouldn't be by fighting. Her limbs still felt weak and limp. Alexander's gray eyes stared at her. His hands were at his sides, but she could see them in fists, slowly uncurling. Ready to grasp at something. Unhurriedly, he hung the lamp from an iron hook above a table.

"It's brilliant," Cora said quickly. And then she waited a beat and stepped forward, decisively. "What you've done, Alexander. Brilliant. I don't know how to thank you."

His expression thawed, and his hands relaxed at his sides. He studied her. "Do you mean that?"

"I found the ledger. I saw what you've done." She softened her tone. "You did all this for me, did you not?"

Alexander reached out a hand and leaned against the dusty wall, and Cora drew closer because she knew he wished it. He seemed suddenly very tired. "I have. To keep your business alive—" He paused after his last word. "Solvent, I should say. You kept refusing my help directly, so I did what I could do."

"Puck?" Cora asked. "You had him kill the people on my list for me, didn't you?"

"Yes, and no. Only a few. I needed help, but Puck was a blundering idiot. I gave him some clever methods to dispatch them with, to make the dissections more interesting. He was instructed to leave the bodies be, so you could dig them up and sell them like normal. But one he sold directly to Duncan, and the other he lost to the police."

Ruby, and William Timothy. The ones she never got.

Alexander drew a finger from Cora's left collarbone to her right. She shivered, but not for the reasons Alexander hoped. "He was sloppy," he said. "Greedy. So, I started sending you letters to make sure you found out about the bodies, before Puck did."

Oh. That would explain the torn-off letter about Conall Culligan. And what he said was true—after that, they'd never had another body stolen from them before they could do the resurrection.

"I knew you were a clever man. A thinking man. But this is beyond my imagining." Cora smiled again. "All of this to protect me. To provide for me."

"Yes." He put a single finger to her chin, lifting it. "Yes. Since you were a child, everything I've done has been for you."

"I thought you loved Charlotte," she said in a small voice.

"I thought I did. But you eclipsed her, utterly. Even as a child, you were my sun." He leaned forward, his face close to hers.

Cora couldn't stop herself from asking, "And what about the mab? I thought you had a taste for boys."

"I had a taste for you. But I knew you weren't ready for such things." His face darkened. "I've been impatient, and for that I despise myself. I drank plaster and water, when I wanted milk. But waiting until now, I believe, has been worth it."

He bent forward, his eyelids lowering for a kiss. But at the very scent of him, Cora jerked away reflexively.

Alexander drew back, stung. "You've been in my mind and heart for a long while, Cora. In time, you'll come to me. And we have forever ahead of us." Despite this, he grasped her hand and held it to his face. Cora flinched, as if touching a rotted carcass.

He studied her again, frowning at her reaction. But then he seemed to remember something. "Ah, I have one more task. Look here."

He went to the entranceway, where he'd left a parcel wrapped in several cloths. It had dripped a little, leaving a small pool of maroon liquid beneath it. He unwrapped it and held it out for her.

"A gift, for you. Well, for us. To complete the end of your story, and for the beginning of another. I stole Dr. Grier's diaries, thinking we could erase your history, but this is better. This is bringing it full circle, and with closure, you'll have a new life."

Cora stepped closer, and pulled the cloth down, to peer at what lay inside.

It was a heart. A real one. Pink and glistening in some parts, matte in others, it still had flat gobs of fat and smears of blood clinging to the muscle. It was rather on the small side—not the size of a heart that might have come out of a full-grown steer.

"It's from the butcher. A pig's heart. I looked at several, to see which one would most likely be the size of a woman your age and weight. Look," he said, clasping her hand in his free hand. He pulled her to Audrey's body, seemingly unperturbed by the dead woman's blank stare, her unpoetic body lying sprawled over the wooden bench. "See, we'll make an incision in her chest and nestle it next to her other heart. And we'll shred the connective vessels. Say she was stabbed, or some such, to make up for the damage. I'll have the same resurrectionists deliver her today to Duncan."

"Five hundred," Cora said. "Duncan knows now? That I was the girl?"

Alexander nodded. "And Audrey will take your place. Her face is similar enough to conceal the truth. I'll pay back Suzette Cutter, so that debt is laid to rest. No one to chase you anymore, because Cora Lee's prized hearts will be on display forevermore."

"It's wonderful," Cora said hollowly. She reached for the stained white cloth and carefully covered Audrey's body. Her eyes stung, and her throat felt swollen. This poor girl, who had been in the arms of this decrepit monster. She didn't deserve this. And now she'd be laid out on a table for an audience of hundreds of eyes hungry to watch the dissection. Later, her hearts would be preserved in a glass jar to be viewed for years and years. The girl with two hearts, the mystery revealed.

Alexander laid the pig's heart atop the shroud.

I need to get out. I need to get away from him, Cora thought. Her hands were trembling, but she had to be calm. She had to pretend she was perfectly content with everything that Alexander had done so far.

A loud knock sounded.

Alexander's head swiveled toward the front of the studio. Cora opened her mouth, not to yell or scream, but in surprise. But at the drop of her lower lip, Alexander sprang at her and clapped his hand over her mouth. After spending countless hours in the casket that was almost the death of her, she found the smothering was too much.

A voice yelled, muffled by space and wood. "Alexander! Alexander Trice! It's Theodore Flint. Open the door."

Theo. She'd told him once that Alexander's studio was on Henry Street. Cora thrashed and grasped at Alexander's hand and wrist, kicking him with her boots.

"No. No. No. Stop it now, Cora. Stop it, love. I can't have you say a word. Will you be quiet?"

Cora nodded frantically. Anything to release his hand from her face.

Theo pounded on the door three more times.

"I know you're inside. I watched you enter, and there isn't an exit anywhere else. Open the door. I'm looking for Audrey March, the girl from Madame Beck's. She's gone missing, and Madame Beck says she was with you the last evening. I need to speak with her."

"Go away, go away, go away," Alexander murmured quietly, almost like the chant of a madman, constructing a curse. "Go away."

"I know you're here. I'll call the watchman and have him open the door. Come now, Alexander. I must speak to Audrey."

Alexander threw his other hand around Cora's waist, lifted and carried her into the bedroom chamber. With his hand still over her mouth, he whispered into her ear.

"Not a word. I'll get rid of him. And if you say anything, I'll kill him."

Cora went motionless. Her eyes widened, and she stared at Alexander. But she no longer recognized the man. His gray eyes were like a dense, suffocating fog. At her stillness, he nodded.

"Ah. You care for him, even now. Very well. He'll forget about you soon enough, but only if he's alive. And for that, you'd best be still and quiet."

Cora nodded, and Alexander removed his damp hand. He left the room, returned with Audrey's body, and laid it at her feet.

"Your twin. Luckily, she'll stay quiet too."

With that, he withdrew from the bedchamber and locked the door.

CHAPTER 32

Cora scrambled to the door, listening with her ear pressed against the whorls of wood.

"Ah. Mr. Flint." Alexander sounded distant, but she could hear well enough. His voice was calm and slow, in the intimidating way it always was. "What brings you here? I apologize, I couldn't hear you from my studio."

"I'm looking for Cora."

Cora's breath caught in her throat.

"I'm sorry? I thought you were asking for Audrey. Did you not hear the terrible news about Cora?"

"That she's dead and buried? Yes, I've heard. I laid eyes on her myself at the Cutters' house after she died. Except she wasn't dead."

This time, Cora clamped her own hand over her mouth, to keep herself from squealing. How could he know that she'd been fabricating her death? He knew. Which meant, he also knew she would be buried alive, and he had done nothing.

"I figured she was hiding here. I told her crew to dig her up, but they never came back to meet me. So, I went to her grave myself, and guess what I found?" Silence answered him. "I found an empty casket, and two dead men."

Two. That meant that her fears were correct—Otto and Tom were dead. But it also meant that the Duke lived. She waited, but Theo said nothing about him.

"So," Theo said, "may I see Cora?"

"I thought you were looking for Audrey," Alexander said.

"I am. Audrey has been missing since last night. Madame Beck called the police. Is Audrey here too?"

"Of course not. Neither of them is. And Cora *is* dead, but someone else must have taken her body. I have no idea where."

Footsteps drew near. "May I look around?"

"No." A second set of footsteps came closer as well, as Alexander followed Theo. "And I'd like to ask you to leave. My niece has just died. I'm in no mood to talk to anyone who gives life to lies. This is a time for grieving."

The doorknob rattled. "What's in here?"

"You want a look inside? Very well. I'll get the key," Alexander said, almost as if bored.

Cora stiffened. He probably already had the key in his pocket. The footsteps drew away, and she knew with the certainty of recognizing her own reflection that Alexander was about to kill Theo. Theo, who she'd once thought was angling for her demise. Theo, who'd loved her when she was Jacob and hadn't revealed the secret. Had she been too hasty when they fought? Had she been wrong? There wasn't nearly enough time to consider the question now.

She inhaled long and deep, before bellowing as loud as her voice could allow.

"Theo! Theo! I'm in here!"

She heard a gasp, and footsteps, and a huge clank of metal hitting something softer. Yells followed, and the walls shook. They were fighting; they must be. But it was Alexander's home. There might be weapons about, and Alexander would have the decided advantage. Despite her weakened state, she gathered herself and recalled what the Duke once taught her early in her career.

Use your boots. Take out a man's knee with a well-aimed kick, or take down a bad door—it's all the same.

A bad door. It was worth trying. She stood up, gathered the silk of her gown in her fists, and kicked at the door as hard as she could with her stronger right leg. The boots were stout, and the thump satisfyingly solid, but the door didn't move. She threw another kick at the door, again, and again. Her chest hurt from panting, and dizziness swirled behind her eyes. The hinges set into the wall were strong, but the wall itself had become softer from the constant dampness of the area around the old Collect Pond, now filled with streets and houses. The wall was becoming loamy, and on her tenth kick, the hinge buckled softly into the meat of the wall.

She heard a yell and more knocks as the men continued to fight. Her thighs burnt from the effort, but she aimed two more kicks near the hinges. On the third strike, the door dislodged from the wall by a mere two inches, but it was enough. She pried it inward, its hinges biting into too-soft wood, and squeezed her way through, tearing her gown in the process.

She ran down the corridor to find Alexander standing over Theo's inert body, next to the extinguished hearth. Alexander was holding an iron poker, ready to thrust it into Theo's chest.

"Stop it, Alexander! Please!"

Alexander wiped the sweat from his face with a hand, and pushed the mess of silver-and-dark hair from his face.

"No. The rumors have to die, and if that means that he has to die with them, so be it. He's already nearly dead, Cora. We must be sure he's gone."

"There is no *we*. There never will be. You cannot do this."

"I can. And this has gone far beyond what you want." Alexander stepped over Theo's body and walked forward with the poker in his hand, letting it slap lightly against his leg. The muscles of his forearm rippled as he gripped it harder. "I would prefer you stayed with me, alive, Cora. I've helped to keep you alive all this time, all these years. I've provided for you, in ways that you didn't even realize. But I've come to know that sometimes, being surrounded by beautiful, quiet, objects that can't disagree with you—well, that holds a certain loveliness as well."

Cora backed away, shrinking to make herself look small. She played up her fear—she had to use whatever she needed to her advantage. If she must fight in a gown, she would. And could.

"Don't do this, Alexander," she whispered, eyes wide. "I'll go with you quietly. Just let Theo be."

"You've proven you can't be quiet. And I know when you're lying, Cora. I've known you since you were an infant. To be honest, I was perfectly content at the possibility that the resurrection men would bring me your corpse. There are at least a dozen ways to preserve the dead. You of all people should know that—an everlasting bath of spirits, or desiccation, or a rather modern method, preservatives through the blood vessels. They'll swirl through both of your hearts. I can change your eyes out for lovely glass ones—blue, if you like—and dress you any way I see fit. You'll not beg for anything then."

Cora whimpered. Alexander didn't smile with any satisfaction at her supposed fear, only strode forward with the iron rod. The voluminous skirts of her gown hid her legs, which she had used to crouch down in preparation. Her fingertips touched the ground not in weakness, but to keep her balance.

As soon as Alexander was two arm's lengths away, Cora sprang up, a tight coil finally released. She dove under the iron-fisted hand, her hand reaching for the rod while her shoulder shoved him off-kilter. Alexander grunted in surprise, hand splayed out to catch himself as he fell leftward. Cora twisted the rod laterally, forcing him to let go. As she dodged to the right, she found her footing and pulled the iron in both fists, bringing it down hard on Alexander's body.

The iron slammed against his arm, splitting the fabric and leaving a bloody welt where it split his skin as well, but he did not cry out. He'd hurt his arm and knee in Puck's fight. Surely this would weaken him. But Alexander scrambled back, making his way to his hand and knees as Cora struck his back and thighs. She stepped forward, panting, and raised the iron over her shoulder. One more strike to the head—to his already bruised skull and brain—and Alexander would be dead.

She had never killed before. She had never possessed the intention; bringing the dead elsewhere had been her job. But now, a second away, an arc of her arms away, was death itself—the passage, the moment, the incandescent slipping away of life.

Cora hesitated.

And that was her mistake.

Alexander shot out his arm, snatched up two fists of the blue silk of her skirt, and threw himself backward. Cora fell, air escaping her lungs in a grunt as her back collided with the ground. The iron had fallen out of her hands, and she was scrambling to reach for it when Alexander straddled her torso. He had the poker in his hands, and up close, she saw it possessed a nasty hook on the pointed end, for pulling chunks of wood in the hearth.

"Is this what you were looking for?"

Cora wriggled and punched, but Alexander was seventy pounds heavier than she. She couldn't kick, couldn't escape him. He raised the iron, looking at her bodice.

"We'll start with the extra one."

He raised it up, and Cora barely had time to think. She punched toward him as he thrust the iron down. Instead of impaling her right ribs, where her second heart was, it stabbed her right arm, pinning it. She screamed. The pain was like a gunpowder explosion. Warm liquid seeped down her sleeve.

"I find that to be a rather pleasurable sound. Let's try again."

But this time, unable to move her right arm, she could only dart out with her left, and her aim was poor. She missed completely. He forced the pointed iron, now shiny with blood, down to her right ribs with the precision of an artist's eye.

It was pain she never could have imagined. The point burst through the silk, slid between her ribs, and twisted with a sickening crunch. She went breathless and felt blood quickly and efficiently saturating her bodice. She looked down. The iron point was still embedded in her chest. Alexander began to lift himself off her and casually yanked out the iron as he did. Cora shrieked in pain again as it exited her body. Crimson liquid, thinner than syrup, dribbled off the tip.

Cora stuffed her left fist against the wound to stanch the bleeding. Her breath failed her, and she began to pant in short, quick bursts. Her lung must have been punctured. Her fist was already covered in warm, sticky blood.

Alexander stood over her, walking in a lazy circle as he pointed the poker at her. "One more heart to go."

"You miscounted. Two more to go," said a voice behind him.

Alexander twisted his torso, just as the pole grasped in Theo's hands made perfect contact with Alexander's temple. The blow stunned him, and the iron clattered to the ground. As Theo pivoted to strike again, Cora grabbed the iron and scrabbled backward. This time, Theo struck Alexander across the spine, and Alexander, still silent, fell to his knees. There was something purely inhuman about how he wouldn't cry out, wouldn't shriek from the blows.

Cora raised the iron in her good fist. There were a thousand ways to kill a man. She'd seen only a fraction of them. This was not a time for imaginative revenge, but a quiet exit. She owed him this—as the one handing him his death.

With a simple thrust, Cora stabbed the pointed end of the iron into his neck, twisted, and pulled. A gush of blood spurted outward, messy and bright. The thick tide of red was forceful at first. But with every beat of his heart, the spurting lessened in intensity and reach, until it was a limpid crest that ran down his neck. His shirt was now more maroon than cream, wet and shiny. Ever silent—for Alexander had always been a man of economy, even in death—he simply collapsed to the floor and closed his eyes.

Theo crumpled to the ground, pole clattering beside him. Cora's hands went back to her bodice, now half-blue, half-crimson. The last thing she managed to say before she fainted was, "I believe I'm dying for real this time. Hearts and all."

ALEXANDER TRICE

When I was a young boy, I walked by a pond near my home in Kingsbridge, not half a mile from Boston Post Road. I'd been sent on an errand to purchase a new needle from the general store. It was well below freezing, and the ice cutters had been at work harvesting all week. The center of the pond had been completely carved out, with only a jagged toothlike edge left over. They had done quick work, taking where the ice had been thickest, a foot even.

And there, sitting at the edge of the pond was a fox, frozen in a block of clear ice. The cutters had found him, enjoyed the surprise for an allowed minute, then placed the frozen beast aside before finishing their work.

The fox must have fallen in when the ice was only irregularly thin, solid to the eye but too weak to support much more than the leaves that fell upon it. The animal looked as if it had been running when the ice had encroached and captured it, fur fluffed and dry looking, despite being encapsulated in solid water. Its eyes were shiny and dull at the same time, mouth open and thorny teeth bared at nothing.

Since the day that you were born, Cora, I thought often of the fox. I thought of how it was so wholly overwhelmed, just as I was when I first laid eyes on you. Your soft pink skin, the gentle pulsations of your second heart. I knew you were everything that God never hoped to create: your blood seasoned with the essence of another people, a duplication of the organ capable of crushing ardor or hatred. I would keep you safe. I would contain the borders of your world and make them mine.

Charlotte would watch me greedily doling out my care for you, in measures of sugar lumps and deliveries of Sunday fowl, lessons of arithmetic and geometry. She said once, "You love that child more than you love me."

"It's like she's mine," I said, which was true. "Like the child you and I lost," which was a lie. But it is easy to lie, when it comes to preserving what is the most salient in your life. Charlotte sighed with resignation. We didn't share a bed after your birth, but I was still allowed under her roof, because, as everyone said, I loved you like an uncle.

And as you grew, first in your boyish disguise, my affection deepened. What I didn't expect was how my body began to make demands upon me while you metamorphosed into a woman. I studied the angles of your rising breasts, the curve of your lumbar spine under your new dresses. My body created prurient thoughts that were utterly distracting. You were not ready to see me with my eyes beneath a hazy veil of desire. You were still innocent, unable to accept me not as family, but as a man. In time, you would. But for now, I needed release. And I found it at Madame Beck's, in the form of the mab who looked so much like you. I could ravage this portion of flesh, this duplicate doll, and save my quenched temperament for my dearest niece.

I gave you everything. Every wire I ordered pulled to closure, every ribbon I gave to knot a breath away, every dose of poison I poured. They were all for you.

Cora. My Cora. With hair like aged ebony and eyes like wet river stones. I know the angles of your jaw and cheekbone, of your wrists and the arch of your eyebrow. Those angles will pierce me even as the earth eats away at my skin, grinding my bones to powder.

There was something to be learned about that frozen fox. Teeth bared, it was screaming a message at my childish self. Perhaps I should heed what looks solid, but upon thoughtful testing, cracks and shatters. Perhaps I should have considered that there were other ways to cross a vicious body of water; considered that what gives life can drain it as well, drop by drop, or in one quick eclipse of a moment.

But I didn't listen.

I chose the shattering and was consumed.

CORA LEE

When I lost consciousness, they took me—the police, carrying me covered in silk and blood—to the operating theater right in the very same building where I had visited Theo. Only this time, I was exactly where I'd dreaded ever to be—on the table, my bare body open to the air, and a surgeon ready to split me open to learn all my secrets.

Everything I had done to avoid this moment had come to naught.

Alexander, the only family that I'd had left to trust, took my trust and corrupted it into a fetid heap. Leah, gone with what money we had. And Suzette—if only I'd had an opportunity to wish her well once more.

And then there was Theo.

But I've lost that chance, haven't I?

The surgery wasn't nearly full of the dramatics I'd expected. There were no eyes watching, only one assistant to Dr. Draper, an older gentleman so inured to the bloody work that he would sigh repeatedly from sheer boredom. And Draper hemmed and hummed throughout, asking for a length of catgut to tie off the troubling blood vessels of my extra, tiny heart. And then he asked for another. The catgut was tied in several places, snipped to size, and my skin sewn to close the ragged, gaping wound.

"Well," he said when done, "how very unextraordinary. Second heart, indeed. I knew it was more myth than truth. What a disappointment. But she shall live, after all."

Oh.

Oh! Where am I to go then? Where—

EPILOGUE

The news ought to have been entertaining.

> The Two-Hearted Girl Lives!
> Murder Scandal Near the Five Points!
> Artist Courts Lady with Dead Bodies!
> Lady of the Dead Resurrectionist Discovered!

But somehow, the *Herald* and the penny papers were silent on the subject.

Perhaps it was because Cora, retired resurrectionist and recent owner of two hearts, no longer had two hearts.

It was true. Cora would hear later about how it had happened. After Alexander had stabbed her, she had swooned from the loss of so much blood. Theo had collected her and run to the door, screaming for aid. He'd refused offers to take her to Bellevue, or the dispensary, and demanded she be taken directly to the surgical theater at the University of the City of New York, albeit without an audience.

Dr. Draper had been called, the ether administered, and Cora's wounds explored.

"It was rather a tidy mess, for one thing," Draper had explained afterward. "I can see why some thought she had two hearts. A tangle of arteries and veins, pulsating like a heart. A vascular hamartoma. Quite an enormous size. I was able to tie off the main vessels after some difficulty. She ought to recover well enough."

Theo had thanked him, but Draper had taken him aside late that night while Cora was brought to the home of one of his nurses, to be cared for. Theo had told him the entire story, the same one he'd given the watchman and police when they had surveyed Alexander Trice's studio, along with Audrey's body and the ledger detailing the list of recent murders.

"Look here," Dr. Draper had said. "We're on the cusp of certain legislation that will greatly assist our anatomic studies. Imagine, all the cadavers we need, from the unwanted poor of the Almshouse! But these unfortunate events with this girl—a girl, of all things, performing resurrections—all of this will muddy the waters and bring unwanted, sensationalist attention. Be quiet about it, and I'll see if the police can do the same. There's an ending to this, and it would be better for all if it stays far from the *Herald*."

Theo was too tired to disagree. He looked rather sorry with his head bandaged and eye swollen so tightly shut; he felt like all the world had been transformed into a flat daguerreotype instead of three dimensions. He nearly injured his other eye after walking into a partly opened door during his recovery.

But recover he did. As did Cora.

As soon as Cora was able to receive visitors, Suzette and Dr. Blackwell had come. Daniel Schermerhorn did not. The scandal, though not in the papers, was still on the lips and tongues of the uppertens.

"I won't look for an invitation to the wedding," Cora had said as Suzette sat next to her sickbed. She had been moved to an empty room in Theo's boardinghouse and was situated in a room down the hallway. The landlady had been adamant about no ladies amongst her boarders, but she softened at the knowledge that a nurse would visit frequently. Also, there was Suzette's double payment for the room and board. Dr. Blackwell had supplied the physician visits afterward.

"There will be no wedding," Suzette had explained, looking unruffled throughout. "The reduction of my inheritance was intolerable to Daniel. It didn't help that my affection for you was as strong as ever once we heard you had survived."

"Your mother still hates me, I am sure," Cora said matter-of-factly.

"Indeed, she despises you! But we have the rest of our lives to reconcile. Do we not?"

"We do. Though I am very sorry about Daniel." Cora raised her eyes. "Are you quite all right?"

"Yes. I am young, as are you, and this island is fairly crowded with eligible men, though perhaps not as lofty as the Schermerhorns and Cutters." She frowned. "Mother will barely speak to me. But I'm her only daughter, and though it may take a season or two, she shall forgive me. And you as well." She smiled cheerfully. "I should like to help Dr. Blackwell with maintaining a dispensary once she finds a position. There is good I can still do in my position, you know. I have my books for now, and I'll have you."

"Not in New York, you won't. I shall be leaving once I'm healed."

Suzette looked forlorn. "Why must you leave? There is no one to fear here any longer. Except my mother." She grinned. "How else will I keep you abreast of the gossip surrounding Dr. Blackwell and her quest to rule all of New York?"

"I am not on a quest!" Dr. Blackwell said, obviously ruffled. She had been in the corner of the room, arranging the tinctures she'd procured at the druggist. "And you! What will you do now? I'm very satisfied that you will not be doing any of this resurrection business any longer."

"I don't know," Cora said, wincing as she adjusted her position. "Goodness, I'm hungry. Hand me that other plate of cheese and apples, will you? I can't seem to get full." Mouth crunching, she added, "I doubt the city is ready for another female physician. They don't even know what to do with you." She pointed her nose at Dr. Blackwell.

"Goodness, don't speak with your mouth full. And you have been eating nonstop since I came here. I'll have the grocer deliver more food later today," Suzette said. Dr. Blackwell glanced at them both, before going back to her organizing. "Mother has said that we can provide for a small income, as long as you . . . What were her words? *Behave like a Cutter woman.* What on earth that means, I don't know, because we behave abominably!"

"I appreciate her gesture, but I'm used to having a vocation," said Cora. Though she knew much about anatomy, she had no interest in teaching, or drawing figures, or any such work. "I've thought of midwifery." Perhaps it would be a pleasure bringing little ones into the world instead of spending her hours with the dead.

"The physicians have been battling the midwives in this town," Dr. Blackwell warned. "It's a war. Men and women, babies and power."

"I'm used to a challenge," Cora said. "But I have time to decide. I've been considering a different option, actually."

"What option?" Dr. Blackwell asked.

"Becoming a druggist, or chemist," she said. "Not many women are in the business, but there are some. I find it interesting how those medicines nearly killed me."

Suzette groaned. "That's interesting? You are peculiar, Cousin."

"Interesting, but they can do so much! Every year, there is more to discover. I may not have an ailment anymore," she said, touching the bandage on her belly, "but I remember well enough how it feels to live with one. Perhaps I can still help someone who can't escape their illness."

Dr. Blackwell nodded appreciatively. She walked to Suzette and grasped the novel in Suzette's lap. She lifted it to display the title to Cora.

"*Frankenstein; or, the Modern Prometheus*," Dr. Blackwell read. "This paper rubbish? You're both peculiar, and we'll leave it at that."

"Curiosity is not a moral failing!" Suzette said, taking the book back and hugging it to her chest. "There is brilliance in here. It's fascinating."

"I'll have to read it then too," Cora said, smiling. "Medicines are fascinating also." Then she said, "*Alle Dinge sind Gift und nichts ist ohne Gift; allein die Dosis machts, dass ein Ding kein Gift sei.*' It's the only German I know."

"Ah," Dr. Blackwell said. "'All things are poison and nothing is without poison. Only the dose makes a thing not to be poison.'"

"Who said that?" asked Suzette.

"Philippus Aureolus Theophrastus Bombastus von Hohenheim," Cora said, before biting into another thick slice of cheese.

"That sounds like a terrible rash."

"Doesn't it?" Cora said, chewing. "Well, if I am to become a druggist, I'd have to find someone who would let me apprentice, and go to school perhaps, but first—"

"First, you need to recover," Suzette added.

"And then she'll need her lying-in time," Dr. Blackwell said matter-of-factly.

"What?" Suzette went pale.

"Well goodness. You have to tell her sometime," Dr. Blackwell said, turning about. She brought a tiny cup full of amber liquid and set it before Cora. "This is to strengthen your womb. Come now, after all that stress, you need it. It's a miracle that the medicines we gave you didn't cause you to lose the child."

"You're with *child*?" Suzette stood up and fanned her face with her hands. "Oh, my dear Cora, you really are a Cutter. Is it Mr. Flint's child?"

Cora said nothing.

"It is! Does he know?" Suzette said.

Cora said nothing.

"He doesn't! Why won't you tell him? You ought to be married—immediately. Why have you not—"

"Give her a moment to breathe, Suzette!" Dr. Blackwell said.

"You're one for secrets. I thought a physician didn't speak of such things to strangers," Suzette said, tilting her head.

"Suzette Cutter, you are no stranger. And she was afraid to tell you, so there. I made it all very easy for the both of you. Do you still love your cousin?"

Suzette's face went pink. "Yes. Of course."

"Then it's settled. Cora, stop looking so discomfited. You can dig up a dead body but cannot speak the truth to your own family? For shame. Be done with it, and tell her what you must."

Cora had said nothing throughout their back-and-forth, just blushing furiously and attempting to stave off further conversation by eating more cheese. But finally, she did. She told Suzette that the baby's father was Theo, and how far along she was, and that no, he didn't know.

"And you're planning on moving to Philadelphia? With no family, no connections, and with a child? Are you mad?"

"Of course she is," Dr. Blackwell said. "Not the usual kind of madness that rarely improves from a thorough bloodletting. This is the irritating kind that can be helped. Come, Suzette. I've some medicines to distribute to my patients, and you've got an hour and two good legs and arms to help me. And I'm your chaperone, so you must. Let's leave Cora to rest."

They left. Though Cora had the ministrations of a nurse visiting every few hours, Theo never came to visit. And she never asked for him. She listened to see if he came home to his boardinghouse room, just down the hall, but he seemed to be avoiding the entire building. It was as if he'd decided he'd done what he could, dropped her off at the university to be healed, and then flown away without a goodbye.

A week passed, ten days since she had poisoned herself.

Cora's wounds healed remarkably well. Her bruises had faded to a sickly yellow, and though her wounds were still knit together with fuchsia scars, they were improving by the day. Already she had gathered more plumpness to her body and her cheeks, and her hair was a messy shag that she'd combed and held back with a thin ribbon. She had been well enough to dress that day, and the landlady knocked on her door.

Cora walked slowly to answer it.

"There's a man waiting for you. Says his name is Mr. Duke."

Cora drew a thick shawl about her shoulders and carefully descended the stairs. Outside, waiting on the street was a small hack, and the Duke was standing outside it, with a woman holding his arm. She had an upright carriage, black hair tucked beneath a lace cap, clear brown skin, dainty dark eyes, and was perhaps a good ten years older than Cora herself. The Duke leaned heavily on a cane, and there was some puffiness to his cheekbone that showed he was still healing from the blows that night at the graveyard. He removed his stovepipe hat.

"Oh! You're well! I'm so happy to see you!" Cora said, clapping her hands together.

The Duke smiled. "Miss Lee. My wife, Annie Preston."

Cora bowed awkwardly and smiled. "It's very good to meet you finally."

"And it's good to meet you too," she said, bowing in turn. Her voice was rich and low. "Lewis has mentioned you before, but he said you were a very private person."

"Lewis?" Cora raised her eyebrows at the Duke. "Is that your real name?"

"It is." He smiled. "Apparently, we both had names for our trade work, which we are leaving behind us, it seems."

"Yes. Leaving behind more than just the work," Cora said, her eyes smarting. She'd thought she was through with crying over the death of Otto and Tom, but grief has a way of insinuating itself into hearts. Her stitches threatened to rend at any moment, and Cora pressed her lips together, trying not to cry.

"It's, ah, good to see that you are doing well. In person, perhaps not so in spirit. We are all still healing from our losses," said Lewis.

Mrs. Preston smiled kindly. "We were going uptown and were hoping you would join us, Miss Lee."

"Uptown?" Cora asked. Lewis had given her a handkerchief to wipe her eyes.

"Yes," Lewis said. "We'll tell you when we get there. Not to worry, it's safe. I hoped you and I would both be well enough for this trip."

Cora let the driver help her into the hack, and soon they were driving uptown. Once they reached Fiftieth Street, they turned past the orphan asylum and then drove north again. From a distance, she saw Lightbody's Ink Factory, and the Phelps, Riker, and Schermerhorn estates (minus Suzette's company, of course) looking out over the East River. Wooded wilderness covered both sides of the roadway. Finally, they stopped before a tidy planting of trees surrounding a small but beautiful outdoor pavilion.

"This is a private botanical garden, isn't it?" Cora asked when Lewis held her hand to assist her out of the carriage. She was tired but perked up at the sight of the trees and the crystalline-blue October sky.

"You are correct. My brother works for the owner, and he has allowed us special permission to stop by. Come."

They walked slowly as a threesome deep into the garden. The trees were turning all manner of color—brown and golds and red maples, and the manicured lawn between them was well kept. As it was so far uptown and late on a Sunday, there were no visitors, and it was a chilly day. After a long walk down the middle of the garden, they stopped. There was some recently turned earth in an irregular fashion, surrounding a young oak tree, only about ten feet tall.

Lewis removed his hat and held it against his chest.

"Otto the Cat. Or rather, Otto Donnelly," he said, pointing to one area. He swept his hand a few feet to the right. "Friar Tom, known before as Moses Thomas Burnshed. And of course, you remember Audrey March. The owner allowed us to bury them here, privately and under the utmost secrecy, so they wouldn't be disturbed."

Cora's eyes welled. Every time she considered that her friends were gone, and gone because of her, she cried. It was too much. Lewis and Annie each placed a warm hand on her shoulder and left her, walking to the shade of some trees behind her.

Cora stood there for more than an hour. She thought of the first times she'd met each of them at Madame Beck's, when Audrey was quietly refusing Jacob's invitation to spend time together; or when Tom had ticked off a list of pies he wished to eat; or when Otto's tail needed mending and she'd brought it to Leah for repair. Her mind danced with memories, a strange concoction of mirth, pain, and regret. She thought of Ida, Ruby, Randolph, Conall, and William, and regret burnt within her. Her face was wet with apologies.

The air grew colder, and the sun began to dip below the tree line, sending dappled arrays of light that flickered on her skirt. The Prestons would want to leave soon. She heard their footsteps behind her and felt a hand laid upon her shoulder. The Duke—Lewis, though she might never get used to calling him by his real name—stood beside her.

"How did you arrange this? You were nearly dead yourself," Cora asked, wiping her eyes.

"I didn't. Today is the first time I've been here, like you. He told me where to go."

"He? Who's he?" Cora turned to him, confused.

"Ask him yourself. He's been waiting a good week to see you."

Lewis motioned to his left, and there between two ash trees stood Theodore Flint. He looked thin, with darkened circles beneath his eyes, and a sallow complexion that begged for sunlight and at least a dozen hearty meals.

Wordlessly, Lewis left her side, and Theo replaced him. Cora said nothing to him for a while, just stood there. Her hand went unconsciously to her belly.

"Are you well?" he asked softly.

"I am. Much better. Thank you for finding the room for me."

"Thank Miss Cutter and Dr. Blackwell. They arranged for the nurse and the financials. All my money's gone."

"Gone! What did you spend it on?"

Theo said nothing, only looked down at the turned earth. "I thought of adding headstones, or an obelisk. I would have gained a debt for it, but then I thought—these things all crumble with time. After you and I pass someday, hopefully when we are very old, no one may ever know that they rested here. And a tree is a living legacy to leave behind instead, don't you think?"

Cora said nothing. So, he'd arranged for this. A safe place for their rest, though Cora and her boys had personally ensured that a hundred anomalous but well-to-do New Yorkers had not rested so peacefully. For so long, Cora had thought that it seemed right and fitting that after death, one's body no longer belonged to anyone, including themselves. Her own body was a commodity, as were those of so many others on this island. The victims of slavery who had fled here for safety and freedom. The dockworkers whose labor was paid in small coin; the Irish kinchin running the streets whose worth was doled out by the number of rags they'd gathered or sugar they'd skimmed off barrels. Worth and bodies, decided everywhere.

But Cora regretted it. She regretted it all. And she regretted that she had snatched away their modicum of peace, after they had suffered a lifetime of struggle and pain (for even for the wealthy, there was pain to be had).

"I hear you are leaving for Philadelphia soon," Theo said, interrupting her thoughts.

Cora nodded, and blotted her eyes with Lewis's handkerchief. "I am."

"Why won't you stay here?"

Cora shook her head very slowly. "I can't stay here."

"You won't know a soul in that city. I can transfer, you know. To the College of Physicians of Philadelphia."

"I thought your career was set in New York."

"It seems I have collected a variety of thoughts that have needed amending."

For a while, there was nothing to say. Everything in Cora told her to flee. To conceal, to protect, to divert—a useful and comforting trifecta of practices. Finally, after being unable to bear it any longer, she turned and walked toward the edge of the garden.

"I'm going home. It's late, and the Prestons have been waiting a long time."

"They've gone already, Cora. It's just me."

"Very well. I'll walk."

"Wait." He ran to her side, keeping stride with her. "I have a carriage waiting. And if you don't want me in it, you can take it alone and I'll walk back. It should take me all of three hours, but I'm happy to do it. I don't think you should walk in your condition."

She stopped walking. Did he mean what she thought he meant? She looked up at his face, and he seemed almost more terrified than she was.

"Yes, Cora. I know. Suzette told me."

Cora dropped her eyes and stared at the grass. "She had no right."

"Well, she didn't exactly tell me—she sent me a note saying you were doing well, considering your delicate condition. I made an assumption, and you confirmed it."

"I see," Cora said, hugging her shoulders.

"And I was a stubborn pig about making decisions on our future before we'd even had a proper dinner together." Theo sighed, and he blinked quickly. "I just wish we could start over. I've made ever so many mistakes, Cora."

"I need time to think about this, Theo," Cora said. She was shaking now. Theo raised his arm and ushered her toward one of the passageways out of the botanical garden. There, a small carriage was waiting. She allowed Theo to help her inside. Nestled on the seat was a basket with a corked bottle of Croton water, several apples, a wrapped bundle of small cakes, and a meat pie. Cora was starving. The little thing inside her was a ravenous beast. But she pretended as if she didn't care. Theo brought from the driver a thick woolen lap blanket. He spread it over Cora's lap and tucked it in on the side.

"Take all the time you need," Theo said. "If you wish to speak to me, you can leave a message with the boardinghouse keeper."

He slapped the hindquarters of the horse, and the carriage jerked forward.

Cora sat facing forward as the carriage drew farther and farther away. Her jaw was chattering, no longer from cold, but from fear. She was a step away from an irreversible decision. Breath drawn, ready to speak.

She missed Jacob. She wished she could don his clothes again, slip into the crowd, and not be herself for a while. He could make decisions for her, fight for her, drink for her, steer their common future. But Jacob was no longer needed, and she missed him acutely. What would he say? What would he do? The clarity of his mind was a very real thing, and hers had been clouded by sickness and sleep and too long spent in flight, never landing, never taking a breath to actually live.

Jacob, what do I do? Cora thought.

But he was silent within her. He'd gone away the moment she had taken those drafts in Suzette's parlor room, the day she'd claimed her identity and all the nuances of herself.

The carriage continued to rattle and move forward. She could sense Theo disappearing into the distance behind her. And somehow, she could almost hear Charlotte and her mother, Elizabeth, chiding her from elsewhere on the edges of the wind.

Stop running, dearest. There is an end to everything, but some endings are very good, indeed.

Stop.

Stop.

"Stop!" Cora cried out to the driver, who pulled on the reins. Cora pushed the blanket off and turned in the open carriage. In the distance, Theo stood there, watching her, his expression unknowable in the dim twilight, but his stance was like that of a man on a precipice, expectant. She stood up in the carriage and hollered as loudly as she could. Louder than her one heart beating, louder than the rising wind, louder than the fear shrinking rapidly within her.

"Theodore Flint!" she yelled, loud and brash as a man. "I think I love you!"

AUTHOR'S NOTE

There is a single rite of passage that physicians have gone through as part of their medical education, one that stays in their memory forever—Gross Anatomy. I recall the first time we met our cadaver, carefully wrapped in plastic, the air filled with the stench of formaldehyde. I was filled with a confusing array of sensations—awe, intimidation, worry, disgust, fascination, and gratefulness. At the end of our first-year class on gross anatomy, we held a vigil of deeply felt thanks to those who had donated their lives so we could educate ourselves and save others.

But the study of anatomy has had a rather dark and nefarious history. It was the history of body snatching and resurrectionists that gathered my interest years ago. I soon learned that in order to steal bodies, resurrectionists occasionally employed a lady who would scout out cemeteries during funerals for fresh finds.

That was when the concept of Cora Lee's character was born. But many of the details of this book are anything but fictional. The 1788 Doctor's Riot in New York City—sixty years before this story takes place—occurred as a result of the inhumane objectification and pilfering of graves belonging to the poor, and often disproportionately to blacks. Despite dissuasive statutes and laws that followed, grave robbing continued into the turn of the twentieth century. Today, the majority of cadavers used in medical schools are voluntarily given and, by and large, from white donors.[1]

Mort houses, used to rot bodies to prevent stealing, were real. In the UK, there were cages placed over graves. Coffins were created with locks and metal cuffs around cadavers' necks, to prevent bodies from being pulled out. And let's not forget those evil gents, William Burke and William Hare, who killed for the sake of selling the bodies to anatomist Robert Knox in 1828, in Edinburgh, Scotland. Their notoriety created a new verb for murdering for the sake of selling dead bodies: *burking*.

Picking a time period for this story took some effort. Though grave robbing occurred throughout the nineteenth century and into the early twentieth century, the passage of the landmark Bone Bill in 1854 changed the landscape of grave robbing significantly. Championed by John William Draper (who appears in the book), cofounder and then-president of what is now the New York University School of Medicine, it allowed the unclaimed dead from the city's Almshouse to be used for anatomic study. It was intended to greatly lessen the frequency of grave robbing, but it also meant that the poor were callously penalized for being poor. As a result of the Bone Bill's dates, I wanted the story to take place before its passage. For more on the history of the resurrectionist trade, Michael Sappol's *A Traffic of Dead Bodies* and Ruth Richardson's *Death, Dissection, and the Destitute* are excellent.

As for Cora's double hearts? She was, in fact, the impossible girl, in that she did not have a second heart at all. Her second heart was designed to be an arteriovenous malformation, or AVM. In the mid-1800s, it was called a vascular hamartoma. It's a tangle of blood vessels, in which an artery connects directly to a vein without the normal progression of artery to arteriole to capillary to venule to vein. Symptoms include hearing a murmur, feeling a "thrill" (a pulsatile, vibratory sensation when felt with the hand), and if the vascular hamartoma is large

---

1   Halperin, Clin Anat. 2007 Jul;20(5):489–95

enough, mini strokes, or transient ischemic attacks, two of which Cora suffered in her life. Ones as large as Cora's are unusual, but do exist, and they are a matter of bad luck, as opposed to being inherited genetically. Today, such a medical problem is more easily discovered and cared for by experienced physicians.

A few notes on these fictional murders. Paris green was the paint employed as a poison to kill the first victim, Randolph Hitchcock, and was a lovely emerald-green color used throughout the nineteenth century. Also called Scheele's green and Emerald green, it acquired its other name because of its usefulness in killing rodents in Paris. Arsenic was the element responsible for its deadliness. Paris green was also used as a colorant on wallpapers, and likely sickened a good many people who lived in these beautiful but poisonous surroundings. I hadn't read of a case where Paris green was actually used as a murder weapon, aside from being used to kill insects and rodents. I suppose there had to be a first! For more on the fascinating history of arsenic, check out John Parascandola's *King of Poisons: A History of Arsenic*.

Strychnine as a murder weapon came to my attention after my cowriting with Nate Pedersen our book *Quackery: A Brief History of the Worst Ways to Cure Everything*. I learned that strychnine poisonings had symptoms very similar to tetanus, and knew I'd tuck that away for my next mystery novel. Thanks, Nate!

And finally, a note on one of the most important characters of the book: the setting. New York in the mid-1800s was a colorful, noisy, stinky place. For a deeper look into life at that time, I highly recommend reading Herbert Asbury's *The Gangs of New York: An Informal History of the Underworld*, Edwin Burrows and Mike Wallace's *Gotham: A History of New York City to 1898*, and George Foster's *New York by Gaslight and Other Urban Sketches*. The city was abloom with personages who often eclipsed the very backdrop of their world—Afong Moy, Edgar Allan Poe, Walt Whitman, Phineas Taylor Barnum, Elizabeth Blackwell, and Jenny Lind, to name a few. I had to include several on the page, and I tip my stethoscope to Dr. Blackwell, a brave and brilliant pioneer for women in medicine.

And finally, navigating the language of the notorious Five Points—flash—was a lesson unto itself. For those who wish to perplex and impress their friends, you'll need *The Rogue's Lexicon*, by George Matsell, so you can rake the lingo, drop a gapeseed for a glass, and act a chaffing pickle![2]

---

2   Translation: Share the language, tell a wonderful story for an hour, and appear to be a talkative, smart fellow!

ACKNOWLEDGMENTS

Thank you to my husband, Bernie, to my lovely children, to my scamp of a dog, Piper, and to all my extended family and close friends, who encourage me endlessly. To Sarah Fine, enormous hugs for always being there. And to Nate Pedersen and April Tucholke, for never blinking at the bizarre subject matter that pops up on our emails. To Emalee Napier, who keeps me calm and organized all the time—you're a lifesaver.

To the wonderful Lake Union authors who have become my colleagues and friends, thank you! And a huge shout-out to the Physician Moms Group on Facebook. It's quite a thing to have tens of thousands of smart women supporting my stories.

To Kate Brauning, for her thoughtful words, encouragement, and insight—you rock. And to Eric Myers, my wonderful agent—thank you for never thinking my stories are way too strange! And finally, to Caitlin Alexander and Jodi Warshaw, and my team at Lake Union—you guys are brilliant, and I thank you for making this book a reality!

ABOUT THE AUTHOR

Photo © 2012 Chelsea Donoho

Lydia Kang is a physician and the author of *A Beautiful Poison*. She was born in Baltimore, Maryland, and graduated from Columbia University and New York University School of Medicine. She currently lives in the Midwest with her family, where she continues to practice internal medicine. Visit her at www.lydiakang.com.